Down the Aisle

Rose Chase

Copyright

Content warning

Dedication

To ALL THE VICTIMS and survivors: You matter. Don't give up. You are important to someone out there, your true family, your child(ren), and, most importantly, yourself. You are a rose waiting to bloom, so don't stop until the world sees your beauty and worth.

Dedication

To the single mothers out there (and every book girlie) who wants a morally grey man to sweep them off their feet and spoil them, Adam's gonna take care of you real good. So, spread your legs and be good ;)

Other works

Volkov Bratva:
Bratva's Bride
Bratva's Beast
Bratva's Bounty
Bratva's Belle (2025)
Bratva's Beloved (2026)

East Coast Syndicate:
Cardinal
Wicked Butterfly (2025)
Dove (2026)

Serial Lover:
Killer in the Sheets
Guilty of Love (2025)

Umbra Demons:
Under My Bed
In My Closet

Blurb

As a mafia boss, Adam Santini has spent years building his empire under a façade of normalcy. The last person he expects to capture his heart is sweet, single mother Eliza. His obsession is instant, and he's determined to be a light in her dark world, even as he hides his own demons.

Eliza Huyen is barely holding her life together in the windswept town of Seaside, Oregon. The last thing she needs is complications while watching her back, but that's exactly what she gets when her son tugs on the sleeve of a charming man who seems too good to be true.

As Eliza lets him into her life, she feels something she hasn't felt in a long time—hope. But when her past comes for her with fury, everything falls apart. Even Adam's dark secret comes into the light to protect the woman he's come to love.

Adam refuses to let her go, so can Eliza embrace his darkness and find safety in his arms, or will her fears tear them apart with everything else?

Down the Aisle

Single Chances Book 1
Rose Chase

Contents

Prologue: Eliza

"Shh, shh, shh, it's okay, baby, it's okay. Mama's here. Mama's got you."

Please, God, if you are out there, please keep him asleep.

I hoped to all that was holy out there that my husband would stay asleep and my baby would remain peaceful, despite all the jostling around I was doing as I haphazardly gathered our things.

The bottle of Xanax still sat open on the counter sat open on the counter and glared at me menacingly every time I passed it in my hurry to grab and stuff last-minute items into my duffle bags. I felt judged by the damn bottle and scattered pills, which made me feel guilty about my sleeping husband on the couch.

Even though I hated him, I couldn't help but slow my steps to observe the slow, steady rise and fall of his chest to ensure he wasn't dead. I wanted him out cold—not dead. Well, actually, that was very debatable, but I wasn't a killer. It would have been very easy to overdose him and send him into respiratory distress, but my conscience kept me from crushing up more pills to spike his drink and food with.

God, maybe this is a mistake.

My body came to a halt when I caught a glimpse of our wedding picture hanging in the hallway. We were so happy, genuinely happy. Tears welled up in my eyes the longer I admired the past, and my heart clenched painfully at what I was about to turn my back on.

The adrenaline surging through my body slowly ebbed the further I looked down memory lane. My grip on the strap of the duffle bag slackened with each step down the hallway; every smile on every picture lining it chipped away at my resolve until I nearly dropped the bag. If my newborn hadn't stirred in my arms, I might've made the biggest mistake in my life by changing my mind.

His small grunt and movement jarred me back to stark reality. I couldn't cling to the past anymore, not when I had my son to live for now. He needed me. Asher deserved better than a broken home. I didn't want to raise him to walk on eggshells like me, or worse, raise him to be like his father.

Closing my eyes, I tore myself away from it all, recollecting myself and steeling my nerves to carry out my plan. A plan which should have been implemented long ago. If I hadn't been so naïve and ignorant, then maybe I would have been better off by now. But, if I'd grown a backbone sooner, then I wouldn't have Asher.

Yes, a part of me felt guilty about bringing a child into this mess, but it wasn't supposed to be like this. Things were supposed to get better, *be better*.

Sighing sadly, I looked down at my infant son, all swaddled up and comfortable in my arms. This was all for him, and deep down, it was for me, too.

Tightening my grip on my bag, I walked with a purpose to the front door, where I had three more duffle bags sitting.

I paused by the side table to take one last look at everything, including my husband, passed out on the couch in the living room with a fallen beer bottle by his feet.

This was it. The moment I head out the door, there would be no going back. Well, there was no going back the moment I sprinkled the Xanax into the food, but it was *really* going to be over once I went out the door.

With a heavy sigh, I grabbed all the keys in the bowl and walked out.

The hit of fresh air filled my lungs, causing a surge of renewed energy to pump through my body, aching my muscles with an urge to move. My body spurred into a run before my mind fully registered everything.

My car, at least ten yards away, appeared before me in a few strides, and the gust of wind from throwing the door open knocked some sense into me. Quickly, I strapped Asher into his car seat before rushing back into the house to grab all the bags. I didn't bother with the trunk because this car was temporary, and opening the trunk to shove things into it would have taken a minute too long.

Right before I climbed into the driver's seat, I took apart the keyrings and randomly threw the keys around the area, except for the key to my car. The plan was to slow him down as much as possible once he'd regain consciousness. I didn't know how long the scattered keys would slow him, but it was going to be a pain in the ass to crawl around on the ground to find and pick up the keys. We lived on about an acre of land, and I threw those keys good.

Good luck finding a needle in a haystack.

One last longing look at the house I'd spent the last eight years of my life in, and I gave it a bittersweet farewell. The crunching of gravel filled my ears as we drove off down the driveway. Every crackle zipped straight down to my heart, cracking it until the tears spilled over uncontrollably.

Ten years. Almost half of my life. Gone, just like that.

It hurt so much, and a part of me wanted to spin the wheel around and bust a U-turn back to the place I used to call home. But I kept strong, death gripping the wheel until my fingers tingled and cramped.

Turning back now would be a huge mistake; I might as well be gambling with my life if I were to walk back through the door now.

So, for the sake of remaining on this earth and Asher's life, I pressed on through the two-hour drive to my friend's house.

Thankfully, the drive was smooth. No one was on the road, probably because it was 2 AM, so I might have broken the speed limit quite a bit. I should probably be more thankful there weren't any cops on the lookout tonight. I really would have been screwed if I had gotten pulled over.

The second I pulled into my friend's driveway, a figure shot up from the porch and ran over to the driver's side of my car, throwing the door open. "Oh my God, you actually did it." Eve greeted me with the most elated smile. A smile so big I thought her lips would rip.

Pulling me out of the car, she suffocated me with a hug. "I didn't think you were actually going to go through with it, no offense." She chuckled dryly after pulling away. "But I'm so happy you didn't dip again." Smiling at me sympathetically, she wiped my tears away. "Everything will be fine. You are doing what's best for you and Asher, and everything will get better with time. I know it's hard, but good and right things are never easy."

Exhaling deeply, I forced myself to smile and nod in hopes of faking myself into a better mood. "Is everything still ready?" I asked, looking around warily to make sure no neighbors were being nosey.

Giving me a confident smile and nod, Eve told me to wait and disappeared around the house. Moments later, a midsize SUV pulled around to the front right next to me. "Alright, get Asher settled. I'll move all your bags over," Eve told me in a rush, after hopping out of the driver's seat.

She handed me a set of keys. "There's a bag in the passenger's seat with all your new documents in it, along with documents for Asher."

She pointed over to a black briefcase which looked rather ominous under the dim lighting of the car. "And I know you said you don't want any more help from me, but I'm not going to take no for an answer." Her eyes drifted to the floor, where another briefcase sat. "And the trunk is packed with water and food for the road trip and a lot more than you need probably, but better safe than sorry."

Tearing herself away from me, she opened the doors to my car to start transferring things over. "Got a phone set up for you, and don't worry, it's untraceable and shit, and my number is programmed in there along with Jag's and Hartley's." Taking a second to breathe, she shut the trunk with a grunt. "Your new place is set up, and the address is on the sticky note on the wheel."

Huffing, she stood next to me as I set up Asher's car seat. "From what Hartley told me, there should be a list of employers at your new place, too," she added after tapping her chin in thought. "But you're mostly set for a few months if you stretch the funds well."

Shutting Eve up with a hug, I rubbed my teary face onto her shoulder. "Thank you. Thank you so much. I really don't know how to thank you properly or repay you." It was a damn miracle I had *a* friend in my life still; it was some act of God for Eve to be as helpful as she'd been.

"Getting away from James and living a good life is more than enough. I expect more updates and shit, though, especially now that you can." Eve grinned with a giggle before urging me with a shove toward the driver's seat. "It's a long drive, but take all the breaks you need, and stay safe."

Guilt sunk into my bones as I slowly dragged myself behind the wheel. "Are you sure you're going to be fine? I don't want to give you so much trouble after you've been so helpful and supportive." I knew for a fact James *would* go after Eve the moment he woke and got his thoughts together.

Eve reassured me with a smile before shutting the door. "Don't worry about me. I do this for a living, remember? Besides, if he has half a functioning brain cell in that empty space of a head, then he won't come after me." I barely caught her words through the cracked window. "Now, quit stalling. Go. The more distance you make before he wakes, the better," she urged me before any words could come out of my open mouth. "Be safe."

I opened the window and, with one last tearful smile, reached an arm out to hug her. "Thank you."

Wasting no time, I punched the address into the GPS and practically floored it the moment we pulled out of Eve's driveway.

Twelve hours.

Well, probably closer to fifteen or more, factoring in the needed stops for rest. If I was traveling alone, the ETA might've been accurate, but I had a three-month-old with me.

No matter, as long as I could make it to Seaside in one piece with Asher. The major task right now, besides making it alive, was to get out of Idaho as fast as possible to minimize the chances of being caught.

God, I'm fucking insane. A twelve-hour drive by myself with a baby?! What am I thinking?! I'm not going to make it. I'm going to be stopped at the border, or some shit, and James is going to show up and drag me back home where I'm never going to see the light of day ever again.

Endless doubt flooded my weak mind the further I drove. My confident and determined grip on the steering wheel slowly faltered until my hands slipped to the bottom, and only the tips of my fingers remained in contact with the wheel.

I mean, what if I didn't drug him enough? If he woke up sooner than expected, then I would have even less time to escape the state. On the other hand, what if I had overdosed him? Even though his vitals were stable when I left, what if the faint and steady pulse was my imagination? What if his chest really wasn't rising and falling as it should?

No. Stop it! Stop.

Mulling over what-ifs would do nothing but stress me out.

This was all for the greater good. I had to remember that.

For me... And for Asher.

Chapter 1
Eliza

~1 year later~

I don't know what gave me more of a heart attack, my blaring alarm, or my toddler whacking me in the face with his sippy cup while babbling nonsense at me.

"Mama mum mum!" Asher demanded while continuing to beat me with the empty cup.

Even if the dull aches got annoying, I couldn't help but chuckle in amusement as I marveled at my 15-month-old. It was still so bizarre to me how much he'd grown in a year. Well, and the fact it's been a year since we ran and started new lives.

Having a fresh start was a godsend, and not a day went by where I didn't thank whoever was up in the sky for this new life. The part I was most thankful for was how my ex-husband hadn't found us yet.

I still kept in touch with Eve on a near-daily basis, and she kept me updated with anything regarding my ex if it pertained to me.

Unfortunately, he hadn't thrown in the towel, even after a whole year.

It was probably too much for me to hope James would give up on me. To be fair, it was a good fifty-fifty shot in my perspective. We were together for a long time, and forgetting someone overnight after ten years wasn't easy. Even though I despised and resented him, I still couldn't get him out of my system completely. I was trying to be fair to myself and not push to get over it faster than I could.

A part of me held out hope for him to finally change so we could be one happy family like we planned. Of course, the larger and more practical side of me knew better and fought endlessly to keep my naïve self from packing it all up and going back to Idaho.

There was no hope for James and me, not after everything.

"Mama." Asher's voice pulled me out of my mental hole.

Then there was my son, my sunshine, my life. If it wasn't for him, I would still be James's punching bag. Becoming a mom really kicked my ass into gear when the prospect of Asher ending up like James plagued my mind. I mean, James used to be good, but given how things turned out and his interactions with Asher, I couldn't chance it. Thinking back to how James barely tended to Asher as an infant and how crude his goals were for him made my skin crawl and burn with an itch to slough off my body.

Shoving my thoughts away with a long sigh, I smiled at Asher as I got out of bed and picked him up. "Good morning, my little chunkers." I giggled, pinching his chubby little cheek.

Thankfully, today was an off day for me, so I could finally do some much-needed grocery shopping and cross out other chores on my never-ending list. I didn't know how much I'd get done today, but I had to try.

Being a single mom was a lot harder than I'd thought, but I'd gladly take the struggle of it for Asher's sake and mine. Even though

I wanted to pull my hair out on more days than I could count, it was worth it in the end. I wasn't cooped up in a house twenty-four-seven, getting beaten every day, worrying about whether I would see the next day, nor did I walk around on eggshells.

Now, the only bruises on my body were from my clumsiness, not belts and fists. Well, that and occasionally from Asher, but not like my toddler could help it. I was mom, the love of his life... and human teething toy. There was also the random pinching here and there when he'd get bored and want attention, but he'd gotten better at not doing it.

If only he would learn to not grab my glasses anymore, that'd be great.

"Asher, stop," I sighed tiredly while leaning my head away from his grabby hands.

Cleaning baby prints off my glasses was next to impossible. I swear, his hands were coated in magical smudge or something that stuck to objects–like glue.

At least Asher was an easy kid overall. He was perfectly healthy, always hitting around the upper 90th percentile in his growth milestones, not a picky eater (seriously, if it was edible, then he ate it), listened as well as a toddler could, and was a smart little turd with a bright future ahead of him. The only complaint I had was his sleep; he rarely slept through the night because he was so used to nightly feedings. Granted, his habit was my fault because I always felt bad about him being hungry in the middle of the night and fed him. It was almost impossible to break the habit now, but since it wasn't detrimental to him, I just bit my tongue and kept it up.

Other than that, Asher was perfect. Just like now with going through our morning routine, he was perfectly content with me getting him ready for the day and feeding him before letting him play a little with what toys he had.

Sometimes, I wished I had more to give to Asher. Yeah, that was probably the cheesiest mom line ever, but it was the Gods-honest truth. Asher was so bright, smart, and friendly, and he deserved so much more than the meager life I could give him. I wanted to put him into daycare for socialization, just for a few hours a day, but I couldn't afford it. Same with more stimulating toys, they got too costly.

If I had a good-paying job, then I wouldn't really care much, but working as an on-demand housekeeper didn't necessarily bring in the dough. We weren't struggling, but I had to be conscious of my spending quite a bit. Even with the money I got a year ago to start our new lives, most of it was spent starting them while the rest sat locked up just in case—God forbid—something bad happened, and we had to start over elsewhere.

Well, at least we were in a decent spot, so I was more than grateful for our situation. We could be living paycheck to paycheck or really struggling to where I was insufficient, and thankfully, that wasn't the case. We also had a roof over our heads, lived in a decent area of the city, and I had a job which was flexible with my conditions.

Honestly, we had it good, in my opinion. It'd be better if I knew for a fact James wasn't after us still, but that was a little too much to ask for, given the good hand we were dealt.

Also, no complaining about anything now. Was this the dream? No, not really, but it was a hell of a lot better than what could have been.

Resetting myself with a deep breath and sigh, I stretched a smile on my face as I picked Asher up and gave him some kisses. "Alright, my lil bun, we gotta go to the store for some milk and food."

I didn't know how much he understood, but he responded by smiling, giggling, and clapping his hands. Granted, he did it for half the things I told him, so it was hard to gauge whether he was comprehending or just reacting because he was amused.

After a few minutes to get my life somewhat together, I got us into the car and to the grocery store in one piece—the trip home might be a different story.

Slowly, I made my way down the aisles, mumbling to myself to keep my list at the forefront of my mind. "Alright... Snacks for me and Asher... Milk... A shit ton of milk..." Honestly, I don't know how, but my little chunkers went through nearly a gallon a day.

A restocking grocery run shouldn't take forty-five or so minutes, but I liked to take my sweet time whenever I was out with Asher to give him more fresh air and more stimulation with seeing new things. Actually, I'd be surprised if every inch of this place wasn't perfectly mapped out in his mind by now with how often we went. Pretty sure if he was more sentient then I could give him a list and he'd be able to find everything in this place with no problem.

Pulling myself away from my thoughts, I focused back on my babbling toddler who was blowing me sloppy kisses with giggles. "You are the sweetest lil chunk," I cooed with a wide smile.

Asher laughed at me before reaching out with grabby hands. Shaking my head with a smile, I gave him one of my hands to hold and play with. "Alright, alright, just don't gnaw my fingers off," I joked with a chuckle.

Carefully, I pushed the cart along with my other hand. "Let's see... Crackers?" I mumbled my thoughts aloud as I scanned the shelves with my eyes.

Damn it, not on sale.

"Sorry buddy, looks like the goldfish gotta wait until next time maybe," I apologized to Asher's confused face with a sad smile.

Shopping on a food stamp budget was never fun, but at least Asher wasn't aware enough to care or throw a fit about things yet.

Flashing him one more smile, I went back to looking at the shelves to see if there were any similar alternatives for my little chunkers.

I was so focused on checking prices and labels; I failed to notice Asher being a cheeky little turd until it was too late. As much as I loved my child's laughter and squeals, it was never a good thing when it was paired with him tipping over.

My heart nearly burst out of my chest with a sharp inhale when I caught Asher leaning over the side of the cart. Strapped in or not, he could still slip out of the single restraint on the grocery cart with enough effort. The instant fear of him falling over and busting his head open or breaking his neck chilled every nerve I had. I wasn't even thinking as my body went on autopilot and whipped around, prepared to catch my falling child.

Thank goodness that wasn't the case.

Seeing what—well, who—Asher had in his grasp sent a different kind of chill through me.

"Oh my gosh, I'm so sorry!"

Chapter 2
Adam

"ADAM, IT'S FINE, I can—"

Holding a hand out, I cut my sister off with a smile and a shake of my head. "Hailee, it's fine. I needed to run out to grab some stuff anyway, so it won't be any trouble. You stay home with Adelaide," I told her while gathering my keys from the door-side table.

Just as I opened the front door, I turned my head around and smiled at Hailee. "And yes, I'll get you some wine." The playful, deadpanned face she threw at me along with her middle finger got me chuckling.

The thought of walking to the store played temptingly in my mind, but a chilly coastal breeze quickly changed it. Well, it was a hopeful thought to begin with. It was the beginning of fall on the West Coast, so things were starting to take a turn for the cold. Not that I minded; I actually liked the colder weather over here. If I didn't, then I would've packed my ass down to California or some other warm state.

Living a good life on the coast of the Pacific Northwest was always the dream. Thankfully, life was good to me; successful casinos along the coastline of Oregon, clubs and other entertainment places in major cities like Portland, and, of course, other small businesses around the rest of the state. Then, the cherry on top, was that everything was smooth enough that I could let my lieutenants run the front sides while I sat back and ran things underground.

Oregon was locked down tight under West Coast Mafia control. The rest of my life was set, and I was only thirty-six years old. Honestly, if I chose to give my position as one of the mafia heads up, I'd be set for three lifetimes with how much money I had stocked up.

Of course, I never thought this was where I'd end up in life. I graduated from business school with full intentions of being a clean businessman, but somehow, I ended up on the mafia's radar. By the time I figured out what was going on, it was too late. I was in way too deep, but it wasn't as bad as I thought.

Growing up, I always thought the mafia was violent and dirty, but that wasn't the case. Yes, there were some bloody moments, but for the most part, I was safe from it behind a desk or I had others to send out. Honestly, it wasn't how a lot of movies and history portrayed it to be.

Granted, we were in a new century, and things had changed drastically. There weren't fist fights and guns around every corner like in the movies. For the most part, we sat in meetings and were civil. It was only after peace fails would things got messy.

Not gonna lie, for someone who grew up in a rather peaceful household, I had a bit of a violent bone in me once I got a taste of bloody victory.

I wasn't a horrible person by any means. I, along with the other mafia heads, ran business as cleanly as possible. People had their choices, and I merely gave it to them. I was just there to ensure they kept to their end of the deal. If they fucked up, then that was on them; all I had to do was be their executioner if they reached such a point of their deal. No one could accuse me of being an unfair or horrible person. I, along with the other mafia heads, ran my businesses as cleanly as possible. I gave people choices, but it was on them how those decisions played out. My job was to ensure they kept up their ends of the deals, and if those deals were fucked up, I became the executioner of the consequences—which sometimes included being an executioner.

Speaking of which, a trip to the city was needed soon. Even though I could handle everything fine in the comfort of my home, I liked to get involved in the midst of it to keep my presence known to everyone and lay eyes on things personally. Well, that was something to plan later once I got home from the store.

When I got to the store, I instantly grabbed a basket and made my way down specific aisles with a purpose. I didn't have time to idle around the store today. Actually, more like I didn't *want* to because I had a date to get ready for. This grocery store run was for me to grab something sweet for my date tonight and a quick restock of my drink fridge. And stuff for my sister and niece because I adored the two and didn't want my sister to have to frazzle herself with going out. Besides, it was convenient for me to grab everything to save the household unnecessary trips.

Also, it probably would have taken my sister forever if I had let her go. I mean, I've barely been in the store for ten minutes and already had my basket filled with nearly everything I came here for. All I was missing was some treats to spoil my niece and the chocolates.

Those two items shouldn't have taken me more than a minute to grab, but I found myself lingering a bit in the aisle when I caught a glimpse of a lovely—damn, she had a kid, and she looked like the straight and narrow type. Don't get me wrong, nothing against her for having a kid, but she held herself rather neatly. Paired with the faint indent of a ring on her finger, I felt safe to assume her relationship status to be taken, or complicated, at the very least.

Still, I couldn't help but look more than I should at the petite lady. I was quick to kick some sense into myself and put my attention to the shelves filled with sweet treats, taking a gross interest in the teeth rotting delicacies. At least, that's where I occupied myself until I felt a firm tug on my sleeve, followed by a happy squeal and a giggle.

Turning my body a little to look, I couldn't help but crack a genuine smile at the sight of a baby clinging onto the sleeve of my t-shirt. Some people might get irritated in such situations, but not me. Kids will be kids was how I always saw it.

"Oh my gosh, I'm so sorry!" A frantic voice apologized.

My playful dismissal lodged in my throat when I felt a wave of warmth assault my body. Automatically, my gaze went to the source of the feeling. When I saw the cause, I wanted nothing more than to place my hand over hers to hold her hand against my upper arm.

Everything around me faded into the background the moment I got a good look at her beautiful face. I don't know what it was about her tired face that captivated me so much. Maybe it was the way her cheeks were prominent on her oval shaped face, giving her an almost model-like look. Or maybe it was those dark brown, amber eyes of hers that drew me in completely to the depths of infinity. The gem-like orbs popped on her face, making her look like a doll almost, especially paired with her heart shaped lips.

A slight tug on my arm snapped me out of my stupor. Awkwardly, I cleared my throat and offered the woman a warm smile as I carefully freed myself from her child. "It's okay, nothing to apologize for," I assured her, chuckling a little to diffuse the awkward air around us. "Kids will be kids, especially at his age. He really doesn't know any better quite yet."

Was it weird to be making excuses for a kid who wasn't mine? Maybe, but I couldn't stop my mouth from moving. I wanted to slap myself because I needed to get a grip. I was a grown ass man and a mafia head; I couldn't be losing my cool like this to some woman in the grocery store, no matter how stunning she was.

"Still, I'm so sorry." The woman was insistent with her meek apology, making me strain to hold the smile on my face. "I'm sorry for the bother, we'll leave you. Again, sorry."

She didn't give me a chance to say or do anything further with how fast she tucked her head and sped off. Alone in the aisle, I stood there with a dumbfounded expression and an outstretched hand in the direction the woman took off in.

Well, shit. I didn't even get a chance to ask her for a name.

Sighing, I withdrew my arm and took a minute to recollect myself. I tried to shove her out of my mind by thinking about my date later tonight, but it didn't make the burning want in my chest die out. Even when I tried to shift the excitement to later, I found myself rebounding to the mystery woman.

God, I just need to get laid.

That had to be the issue. Otherwise, why else would I react so overtly to a random woman in the grocery store? But that excuse only went so far. I had my pick of the crop, as some would say. Nothing was out of my reach. If I wanted something, or someone, then I got it.

So, why didn't I have that mystery woman?

A small wave of irritation irked my mood as I forced myself to finish the rest of my trip. I shouldn't be pissed about the woman slipping away, not when I had a hot date in a few hours. Yet, thinking about the date later sparked no joy or excitement like before. If anything, it made me feel exhausted, and the idea of calling it off dangled in my mind teasingly before I whacked it away.

A mess of muddy emotions churned within me as I moved through the aisles robotically, my hand snatching up what I needed without much of a glance as I was familiar with these products and easily recognized them.

The last thing I needed to grab was a tub of ice cream, so down the frozen section I went. It should have been a simple grab-and-go, but the hairs on the back of my neck stood on end before I heard it–the shrill cry of a baby.

Not just any baby, though.

I barely managed to run up in time and catch the falling baby when he reached out for me a little too far. "Whoa there, buddy!" I chuckled a little nervously with how close of a call it was.

"Oh my God, Asher!" I felt bad for his poor mom, whose face was as white as a ghost after the almost accident.

When she tried to take Asher back, he instantly clung to me and screamed in protest. The poor woman's face paled and fell even more with her embarrassment. Her eyes remained avoidant of me for as long as possible, keeping them fixed on her child until she could no longer.

I felt a little bad about wanting to laugh at how wide her eyes got and how her mouth opened slightly at the sight of me. "Oh my—I'm so sorry for bothering you again." Her face instantly blushed up until it was cherry red, which made me worry a bit because she looked like she was about to pass out with how she swayed a little.

Once again, she reached for Asher, who screamed and clung to me for dear life the moment her hands slipped around his midsection. "Asher, please don't do this." Her small voice cracked along with the apologetic smile on her face.

Setting my basket down, I took her hands in mine and held them together between us. Firmly holding her there, I turned my attention to Asher, shifting him in my arm a bit to hold him better. Then, I looked back at my blushing beauty with a warm smile.

My blushing beauty...

She wasn't mine by any means, but fuck did it sound right.

Forcing my face to maintain the smile, I brushed aside my budding desire for her. "There's nothing to apologize about. I mean, I'm not exactly mad at you or anything, so it's fine, really," I assured her warmly while brushing the back of her hands with my thumb.

Reluctantly, I let go of her in order to hold the squirming toddler properly. Chuckling softly out of amusement, I held him firmly in my arms. "You're gonna fall again, bud." I kept my voice soft and playful as I spoke to Asher, sounding atypical for a rugged-looking man like me.

Asher laughed as I poked his midsection with a wiggling finger. "Five seconds, that's all I need to talk to your momma, alright, bud? Think you can be good for me for five seconds?" I doubt any of my words were understood, but I knew how important it was to communicate and work on those little neural pathways in the growing brain.

Grinning at the woman, I proposed my idea to her, "How about this, and you are free to say no, but how about I carry this cute little sucker around and help you finish your grocery trip in peace?" A sudden grab of my cheek pulled a laugh from me as I glanced at Asher. "He seems to like me, and I don't want to leave you to deal with a screaming kid the rest of the trip. I know how stubborn they can be if they don't get their way."

Her eyes lit up with curiosity for a split second before they averted to my hands and clouded over with disappointment. "Y-you have kids of your own?" Her reluctant eyes looked back up at my face as she chewed her lip nervously.

A smiling chuckle and a shake of my head was all it took for her tense shoulders to relax with an exhale. "No, I don't have kids of my own, unfortunately. But my younger sister has a daughter, and I babysit my niece a lot for her so she can go to classes and work."

Looking closely at Asher, I surmised he was around Adelaide's age. "I think Adelaide is around Asher's age. I mean, they kinda look about the same, like size-wise and all, but I could be totally wrong," I commented with a warm chuckle, poking at Asher again when he started to get handsy with my hair. "How old is the little guy? If you don't mind me asking."

Cracking a warm smile, she hid her face a little from me shyly as she reached up to help pry her kid's chubby hand from my hair. "Asher's about sixteen months old," she replied with a proud smile.

"Oh, Adelaide is sixteen months too." I beamed, making faces at Asher to keep him entertained.

Holding my hand up to him, I wiggled my fingers around to distract him so I could give his mother my full attention. "But my offer, what do you say?" I did my best to put on my charming smile to rope her in.

I probably should be getting home to prepare for my date, but that was the last thing on my mind. Like hell would I let this second chance of mine slip away. I mean, what were the odds of us running into each other again on the same trip? And for her son to cling to me like this. It was obvious that whoever was writing our story up in the sky wanted to line things up for us.

"You don't have to." She hesitated with a reluctant smile. "I mean, you have your own trip to finish, and you probably have a lot of things to do besides this, and I don't want to be a bother to you, or more of a bother than I already have." Her soft voice grew shakier and shakier the more she rambled, until she was practically mumbling to herself with her head down.

In a somewhat bold move, I reached out and curled a finger under her chin, lifting her head. "I wouldn't have offered if it would have been a bother," I assured her with a firm smile. "I'm not the type of man to waste my time either. Not to sound like a dick, but I would have just plopped your son back into the cart and left if I didn't want to stick around." Yeah, that really sounded bad of me, but it was the truth.

I wasn't the type of person to beat around the bush or idle with time because, well, I didn't have the time or energy for it. I only ever put myself toward things I deemed worthy, and apparently, this woman and Asher fell into the category.

Brushing the tip of her chin with my thumb, I warmed my smile up as much as possible. "So, what do you say? Put up with me for about ten more minutes, for Asher's sake?"

Instantly, her eyes trembled with nervousness as she looked at me with uncertainty and... fear?

Had I tried too hard and ended up making myself creepy? What did I do to scare her? Why was she scared? I really haven't done or said anything too strange... Hopefully... I think...

Her neck tightened as her throat bobbed with a hard swallow, and I was fully prepared for her rejection when she surprised me. "W-well, you should at least tell me your name if you're going to be tagging along." It was so cute how she struggled to sound coy, and the way her cheeks flushed up made her more adorable.

Trailing the back of my index finger up her jaw, I tucked her silky chocolate-colored hair behind her ear. "Adam, and I apologize for being rude and withholding my name from such a beautiful woman," I replied with a smooth chuckle and playful grin. "A lovely woman who hopefully has a name as well?" I couldn't keep referring to her as 'the woman' or 'grocery store woman.'

The redness in her cheeks dissipated with her giggle and shy smile. "Sorry, I'm Eliza." Nervously, she rubbed her bunched hands together. "Are you sure you're fine with holding Asher for another ten or fifteen minutes? I mean, I'm almost done, but I like to take a close look at everything."

Throwing her a knowing smile, I nodded my head with certainty before reaching down to pick my basket up, only to have her take it from me and set it in her cart. "You're already carrying my sack of potatoes," she joked with a playful chuckle. "You don't need to lug around extra weight."

Deciding not to fight with her on it, I let her have it her way. "I mean, these muscles aren't just for show, you know." I lightly boasted with a slight puff of my chest.

"Oh? I didn't notice them," she snarked with a stifled smile.

Unfortunately, her little ray of sunshine cut off with a quick frown and a turn of her head. "Sorry, I don't mean that in an offensive way, not saying you don't look good, or your efforts aren't clearly seen," she quickly apologized with trembling eyes.

A slight pang to my heart caused me to wince internally as I smiled at her sadly. "Hey," my finger reached back out and tilted at her chin. "That means I didn't flex enough for you," I joked with a cheesy grin and chuckle. "You don't have to apologize for a harmless quip," I assured her. "Besides, do I look upset by it?"

I actually found it quite amusing and a little refreshing because not many people made such jabs at me. To be fair, joking around with a mafia boss wasn't a good idea all around. Eliza probably wouldn't have talked to me or looked my way if she knew of my career.

Which is why she will never know if I can help it.

Pinching her chin, I flashed her a friendly smile before nodding at the freezer. "Are you done looking at dino nuggets," I asked with a chuckle before looking down at her cart to see a missing bag of the fun-shaped chicken bites.

"Uhh yeah, I remembered I still have a lot at home..." If her voice hadn't wavered as it did, then I wouldn't have doubted her words.

Hiking Asher up because he was slipping, I gave most of my attention to the smiley toddler. Glancing at her out of the corners of my eyes, I told her, "Well, I'm perfectly fine and dandy with the lil' dude, so you take your time." It also meant more time to spend around her if she took her sweet time.

Giving in with a smile, she started to push her cart along the aisle at a slow pace. Her eyes never ceased scanning each item and tag as we passed by the shelves. Besides watching Asher, I found myself being the cart police with Eliza. She was so engrossed with the items she kept veering her cart into the middle of the aisle, so I had to keep nudging it back or steering it clear from hitting people. Along with Asher duty, I found myself being the cart police. Eliza was so engrossed with the items and tags that the cart kept veering into the middle of the aisles. Discreetly, I carefully nudged it back, keeping it from hitting other customers and avoiding embarrassing Eliza in the process.

Even if most of my attention was on Asher, I didn't let Eliza slip from my radar. I noticed every scrunch of her face, frown of her lips, deflate of her chest as she sighed inaudibly, and downward turn of her eyes.

Was she just picky? Was it something at home? Why did she seem so stressed?

"You usually take these trips alone? Like, just you and Asher? Or does your partner help out usually?" Hopefully, I wasn't too straightforward or offended her, but I was curious as to whether I had to get rid of a body or not to get her.

Her cheeks tensed up in an awkward smile as she looked at me with half-hooded eyes. "Uhh it's just me and Asher..." she dragged out, her voice a little flat as she scratched at the side of her head with a finger.

She didn't sound *to* beat up about it. If anything, her voice softened a little with relief before fear tightened it up a little. "But yeah... Uhh just us..." Her bottom lip reddened as she gnawed on it and nervously chuckled. "Hopefully, your girlfriend won't get too upset at you staying out long..." her voice wavered heavily between confusion and coyness with a tinge of regret when she looked up fully at me.

This poor woman really needed to grow a backbone, or at least, she needed to let her confidence out. I could see the sparks of confidence and trouble in her eyes, but they were always extinguished before they could rage into a wildfire.

Who hurt you, my dear Eliza?

Chapter 3
Eliza

I TRIED NOT TO take long with the rest of my trip, not wanting to take up more of Adam's time than necessary. I mean, I wasn't exactly complaining about having him around. Strangely, I found his presence rather comforting. Well, mostly comforting. There was something about him that made my gut uneasy.

Adam was friendly and charming, but it felt a little overly so. Sure, he could very well be a wholesome man, not like they were extinct in the twenty-first century. But Adam... I don't know... There was this strange, nagging feeling.

Although, such feeling of distrust could be me in general. I wasn't exactly trusting of people after being constantly let down nearly my whole life, but with men it was worse. I had a natural distrust of them because of all the abuse my ex-husband put me through. Even if they were harmless and friendly, like how Adam presented, I could never lower my guard.

I refused to open myself up to another potentially harmful situation. I won't ever put myself back into a vicious cycle of domestic violence. I couldn't. I had Asher to care for, and I refused to expose him to an environment where he could grow up thinking abusing women, or anyone, was okay.

His heartwarming chuckle of amusement put a stop to my mental walk, making me tuck it away for later. "If I had a girlfriend *that* obsessed with me, then I'd never leave her side." Was he insinuating something with his answer? "I only have my work to go home to and my sister and my niece, but that's about it." Or maybe I was thinking too much into it.

But why am I relieved that he's single?

I shouldn't, and I definitely shouldn't feel hopeful. After all, I was probably never going to see him again. Also, it wasn't as if there was anything for him and me anyway. I wasn't some hot model; I was an average plain Jane.

Well, I was probably a little worse than average. I was a twenty-eight-year-old single mom with no college education—correction; no college degree—and no positive projection in life anytime soon or ever. Career-wise, I was stuck. Sure, being a house cleaner paid okay, when paired with my nightly gig as a delivery driver, but the dream of working some nine-to-five or being a pharmacist was galaxies away.

Most of my earnings went to rent, bills, and necessities for Asher and me. What little extra I had was split between savings for Asher and our emergency funds. I didn't have enough to pay for daycare or babysitting; I took him to my job sites, and I always had him in the car. Besides care for him being out of the question, the cost of college was way beyond my means. Financial aid existed, but it was too risky to apply. Eve might have gotten me a new identity and background, but I didn't want to risk things coming apart if the government ran my information through the system.

Forcing my thoughts away with a smile, I averted my eyes from him as I reached up and pinched Asher's smiling cheek. "Well, I'm just about done, so let's head to the checkout?"

Was this where we parted ways? Or was he going to follow me to my car, too?

Smiling at Asher, Adam tickled him a bit before talking to him. "Alright, buddy, it's almost time for me to go bye-bye for now."

Did I hear him right?

Chuckling awkwardly, I looked up at Adam quizzically while doing my best to keep my hope at bay so I didn't seem like some lonely and desperate woman. "For now?" I inquired with a slow raise of my eyebrow.

Leaning close to Asher with a cheeky grin, he spoke to him in an upbeat voice, "Do you think we can convince Mommy to give me her number? Think a big smile from you will be enough while I make puppy dog eyes at her?" His playful eyes flicked to me as he spoke to Asher and made funny little noises to get him giggling.

Adam's playfulness and natural flow with Asher had me smiling uncontrollably and giggling as I watched. It was too adorable and heartwarming of a sight to not appreciate. Especially since Asher seemed to have taken quite a liking to Adam in a very short amount of time. Usually, it took my son a good few minutes of sweet talking and urging from me before he would even let go of me to go check another person out. So, the fact he grabbed onto Adam and even went as far as lunging for him was a huge surprise to me.

Giving me his full attention, Adam leaned in close to shine his bright, pleading eyes right in my face. "What does the beautiful Miss Eliza say?" The eager grin on his face stretched wider when Asher hugged his face. "May I have your number?"

Though eager, he kept himself pretty calm and collected, sounding rather charming. "We can set up a playdate for Asher and Adelaide. Then my sister can watch the two while we go on an adults-only date," he suggested, his face softening with hope.

Is he serious?

I was tempted to whip my head around to see if I could find some kind of hidden camera or crew because surely this had to be a prank of some sort. But the longer I studied his patient smile, the more my resolve chipped away.

I don't know what it was about him, but he was quite irresistible. And, I mean, it wouldn't hurt me in any way to give him my number. Worse comes to worse, he ghosts me, and I get a bout of disappointment before moving on with my life.

I should probably prepare for that anyways, since there's no way he's actually serious about me.

Relenting with a small smile, I nodded my head. "Only because you asked so nicely," I snarked at him playfully with a giggle.

Grinning victoriously, Adam looked at Asher and did a small fist pump. "Yeah, you hear that, buddy? I just hit the jackpot," he playfully squealed. Whisper spoke? Something between a manly squeal and over-excitement.

He honestly did look like he'd won a billion-dollar jackpot with how much he beamed. His joy even managed to infect me, and I found myself smiling uncontrollably back at him.

Carefully, he held Asher in one arm and used his free hand to pull his phone out of his pants. "Come on, let's get in line while you do that because it looks like it's getting long." Grabbing my cart, he began to push it toward the checkout lines while I followed behind with his phone in my hands.

"Oh, hey, Eliza," the cashier greeted me with a friendly smile. "How are you and Asher today?" The cashier was an old lady who'd been working here since the dawn of time—her words, not mine.

"Mary, hey, we're doing just dandy. Same old, same old and all," I replied with a warm smile of my own as I made my way past the cart to the card reader. "How are you and Rob? Not partying it up too much are you?" I asked with a chuckle at the end.

Laughing in response, she shimmied a bit in her spot. "Hey, as long as these hips can sway, then we will dance away." She was such a lively person, and I kind of envied her, not gonna lie.

After many trips throughout the year and regularly having their house on my delivery route, I learned that she and Rob, her husband, have been married since their late teens after they ran away from their parents. I was kind of jealous of how she seemingly led a perfect life. Well, it more so made me disappointed in my own life with my failed marriage.

Where did I go wrong?

James and I were the perfect couple in high school. We had known each other our whole lives because we grew up together. We initially met through church, and we ran around in the same friend group ever since I found out he lived only three houses down from me.

Sighing softly, I forced a smile on my face as I kept my eyes trained on the card reader's screen. "You and Rob are going to be waltzing up those stairs to the pearly gates one day instead of just flying up," I teased her with a soft chuckle. "Does Rob want any more sticky rice buns?"

Leaning over to me, Mary placed her arm on mine, "Honey, his buns are going to turn into hamburger buns if you don't stop spoiling him." She smirked and we shared a laugh at her joke. "Don't worry, he still has some stashed away in the freezer from the last time you gave us some. Besides, you gotta save your money for that one," her finger playfully wiggled at Asher, who laughed in response to the attention, "right there."

Then, her eyebrows rose up, and her eyes sparkled with interest and amusement when they landed on Adam. Slowly, her lips curled into a teasing smirk as she glanced and winked at me. "Adam, how are you sweetie? How's Hailee and Adelaide? I see you're still getting lucky and getting yourself once-in-a-lifetime opportunities." Her eyes trailed over to me when she said the last part. "Sweet little Eliza and Asher here are diamonds waiting to shine."

Heat flooded my cheeks from the embarrassment of all the attention and doting. "Mary, what happened to not telling lies," I bit back playfully behind my blushing cheeks.

Laughing softly, Mary waved me off. "Because it ain't lies," she remarked sassily. "You two really are diamonds in the rough."

Rolling my eyes, I lightly shooed her off. "Oh, Mary, you're too much sometimes, I swear." My own sassy response came out before I could control the snap of it.

"Sorry, I didn't mean for that to come out so... bitey?" I quickly apologized, pressing my lips together to zip my mouth.

Mary didn't seem to mind, though. If anything, she rather liked it with how elated and proud her smile was. "Oh, that's what I love to see. I know there's a fire in ya somewhere just waiting to rage."

Patting my arm, she widened her smile for a split second before going back to scanning the rest of the items while I fished my wallet out from my bag. Okay, let me rephrase that last part: while I tried to fish out my wallet from my bag. A large hand stopped me from fully doing so. "Don't worry about it, I got it," Adam assured me warmly and confidently as he pulled my empty hand out of my bag.

I quickly denied him with a shake of my head and a light frown. "I can't trouble you like that, and besides, you already had to carve some time out of your day to watch Asher when you really didn't have to." I also didn't want a handout like this.

As if I already didn't feel bad about troubling him thus far. The last thing I needed was to feel indebted to him because he paid for my groceries. Looking at everything, it was a lot less than what I'd usually get on a typical trip, but still.

Or was that his angle? Warm his way in and keep me trapped with debt?

Before I could spiral down the well of doubt and smear his seemingly good image in my mind, his chuckle yanked me back to reality. "If it was a bother, then I wouldn't have done it," he remarked while tucking his wallet away.

"Huh," was my stunned response, and I stood and watched Adam like a deer in the headlights as he loaded the bagged groceries into the cart, bid Mary goodbye, and put Asher back into the cart. I obediently allowed him to take control of the cart with one hand and pull me out of the store with the other, our hands clasped together like it wasn't a big deal, all with a single thought in my head.

What the hell just happened?

With how boggled my mind was, I barely managed to catch Adam's question. "Which car is yours?"

Of course, like a total idiot, I just stood there blinking at him in silence, making a fool of myself for a good solid minute before I managed to slap some sense into myself. "Uhh, it's the Rav4 over there," I answered in a slight daze, pointing over to the silver Toyota Rav4 a little way from us.

Casually, as if we'd been dating for a while, he slipped his arm around my waist and held me rather protectively as he made his way to my car with me and the cart in tow.

I felt kind of bad about tensing up at his touch, but after equating a man's touch to nothing but pain for so long, my brain had become rewired. Now, men, in general, left a bad taste in my mouth and got the hairs on the back of my neck standing up.

As friendly as Adam was, I still couldn't settle my thumping heart that squeezed so slowly and painfully in anticipation of something bad coming. Bile churned in my stomach in response to my body's stress levels ramping up. Then, I was torn between wanting to shove his arm away and wanting to lean into him for safety and support.

No matter how damaged I'd become, there was always a small, hopeful part of me that yearned for the good in people—even if there wasn't any to be had.

I hated that part of myself.

If I had just...

"Eliza?" Adam's voice stopped my train of thought again before it could leave the station. "Open the trunk?"

Completely snapping out of it, I quickly fumbled for my keys and opened the trunk with an awkward chuckle. "Sorry, I uhh get lost in my head a lot." I hoped my half-assed apology would be enough to keep him from pushing.

I was prepared to throw excuses at him to stave him off, but he just let it go. "You probably have a lot going on handling Asher all by yourself and working, so I don't blame you."

My lips curled in a quick smile to show him some silent gratitude before I opened the trunk. "Have you lived in this town long?" All the friendly greetings he'd been receiving in the store hadn't gone unnoticed.

"About ten years, give or take," he answered without breaking a sweat or losing his rhythm while putting things into my trunk.

"What about you?" His eyes quickly looked at me for a few seconds before he had to give his attention back to the groceries. "I don't think I've seen you around until today."

Seeing him do everything while having Asher on his hip made me feel a little bad, but it also made me feel a little warm on the inside. He was such a natural as if he'd been doing this forever. I didn't let the feeling fester, though, dumping a bucket of water on the growing fire before it could blaze.

Taking a calming breath, I centered myself before replying, "Oh, I've only been here for about a year, and I kinda don't go out much." Reaching out, I pried Asher away from Adam to give him a rest from my clingy toddler. "If I'm not at work, then I'm with Asher, either at home or at the park if the weather is pretty good, and I usually only go to the grocery store like once a week when I can."

Honestly, with no set schedule, the chances of running into Adam were probably slim to none. Even if I'd been living here long, it would've probably been impossible to cross paths with Adam. Maybe I should take this as a sign, because coincidences didn't just happen for no reason. However, I don't think I could make room for anyone else in my life right now.

Grinning at me, Adam quickly shut the trunk before reaching out and ruffling the top of Asher's head. "Well, better late than never, I say."

Then, awkwardness... I mean, obviously, this was where we said bye to each other and made promises to see each other later, but this felt weird. Of course, it could also be me being an awkward little duck and making a big deal out of nothing.

Luckily, a warm chuckle from Adam broke the icy tension—thank God. "Let's get Asher into his car seat." Lordy, that should not sound so natural, as if we were a family.

Humming in agreement, I made my way over to the door of the backseat with Adam, thanking him softly when he opened the door for me. I quickly, I buckled Asher in and stepped aside so he and Adam could wave goodbye. Then, I stepped back fully to let Adam shut the door.

Swallowing the lump in my throat, I looked up at Adam with a lopsided smile. "Well, thank you again. You really didn't have to do any of that." This felt awkward, especially with the fact he'd paid for my groceries dangling in front of my mind. "Listen, about the groceries—"

As if he knew what I'd say, he held a hand out and shook his head. "Eliza, it's nothing to me. The cost, I mean, so don't try to insist on paying me back." He really didn't sound bothered by it one bit, which really threw me for a loop.

Then, his warm smile curled playfully as he leaned so that our faces were inches apart. "Well, actually, you could pay me back..." Damn, I knew there was a catch. "...by agreeing to a date with me when we can work something out."

Okay, never mind, maybe I was a little harsh on him.

Unable to help it, I cracked a small grin and giggled. "I mean, no promises since I'm a pretty busy person, but I'll try." If he was even serious about it.

Again, I was convinced he would delete my number or forget about me in the days to come. I'd probably just be 'that grocery store girl' to him sooner rather than later.

Straightening himself back up, he slowly reached out and took my hand, rubbing the back of it with his thumb. "Drive safe, and have a good night, Eliza." His body twitched toward me for a split second as if he wanted to lean in, but he was quick to recompose himself with a smile. "I *will* talk to you later, promise." The depth of his stoney gray eyes made them shine in a way that made my doubts dissolve.

Chapter 4
Adam

WELL, I WISH I could say I was surprised, but I really couldn't. Eliza Huyen really wasn't much. As harsh as it was to say, she was a sad and boring person.

Honestly, her file was probably the saddest one I'd seen in a long while—or maybe ever. Seriously, the thing wasn't even an inch thick!

Her life was boring. She was born in Salem, Oregon, in 1998—which put her at twenty-eight years old. Her grade and high school educations were received through the public school system, and rather than attend an out-of-state college, she went to the local community college. Hell, she only remained there for a short time, before dropping out over a year ago, when I assume Asher was born.

True to her word, her record showed that she moved to Seaside about a year ago, a few months after her son was born when her parents relocated back to their home country of Vietnam and passed from the land of the living shortly after. With no college degree in hand, she'd been working a low-end job as a housecleaner, contracting herself to a local company here in Seaside. Outside of her housecleaning job, she worked as a delivery driver for various food delivery apps.

She was a simple girl stuck in life, simple as that—in my opinion. *So, why the hell am I so enamored with her!?*

Biting out a frustrated sigh, I closed the folder with a little force before throwing it into the top drawer of my office desk. Running a hand down my face, I racked my brain for a reason as to why I couldn't get her demure smile out of my mind.

She was a girl down on her luck who would probably use me in the end, so why was I obsessing over her?

Mentally slapping myself, I shook my head in denial because thinking about her like that felt wrong. I shouldn't think ill of her, not with the goodness I saw in her sad and broken eyes.

God, those eyes. Those lovely, amber brown eyes with a perfect ring of black flecks, haven't stopped haunting me since the grocery store. Even when I was out on my stupid date that night—all I could see, whenever I looked across from me, was her shy figure and smile instead of the busty and leggy brunette who was more interested in her phone than me. Yeah, that was one of the worst dates of my life. Thankfully, I don't think she cared enough when I told her it wouldn't work out and threw a few bills at her.

Sighing heavily, I picked up my phone and opened my messaging app to send Eliza a quick text.

Good morning, Eliza, how are you and Asher this morning?

At least she hadn't ghosted me, thank God. When I texted Eliza three nights ago, I was surprised when she responded. It wasn't much; just a quick 'good night' exchange as it had been late. The next day our text exchange was also short and to the point, but yesterday was a little smoother with her opening up a little to me.

Good morning, Adam! We're just busy as always lol! Hopefully we won't be too busy this weekend because it seems like it'll be nice, so I wanna take Asher to the park.

Oh, I was planning on taking Adelaide to the park this weekend too while her mom works. Let's make it a playdate for the two and we can grab lunch as well?

I couldn't help but smile in anticipation as I watched the three dots pop up on the screen. I mean, it was perfect timing!

Yeah! I'll let you know if anything changes, but for now, let's put it down.

It's a date!

I mean, if that's what you want to call it lol. You don't want to date someone like me, you're too good!

Well, too bad you don't have a say in who I date lol.

Pretty busy schedule today?

Yeah, but busy means money, so I'm not complaining. Wbu?

It's a steady day.

Do you want me to bring you something between your houses so you can eat?

Oh no that's okay! You don't have to! I got my lunch packed for the day too but thanks. :)

Somehow, I doubted that very much, but I didn't feel like I could say anything because I didn't know if she was lying to me. So, I let it be, begrudgingly.

Alright, if you do want or need anything, I'm here, alright? I might be a little quiet today because I have to go out on some errands later, but I'll do my best to respond when I can.

Have a good day at work. :)

You too.

Tucking my phone away, I leaned back in my seat as I studied her scheduled houses for the day. She wasn't lying; she was very busy today. As bad as I felt for her, because it looked like she was going to be cleaning house after house after house for the next six hours, I couldn't help but feel grateful. Her being out longer meant more time for me to snoop around and do what I needed.

Speaking of which...

Where the hell is Max?

Of course, speak of The Devil, and he shall come.

Not even a minute after I thought about texting him, Max barged into my office with an unamused glare. "You gave me the wrong code," he deadpanned, flipping me off.

Barking out a brief laugh, I stood up from my desk and rounded it. "Or you could have punched it in wrong," I retorted, smirking at him smugly.

No, I gave him the wrong code to fuck with him, but I wasn't going to admit it. "How long did it take you this time, genius?" I asked with an innocent smirk, stuffing my hands into my pockets and leaning back against my desk.

Rolling his eyes, Max flipped me off—again—before going over to my liquor cabinet and grabbing a bottle of bourbon. "Considering how it's *my* security system, it took me no time," Max remarked.

Popping the bottle open, he grabbed a glass and poured himself a heavy one while looking at me knowingly with a raised brow. "So, are you going to tell me what you need me for before or after I drink?" he questioned while swirling the drink around. "Or am I going to need the drink first?"

"Oh, come on, it's not like I'm asking you to do anything *too* illegal," I joked with a soft laugh, making Max roll his eyes harder at me. "Just need some cameras in someone's house, that's all. Not like we haven't done anything like this before." It wasn't a very common thing we did, but we had our fair share of breaking and entering to rig a place.

Leaning his head back with a confused frown, Max tentatively sipped at his drink. "Are you really that hung up over this Eliza chick? I mean, not to knock your tastes and shit, but she's boring," Max commented, his words slightly hollow from having spoken into the glass. "Literally, there is *nothing* interesting about her life."

My chest heaved with a deep breath as I ran a hand through my dark locks, pushing them back. "There's just something about her, man." I could feel the corners of my lips pulling up into a dopey smile as I thought about Eliza's soft face. "I don't know how to explain it, but it's just a feeling." The mere thought of her always brought a flare of heat to my chest, as if someone tossed a match at my heart and lit it up in a blaze of passion.

"Holy shit." I faintly heard Max gasp. "Dude, are you okay? Did this girl drug you or something?" His concern was playful and teasing in nature, but it was genuine.

"No. God no. Nothing like that, but it honestly feels like she's giving me the best chase of my life. It's like a never-ending high." Shaking my head with a chuckle, I sighed happily and looked out the window for a moment. "That's what I mean, man. She's just..." Letting out a frustrated sigh at the nagging feeling gnawing at my chest, I looked back at Max. "I can't get her out of my mind. Every time I close my eyes, she's there. Everywhere I look, I see glimpses of her. And yes, there's technically nothing special about her. She's plain and boring, but I don't know. Something about that makes me kind of happy." I was beating around the bush now because I couldn't make heads or tails of my confusing feelings.

Clearing my muddled thoughts with a firm shake of my head, I looked back at my friend with a lopsided smile. "Sorry, probably not an answer to your question, but no, she didn't drug me." Even if it felt like it, or at least it felt like I'd been stabbed in the ass by Cupid. "I just... I don't know, Eliza is just perfect..."

Seems like I couldn't get past Max, though. "But?" he bit out with an urgency for me to spit it out.

"Just a gut feeling that she's not as simple as she seems." Maybe she had some kind of addiction or a strange personality trait or two. Perhaps that's what set off my caution radar.

Dragging out a long sigh, Max downed his drink. "Well, whatever she's up to or hiding, you'll find out sooner or later after we rig her place." Clapping his hands together, a habit of his to reset himself, he pointed a finger to the open door of my office. "Well, we haven't got all day, so let's go."

We had about an hour before Eliza would leave her place, and her apartment complex was right across the creek from me—literally fifteen minutes tops. So, I took my sweet time going over the plan to break into Eliza's place one last time with Max, before taking stock of all the equipment we'd need. One can never be too careful is something I'd always believed, and better to be over prepared than under.

"I still think you're a little crazy for this," Max commented as we started the drive in his truck.

Shooting him a flat glare, I scoffed. "Says the man chasing after a nurse he bumped into. One who couldn't give less of a shit about you." He really had no footing against me because we were both in the same shit hole together.

"Hey, hey, hey," he chuckled in protest. "Amira is just playing hard to get, that's all."

Unable to help it, I snorted out a laugh. "Dude, how many times has she rejected you just this week alone?" He was persistent, and this latest venture of his was too patient for her own good.

Beaming with a victorious grin, he chuckled happily. "Only three times out of the four I've asked, so I'm making progress."

Rolling my eyes, I scoffed playfully. "Whatever makes your boat float, man." If he wanted to be a little delusional, then who was I to pop his bubble.

Also, given that I was now pining after a random woman I met at the grocery store, I was the last person who should be giving him shit about the situation. A seeming down-on-her-luck kind of gal, but again, there was this gut feeling about her I couldn't shake. It wasn't a bad feeling or anything, but one cautioning me to dig deeper.

Sure, some people were fine and happy living a simple life, and usually they radiated genuine joy. Yet, I got none of that with Eliza, especially when I looked into her eyes. The only time her eyes even remotely lit up was when she looked at Asher, but other than that, they were muddled with dullness and, occasionally, fear.

No way a 'boring girl' would have such broken eyes.

Something was up with Eliza; I had no doubt about it, and I had every intention of figuring out the reason behind her troubles.

It didn't take us long to reach her place, and we had no trouble gaining access after slipping the shady landlord a few Benjamins. I was thankful for the easy entrance to her private abode, but it also pissed me off.

"Remind me to have him replaced," I grumbled to Max as we stood in Eliza's small studio apartment.

Scoffing in disdain, Max scowled at the door. "Imagine if we had been bad people."

If I wasn't so pissed, then I would have cracked a laugh at his comment because, well, *mafia*.

In all honesty, if all it took were a few hundred-dollar bills to gain access to her place, then what was to stop someone from walking in and stealing her things while she was out? What was to stop them from bugging the place with cameras to spy on her? What about in the middle of the night? What if they just waltzed in and assaulted her one day on a whim? Or hell, what was to stop the creepy landlord from abusing the master key himself?

I didn't like the way his face lit up at the mention of Eliza's name, nor did I like how he lingered at the open door for a minute too long with his beady eyes scanning the place.

The thought of anyone violating and invading Eliza's personal space with bad intentions, or just in general, caused a surge of hot anger throughout my body. Tension tightened my jaw and made my teeth grit and grind against each other as I stood there with my hands balled into fists inside my pockets.

My glaring eyes glanced over at the nonfunctioning secondary lock currently on her door. "Remind me to replace the locks at her place, too, especially that secondary lock." The thing wasn't even screwed in properly, so like hell would it keep the door from being thrown open without much force. "Hell, remind me to replace the entire door with something sturdier."

"Want to replace him with one of our men? Or do you want me to filter through some people and hire someone?" Max inquired as he started to unpack his tools and equipment from the box he had been carrying.

Calming myself with a deep breath, I ran a slow hand through my hair, holding it there for a moment as I carefully scanned the apartment. "For the sake of keeping it simple, and our sanity, just see which of our men will work," I replied before slowly stalking around the place.

Max was so much more than my best friend; he was also my lieutenant who kept things afloat so I could be in the background. My tech whizz of a friend was a godsend, and I honestly wouldn't be here if it weren't for him. From hacking college exam answers to my enemy's network, I would have flunked out and been on the street by now if I didn't have him. Any and all information which found its way into my hands was courtesy of Max and his crew. Even Eliza's profile was all because of him.

"Consider it done." Max's casual reply filtered through the air before things went silent as the two of us got to work.

Contrary to what many believed, hiding cameras around a place and fully rigging it was more complicated than what movies made it out to be. You couldn't just stick a tiny little camera in a teddy bear or in a dark corner and call it a day.

Finding the ideal place for a camera was tricky, and then the wiring or transmitter for it was the next issue. Honestly, if it was as easy as slapping a mini camera into a vent or placing a teddy bear camera, then everyone would be spying on each other.

I let Max handle all the finding and rigging, for the most part, because it was his forte. While he was occupied, I busied myself with snooping through every inch of Eliza's place.

Naturally, I started with her dresser, if it could even be called such. It was one of those plastic drawer things someone would get from Walmart or Target that barely reached my mid-thigh. She had, like, the bare minimum. Only about enough for a week's worth of clothes, it seemed. About seven to ten sets of clothes lined the three drawers, and there was a small cubby box filled with cheap underwear and bras right next to it.

The tiny closet housed an even smaller dresser, this one filled with children's clothing. Hanging on the rack were some work uniforms, or some kind of ratty clothes that had bleach stains all over them along with other smudges and discolorations. The floor was lined with three pairs of very worn sneakers.

Sliding the closet door shut, I made my way over to her kitchen to see what she had stashed away. And surprise, surprise, there was nothing. Okay, by nothing, I meant it was barely stocked. There were plenty of jars containing baby food and other child-friendly food items plenty, but there was barely anything for Eliza. The only things I found that were suitable for an adult were packages of ramen, cans of soup, bulk frozen food packages, and some stuff for simple ham and cheese sandwiches.

No wonder she's so fucking skinny.

Hell, after seeing the sadness of her kitchen, I was convinced that a homeless person had better options and ate better than her with a free meal from the shelter. It seemed like she only fed Asher more than well and didn't take care of herself, or forwent her own health for his.

The thought of her suffering for her child made the corners of my lips drag into a frown as an anchor pulled my heart down to the depths of despair. Yes, people struggled, and when it came down to it, a good parent sacrificed a lot for their child. But I didn't want Eliza to be in that pit hole. She shouldn't have to decide between feeding herself or Asher.

Honestly, she shouldn't be struggling as much as she was, with housing assistance, cash assistance, and food stamps—the only thing missing was childcare support. Even with all that assistance, she hustled two jobs with Asher strapped to her.

My sweet Eliza shouldn't be struggling so much. She deserved to have a moment to herself, to be spoiled. I wonder what she'd choose to indulge herself in if she got the chance. Well, slight adjustment; I wonder what she'd pick when I gave her the chance. It wasn't a matter of if, but when.

God, I couldn't wait to finally take her out on a date and make her face light up with so much with joy, she'd outshine all the stars in the galaxy.

While mulling over the endless fantasies of us going out, I made my way over to the last area to be searched—her bathroom. Like everything else, it was scarcely stocked with the bare minimum. Well, at least everything but her cupboard under the sink. Besides toilet paper and extra soaps and shit, over half of it was stocked with boxes of brown hair dye.

Now, why on earth did a woman like her hoard this much hair dye? Was she going gray already? Highly doubtful, and my gut didn't settle with that thought one bit.

Making a mental note to myself, I closed the loose wooden doors and went back out to the couch to regroup with Max.

Remaining occupied with his task, Max took a minute to take note of my beady eyes, which were locked on him. The sight of me made his eyes roll as he let out a heavy sigh, "You know, I have to say... This Eliza chick you're obsessed with," his words trailed off as his eyes glanced at me. "Something isn't fitting..."

Plopping down on her ratty couch with a sigh, I hung my head in my hands. "I feel it too, but I can't even begin to place my finger on where to start trying to figure things out." Letting out a frustrated sigh, I ran my hands through my hair. "Like, where do you even begin to grasp and unravel someone so plain? Her records are solid, so there's nothing there. Her parents are dead, so I can't pick up the phone and talk to them." It didn't help that she had no other family around.

"Okay, but no one has a perfect record, man," Max mentioned with a soft huff of frustration. "The fact *everything* about her record is spotless is a huge red flag. I'll dig into her further later, when I get a chance, and fill you in as things come up."

Max's voice droned on about being careful and shit, but I paid no attention because I was in a mental sinkhole.

I mean, what could a person like her be hiding? Was she some ruthless killer?

A snort scratched at the back of my throat at the thought of Eliza being a violent criminal on the run.

Yes, there was something about her, but being a criminal couldn't be it. She was much too frail to do any damage in a physical struggle, and she was much too soft. Honestly, I wouldn't be surprised if she couldn't hurt a fly; hell, I wouldn't be surprised if she cried about hurting a fly. Also, she had Asher. If I were a criminal on the run, the last thing I'd lug along with me was my child, a toddler at that. It would already be a shit ton of work to watch my own back, so the less responsibility I had, the better.

Sighing, I leaned back against her couch, letting my heavy body sink into the mushy couch. "But what if..." No, I couldn't finish that absurd thought.

No one was perfect, even my Eliza.

Forcing the nagging feeling away, I attempted to alleviate the tension with a joke. "You know, at least she's not hiding a body in her closet." As if she could fit one in that tiny thing.

"Man, did you listen to a single thing I said?" Max grumbled with a scowling glare. "It'd be better if a body had fallen out of her damn closet, because then, at least, we'd have an answer as to what the fuck is up with her."

He had a good point. Also, a body would've been a lot easier to deal with than whatever her unknown secret was. Disposing of a corpse and covering up whatever crime she'd committed would have been child's play. The more I thought about it, the more I wished I had found something physically damning to confront her with.

Since nothing had been found, there was literally nothing I could do at that moment. The only thing remotely out of place, had been a vibrator and dildo I'd found in her nightstand. Poor thing would need to upgrade and level up in size before I could take her. The toy had nothing on me; and no, I wasn't tooting my own horn and exaggerating my dick size. I was much bigger than the meager six-inch toy, and much girthier too. Not to mention, I would far outlast the battery on that thing.

Taking a deep breath, I slapped my hands down on my thighs and shot up from the couch. Grinning cheekily, I snickered softly. "Alright, let's finish this up so I can go make a list of things to charm her with."

Unamused, Max threw a bundle of wires at me after rolling his eyes. "Go make yourself useful then and start connecting."

"Hey," I snapped at him playfully, "don't forget who's the boss between us."

Chapter 5
Eliza

~1 week later~

The sound of my notifications going off felt like a hammer to the head, reminding me of my cowardice and really driving that nail deep into my bones.

"Mama." And Asher didn't help either.

Of course, I couldn't fault the little guy, nor could I be mad at him. I mean, watching him waddle over with my phone in his hands to give it to me was too adorable. He was only trying to help me and be my good boy.

Bending down to his level, I took my phone from his outstretched hands with a big, warm smile. "Thanks, baby." I gave his little head a rub and kiss before standing back up to look at the contents.

Besides reminders about upcoming jobs, and texts from my boss about said, and new, jobs, the main reason why I dreaded opening my phone was—

Ding!

Hey, check your door. :)

Oh, like that's not creepy at all.

Rolling my eyes, I went against all caution and headed to my front door, opening it with the expectation that he'd be crowding the doorframe. So, it surprised me a little to see the nearly empty parking lot in front of my apartment complex with no hot man in sight. Instead, the only thing I found was a single rose with a to-go cup from Controversial Coffee and a little folded-up note.

I shouldn't be giving you a coffee addiction, but you deserve it.

-Adam S.

P.S. throw away that crap in your cupboard before you burn a hole through your stomach.

Should I be drinking from a random cup delivered to my door? No, probably not, but it smelled rather nice. Well, at least I was home, and the door was locked... though, I wouldn't want to leave Asher stranded for any amount of time if it was drugged. On the other hand, I didn't see why Adam would tamper with my coffee when he wouldn't even be around to reap its effects. Wait, actually—

Okay, this was sweet and all, and thank you, but how do you know where I live? And what I have in my cupboards?

I most definitely did not give him my address during the two weeks we'd been casually texting back and forth. Really, I wasn't ungrateful for the rose and coffee; they were nice—honest! And if this situation of ours was different, then I'd be gushing with so much happiness that the walls of my place would turn pink and bubbly.

But it was a little weird... Very creepy.

Did you forget I went grocery shopping with you? I saw every-thing you had in your cart, and I still have the receipt.

Fine, I guess I'd accept his answer. Not like I could argue with him about it because it was all true.

Mary gave me your address the other day when I was at the grocery store. We chit-chatted and I mentioned I wanted to do some-thing nice for you.

Don't worry, I didn't follow you around like some stalker or anything lol!

The ball of tension in my chest unraveled and left my body with a long exhale. That was a relief to hear. Mary knew where I lived because she'd been by a couple of times to drop things off for me and Asher, or to pick up some treats from me for her and her husband.

Oh, okay then!

Thank you :)

It's so lovely! I really love the rose! Roses are my favorite, espe-cially pink and cream ones, and I haven't tried the coffee yet, but it smells good!

Feeling more at ease, I eyed the coffee cup for a second before taking a sip of it. My body tensed up slightly as I prepared myself for the bitterness to bite my tongue, but I found myself relaxing with a surprised raise of my brows when silky, sweet smoothness bathed my tongue.

I rarely got coffee from shops because I hated the bitterness of it; the coffee I made at home was usually drowned in creamer and sugar, basically making it a frappe. Honestly, I was probably breaking all the rules of coffee drinking, but I needed the caffeine to get myself through a whole day; I'd tried energy drinks, but they usually gave me headaches.

Happily smiling to myself, I sipped away at the drink, humming and giggling to myself as I zipped around the house to gather things.

I actually had no cleaning jobs scheduled for today, and the weather was pretty decent for once. So, I figured a day at the park would be nice for Asher and me.

Just as I was about to grab Asher, I became distracted when my phone dinged again.

How's the drink? Do you like it?

Also, you busy today?

And there goes my mood. It wasn't Adam's fault for the sourness to my pep. I was a coward who kept avoiding him like the plague. A part of me wanted to give in, go on that date, and have some fun for once. Yet, I couldn't. The thought of leaving Asher to take a moment to myself like that, made my chest tighten with guilt. Also, I didn't think I was ready yet.

What if I put myself out there and got rejected? Yes, Adam might be the one initiating everything right now, but what if he pulled back after finding out the truth? I had so much baggage, and honestly, I probably should have shot him down at the store for both our sakes. Honestly, I have no idea what I'd been thinking!

I was setting myself up for failure. There was no way anything good could come from any of this. I mean, how would I even begin to tell him the truth if, or when, the time came?

'Hey, so my name isn't actually Eliza Huyen, I'm a total loser because I let my ex-husband abuse the shit out of me, who by the way I ran away from in the middle of the night, and I am now hiding from. Oh, and I'm still technically and legally married.'

Like that conversation would blow over well for anyone.

I had to keep my head low, dating right now was not an option. I couldn't bring myself to reject Adam. Stringing him along wasn't any better, but I just couldn't do it. I couldn't let him go. I couldn't give up the way he made me feel, but letting him closer wasn't an option either!

Letting out a frustrated groan, I gripped and tugged at my hair, hoping the pain would kick some sense into me. Of course, that did nothing but give me pain without the sense. "Oh my God, why am I like this?" I asked no one in particular. Well, Asher did look at me with a confused look for a moment before going back to chewing on his toy.

Huffing to myself, I plopped down on my couch with a pout. "Why did I think starting over would be easy?" In hindsight, it was.

In hindsight, it should've been, but that was before all the nuances and paranoia set in. I didn't have to worry about Asher and school right now, but he only had a few years left before I had to send him. Sure, homeschooling was an option, but I couldn't be doing that while busting my ass to make sure we had enough money for bills and food. The fear of James finding us once he went to school, made friends, and spread his wings kept me up into the late hours of the night more often than not. What if James just showed up and kidnapped Asher? What if he just showed up at the school, picked Asher up, and took him back to Idaho?

The soft thumps of Asher's thundering steps made me peer up at him. I couldn't help but smile at the sight of my chunky man barreling towards me and then hugging me. "Mama?" He was so young but so in tune with me. He probably didn't have a lick of an idea about the situation, yet he worried over me.

Asher had always been so sweet and intuitive. I mean, I didn't know how his little brain was wired, but ever since he became more and more aware, any time he saw me frowning or crying, he'd instantly run over to comfort me. I had to be doing something correctly with him then, right?

"Oh, baby." I forced a laugh through my budding tears. "Come here." With a strained groan, I picked up my heavy toddler and held him tightly with a growing smile. "I love you so much, baby."

And the sweet moment lasted two seconds before he squirmed with a whine, meaning he wanted to be free to do whatever his mind was on now. So, with an amused chuckle, I set him down, watching as he waddled off to his pile of toys.

Resetting myself with a deep breath, I picked my phone back up to reply to Adam.

The drink was so good. I usually like sweet coffee drinks, so this is perfect. Thank you :)

Also, I don't have work today, but I want to spend time with Asher today and just try to unwind. I hope you understand.

Good to know for next time lol

And hey, don't worry about it, you enjoy your time with Asher. Tell him I said hi :)

Of course, Adam being a good sport about it all didn't help. I mean, who allowed this man to be such a golden star? Like, God, why couldn't you make him snap at me? Send a red flag my way! Something!

I needed this man to be less perfect, like yesterday, so I could drop him like a brick into the ocean. Seriously, life was not fair to me. Granted, it hadn't been for a while, but this whole placing Adam in my life was just beyond cruel.

Letting out a drawn-out groan, I stared up at my ceiling for a long moment before shooting up from the couch, startling Asher. "Sorry, baby," I chuckled with an apologetic smile.

Warming my smile up, I bent down and reached out for him. "Come on, bud, let's go to the park."

Asher instantly perked up and scrambled over to me with a toothy grin, tackling me in a hug and squealing. Again, I didn't know if he fully understood or if he just took my open arms as an invite, but either way, it was too cute, and I wanted to give him a little credit.

Maybe he was starting to understand. I mean, kids did grow smarter by the day.

Grunting softly because my damn kid felt like a sack of rice, I picked him up and got him into the stroller. Then, I grabbed the prepped bag and left.

Ten-ish minutes of walking later, and we made it to the park in one piece. Asher was still too small and young to enjoy the whole park, but he always had fun running around, climbing what structures he could, going down the slide (with my help), and swinging on the swings.

Wonderful little moments like these always tugged at my heartstrings. I couldn't help the thoughts of Asher growing up from fluttering through my mind. Soon, he wouldn't want to go to the park anymore, nor would he ever be this carefree toddler again. All the smiles and giggles right now, they were only now and never after. These were the moments I would miss, but they were also the ones that made me appreciate motherhood.

It really was special, and I wouldn't trade it for anything else in the world.

Capturing these moments on my phone didn't do them any justice, but it was the least I could do to preserve the memories.

Everything was perfect for a long while until Asher decided to go rogue. "Asher!" Of course, my clumsy ass managed to trip on thin air when I went after my speedy toddler.

"Wait!" I paid no attention to the sting on my cheek from my face plant, nor the dirt in my mouth as I struggled to chase after him; I was too worried about my son crashing into someone or something—or, God forbid, a car.

My racing heart stilled with warmth at the sound of a familiar voice. "Whoa, there, bud!" A sense of relief and security blanketed me when my wide eyes caught sight of Adam holding a giggling Asher in his arms. "Where's—"

His worried face instantly relaxed and brightened when his head did a quick sweep, and his eyes landed on me. One look at his face as his sharp eyes locked onto mine, and you'd probably think he'd won the lottery or something. "Eliza." And that billion-dollar smile made me feel like someone important.

It only took him a few strides to close the distance between us—him and his long legs. I couldn't stop my eyes from wandering to his muscular legs, appreciating how nicely toned they were. Of course, I didn't stop at his legs. Slowly, my eyes worked their way up his fit body.

Fuck you for being so damn perfect.

Seriously, he looked like those damn statues carved by ancient sculptors. Every part of his strong, athletic build was perfectly proportionate. I was willing to bet that every inch of his six-foot-something body was perfectly toned with muscle. He wasn't bulky and built like a tank like a bodybuilder, but I could see the nice definition of his triceps and biceps, and lordy, those forearms of his were so perfect. Then those nice veins... God, it'd be so easy to just stick a needle in him. Hell, forget about anatomy models and diagrams on paper; this man would be the perfect study model.

"Eliza?" A chilling shock to my body made me flinch when Adam waved his hand right in my face.

Whatever awe and wonder checking his body out had blessed my mind with flew away as the demons came crashing in like a stampede of raging bulls. Out of pure instinct, I flinched away from Adam, cowering and covering my head protectively with my arms. The ache in my tense muscles worsened at the feeling of large hands wrapping themselves around my wrists, and I only resisted more when I felt the tug.

"Mama."

"Eliza."

Their voices muddled together in my adrenaline-filled mind. I didn't try to fight the sensation of my curled-up body being moved. The anticipation of blows on my body caused me to clam up even more to where I probably looked like an armadillo. Yet, they never came. All I felt was warmth.

A part of me dreaded the crushing pressure that would come when I felt the pair of strong arms wrapping around me. I wanted to take comfort in Adam's embrace, but I was too terrified.

Adam was probably pissed I let Asher get away, that he could've been severely hurt. He probably thought that I should have been more mindful, paid more attention, and been better. There were so many things he could beat me for, and I wasn't ready for it. It'd been too long since...

I can't...

"Hey." The softness and warmth of his voice took me by surprise, making me freeze because I didn't know how to process it. Was it a ploy to get me to lower my guard? It had to be, right? I mean, hitting me while I was all clammed up wouldn't be any fun.

A slow trickle of fingers flowed down the back of my hair as Adam soothed me with soft shushes. "Hey, you're okay. You are okay." His rough fingers slowly pried at mine, peeling my stiff hand away from my head.

Resting his head against the side of mine, he spoke in a calming voice, "You are safe." His words vibrated against my head, making me shiver a bit from the ticklish sensation.

Deft fingers danced down my head, and a gentle hand caressed up and down my spine warmly, easing the nasty tension out of my body layer by layer. It probably helped that Asher had joined in, rubbing my back haphazardly in a way that felt like he'd give me a skin burn.

Carefully, Adam lowered my other hand down into my lap, holding both my hands with his while he kept an arm wrapped around my waist. "There you go, good girl." His deep voice sent a hot wave of calm and pleasure throughout my body, causing me to shudder slightly. "Keep breathing deeply like that for me. In through your nose, out through your mouth. Keep coming back to us." He continued to soothe and encourage me with his calming touch. "There's nothing to be afraid of. You are safe here, with me."

Am I, though?

Was I ever truly going to be safe?

Going against my better judgment, I gave up the fight and let my body relax into Adam's embrace. "There you go, Eliza, that's a good girl."

Another zap of pleasure clenched my shuddering body when I heard those two words being uttered from his mouth. Then again, this whole thing felt... Weird... *I shouldn't be so calm in his arms.*

By all means, Adam was still very much a stranger to me.

Both our arms were nudged around as Asher forced himself between us to get into my lap. "Mama?" His big, rusty brown eyes peered up at me blankly as he scrunched his face pensively.

I had no idea what thoughts went through his little brain, but he instantly threw his arms around my neck, strangling me with a hug. "Mama?" Leaning back, Asher flashed me a toothy grin as if to cheer me up.

Well, it worked because it got me cracking a smile and laughing, along with Adam. "I'm okay, baby." I tried my best to believe my own lie as I put on a strong smile for my son. "I'm okay." Eventually, I'd believe the lie after telling myself so many times.

Fake it until I made it... At least, that's what I wanted to believe. I mean, I probably could lull myself into that false sense of security, but again, nothing good would come from letting my guard down. It was only a matter of time until something bit me in the ass.

Sliding out of my lap, Asher sat beside us, picking at the grass and flowers within his reach. It amazed me sometimes, how short of an attention span he had. It also brought a warm smile to my face, because it reminded me of how innocent he truly was.

Adam's heavy voice called out to me, "Eliza," making my chest feel like it caved in with the dread that pulled at me from the inside. "Look at me," he demanded sternly, yet it wasn't harsh.

Reluctantly, I bowed my head and glanced up at him half-heartedly. "L-listen, I know what you're going to say, and I'll do better next time." Shame on me for thinking I could get away without a scolding; the least I could do was try to mitigate it.

When Adam didn't respond, I frowned and furrowed my eyes together slightly. Why wasn't he yelling at me for being careless? Where were the harsh words about how stupid I was to let Asher get away from me?

A reflexive flinch shocked my body at the feeling of his skin against mine. "Eliza..." His finger curled under my chin, and his thumb held my chin softly as he tilted my head up to fully look at him.

I instantly regretted meeting his eyes when I saw how sharp with anger they had become.

Oh God, this is going to be worse than I thought.

All I could think about was how I would brace myself for his fury, but before I could cover myself with my hands, he stopped me by grabbing both my wrists into his large hand. His gray eyes turned into stones under running water when they softened with concern. "Did you think I was going to hit you just now?" I didn't expect such a question to come out of his mouth, especially with how torn and angry he sounded.

Forcing my nerves down my throat, I held myself together enough to answer him. "Y-your eyes were angry at me," I replied to him meekly, while averting my gaze.

His head instantly shook in denial as his face twisted with a guilty frown. "Oh, no, Eliza, no." Cupping my face, he steadied my eyes back on his. "No, that anger was *not* for you. No." He quickly shook his head. "Any anger you see from me will never be for you or because of you," he assured me with such sweet confidence that I felt it down to my very bones.

Exhaling shakily, my question slipped out with my breath, "Then why were you mad? If not at me?" The question festered in my mind, but I didn't want to manifest it out into the world.

Well, it was too late now.

"I will answer your question if you agree to answer mine," he bargained with a hesitant yet charming smile. "Deal?"

Something about his smile set me on edge, as it reminded me of a snake. I shouldn't agree, that's what my gut told me, but I decided to be stupid today. "Okay." My reply barely came out above a whisper.

The corners of his lips curved ever so slightly in victory, before his mouth moved. His silky-smooth voice started out calm, but it slowly dipped with a rasp as his seething rage seeped into his words. "I was angry at the thought of someone daring to raise their hand at you." The softness in his eyes had hardened so much that his gray eyes looked like sharp stones. "Angry at how someone can be so cruel to crush such a beautiful thing like you to pieces, break you down so much that your first instinct was to ball up and protect yourself at the sight of me running to you."

I didn't know how to react to that. I expected some kind of gaslighting from him, or for me to be the main reason for the fury that lit up his eyes. I mean, I was the subject, kind of, but not in a bad way as I'd thought. He was mad, not *at me*, but *for me*.

"But why?" Once again, my thought slipped free from my mouth before I had an inkling to hold it back.

Chuckling amusingly, Adam licked his lips almost playfully and teasingly. "That wasn't the deal, but I'll bite," he mused playfully, flashing me a quick grin as he held me tightly against him. "Besides it being wrong for anyone to raise their hand to a woman, it's even more wrong, just downright sinful, for anyone to hurt you." His thumb lightly brushed along the tip of my chin and jawline. "And since you aren't going to feel angry about it yourself, then someone has to. So, it might as well be me."

A dry chuckle shook my slumped shoulders. "I don't deserve it, so save it for someone who actually matters," I remarked with a pressed smile, holding back a wince at my harsh words toward myself.

His eyes narrowed at me almost daringly with a raised brow. "You don't think you matter?" He almost sounded a little peeved at my low self-esteem.

Frowning deeply, I hung my head shamefully and shook it. "I don't *think*—I *know* I don't matter." Probably not what he wanted to hear, but it was the truth.

A faint click of a tongue followed a tick in Adam's neck muscles. Then, I felt some pressure on the back of my head as my hair was grabbed into his fist. It wasn't a harsh or painful tug by any means, but I got fearful chills standing every hair on my body up when he pulled my head back. Every vertebra creaked softly in my skull as my stiff neck was forced back until I couldn't budge my head from him. All I could do to avoid his gaze was shut my eyes tightly.

Unfortunately, that only lasted a sweet second before his dominating voice shattered me. His tone was stern but stable and calm. "Eliza, open your eyes and look at me."

Relaxing my eyes, I let them open to his command, against my better judgment. I wanted to fight him off and curl up in a ball again. Yet, I found myself staring at him in confusion and awe as I anxiously waited for his calm face to contort in anger.

Why isn't he getting mad? Is he trying to lull me into a false sense of security before slapping me? Why was I so eager to obey him? Why am I not pissing myself right now?

Slowly, his eyes darkened, making me shiver and cower a little under him. I couldn't discern the mess of emotions that made his gray orbs darken so much that they almost seemed black. His deep voice was so calm and orderly that it didn't feel like I was getting chided by him. "You are anything *but* worthless. You are busting your ass day in and day out to provide a good life for your son. You work yourself to the bone to be the best mother possible and to just make it." His grip slackened until his hand cradled the back of my head tenderly. "That in itself makes you worth so much."

Letting go of my waist, he raised his other hand to cup my face, stroking my cheek with his thumb. "Besides being an amazing mother and hard worker, you are kind, caring, and selfless." He almost sounded envious of me as he spoke with a proud smile. "I don't know what happened to you, but you hold nothing against the world when you should. There isn't a speck of malice in your tired but bright eyes."

Softening his smile, he leaned in and pressed his lips against my forehead in a chaste kiss. "And I am going to spend every second of every damn day trying to show and prove to you that you are not worthless." His promising words made a wave of warmth cascade down my body.

I wanted to believe him and give him a chance—really, I did.

But it wouldn't be fair to him.

I had nothing to give.

My heart was broken beyond repair. It had been broken long ago, and there weren't any pieces left to try to put back together. It was nothing but a pile of dust. Well, there might be one sliver of a piece left, but that was reserved for Asher.

"Please," he begged, his whole face softening rather convincingly. "Just one chance."

Chapter 6
Adam

I would kneel at her feet and kiss them while begging her forever if it meant she would give me a *single* chance.

I wanted to ease the burden off her shoulders, give her more time to enjoy life and spend time with Asher. Even if she took Asher everywhere with her, it wasn't quality time she spent with him because she couldn't give him any attention while she cleaned the houses. Sitting down to play with him was impossible when she had to focus on driving around to deliver food.

She yearned for more when it came to Asher, and I wanted to give her a chance to do all she wanted. I'd seen how sad her eyes got every time she settled for the night and looked down at her sleeping son in her arms. All the tears she'd shed over him never escaped me as I would watch her through the screen of my phone while I laid in bed at night and watched her through the monitors we'd set up and connected to my phone. Every single apology she'd given Asher about how she couldn't give him more, felt like a nail in my aching heart.

Taking in a trembling breath, I begged one last time with a cracked voice, "Please, just one."

Hope filled her eyes for a split second before she withdrew from me. Her mouth opened slightly, but no words came out as she shook her head slowly at me while she pushed my hands away from her body. "I don't know if I can do it..." At least she didn't outright reject me. "Can I have some time to think about it?"

Unable to help myself, I eagerly grinned and nodded my head in response. "Of course, take all the time you need." As long as it ended in a 'yes' or some form of agreement, then she could take forever.

Well, preferably not forever because it'd defeat the point, but I was more than willing to wait that long. Okay, maybe that would be stretching the truth too much. If she dragged it on for longer than six months, then I'd find ways to force her hand. Some vandalism here and there, maybe a few threats to chase her into my arms, and eventually, I'd get her into my house and life permanently.

I sat there on the ground with her in my lap for a peaceful moment, watching Asher waddle around and pluck at whatever his chubby hands grasped. We probably could've stayed like that forever, if it weren't for the sound of Eliza's stomach coming to life. I felt a little bad for chuckling at the sound of her stomach rumbling with hunger, but it slipped before I could stop it.

Then, as if on some cue, Asher ran over to us and flopped his body into us. "Mama mum mum?" The toddler looked up eagerly at his mother while tugging at her shirt.

Standing up with a light groan, I lifted Eliza to her feet before bending down and picking Asher up as he held his arms up to me. "Let's go get you two fed," I decided with an insistent grin at Eliza, who deadpanned at me.

Going over to the stroller, I settled the protestant toddler in before facing my Eliza. "Come on. We're already out, and there's a lovely place not far from here," I told her, nudging at her hand playfully with my finger. "They're kid-friendly, too, so Asher will have plenty to eat."

Sighing, Eliza rolled her eyes and crossed her arms stubbornly. "Adam, I told you I need time."

Holding my hands up in defense, I shrunk my body a little. "Technically, I'm not asking you out on a date," I retorted with a sheepish smile. "Just a friend taking another friend out for some food," I continued to play around with the situation a little in hopes of convincing her. "Besides, it's closer than your place, and the little guy is hungry. It's best to get food in him sooner rather than later." Okay, that might have been a cheap blow to her motherly nature and whatnot, but I was a slightly desperate man.

Relenting with an unamused frown, she narrowed her eyes at me as she sighed, "Fine, but only because Asher needs to eat."

The urge to fist bump the air in victory was hard to resist, but I kept the itch at bay. Instead of making a fool of myself, I channeled the energy into throwing my arm around Eliza's waist and pulling her close. "You're going to love Gia's, promise."

"I love all food regardless," Eliza remarked with a weak chuckle as she let me drag her along. "Unless it has mint in it and raw tomatoes."

Intrigued, I quirked a quizzical brow at her as I continued to lead the way. "Oh? Why? Don't like them?" Not like she ate anything besides fucking packaged ramen, frozen foods, and canned food for me to pick apart her eating habits.

Answering me with an unsure bob of her head, she shrugged her shoulders. "The tomatoes, kinda, but it's more like I avoid them because they make me nauseous." Her words kind of dragged awkwardly, as if she struggled to put her answer into actual words.

She regained her footing quickly before moving on to the other part of her answer. "I'm allergic to mint, though." That time, there was no fumbling as she stated the fact.

"Oh? Interesting." Honestly, it was, because that was nowhere in her file. "Anything else you're allergic to? Before I accidentally send you into a medical crisis?" Well, now I had to question everything in the damn file because there was no way a food allergy went amiss in medical records.

Chuckling and waving her hand dismissively, she gave me a flash of a reassuring smile. "Well, I'm not like deathly allergic to mint. It just kind of makes my throat itchy and mouth numb, for now," she said so casually, like a lactose intolerant person waving off the fact they are while eating a bowl of ice cream. "Other than that, no other allergies I'm aware of, so don't worry about killing me with food."

Well, that was good to hear and know. It barely changed the fact I didn't know her as I thought I did. Honestly, what else in the file was false, inaccurate, or missing? Was it all false? Was that why her life seemed so perfect? Could I believe anything from the file?

"Do you ever miss Salem?" I prodded with an overly curious voice as I continued to push the stroller with one hand.

"Hm?" Her confused face looked up at me for a second before a blank smile smeared across her face. "Oh, no, not really. I much prefer the coast, and the smaller city feel here compared to Salem." A fair reason, but her lack of emotion made me doubt her.

The answer didn't sound organic; it seemed crafted with how blank her eyes were when she spoke, along with the lack of warmth in her voice. I couldn't really call her out on it, though. What if she just didn't like Salem, or found it boring? Home or not, if she had no affinity with it, then of course there wouldn't be any affection in her voice while speaking about it.

On the other hand, that shouldn't matter because there was always some kind of nostalgia in a person's eyes whenever they spoke about where they came from, even if they hated it. So, time to prod. "Oh, come on, there has to be something you miss there, like a restaurant or store or place?" Unless she spent her whole life locked in a basement, there had to be *something* about the place she enjoyed.

Another fake smile as she shook her head in response. "No, I didn't really go out much there, and my ex kind of ruined a lot of it for me. So, I don't have much of a fondness for the place or anything there." If there was more firmness behind her voice then I'd be inclined to somewhat believe her, but again, everything was empty.

Deciding not to press her further because of how she was shying herself away, I changed the subject. "You planning on staying here for a long while then? Or forever?" The future was what really mattered.

Sure, knowing her past was probably important, but the past was the past. That could all be dug up some other time. For now, knowing where she saw herself years from now was where my curiosity led me. I also needed to know for my plans. If she planned to stay in Seaside for the long run, that would be great; if not, then I needed to come up with a way to trap her with me.

Looking down at Asher with a natural smile, she reached down and poked at his chubby cheek with a giggle before turning her gaze up at me. "I love it here, so if I can stay here forever, then that's the plan." Though genuine, I could hear the slight dip in her hopeful voice.

Keeping my voice light and curious, I pressed, "What would stop you from staying? I mean, you might be hustling a little, but you're getting by okay from the looks of it." I wanted to see if she would let slip any information I could use. "And you seem pretty content here." I sweetened things a little with a hopeful smile.

Her hopeful smile saddened with her dry chuckle. "Well, sometimes life just kind of happens, ya know?" There was that distant and broken look to her brown orbs again. "Never know when shit crashes into your life."

There was definitely something going on; I just had to figure out what it was. And if I couldn't, then I had to figure out a plan B real fast. Well, I could wait around for her problem to come and deal with it, but then I'd risk her running.

Sighing internally, I softly shook my head to throw the thoughts out. "Well, no shit will come your way while I'm around," I assured her with a determined grin.

Squeezing her hip firmly and reassuringly, I leaned over and placed a brief kiss against the side of her head. "I'll take all the hits, and as long as it means I get to see your beautiful face every day, then bring it on." They'd only get one hit before their body ended up in pieces in the ocean and eventually in some shark's stomach.

Rolling her eyes at me, she gave me a light shove with her shoulder. "You're too much, you know that? Giving all your efforts to someone like me with nothing special going on."

Before I could help it, I found my hand slipping around to her bubbly butt cheek, pinching it and making her jump and yelp in response. Eliza tried to jerk her body away from me, but my hold locked back around her waist and hip, preventing her from inching away.

Growling softly with a scowl, she glared up at me. "What was that for, you pervert?" Her hand lightly whacked at my arm in a pouting manner.

Amused by her cute face and reaction, I chuckled in response. "That's for saying you don't have anything special." I loved the way her cheeks blushed up with her wide eyes as she stared at me in wonder. "Keep downplaying yourself and putting yourself down, and you'll find yourself over my knee eventually."

Eliza instantly dug her heels into the ground, forcing us to stop. "W-whoa, wh-what?" Her soft face was twisted in shock, horror, and slight excitement. "W-why would you do that?" Her head bowed as her hands covered her ass. "I thought you said you would never hit me." Okay, I felt like a bit of an ass when I heard her voice crack with those words.

Turning to face her fully, I slipped my arms around her waist, pulling her close. "Eliza." Keeping one arm secured around her waist, I brought the other up to her face. Running a finger along her neck, I curled my finger under her chin, tilting her head up. "Spanking you to punish you for putting yourself down is not the same as flat-out hitting you for the sake of physically abusing you." Though, I could see why the two concepts could be easily mixed up.

Her frown deepened along with the scrunch of her eyes. "You're still putting your hand on my body," she retorted with fear clouding her once shiny eyes.

Keeping my mouth shut, I mentally debated how to explain this to her. It was obvious from her extreme reaction earlier that she had suffered at another person's hands, so she probably saw physical impact as abuse either way. Though, I wouldn't fault her for the misunderstanding because the line between abuse and certain BDSM activities was very blurry.

"Yes and no." I struggled to get my words out confidently. "Yes, in the sense that I would be putting my hands on you, but no, in the sense that it won't be to harm you." Okay, how the hell could I word this without scaring her into the next state?

Dragging out a sigh, I ran a hand down my face and held it across my jaw in thought for a good moment. "It's the intent." Was that the right thing to say? "I'm not going to 'hit' you because I want to hurt you or find some sick joy out of it. I'm not some woman beater." I didn't mean to sound a little accusatory toward her with my last words, but my anger slipped out.

"If I were to take you over my knee..."

Or a spanking bench.

"It'd be to help you to grow better." Or maybe I should shut my mouth because I might very well be digging my grave; too bad I was already digging. "For example, just now, with you downplaying yourself. I'd punish you, within reason, so that you will think twice about doubting yourself next time."

Pursing and twisting my lips in thought, I sorted my words as best as possible in my mind before spewing them. "There is a purpose to it all." I probably sounded like some serial abuser gaslighting their victim. "I don't want you to discredit yourself or talk yourself into a negative headspace, so the punishment is for your benefit. Seeing you lower your self-esteem like that displeases me because of the impact it has on you."

I let out a sigh of defeat when her face remained twisted with confusion. "I'm sorry if I'm not making much sense. It's just a little tricky to put it in a way that won't scare you off."

Sliding my hand to the back of her head, I tightened my hold on her to hug her firmly. "I don't want to harm you like whoever did in your past, and it might be better if you just Google it and looked into it yourself on your own time because there are others out there who can do a hell of a better job explaining it than I can."

I might be involved in the community and scene, but I was not an instructor or informant about it. If Eliza needed a simple explanation, then I could, but her situation had so many layers to it that I didn't want to uncover them too fast and end up harming her. If I knew more about her situation, then I probably could work my way with her, but I was blind. Trying to talk to her about it was equivalent to walking around a field of landmines with no idea about the amount or general location of the explosives.

One wrong step was all it would take for my chances with Eliza to blow into space.

Humming softly against me, she let me hold her for a somewhat awkward moment. "Sorry if that was a little confusing and much for you. I promise I'm not trying to get in your pants and to get my hands on you in a harmful way." Said the killer before stabbing their victim to death—it seriously felt like it.

"Space and time, Adam," she reminded me with a weak sigh and chuckle. "Space and time." A few soft pats hit my upper arm, indicating my cue to release her and resume our journey for food.

Both of us continued the rest of the way in a—surprisingly-ly—peaceful silence. Thankfully, it wasn't awkward because I put her off by trying to explain myself. And if she did feel awkward around me, then she didn't show it.

The moment we came to a stop at the restaurant, Eliza's face instantly lit up. "Oh, I've picked up for this place so many times, and it always smells and looks so good! I also hear a lot of good things about it," she beamed, her body trembling with excitement.

"And you've never set foot inside for yourself?" I questioned with a quizzical look as I opened the door for her to push the stroller in first.

After muttering a quick 'thanks' to me, she busied herself taking in the warm place with a big smile. Then, she looked at me with a flat and sad smile. "No, I just never had the time and money," she replied with a downward turn of her eyes.

Giving her a bright smile, I stepped up to her and threw an arm around her shoulders, squeezing them slightly. "Well, order and eat to your heart's content today because it's all my treat." What kind of man would I be if I let my girl pay?

Granted, she didn't need to know all of that quite yet.

Denial pulled her facial features down as she vigorously shook her head at me. "No, Adam. I can't do that. It's not like I'm going to eat much, but I should at least—"

Cutting her off with a playful scoff and roll of my eyes, I prevented her from spewing any more words by pressing my forefinger against her lips. I spoke to her in a very sure and determined voice. "You're not doing anything but making me happy by letting me spoil you and give you what you have deserved all along and then some."

Stubbornly, she glared at me softly, her bottom lip tucking itself between her teeth as she struggled with herself a bit before relenting with a huff. "Fine... But only this once!" The way her voice wavered made me smirk victoriously because she knew this wouldn't be a one-off thing with us.

"Adam! Hey, how ya doing?" A cheery voice broke through our little moment, making us turn our heads to a friendly waitress. "Do you want your usual spot at the bar, or do you want me to work a little magic for you and your beautiful guest today?"

The old woman wiggled her eyebrows at me teasingly as she leaned in and nudged my arm with her elbow. Teasing me with her words, she spoke in a low voice, "I may be an old fart, but I still got my magic touch with you younglings." She snickered with a wink.

Standing up straight, she smiled warmly at Eliza before bending down and pinching Asher's cheek. "How are you today, my dear? I would ask which order you're here for, but I doubt you're running yourself ragged while pushing this heavy little nugget around." Well, at least Claire and Eliza seemed friendly with each other.

A grateful and eager smile brightened Eliza's face when she looked at the older woman. "I'm doing wonderful, Claire, and so is the little chunkers. How are you? What about Steven? How's his wrist? Is he wearing the brace like he's supposed to?" The slew of questions flew out of her mouth, making Clair laugh while her hand waved dismissively.

Reaching out, Claire patted Eliza's arm while smiling at her warmly and reassuringly. "Oh, we're both doing as well as two old farts can do, and he's being stubborn and crabby about it, but I make sure he wears it." Then, she turned her full attention on both of us. "So, are we going to try my magic booth, or are we ordering to-go?" she asked, grabbing the menus and straightening them against the hostess booth.

Chuckling in response, I looked down at Eliza with a widening smile for a second before looking back up at Claire with determined eyes. "If she doesn't leave here with my ring around her finger, then you and Steven are going to take that week-long vacation you've been talking about, alright?" I bargained playfully with a hearty laugh when Claire playfully smacked me with the menus. Seeing Eliza's bright red face brought some amusement to me, too.

"Boy, I said magic, not a miracle," Claire remarked with a roll of her eyes. "If you want to score a queen like Eliza, then you best start getting on your knees and kissing her feet and thanking her for gracing you with her attention."

Then, a bellowing male voice joined in on our conversation, "I'd listen to her if I were you, boy! She knows what she's talking about!" Steven, Claire's husband, and the head chef of the place peeped his head out from the busser's window. "She might be a nag, but she knows things!" His teasing words were more for his wife, who spun around and waved a fist at him.

Placing a hand over my heart, I leaned back and feigned hurt as if I'd been shot through the heart. "And here I thought you were my fairy godmother to turn my rags to riches to impress the beautiful and illustrious queen Eliza," I joked with a cheeky grin, making

Claire scoff and roll her eyes, while Eliza blushed harder. I wondered if she had blood rushing elsewhere in her body.

"Oh, stop it, you little cheeky bastard," Claire scolded me playfully with another smack to my arm, courtesy of the menus. "You're going to make the poor girl faint from all the attention."

Honestly, looking at how cherry-red her face was, that was a slight worry. Well, at least I'd be there to catch her if she did keel over. Also, I wouldn't mind having her in my arms one bit.

Chuckling with a shake of my head, I urged Eliza to follow Claire as she led us to our table, a nice little corner booth with a view of the streets on one side and the beach on the other. "You look so beautiful right now, just like a morning rose shining under the first sunlight." Was that overly sweet and cheesy? Maybe, but I didn't care.

Turning her face away with embarrassment, Eliza scoffed playfully and reached over to lightly shove my shoulder from across the table. "Oh, stop it, you. You're going to make my teeth fall out if you get any sweeter." Yet, the lovely smile remained on her appreciative face as she sat there trying to hide her gorgeous face from me.

After setting the menus down in front of us, Claire left for a moment to grab a highchair for Asher. "Is it alright for him to have some pasta with meatballs and some cut-up fruits?" Claire asked while looking up at Eliza.

Smiling and nodding, Eliza replied, "That honestly sounds so lovely for him, and I'm sure he'll love it."

"Steven makes the perfect pasta sauce with carrots, tomatoes, and sweet potatoes that our grandchildren love." With a caring and tender smile at Asher, Claire let him play with her finger as she looked at Eliza with a cheeky smile. "We like to sneak some veggies into the meatballs, too, but don't let them know that." She snickered, playfully putting a finger to her mouth and shushing softly.

"Well, Asher's just a blackhole when it comes to food, veggies and all," Eliza mused with soft and warm eyes that held so much love for her son.

Straightening herself, Claire rubbed the top of Asher's giggling head before flashing a smile at us. "What do you want to drink? I'll grab those while you two look at the menu."

Eliza didn't even take a second to debate before answering, "Water is fine with me. Thank you, Claire."

Yeah, no. Not on my watch.

Smiling warmly at Claire, I leaned back in my seat a little. "We'll have a pitcher of your oh-so-famous sangria lemonade to share, but maybe go a little light on the good stuff for today because I don't know how Eliza's tolerance is." I felt like a jerk for stepping on her toes, but like hell would I let her cheap out.

"Got it!" Claire beamed. "I'll be back with drinks and silverware and all that stuff in a minute," she informed us, turning around and leaving after giving Asher's cheek another loving pinch.

"A-Adam, I'm really fine with water, promise," Eliza squeaked up with a soft frown.

Feeling bad, I leaned onto the table with my elbows, reaching over and taking her hands in mine. "Hey, I'm sorry for dancing on your toes, but I want you to enjoy lunch today. You have water at home and everywhere else, so can you indulge a little today with some delicious lemonade?" I did my best to put on a soft and charming smile to sweeten my apologetic eyes.

Rubbing the back of her hands with my thumbs, I slowly brought them up to my lips to kiss her fingers. "Don't worry about the price or the financial burden this is going to be on your bank account for today." It really wasn't any bother for me, and I didn't know how to get through to her. "I want to spoil you, Eliza, because you deserve every bit of joy and happiness this world has to offer to you. I'm not doing this to get you indebted to me." I tried my best to assure her with a serious smile, but from how unsure she looked, I wasn't sure if I was moving toward success or failure.

"I've more than enough money to last me many lifetimes, so please, if you're worried about my financial situation or anything like that, then don't. And I'm not trying to sound like some rich asshole, either. It's the truth." I really wasn't trying to brag about my seemingly endless wealth, but I wanted to assure her that I could more than provide financially without taking a blow.

Dragging out a deep breath, I peppered kisses along her knuckles pleadingly. "Please, just let me take care of you, Eliza. Let me spoil you and be your ray of sunshine, at least for today. Let me be your angel."

Pretty fucking ironic.

I wanted to laugh a little at my desperate words because the only ray I was, was one of death and despair. Usually, nothing good came of my presence. If I showed up in anyone's life, then it typically meant they fucked up badly. A visit from The Angel of Death was never good.

If I had to be dragged out of my homey abode, then I would usually be in a foul mood to begin with. Then, to be forced to deal with problems my lieutenants should be handling pissed me off more, because I didn't become the head honcho to waste my time with dirt. Not when I had to run the whole operation behind the scenes.

An angel was the last thing I'd be in life, but for her, I'd put on my broken halo and bloodied, tattered wings.

Chapter 7
Eliza

Too bad my body and heart didn't listen to my reasonable brain with how my hands tightened around his. I gave a lopsided smile, a weak chuckle, and peered up at him warily. "You're not going to let me say no, are you?" Did I really have a choice in any of this?

"Hey, the safe word is Bananas," he joked half-heartedly with a chuckle. "I mean, if it really makes you uncomfortable to the point where you're going to lose sleep over it at night, then I'll back off, but if there's any chance you can try, then that's all I'm asking for." His face softly scrunched with a pleading frown that matched his eyes.

Going against my gut, I shoved away the second thoughts to take the plunge. "J-just today."

God, please don't let me regret this. Please don't let this blow up in my face.

I silently pleaded to the man upstairs as I let out a nervous breath. "You are a strange one, Adam." I chuckled awkwardly as I stroked his palms with the tips of my fingers. "You really are putting so much toward a nobody—" My hand instantly shot up to stop Adam when his mouth opened. "And before you say anything, let me finish and listen, please." My body naturally winced at the firmness in my voice, and a wave of anxiety sickened my stomach as the need to brace myself for impact ached at my muscles.

Shaking my hands off, he carefully reached out and cupped my face gently. "Hey, breathe," he commanded, in a very deep and calm voice. "You are okay. You are safe." He assured me with a soothing smile full of genuine care. "I am so proud of you for standing up for yourself like that," he admitted, his smile widening proudly. "I knew I wasn't mistaken when I saw a spark within your eyes."

Well, color me surprised because I didn't think there was a spark of anything good in me after everything I'd been through. Seriously, I felt like a zombie half the time, just going on complete autopilot to get through the day. Also, I was pretty confident my ex had extinguished all the sparks I had, before drowning all the kindling to ensure I couldn't start anything new.

I was so used to being beaten down and berated for even the slightest hint defiance, that being praised for it by Adam felt almost like being slapped in the face with a pan. Confusion tensed my face as I tried to make sense of it all.

He was proud of me for being strong? Why? Shouldn't he be mad at me for being like insubordinate or some shit like that?

Tension eased from my face in response to Adam's chuckling. I was even more befuddled with this man. "Eliza, stop turning the gears in your head before you wear them out," he teased playfully. "I will never, and I mean it, never get upset at you for using your own voice and setting your foot down. I want you to bloom into the powerful and independent woman I see hiding behind your eyes."

Seeing the fire of excitement and motivation brightening his eyes as he grinned at me encouragingly set some part of me ablaze with vigor. It was hard to believe a stranger, I'd met a little over a week ago in a damn grocery store aisle, wanted the best for me and believed in me more than anyone else had in my life. Even at the height of my relationship with James, he never once stood behind me so closely and eagerly; I practically had to beg him to praise me or compliment me for anything I accomplished. Hell, I'd had to fish so hard for compliments on a simple outfit that it was downright embarrassing to think back on now.

Collecting my scrambling nerves, I smiled gratefully at Adam while moving my hands up to cup his. "You are such a strange man," I mused with a chuckle, not knowing what else to say for now. "But thank you..."

Neither of us had to say anything as we basked in the peaceful silence that fell between us. There were no words to be exchanged, our glimmering eyes said it all. Adam didn't need to further verbalize the encouragement or compliments for me to know he was proud of me, and no doubt I didn't need to repeatedly tell him how thankful I was with how much gratitude and happiness filled my eyes.

Reluctantly, I tore my eyes away from him and removed his warm hands from my face to get some space. "You haven't looked at the menu yet," I stated the obvious as I picked up mine gingerly.

Cocking a rather smug grin, Adam rested his chin atop his interlaced hands. "I already know what I'm gonna get." Well, at least he seemed pretty excited about the food. "Steven makes the best burgers, so I usually get one or the chef's special."

Humming softly, I nodded my head in response before looking over the menu with clueless eyes. There were so many choices—I didn't know where to begin. I mean, everything sounded so amazing.

God, I couldn't remember the last time I went out to eat. I didn't even know what I liked anymore. Fancy dates, or eating out in general, became nonexistent soon after my marriage to James. He always demanded 'homemade' food and shit—always prattled on about how outside food was a waste of money or how it wasn't worth wasting on me.

Huffing out in frustration, I set the menu down with an angry pout because of my indecisiveness. "Everything looks and sounds so good..." I grumbled, mentally running through the menu.

Like the cheeky little turd he was, Adam flashed me a smug smirk. "Well, make a list, and we can slowly knock them out one by one every time we come here." I hated how confident and sure he sounded, but what I despised more was the fact he was growing on me.

As much as I kept telling myself that this was a one-off occurrence, I knew deep down it wouldn't be. If this was how lovely it'd be to go out with Adam, then who was I to deny myself more of it? I mean, for once I found myself happy with giving my time to someone besides Asher, and a man at that. Honestly, I thought if I were to involve anyone in my life, then I figured it'd be a female, given my track record with men.

Biting my tongue so I wouldn't make a fool of myself by denying the inevitable, I darted my eyes around to see if I could catch the board with the specials listed. Unfortunately, it was just a bit out of my line of sight. So, I had no choice to ask Adam for some help, very begrudgingly. "Adam, can you look at the board and tell me what the specials are?" At least the fear ingrained in me over the years kept me from snapping at Adam, so I sounded quite nice.

Those beady gray eyes of his glimmered with mischievousness as his lips curled up into a catty smirk. His delicious lips parted slightly with a quick swipe of his tongue before he covered his jaw with his hand. Slowly, his head tilted as he eyed me for a second, and he gave it a quick shake as if he'd changed his mind about something before turning his attention to the board.

Mindlessly, I watched his index finger travel along his stubbled jaw as he read the board carefully. After his eyes traveled up and down the board a few times, he turned his head back to me to list off the items, "Soup of the day is clam chowder, special of the week is wagyu, chef's special is a halibut and crab pasta with creamy alfredo, and the dessert of the week is a Marionberry cheesecake."

Okay, not gonna lie, all of that sounded delicious as fuck. For a split second, I debated the wagyu, because I honestly hadn't had anything beyond a cheap piece of chuck or skirt if I was lucky enough to get a whole piece of steak to myself. Otherwise, it was scraps from my ex, if he felt generous enough to leave me any.

However, my carb-craving heart decided on the plate of creamy and starchy deliciousness. "I think I'll have that chef's special. It sounds so good." My mouth was watering so badly at the mere thought of it, and I was afraid that if I opened my mouth too much, then I'd start drooling out a waterfall.

Reining myself in, I looked at Adam pleadingly. "If that's fine with you?" I tried to keep my voice stable, but it wavered timidly out of habit.

Although, I probably should have checked with him before even deciding. After all, he was the one paying.

"Eliza." His stern voice made my nervous eyes settle on his una-mused face. "I already told you before to get whatever you want, and even if I hadn't, whether I am fine with it or not shouldn't matter." Reaching back over, he took my hand in his, playfully tickling my palm with the tips of his rough fingers. "Never ask anyone if it's okay for you to eat something, unless it's something questionable looking." He cracked a chuckle at his own joke.

Not even bothering to suppress my chuckle, I let my body relax with the joyful tremble of my amusement. "No promises, but I'll try." Bad habits were hard to break. "I just... I don't want you to be disgusted with the plate of food when it comes and when I eat it... I mean, if you're not fine with it, then I can always get a salad." Or maybe I should get the salad and lie about changing my mind.

Adam's eyes immediately rolled in an exaggerated manner at me as a tiny groan left him. "Salads are for herbivores, which you are not, last I checked," he retorted with a firm but playful look. "As long as I'm around, you are always going to be eating your fill of actual food that's not jammed packed with preservatives."

I probably shouldn't have doubted and challenged him, especially with how sharp his eyes were with determination, but I couldn't help it. "You can't just feed me three meals a day, Adam. That's just insane," I joked with a nervous chuckle, afraid he might actually try to prove me wrong.

"And why can't I?" he smugly asked, in a much too amused voice.

Gulping nervously, I chuckled sheepishly with an awkward smile. How the hell was I gonna argue with him? It was his money, time, and effort at the end of the day. I had no control over him or his choices.

"W-well, I mean... W-what if I don't eat it? Then it's a waste." Yeah, that was probably a stupid rebuttal, but it was the only thing my flustered mind could come up with right now.

Of course, being a smart-ass, he had the perfect response. "Then I guess you better be sure to eat it all so none of it goes to waste." An urge to shoot across the table and swipe my hand across his face twitched at my fingers as I glared at him softly in response. "You gotta take better care of yourself, Eliza, and if you're too busy to do that, then I'll do it for you and do whatever I can to help."

Huffing, I stared at him for a good moment, waiting for him to go 'just kidding' or crack some kind of laugh and dismiss this whole thing, but nothing of the sort came. There was no way in hell Adam was this amazing of a person... Or maybe he was crazy. Seriously, no sane person would stick their neck out so much for a single mother who was way down on her luck.

Adam said my name with a soft sigh, "Eliza." And a squeeze of my hand pulled me out of my thoughts.

"I'm not worth it," I bit out with a frown. "I have nothing to give you return." It felt so unfair the more I thought about it.

I grossly lacked the money to pay him back or to gift him something in return, and my time was mostly spoken for. A pit of guilt already welled up inside my chest at the thought of him putting forth so much of his time and effort into this, only to receive the bare minimum in return.

Scoffing, Adam rolled his eyes at me. "You are worth everything. Every second of my life is worth dedicating to you." The sheer warmth in eyes made me freeze with panic because I'd never seen such intensity directed toward me before. "I am not doing any of this to get you into bed or to get anything in return from you. Honestly, as long as what I do makes you smile and happy, then that is more than enough payment for me."

Okay, that sounded a little too deep and heavy there, bud. Seriously, can I tell him to back up a little?

How could a man be so head over heels for someone like me in such a short amount of time? It felt too surreal, and I was terrified because this sappy shit didn't happen in real life! I mean, how was I supposed to respond to that? Not saying I disliked it or anything because, strangely, I didn't.

Growing up, not even my parents looked at me with endless wonder and grace like Adam, and I got none of that shit from James.

So, it bewildered me to no end that Adam could seem so sure and awestruck with me when he barely knew me. Granted, there wasn't much to me for him to know, but still.

Probably sensing my wariness, Adam shrunk his shoulders a little with a nervous chuckle. "Sorry if it was a little much. It kind of just came out," he apologized with a smile, before bringing my hand up to his lips and kissing the back of it again. "You have a lot on your shoulders, and I really want to help because I *want* to. So, please, let me?"

Before I could try to awkwardly remove myself from him, Claire's hearty chuckle interrupted us and sent me down a different path. "He's not going to take no for an answer, so you might as well make your life easier and agree now before he ups the charm," she told me as she set the pitcher filled with a red liquid down between us with some glasses.

Patting my arm with a warm smile, Claire leaned in close to me with a giggle. "He's a stubborn and persistent one, but his heart is in the right place." Her voice was soft and low as she spoke to me like a loving mother advising her child. "You don't have to carry everything on your shoulders alone, and a person like Adam only comes around once in a lifetime."

Claire's head looked over at a laughing Steven with a nostalgic and content smile. "Take it from me, Eliza." Her voice softened almost pleadingly as she looked back at me. "Don't let whatever is holding you back win. Not everyone gets a chance at miracles, and Adam is definitely one. If he wasn't, then I would have snuck you out the back by now," she joked at the end with a chuckle, making me crack a smile.

Standing back up, Claire finished setting out the table, leaving us with a basket of seasoned fries after she informed us of our food's ETA.

Unfortunately, she took the peace with her, because an awkward tension mugged up the air between Adam and me.

I didn't know what to do or say because I didn't know what I wanted.

Do I let him in? Or do I push him away and slam the door in his face?

"One month," he spoke up suddenly, making me look at him cluelessly. "Give me one month to show you I am worth your time and smiles. Once the month is up, if you really aren't feeling it, then I will remain in the friend zone until you move me out, or forever."

Don't.

Don't do it.

Don't. Do. It.

Do not—

"Deal."

Chapter 8
Adam

I couldn't wipe the giddy grin off my face as I eagerly approached Eliza's door with my arms full of grocery bags.

Obviously, I was still more than ecstatic about Eliza agreeing a few days ago. The little bargain I made, not me showing up at her place unannounced to make her breakfast. She had no idea about me coming over right now because I knew if I had asked her, then the answer would have been a fat no. So, I took it upon myself to be the best temporary boyfriend ever and surprise her.

Getting into her place was easy—I had a key.

Was the key given to me by her? Fuck no it wasn't, and technically it was kind of legally—and possibly morally—wrong, but I'd make up for it with a breakfast so good that she wouldn't even dwell on the fact I cloned a key after breaking into her place the other night.

Well, did it count as breaking in if I walked in because the door was open? I mean, the door might have been open because I had the locks replaced, and I just happened to go by while it happened.

But who cared about the finite details?

After casually entering her place, I made myself at home in the kitchen, mindful to keep the noise to a minimum so as not to wake her.

Surprisingly, I managed to go two hours unnoticed, and I probably could've gone longer if Asher hadn't woken up. The happy little guy screeched with glee the moment his tired eyes landed on me, startling his mother awake.

"Asher, wha—" Eliza's half-closed eyes shot wide open the moment she followed Asher's gaze to me. "Oh my God, what the fuck! Adam! What are you—" Gripping her hair in a panic, she held Asher tightly as she hyperventilated. "What are you doing in my place!? How did you get in!?"

Alright, well, how the hell am I going to go about this?

Without making the situation worse.

After a split-second debate, I answered her nonchalantly, "Spare key, but also your lock is broken." Then, keeping a very cool demeanor, I held up a jug of juice in each hand. "Orange juice or fruit tea today? Also, I hope you don't mind mixed cheese in your omelet today. They were all out of the melty one." No, they weren't out; I didn't buy it because that shit wasn't exactly healthy.

Utterly stunned and confused, Eliza sat there staring and blinking at me as if I were some psycho stalker who broke into her place. "Do you need a moment to bask in the sun and bloom first, little rose?" I teased with a chuckle while setting the jugs of juice down on the dining table. "I can take Asher for a little bit so you can go freshen up a little to wake up," I offered with a kind and warm smile.

Shaking her head vigorously as if to clear it, she stared at me again with bewildered eyes for another good minute before swinging her legs over the edge of the bed and remaining perched there. "Adam, this is not—"

No way she was finishing that sentence, not if I could help it. "Oh! Shit! Hold that thought!" I rushed over to the stove, turned it off, and pulled the pan off. "Didn't want your omelet to dry out or burn. It'd ruin the taste of the mushrooms and cheese," I fibbed with a rather exaggerated smile as I plopped the steaming egg dish onto a plate.

Her lips peeled back in a wary frown as she looked at me very dubiously. "Did you actually make that, or did you buy it from somewhere and put it on a pan and pretend to make it?" Slowly, very slowly, she got up to her feet and took a few tentative steps toward me. "I should really call the cops on you right now for inva—"

She could call me a prick later, but I needed to shut her up. Shy of planting my lips on hers to get a taste, I settled for the second-best option: shoving a forkful of food into her open mouth mid-sentence. "Don't spit. Otherwise, it'd be a waste." Okay, I was just being a cheeky asshole with that comment.

Blushing madly, Eliza groaned and stomped her foot, glaring at me slightly as she chewed the mouthful. Her scrunched-up face slowly softened the more she savored the food. My victory didn't last long because she turned her head away in a pout when she noticed my winning grin.

After swallowing, she glanced at me out of the corner of her glaring eyes. "J-just because you can make good food doesn't give you the right to break into my home," she remarked weakly in a wavering voice.

I settled for an amused chuckle when my laughter became hard to hold back. She was too adorable being all stubborn, and I wanted nothing more than to poke at her to rile her up more.

Quickly, I set the pan back on the stove before going up to her with my hands held out. "Here, I'll take care of the lil' dude while you eat." Nothing but warm assurance and kindness filled my smile as I urged her with my hands. "You'll be able to see both of us the whole time."

Her lips pressed together into a thin line, twisted into a frown for a second, them went flat again. She seemed conflicted as she started to pass me Asher. He giggled and reached for me, but before I could take him, she jerked him back into her body. A moment passed as her eyes traveled around the room, searching for anything else that might be amiss, before coming back to the kitchen. Her nose twitched as she inhaled the delicious sent of the omelet, and she gave an irritated sigh as she caved and gave me the toddler.

With a deadpan expression, she crossed her arms and glared at me sternly. "No funny business or I will kill you." That was one threat I'd be taking seriously.

Never mess with a mother, especially when it comes to her children. As harmless as she seemed, I had no doubt about her removing me from the land of the living with ease if I were to harm a hair on Asher's head—not that I ever would.

Eliza's wary eyes constantly bounced between me and her food as she dug in after she sat down. I didn't take any offense to it; at the end of the day, I was still mostly a stranger to her. All I could do was take careful steps around her and work my way into her life until I had her heart in my grasp.

While she ate, I took the liberty to change Asher's diaper and clothes before I settled him in his highchair, scooting it close to Eliza. Once the little guy was comfortable, I went back over to the kitchen and opened the fridge. "Some fluffy scrambled eggs with some cheese and fruits sound okay for him to have?" I asked, craning my neck back to look at her with a raised brow.

Her lips twisted in a struggle as if she wanted to say something but held it back. The slight frown on her face gave her discomfort away so easily, and I couldn't help but furrow my own eyebrows in concern as I tried to read her deeper. What was she bothered about? Me making food for Asher? I mean, it was a silly thing to be upset over, but maybe I stepped on her toes a bit by snatching her motherly duties out of her hands.

Turning my body around, I closed the fridge and softly frowned, "Eliza? What's bothering you?" I kept my voice soft and tried my best not to sound accusatory or irked at her. "This is your home, so please, don't hold back whatever is on your mind."

Setting her fork down with a sigh, I watched her look at me with somewhat apologetic eyes. "It's not that I'm ungrateful for this, as weird as it is, but I just..." Her face twisted as she stammered and struggled to find the right words.

Closing her mouth, she cleared her throat before speaking again, "You don't have to do all of this. You really don't have to put so much energy and effort into this. I don't want you to get upset if, for some reason, things don't work out." Her voice slowly trailed off, until she mumbled to herself.

Toning down my eagerness, I relaxed my shoulders and approached her side, then knelt down. Naturally, my lips spread into a reassuring smile as I looked up at her. I only broke my gaze with her nervous eyes for a split second to take her hands in mine and comfort her.

"*Mia rosa*, if you reject me twenty-seven days from now, then I will take that defeat with pride and be forever grateful for the time you chose to give me." I sweetened her with assuring words while stroking her hands. "A deal's a deal, and I'm no sore loser," I told her, confident she wouldn't end this between us. "You should never feel like you owe it to anyone, not even me, for their efforts put toward courting you. When we put ourselves into the dating ring, then we always have to be prepared for either outcome."

It was unfortunate, but that's how the game worked. Not every race would be a victory, something I've accepted with every aspect of my life. Well, until now. Even if I was buttering Eliza up with my words, I didn't fully mean them. I would have her no matter what; it was up to her whether it would be easy or hard.

"If someone chooses to chase after you, then that's on them." Steeling my eyes, I gave her a stern gaze. "And don't you ever let anyone make you feel guilty about it. You don't ever let them gaslight you into giving your time and energy in return just because they put out."

Cracking a smile, Eliza briefly took her hand from me to reach out and gingerly stroke my hair. "You're not a shrink, are you?" she asked half-jokingly with a nervous chuckle.

Chuckling along with her, I shook my head in response. "No, but I did think about it in college." Honestly, I did, but I found it a little boring and tedious to listen to other people's problems all day.

Her cheerful sounds died out to a face full of curiosity. "What do you do then? For work, I mean."

Smiling, I brought her hands up and kissed them before standing. "I'm a businessman," I told her as I walked back to the kitchen. "I own a string of clubs in Portland, along with a financial firm. I'm pretty hands-off now in my career, hence why I'm able to be here in Seaside and not in the city."

I wasn't lying to her, technically. I was a legit businessman with a business degree. I just omitted the part about my businesses being tied to the mafia, that's all. I mean, tiny nuances, not like they mattered. It was something she didn't strictly *need* to know. I didn't do *horrendous* things, just some drug selling, money laundering, loan-sharking, gambling, and maybe some prostitution here and there—all voluntary of course, maybe some mild coercion when necessary. It wasn't like I trafficked humans or did anything unto-ward to the elderly or minors.

Smirking, I gave myself a little ego boost, "I have supervisors and managers overseeing everything while I reap the rewards from the comfort of my own home."

As I busied myself with making some food for Asher, I heard a scoff and a dry chuckle. "If you're trying to see if I'm a gold digger, then you can stop waving the stack of cash." She sounded a little offended, but I couldn't tell for sure because I wasn't facing her.

"Eliza, I'm not that kind of asshole, and I know you're not one," I replied, chuckling and rolling my eyes. "You're a good person, little rose, and don't argue because I'm good at reading people. Even if I wasn't, every interaction we've had involving money so far has shown me you're not." I was extremely good at reading people." In my line of work, I had learned hard and fast how to hone that particular skill-set. It came early in my career, after being too soft-hearted caused me to be duped into believing one too many sob stories, only to later find the culprits with their hands in the proverbial cookie jar. Thankfully, I hadn't been played enough to lose territory or business, which is how I became a mafia head.

While plating Asher's food, I changed the subject. "What do you want for lunch and dinner later?" Pulling a chair next to Asher's, I situated myself and presented the small plate of food to the toddler, who responded with a happy scream and clap of his hands.

My eyes glanced over to Eliza, watching her chew her fork for a moment before replying, "Uhh, I'll just bring myself a sandwich for lunch, and you don't have to worry about dinner or anything, I'll be okay to feed myself."

Yeah, no, not on my watch.

Rejecting her words, I shook my head. "Nope, I am going to be your personal chef for the next twenty-seven days, so too bad,"

I jabbed with a cheeky chuckle and grin. "Either you give me an answer, or I will make something random."

Grumbling, she narrowed her eyes at me for a minute before rolling them. For a moment, I thought I'd won until she made one last ditch effort. "W-well what if I want a sandwich for lunch?" It was a shaky retort, making me roll my eyes back at her and chuckle in response. "What if I want a simple ham sandwich? Hm?"

Little smartass.

Too bad I was smarter.

Smirking, I leaned my elbow onto the edge of the table, propping my cheek against my fist. "Then I'll make the best ham sandwich for you, jammed packed with the best ham ever made to mankind." Okay, maybe that was a bit of a stretch, but I had to exaggerate for effect. "I'll use the best condiments, and I'll pack you the best fruits and vegetables, the freshest of the fresh." Alright, I was being over the top.

Groaning in defeat, Eliza threw her head back and arms up. "I'm not winning with you," she admitted begrudgingly, glaring at me playfully before going back to finish her breakfast with a rather satisfied smile.

Even though the morning so far had been going swimmingly, her sense of unease crept through the air like a steady annoyance to me. Unfortunately, as irked as it made me, I couldn't blame her for it.

I literally barged into her life and hunkered down very stubbornly. On the bright side, she wasn't locked away in my basement, as tempting as it was.

The more I entertained the idea of forcing my hand with her, the less appealing it became to me. Don't get me wrong, I'd do it at the very end if all my other efforts met a dead-end.

It'd been so long since I felt this kind of energizing excitement. The kind that constantly buzzed at the end of every nerve fiber in your body until you were forced to act, or you'd risk exploding from all the pent-up energy. This thrill of the chase, for a woman. Fuck, I hadn't felt like this since my younger years, and it was too riveting to let go of.

Yet, even back in my crazy and hormonal years, I never wanted a woman as badly as I did Eliza. If a woman rejected me back then after some effort, then that was it. I never pushed or persisted because there was no urge or need to *have* them, nor did I ever feel the motivation to *possess* them.

In all this time, I'd never had the desire to have a woman so fully by my side, nor did I care enough to put forth so much effort.

Until a little rosebud took root and bloomed right in my path.

Eliza really was a breath of fresh air, as cliché as it sounded. Nearly every moment of my day-to-day life followed the same routine, with minimal deviations. That wasn't the case anymore. No, ever since I met this woman, and especially since I'd gotten my hooks into her, my life had started to feel like an adventure. My dull life had been turned completely around. I felt like I had walked into a scene from the gardens of Eden—she was the forbidden fruit and I couldn't wait to take that first bite.

No matter how long it took, I'd get that forbidden fruit. I wouldn't stop until Eliza was in my arms, and my lips upon on hers. There's no stopping me until I've tasted and marked every inch of her divine body and claimed it as mine. Until my name fell from her lips like a prayer while I was buried deep inside of her, I wouldn't stop. Slowly but surely, I'd get her to worship me on her knees, make her look up at me as if I were her god.

Once I got her under me, I'd fill her with my cock, make her scream my name, and pump her full of my seed. Eliza *would* be mine.

Fuck, to fill her and breed her precious body, the thought made me almost feral. We'd have the perfect babies—she was already the perfect mother. So, giving her more babies just made sense.

"Uhh, Adam?" Her sweet but wary voice cut through the fog of my thoughts, making me snap out of it.

Looking at her, I watched her body shy away from me a little. "Adam, are you okay? Did I say or do something to upset you? You got really quiet and serious, and you're looking at me really intensely." Her soft eyes grew worried and jittery as she reached a hand out and placed it on Asher.

A deep breath relaxed my body, and I slowly leaned back a little in my seat to give her the illusion of space while smiling at her apologetically. "Sorry, it's nothing directed at you or anything like that. A small situation from work crossed my mind at the wrong time," I lied smoothly with another reassuring smile. "It really isn't you, promise."

Telling her the truth was *not* an option, not unless I wanted to scare her off and make my life harder. "Also, I could never be upset at you," I scoffed playfully with a warm chuckle.

Eliza's smile faltered to a flat one as she averted her gaze. "That's what they all say..." I faintly heard her mumbling words before Asher's happy scream drowned her out completely.

Curiosity tempted me to press her to find out what she meant, but for the sake of keeping some peace between us, I zipped my lips.

Clearing my throat, I put on my best charming smile. "You know, you don't have to take Asher with you to work. I can always watch him for you," I offered while picking some spilled food off the table and feeding it to Asher. "It will really make things easier for you."

Eliza's smile tensed up with a deep breath. "It's fine. I prefer to work with him around. It kind of gives me some ease and peace of mind." A look of realization shocked her face, and she instantly held her waving hands up in denial. In a flurry, her words flew out, "Not that I'm saying you're a bad person and that I don't trust you or anything with Asher, because I would. It's just I have attachment issues with him and separation anxiety."

A light-hearted chuckle trembled at my body. "Eliza, it's fine," I assured her.

Reaching over, I stopped her frantic hands by grabbing them and holding them together. "Really, it is, and I totally understand." The warmth in my voice meant they weren't empty words. "It's been just you and Asher for a while, and you're his mother. So, it's natural for you to want him around for peace of mind. You really don't have to try and explain yourself. Asher is *your* baby, little rose. You set the rules for his care, no one can take that from you. Don't let them."

Settling her hands down on the table, I kept mine over hers comfortingly. "I've seen my sister and her kid, so I really do understand."

It probably wasn't too healthy at this point, but if this was how she'd been doing things ever since he was born, then who was I to break such a comfort routine. The last thing I wanted to do was send her into some kind of mental breakdown or episode of sorts because I ruined her ways.

Although, she really did need to start putting that boundary up between her and Asher. Yes, she was his mother, but that wasn't her whole identity. If she kept going down this path, then she'd end up smothering Asher and preventing him from having a fun life. Also, she wouldn't be doing her mental health any favors either if she kept her identity tied to Asher.

"How about this," I started with a cautious smile, "you take Asher with you, do what you need to do, and I'll take the lil' guy when I drop off lunch for you? That way, I can take him back to a nice and cozy bed for his nap, give you some time to just focus on getting work done, and I'll make dinner with him so you can come home to a smiley kid and a hot meal. Yeah?" I tried to convince her with a warm smile as I bargained with her in a pleading voice.

Sweetening my smile to try and rope her in more, I added, "You'll still have him for most of your shift today, and he'll get to sleep in his comfy bed for a nap rather than his playpen. And if you really can't stand to be away from him for too long, then I can drop him back off with you after he wakes from his nap."

There were lots of other things I could have said, and there were definitely other things to be added in not-so-nice ways, but I didn't want to be a jerk to her. Not when I could see that she was really trying her best out here in this rotten world. She didn't need someone harping on her for the wrongs in her life or how she chose to live it. Not that I had an issue with her doing what she did; I didn't have an issue with how she was doing things, I just saw some better ways to go about them, especially with the help I offered her.

But, again, I wasn't going to soapbox her, not when I had no right to.

We sat in tense silence as Eliza debated for a good while. She almost had me a few times when she looked at me forlornly and opened her mouth, but she always promptly shut it and turned her head away before any words came out.

After she did that a few times, I thought she'd reject the idea, so I found myself looking at her in disbelief and victory when she said, "Alright, fine." Before I could celebrate my little victory, she slapped a lid on my budding excitement. "But! But." She looked at me pointedly, making sure my full attention was on her before she continued, "But, if I want Asher back once he is done napping, I expect you to drop whatever you are doing and bring him back to me, a-alright?"

And here I thought her backbone started to come through. She started off so strong and nice, but her voice wavered in the end.

Well, I was still proud of her because progress was progress, no matter how little.

Leaning in, I pressed my forehead against hers and smiled proudly. *"Brava ragazza, sono così fiero di te,"* I whispered, appreciating the way her cheeks flared up brightly in response.

Brushing off the short and tender moment, I gave her some space before brightening my smile into an excited grin. Then, I eagerly nodded in response and switched back to English. "Of course, whatever you want. You are his mother, after all, and it would just be an asshole move of me to disregard your wishes and wants when it comes to *your* child."

I might be an asshole to many people, usually scumbags who never deserve to be treated decently for even a second, but never to a woman. Actually, that would be a lie because I could be a little snappy toward a female if she were a total snobby bitch. That was rare, though!

"Also, you still haven't exactly answered my question from earlier about what you want for lunch, that's not a ham sandwich, and dinner," I reminded her with a cheeky smile, chuckling softly when Eliza rolled her eyes and playfully smacked my arm. "Again, it's either you tell me, or I'll surprise you."

Accepting her defeat with an unamused scoff, she gave me an answer, "Surprise me with any sandwich of your choice, but just keep it small. I usually have a small appetite for lunch." She didn't sound too happy about giving in to me, but at least she didn't try to fight it.

Also, she didn't have to tell me that because I'd seen how little she ate at lunch—if it could even be called a meal. Seriously, her lunch portions were so small they qualified as snacks, in my opinion.

"And uhh dinner..." she drawled, and her eyes glazed over with a distant look for a few seconds. "I guess you could surprise me since I'm not really craving anything or have any idea for what to request."

"You're not going to get mad at me for not being able to read your mind, are you?" I joked with a laugh. "This isn't one of those 'I don't know' moments where you really know what you want but don't want to tell me and want me to figure it out by myself and whatnot, is it?" God damn, that was a mouthful to say.

A soft smack echoed through the area and Eliza rolled her eyes. "I wouldn't do that to you. I really don't know, nor do I really care as long as it's edible food and somewhat good," she replied truthfully, smiling gratefully at me. "Besides, the last thing I want to do is piss you off by making you chase your own tail around." I think that was an attempt to joke around, but it came out so forced and dry I doubt there was any lightheartedness behind her words.

Which brought another issue back to my mind regarding how skittish and overly reactive she was. To be honest, I wanted to bring it up to her the day at the park, but I dropped it and we moved right past it. The last thing I wanted to do at the park was further dampen the mood.

And it was the last thing I wanted to do now. And I definitely wanted to avoid dampening the mood when I was gaining more ground with her.

I didn't want to stress her out before work either; that'd be pretty fucked up of me.

Besides, we were having a very good morning, despite the fact I'd showed up without warning and let myself. I mean, I could have been in cuffs or behind bars had things gone south.

Okay, maybe not that bad because no cop in their right mind would cuff me, nor would I ever face charges. Not with how much dirty money I threw the legal system to turn a blind eye to my activities. The mafia paid good money to ensure smooth operations, so I'd have been really pissed if I had gotten arrested for something as trivial as breaking and entering—not that I did! Pretty sure it didn't count as breaking and entering if I had a key to the place. Granted, I didn't have explicit permission to have the key, but that tiny detail didn't matter.

Either way, the subject of her being tightly wound and hyper-reactive could wait to be discussed some other time.

Pulling myself out of my troublesome mind, I asked, "Is there anything you're craving or have an affinity toward right now? Or do I really have full reign? I have mad kitchen skills, so unless you want something extremely complicated, I'm confident I can manage." Hopefully, staying on an innocent enough subject would set me straight again.

Once again, Eliza pondered for a second, this time humming to herself softly for a bit. "Maybe just something savory? I know it may sound weird and not the best, but like something nice and savory. A nice bowl of actual ramen, or a juicy and fatty steak with mashed potatoes and gravy, or a plate of cheesy and creamy pasta, or just something that would send us into an instant food coma because it's so filling and amazing." I loved how her eyes lit up with hope and excitement as she spoke. "I mean, I guess those are some ideas for you for tonight." She chuckled sheepishly with an uneven smile.

Smiling happily and proudly in return, I reached out and stroked the top of her head. "I'll make you something so amazing you'll have no choice but to keep me around," I joked with a hearty chuckle.

"One lovely dinner for my little rose coming right up."

Chapter 9
Eliza

I PROBABLY SHOULD'VE CALLED the cops. I shouldn't have entertained him. But God, he was right there in my home. I mean, I had no idea when he came in! He could've hurt me while I was asleep, or worse, he could've hurt Asher.

Damn it, stop it. You're being ridiculous.

If Adam had any bad intentions, then surely, he would've acted on them by now, no? Or at least, I would've seen some signs of his malicious nature or plans, right? I know, in the past, I tended to be blind to a lot of things as evidenced by the man I married, but I've been vigilant since we left. Especially when it came to the safety of Asher and myself.

My gut hadn't screamed at me to run for the hills when it came to Adam. My traumatized brain may have, but not my gut. Sure, I still had some inkling of wariness, but it wasn't extreme to where I wanted to shut him out completely. It was quite the opposite, shockingly. I wanted to let him in. Okay, let me rephrase that: my heart and soul wanted to let him in. My stupid gut wanted to maintain a few inches of distance until we figured out what about Adam threw us off.

He was too perfect not to be suspicious of. There had to be some ulterior motive or something seriously wrong with him. I was willing to bet it'd be a punch to my face the moment I found out whatever dirty secret he hid.

I needed to cut him off; that was the best thing to do. Yet, I couldn't bring myself to do it. It was a stupid cycle when it came to Adam, from wanting him out and wanting him in.

The stupid romantic in me fancied his persistence, kindness, patience, and attention. Unfortunately, that side of me was the reason why I was in my current situation. If I hadn't fallen for James's stupid lies and empty promises, then I wouldn't have ended up in a boxing ring with a loveless marriage.

This whole shit show of my life wouldn't have happened if I hadn't been stupid enough to open myself up to love. I shouldn't be on the run as a single mother. I should be living my life, be happy with my career, and have someplace I belonged in life. Instead, I had no career, no life, nothing. The only thing I did have was my son, Asher. The funny thing was, I shouldn't have had him either. If my life had taken a different turn, then I wouldn't be a mother.

Hell, I wouldn't have been a married woman in the first place. I had my reservations with James back then, but I always ignored them because I wanted to be loved by someone so badly. Plans to be a pharmacist before settling with Mr. Right were stripped away the more I let James dig his claws into me. Marriage right out of high school certainly wasn't in my plans, but he convinced me with sweet lies about a wonderful life full of rainbows and sunshine.

Breathing deeply, I shook those bubbling thoughts out of my mind before they could spill over and take root again.

Constant denial had swallowed me up like quicksand until every part of me was snuffed out. The person I was when I met Adam, had felt so foreign to me whenever I took any time to dwell on my life. If I hadn't needed to hold it together for Asher, then a few mental breakdowns, and maybe a trip or two to the psychiatric ward, would've burned themselves into my record. But I had to be strong for Asher. He only had me, and I couldn't let him down.

I already fucked up my own life. No way would I screw Asher's up. Even if I didn't plan for him, I still had him, so he was my responsibility. He'd done nothing wrong to deserve a bad life, and, even if I didn't have much to give him, I'd do my damn best to give him a happy life.

Nothing like a mother's love. I never understood that until I laid eyes on Asher for the first time. He honestly brought something out in me, a spark I'd thought no longer existed after years of suffering at James's hand.

If we weren't on the run, then maybe I could nurture that spark into an actual fire and make something of myself.

"Eliza quit fretting over there. You're going to look all wrinkly and gray like me sooner rather than later if you keep scrunching your face like that and stressing your young mind." Mary's playful chiding slammed the breaks on my train of thought. "Asher is going to be fine. Adam is a wonder when it comes to children, so don't worry." Her assurance did little to ease the mom-guilt that welled up inside of me.

It had only been fifteen minutes since I separated myself from Asher, allowing Adam to leave with him, but the guilt and anxiety gnawed at me like some beaver going at some wood. I knew he was safe, but I had bad separation anxiety when it came to Asher. Even in the past, when I left Asher with Mary, it was only for the briefest of moments. I never took longer doing what errands I needed because the thought of Asher being away from me tore at me. Describing the sheer dread from the constant onslaught of damning thoughts that came from being away from Asher was impossible.

Without Asher, I felt hollow.

It probably wasn't healthy to measure my worth by the type of mother I was to my son, but I had nothing else in the world besides him.

A sudden jolt of warmth on my shoulder brought me back to reality. "It's only just a few hours, then you'll be back home with a doting man waiting on you hand and foot." My ears zoned in to Mary's voice as my eyes glanced over at her appreciatively. "I know it feels impossible, but stop worrying about Asher so much. He is in amazing hands, trust me." At least her warm and affirming smile settled some of my nerves, thankfully.

Her joyful laugh made it impossible for me to keep the smile from showing on my face. "Get on with cleaning while I finish my cookies for you to take with you," she urged me with a soft pat on my shoulder before she left for her kitchen.

It was damn near impossible not to think about Asher the whole time I cleaned Mary's place. The constant photos from Adam did nothing to ease the turmoil within me either. Seeing Asher laughing and having fun melted my heart with pure bliss, but it also cracked it to pieces from the sadness of not being there to fully witness those moments. Pictures could only do so much to capture a memory, and I was greedy when it came to Asher. I wanted every little bit of his life engrained into my own memory bank.

Also, seeing Asher have fun without me felt like a slap to the face. Yes, Asher needed to grow up and become independent; it was only a matter of time before he would be off on his own. But I didn't want any of that yet. I didn't want him to grow up so fast. Like some selfish prick, I wanted to keep Asher and all his baby cuteness to myself—to keep him my baby forever.

The temptation to ask Adam to bring Asher back beckoned me like some twisted demon after my soul. Sending the message would've been so simple. Just a few taps of my fingers and Asher would be back by my side before I knew it.

But I can't.

I shouldn't.

Besides the fact Asher was currently happily napping his tired little baby brain away, it was a little ridiculous. He was fine and content; it'd be bad to ruin things for him. But God, I wanted him back so badly. I wanted to have him sleeping a few feet from me to peak at him whenever I missed him, to reach out and touch and adore him with my eyes.

Almost robotically, I cleaned the house at a faster-than-usual pace because of my agitation. No matter how much I tried to vent it out by scrubbing at the grout of the tiles, running the mop back and forth against the wooden floors, scrubbing at the sink, and shining all the mirrors and surfaces, the irksome feeling wouldn't stop festering in my chest. Every little back-and-forth movement only served to worsen the feeling; it was as if I pulled at a cord to my irritation, revving it up and causing more build-up rather than releasing it with my activities.

"Eliza, don't make me send you out to the barn to chuck hay bales." If it weren't for the stringent look, her playful threat would have flown over my head. "If you need a good outlet for the worry, some time in the barn helps, and the fresh air helps quite a bit, too."

Sighing in defeat, I sucked in a deep breath and held it stubbornly until I felt myself grow lightheaded. "I don't know why it's bothering me so much when it shouldn't bother me at all," I grumbled as I helped Mary clean up the kitchen from her baking adventures.

"Because it is a huge deviation from your normal routine, and it's so sudden. I mean, I remember how antsy you were when Rob and I first offered to watch Asher. You were such a fluster when you came back in half an hour," Mary mused with a chuckle, grabbing out some to-go boxes. "It will take some time, but it'll become your new normal before you know it. Heck, if Adam does become a constant in your life, then you can finally pick back up that college career of yours and finish it out with the time and support he'll be able to give you."

I couldn't help but smile grimly as my hopes sank to the bottom of the endless ocean. There was no way I could go back to school. Not only did I not have the funds, but if I had to keep my head low, enrolling in university and getting out there was the last thing I should do. Also, I couldn't afford to devote six to eight years of my life to a pharmacy degree. That ship sailed long ago and sank after being assaulted by cannonballs from all angles.

Humming flatly in response, I took the boxes from Mary to fully assemble them. "I don't know about having Adam as a constant in my life, though." At least I could admit something truthful out loud. "I just... I don't know him, and he seems kind of too good to be true, and I don't want to get hurt or find out later down the line, after I get involved with him, that Asher doesn't get along with him or he feels different, and I just don't know about him." Well, now everything came out after I pulled the plug.

My worries rambled on and on until Mary grabbed my shoulders and flashed me a stern look. "Eliza, honey, that's what the dating period is for," she reminded me with a motherly smile. "And life is nothing if you don't take chances. You can't play it safe all your life, or you'll get nowhere." Comfortingly, she rubbed my shoulders and upper arms. "And yes, dating is scary, but what is your heart and gut telling you about Adam?"

"Mary, my gut and heart don't exactly have a good track record," I joked dryly with a chuckle. "I don't know if I can trust it with how much it's led me astray," I admitted with a crestfallen smile.

"We all learn from our mistakes as we mature, and it's a part of human nature to stumble here and there," Mary said with a wary chuckle. Turning away from me to the cookies, she started to lift them off the baking sheet before continuing, "But we have to fall in order to learn. If we don't fall, then how will we learn to get up? Or to not do what we did that caused the fall?"

Her warm eyes glanced at me intermittently as she sorted the delicacies of cookies into the various boxes. "No doubt you've learned from your past at this point, and your instincts have honed after becoming a mother. So, you need to trust yourself a little more." Reaching over, she gently patted my arm. "I care for you, Eliza, and I usually don't advise those I care about to take chances easily if I don't have a good feeling about things." The genuine smile on her face, along with her tender look, made it hard for me to resist her advice.

"You don't have to flop at his feet, but give Adam a chance." Her old and worn eyes lit up with a nostalgic and hopeful fire. "Both of you are good people who need to take chances, but you are also both young and stubborn. Your hearts and souls already know before your mind, but you two don't want to admit the sparks that light up the whole world around you."

Furrowing my brows together, I let out a ridiculous chuckle as I hugged Mary tightly. "Okay, I get your point. Let's not get too deep and sentimental because my heart won't be able to handle it." Having it said to my face repeatedly wouldn't make the situation any different.

Unless James disappeared or forgot about me, I wouldn't ever be able to settle or have an ounce of solace in my life.

Pulling away, I helped Mary pack the rest of the cookies. To further pass the time, I decided to break the peaceful silence. "Mary, what can you tell me about Adam?" I didn't know who else to go to for information, and I was at a loss when it came to social media. I could ask Eve for help, but she already had so much on her plate—I didn't want to add something so trivial to it.

Smiling and chuckling warmly, Mary flashed me a cheeky wink. "He's downright handsome, obviously." She snickered, making me roll my eyes. "As I said, he's a good man, always helping people around the town whenever he's out and about, never afraid to offer a lending hand either, as you probably experienced at the grocery store that day."

Yeah, that was the whole problem. He sounded perfect. Too fucking perfect, and no one was perfect. Even saints had their sins, was how I always saw things.

With a warm and encouraging smile, she squeezed my hand with beaming eyes. "Just do both of your sakes a favor and give him a chance and take things slow. You only have one shot in a lifetime at true love, and it's better you shoot and miss than don't shoot at all and live with regrets."

Sighing heavily, I flashed her a lopsided smile. "No promises, but I'll try if I cross that path." I wasn't confident about it, probably because I had little intention to do so.

I couldn't be selfish and let myself be happy like that, not at Asher's expense. If I got comfortable and James found Asher, then our lives would be turned upside down. The last thing I wanted was to have Asher back in his biological father's grasp. I had to keep a clear head and remain vigilant to protect my son.

Changing the subject a little, I asked in a genuinely curious voice, "Is he really a businessman? Or do you know what he does for work?"

Mary instantly gushed over Adam like some proud mother with how her eyes lit up like a beacon in the night. "Oh, that boy has got his life set with how he runs things. Struck it lucky right out of school and landed a position at Goliath Financial, then expanded to some of the casinos along the coast before the hotels and restaurants came, and all the other little businesses here and there naturally came with the years."

Huffing, she hooked her hands on her hips as she finished boxing up the last of the cookies. "And he's such an amazing son. He shared a lot of the money with his parents. Started up a vineyard for them in eastern Oregon to let them live out their dream. That boy is a godsend. Hopefully, you'll snatch him off the market before someone bad can." Looking at me with a kind grin, she shoved a few of the boxes into my arms. "Those are for you and Asher, and since you're going to be seeing Adam, could you give him his portion as well?"

Rolling my eyes, I tightened my hold around the boxes, and smiling gratefully, I leaned my head onto her shoulder in an armless hug. "Thank you, Mary." It was impossible to say no to her whenever she offered me food. Well, it wasn't even so much an offer as it was a demand.

With a warm chuckle that sent shivers of calm down my body, Mary urged me toward my bag with a pat on my back. "Drive safe now, alright? And have a good evening."

"I will," I replied with a widening smile. "And you and Rob have a good one yourselves."

Chapter 10
Adam

THE JOYFUL SOUND OF Asher's laughter warmed the room up, along with the soft scent of herbs, cheese, and boiling pasta as the two of us goofed around in the kitchen.

The toddler sat in his highchair while I bounced back and forth between him and the stove, tossing the occasional shred of cheese onto his tray to keep him occupied between our jamming.

Fortunately, the little dude loved Baby Shark...

... Unfortunately, he loved Baby Shark.

I swear, every child in the whole world was obsessed with that song. Yeah, it was a little annoying, but I'd gotten to the point where my ears had become numb to the song after hearing it constantly around the house—thanks, Adelaide.

Bending down to the child, I tickled his nose with a chuckle. "You think Mommy's gonna like this?" I asked in a baby voice, looking at Asher as if he'd actually answer me. "And you know, don't tell your mommy this, but I think she is the most beautiful woman ever." At least my secrets would be safe with him. "I'd do anything for her."

Anything.

I mean, I already had a man sacked for her safety, even if she didn't know it. Turns out, her apartment complex manager had had quite the record as a Peeping Tom and for abusing his power with the master keys. I still wanted to deal with him, but that was problem for later—not like he'd be going anywhere chained up in the bunker.

"I gotta make sure the bad man doesn't ever snatch any panties ever again." I probably shouldn't be saying that so nonchalantly to the kid with a smile on my face, but not like he could understand any of it.

And I gotta buy your mommy some new panties.

That needed to be added to my to-do list. The thought of that idiot's grubby hands touching my Eliza's private clothes, the ones that touched her so intimately, made my blood boil with disgust. That scumbag wouldn't have any grubby fingers left to use after I was done with him later tonight.

Now, just how the hell would I replace her stock of old undies? I mean, as straightforward as it'd be to give her a box full of them, that'd probably cause her to pull back from me. Pushing my luck with her wouldn't be wise after the stunt I pulled that morning.

Actually...

Soft creaks from the bones in my neck echoed in my ears as I turned to look at her closet. Her outfits were pathetic. No, I wasn't mocking her or anything like that. Okay, maybe pathetic wasn't the right word to describe her poor closet.

How the hell was I gonna go about her bland fashion sense without sounding like a pompous asshole? I wanted to upgrade her bland wardrobe without insulting her or sounding like a pompous asshole, but I didn't know how. Was I the most fashionable man out there? Fuck no, but I knew a boring closet when I saw one. Ironic, given the fact my closet and dresser contained the same damn outfits, or at least I wore the same ones for most of the week, gray sweatpants or basketball shorts with a white shirt, Occasionally, I switched it up with a black shirt, but that was it unless I had an outing, in which case, I cycled between various suits. I had jeans and nice pants as well, but again, those were only worn occasionally.

Just as I opened my mouth to converse with Asher some more, the audible click of the lock and front door opening caused both of us to shut up and snap our heads in that direction. Both of us were practically vibrating in excitement, goofy smiles spread across our faces, as we waited for the door to open fully and reveal a tired but smiling Eliza to us.

Being the more important one between us, Asher instantly captured his mother's attention. "Mama!" The highchair screeched and scooted around as the chubby toddler bounced in his seat. "Mama!" A high-pitched ringing filled my ears from his ecstatic shrieks, along with the chair's plastic legs fighting against the wooden floor.

At least Eliza's delighted laugh made the assault on my eardrums worth it. "I see he hasn't conned you into buying him half of a toy store," she joked after shutting the door and locking it.

Closing the distance to Asher with a few long strides, she plucked him from his seat, and hugged him tightly with an infectious smile. She buried her face into his giggling body and inhaled deeply. "Oh, I missed you so much chunkers." Her muffled happiness pulverized my dark heart.

I don't know what it was but seeing Eliza smile or be genuinely overjoyed made me forget that I was a bad person. She made me feel a sense of normalcy and belonging, and she brought out this thrill in me. I just wanted to be content.

I was convinced that such a TV-perfect scene would eventually become the norm for us. Eliza coming home from work, or hell, me coming out of the office after a long day, to nothing but pure bliss. It really wasn't a matter of if, as I had every intention of making this our routine. I'd condition Eliza to love it to where she wouldn't be able to live without it.

There won't be a life without me in it. I'll make sure of it.

Forcing myself to smile normally, I got up and hugged her briefly in greeting. "Oh, he came close," I joked back with a chuckle. "Why don't you go wash up real quick for dinner," I suggested, turning her body slightly toward the bathroom. "It's almost ready. I just need a few extra minutes for the pasta to be done."

Pressing her lips together into a tight line, her eyes bounced between the bathroom and the lot of us for a long second. It seemed like she'd take a seat and be stubborn, so it astounded me when she reluctantly placed Asher back in his chair. The soft nod of her head nearly went unnoticed by me, along with her hum, "Alright, but it shouldn't take me long either." She didn't sound fully convinced, but I had to praise her silently for trying.

Her slender body looked like a blur, darting to the closet and then into the bathroom. I wanted to question her about whether she actually washed up or not when she reemerged from the bathroom, not even a second after the door had shut. Seriously, I blinked twice, and it felt like she was in and out. I would've honestly questioned her if it weren't for the wet bangs and fresh face.

Smiling like an idiot in love, I snaked an arm around her waist when she came close enough. "Hopefully, work wasn't too bad to-day?" I asked while leading her to the spot I'd been sitting at when she came home.

Her head lulled back to look up at me when I pushed her down into the seat. The soft wrinkles at the corners of her tired eyes deepened with her exhausted smile. "It wasn't too bad," she answered me truthfully.

Then, her face straightened out with a look of realization. "Oh! Mary gave us some cookies!" There was some pressure against my palms when I forced her to remain seated. "Adam, I'm going to forget them in my car again if—"

I cut her off by holding my hand up, though I instantly regretted it when I saw her flinch a little. Remorse locked my knees and buckled them, sending me to the ground before her. "Shit, I'm so sorry, little rose. I should've been more mindful." I really should have, and I couldn't help but scold myself mentally for scaring her like that.

Breathing deeply, I looked up at her with a face full apology. "I swear to you, on my life, on my parents' lives, on everything, that I will never raise my hand at you with any intention of harming you." Gingerly, I placed my hands on her outer thighs, squeezing and rubbing with my thumbs. "Listen, I don't know exactly what happened to you, and I hope that one day you'll trust me enough to let me know, but I will never mistreat you."

Slowly, I bowed my head and kissed the top of her knees tenderly. "You really don't have to tell me anything. Your reaction is telling me enough." Peering up at her with an understanding smile, I leaned my cheek against her thigh. "I won't push for anything either because I trust that you will tell me when you are ready."

God, please don't let me fuck this up already.

Maybe dropping down to my knees might was a little much, but how else was I supposed to show her I was sorry and meant no harm? Words wouldn't have sufficed, and I doubted they'd affect her since the last bastard probably ran them ragged.

Looking up at her, I smiled contently "You know, once I plump you up a little, these thighs are going to be heavenly."

God damn it! Why the fuck did I say that!? That sounds so weird in a moment like this.

I wanted to smack myself for losing my cool with Eliza. I mean, I was a grown-ass man with experience; I shouldn't be fumbling around like some awkward teenager. It wasn't as if I didn't know what to do, because I did. It was more or less not knowing how to go about things with Eliza. I had to be careful with her until I figured out what her deal was.

Once I figured out her tune, I could dance to it to my delight and string her along until she matched my rhythm. Until then, I had to be a goofy klutz around her, not that I minded. Being a charming asshole would've been preferred, but a nice challenge was always refreshing.

Eliza's long sigh made me frown internally, especially when she slowly raised a jerky hand up and held it inches from my head. Was she going to push me off? Tell me to leave? Shut me out?

My hands unconsciously gripped at her tighter out of fear of having her slip further from me. She could shove me away all she wanted, but like hell would I let her go further than an inch.

She is mine.

My darkened gaze went unnoticed until Eliza's nervous voice pointed my face out to me. "A-Adam, why are you looking at me like that? I... I'm sorry if—"

Confused, I picked my head up a little and tilted it while softening my tense face. "Look like what? Am I looking at you funny? Did I offend you? What are you apologizing for?" Great, what had my face fucked up?

Breathing out a short and nervous chuckle, she settled her hand down on her lap. Then, her lips twisted for a few seconds before her words came out rather awkwardly. "I... You... Uhhh... It's just... I don't know how to say this without offending you..." Her upper body leaned away from me despite the back of the chair stopping her. "I don't want you to get mad at me," she admitted in a trembling voice, her eyes averting from me and darting around the room.

Okay, how the hell do I go about this?

Relaxing my shoulders, I brightened my face with a playful smile. "Do I have flour on my face? Sauce? Dressing? Do I look like a clown?" I hoped joking around with her would ease some of the tension before bringing in the heavy subjects. "*Mia rosa*, there's little you can say to offend me, so please, don't ever be afraid to speak your mind with me." Yeah, but how the hell was I going to get that through her thick skull? "And I know you might not believe me much, but I swear, I won't ever get upset at you for anything like that, and if I ever do, then break my face with a pan," I offered with a nervous but serious smile. "And since I quite like my face, I'll be sure to keep to my own promises," I quipped with a sheepish chuckle.

The pressure in my chest eased a little when I caught a glimpse of Eliza's cracking smile and stifled laughter.

And since my silly little plan seems to be working...

"I know you probably might have heard it all before and that you haven't known me long or much, but you can trust me when it comes to your safety and wellbeing," I assured her with a warm and comforting smile, taking her hand into both of mine. "I was raised better, and if my sister or parents caught wind of me hurting a woman, even if it's just with my words, they would drag me out back by my ear and beat my ass." I tried to sound confident with my chuckle, but it shook at the thought of my pissed-off parents having a go at me.

I learned the hard way when I said something mean to a girl in grade school and made her cry. My mother really instilled the fear of God into me, and I was pretty sure I met him for a split second before she dragged me back to the land of the living, only to rip me a new one. Hell, I could feel the phantom pain on my backside still, along with the taste of the rancid soap in my mouth.

I shuddered at the memory and quickly shook it out of my mind, not wanting to dull the moment with Eliza.

Taking a deep breath, I softened my curious eyes at her. "So, please elaborate on earlier," I urged her in the smoothest and calmest voice I could manage. "I want to know if something triggers you or upsets you in any way to avoid it in the future, but I can't read your mind. So, please, let me in just a little so I can avoid passively harming you." If I went off her reactions alone, I could easily take everything the wrong way, become overly cautious, or end up walking around on eggshells.

Eliza hesitated for a moment with some heavy sighs before relenting, "It's just... The way you were looking at me, it kind of... I don't know how to exactly put it into words, but you looked like a hungry wolf preying up on an injured rabbit..." Her body squirmed a little in her seat while her teeth chewed at her bottom lip. "A-and like, it wasn't in a bad way?"

Her hand balled up into a fist as her fidgeting increased, causing the chair to shift and creak under her weight and movements. "You looked like you wanted me... Bad... Like you wanted to tear into me and take your sweet time with me." She didn't sound too comfortable with how her voice wavered, but she didn't sound opposed to it either.

With a deep breath and a kind smile, I reached up and cupped her face with both my hands. "Do you want me to be honest with you?" I should have worded that better. The way she frowned and winced at my question made my stomach sink. Chuckling sheepishly, I bowed my head apologetically. "Sorry, that came out wrong," I said with a nervous exhale and lick of my lips. "What I mean by that is, do you want me to be honest with what went on through my head just then? Why I looked at you like that?"

I really wanted to slap myself again because I didn't think I helped my case any. Backpedaling, I smiled flatly. "I mean, I'll always be honest with you, but obviously, there are some things I won't be so open to divulging because they aren't the most appropriate."

God damn it, stop digging your own fucking grave! Just shut up!

Backtracking some more, I smiled nervously. "N-not to say I always think inappropriately when it comes to you because I don't. I think about cute things too, like what color roses will bring out the best smile or what drinks you might like or if you like candy or how bright your face will light up if I get you a cute little gift." It was the worst time to lose my cool, but my mouth would not stop running. "I mean, I'm not going to deny that I don't think about you in other ways because it would be impossible. I mean, you are so cute and sexy that I can't help but think about how lovely you feel in my arms and against me."

Someone kill me and put me out of my misery.

God, this was so embarrassing, but I couldn't shut my damn mouth! The chilling fear of rejection clawed at my body from the inside out when Eliza's eyes grew wider and wider with astonishment. On the bright side, she hadn't slapped me across the face and shouted for me to get out of her life, so that was a win, I guess.

Still, I watched her with bated breath as her face twisted with confusion and concern for a long while. Her trembling tongue darted out as fast as a snake's, wetting her nervous lips that shook like leaves with her heavy breath. When she finally spoke, her voice came out so small and shaky that I barely caught it. "I... I don't know what to say..." Not exactly the answer I expected or wanted, but I'd take it over 'get the fuck out' any day.

Unable to help it, I looked at her with squinted eyes and a small frown of confusion, causing her to let out a breathy chuckle. "Not in a bad way." Her reassuring smile lightened the weight against my chest a little, making it easier for me to breathe. "I'm just kind of surprised you see me like that, and it scares me a little, but I am really flattered that a perfect man like you desires someone like me so much," she admitted with a red face.

The sweet moment didn't last with her crestfallen expression. "But... If you're just after my—"

"No," I tersely cut her off. Tightening my hold on her face, I looked at her with steeled eyes. "Little rose, I am *not* pining after you just for sex. I genuinely want you because my world is bright with you in my life. There is so much to you deep down, and I just know it and see it every time I look deep into your eyes. I want to help you bloom to your full potential, be there for all your smiles and tears, and be your person."

Alright, don't fuck this up, Adam. Don't. Fuck. It. Up.

I forced my mouth shut so I could properly sort my thoughts out. Otherwise, I'd go down the hill, and this time, I wasn't sure if there was a way back up if I fell. "Yes, sex is nice, and I'm not going to deny that I want you in all the sinful ways of the world, but such acts and wants don't come before your heart." Alright, it sounded much better in my head, but it was too late to say it better.

Taking a deep breath to reset myself, I nervously licked my lips before continuing, "I want you for your beautiful heart, the one that drives you to wake up every morning to work late into the night for you and Asher. The one that makes your eyes light up seeing each new day. The one that makes you unique."

Should I have shut up before I started to make less sense, or just make myself sound utterly stupid? Probably, but I couldn't. "I know you have baggage, and I really don't give a single damn about it, except that it hurts me to know you're hurting. I want you for all of you, chains with weights, baggage, and all. The moment I decided I wanted you, I accepted the fact that you will come with all the bad along with the good."

Pausing, I collected myself and gave both of us a peaceful moment to digest everything. "But despite seeing everything you're dragging around, I couldn't ignore how much I wanted you in my life. I knew I'd help you carry it, if you'd let me, after thirty days." I gently cupped her cheek, my thumb brushing softly over her skin as a smile pulled at my lips. "And before you argue it's not my place—I know. I know it's not my job, and you'll probably say it's unfair for me to take on your burdens, but I don't care. The moment I chose you, I chose all of you—every part, every piece. No one, especially someone as incredible as you, should ever carry it alone."

Letting out a choppy chuckle, Eliza hesitantly reached out and wrapped her arms around my head, bringing me into a stiff hug. Well, it was more like bringing my head into her midsection because I was still kneeling on the floor. "Thank you." Her voice vibrated against the top of my head. "I promise I will take you seriously over the next month, but like I said before, I just need time," she reiterated, almost somberly with how flat she sounded.

Her body pressed against my face with a heaving breath right before she leaned back and smiled at me appreciatively. "I will take all you said into consideration, but we should shelve this conversation for a lot later." Then, her lips curved into an awkward smile. "For now, you should check the pasta before it overcooks."

"Oh shit!" Immediately, I scrambled to my feet, darting over to the stove to turn it off.

Thankfully, it was salvageable. The pasta noodles were a little more done than I'd like, but they weren't mushy. A few quick tosses later, and the nearly perfect carbonara was plated and on the table.

"Bon appetit, my little rose." I couldn't help but grin excitedly when I saw her face break out in a huge smile and her wide eyes light up like a starry night sky. "Just a nice little Caesar salad with some creamy carbonara, a Santini family special straight from my mama's recipe book." Offering her a little wink to make her giggle, I carefully poured some white wine for her. "Some nice oaked white wine to pair it all off."

Looking up at me with smiling, teary eyes, she covered the lower half of her face in disbelief. "Adam," she squeaked. "This is too sweet and too much!" She finished with a soft sob. "I can't even begin to thank you enough."

Chuckling, I waved a hand at her dismissively. "Oh, it's nothing to thank me for." Using her own words against her with a smug smirk, I grinned at her cheekily. "I am only doing the bare minimum and giving you what you always deserve."

There wouldn't be a day went by where she'd be treated any less than like a queen because that's what she was.

A fucking queen.

My fucking queen.

Urging her with a gesture of my hand, I watched her with hawk-like eyes. "Well, dig in, let me know how I did." I mean, I knew I did well, but it has been a while since I took a crack at something besides sandwiches and breakfast in the kitchen. Well, at least it was almost like riding a bike.

Throwing a chuckle back at me, she scooted in closer to the table, picked up her fork, and took some of the creamy pasta goodness into her delicate little mouth. I felt bad for laughing, but she looked so cute with her cheeks all puffed out from taking too much into her mouth. I wanted to capture the moment, so I pulled my phone out and snapped a quick picture of her pouting chipmunk face, while Asher laughed beside her.

A playful but irritated protest left Eliza as she lurched out of her seat, swiping a hand at my phone. I easily evaded her attack while snickering in response. "Adamnth." Her muffled protest came out from behind her hand as she tried to remain mannered.

Growling softly, she stood there for a minute to chew and swallow her mouthful before snapping at me mirthfully, "Adam, delete that! I look stupid." If she had been seriously upset about it, then I would've, but nothing about her bright face and shimmering eyes indicated distress.

"You could never look stupid, little rose," I retorted smugly, smirking at her as I pocketed my phone. "Now, be a good girl, sit down, and eat while I feed Asher." I hadn't planned for my voice to drop with that playful command, sounding like I was actually her Dom giving orders.

I half expected her to clam up and close herself off. But she surprised me with her compliant demeanor and two simple words. Simple words that did decidedly not simple things to my body.

"Yes, sir."

Chapter 11
Eliza

RUN. RUN. RUN!

My lungs ached in my tightening chest with their struggle to fill out properly. Seeing the way his eyes darkened again with such desire and excitement spurred my body into a stress response momentarily. A part of me felt like he'd grab me any moment, rip my clothes off, and take me until he was satisfied.

I'd conditioned myself to take such looks as a bad thing because of James throughout the years. It didn't help that his creepy friends looked at me the same way and had bad intentions, ones they weren't shy about making known to me. Dark eyes equaled bad; that's how I'd always seen and taken it for so many years..

Every time anyone looked at me with such wanton eyes, it meant painful sex was to follow soon after. It wasn't necessarily rough sex or anything like that; it just always hurt me because I never wanted it. No matter how much I tried to get used to the assault, I never could.

I couldn't even bring myself to fake it enough to be convincing, let alone fake it, until I made it.

So, it confused me a little when Adam remained rooted to his spot. He didn't budge a millimeter as he stared at me with his burning gaze, which set my own body ablaze with feelings I hadn't felt in so long. The way his lustful eyes bore into mine was almost adoring, which got my body purring with arousal.

When was the last time I'd desired someone? Thinking back now, I hadn't wanted James in years. When had my fire for fun fizzled out? When had it started? Had it started at the first strike of James's hand? The first time he disregarded my safe word? The first time I opened my eyes and saw him for the monster he was?

Should I even be wanting a man after all of that? It didn't feel right for me to give myself to someone after all I'd been through. I broke away from James to find myself and make a life for myself and Asher. Would it be wrong for me to let another man in after suffering at the hands of so many? I don't know why, but the thought of letting Adam in felt like a defeat, as if I was throwing in the towel and turning back to a bad habit.

I didn't need a man—I knew that... But deep down, I *wanted* a man. A man, not some immature male who calls himself a man, nor did I want some bastard who had a fragile masculinity complex (cough, James, cough). I desired a man who had his life put together, had a decent career to keep him sustained, had the emotional capacity beyond that of a teenager, and was overall a decent gentleman who knew how to treat a lady right.

Okay, it sounded like I wanted a Prince Charming, but that didn't hit the spot for me. Yes, I wanted all of it, kind of, but Prince Charming was nice, and I didn't want nice. At least not all the time.

As fucked up as it sounds and felt, I wanted a man who was a little rough around the edges, or at least a man who could give me a firm and guiding hand for my benefit. Not to say I wanted to be abused again or anything, but I guess one aspect I liked about James, before he turned from a loving husband into a nightmare, was how dominant he was.

However, as our relationship went on, the dynamic between us shifted. Of course, James never saw a problem with it, because he was the bully coming out on top. Too much chatter from everyone and his family eventually got to him, and he went on a whole power trip, which didn't end until I was broken by his feet.

Well, guess that was another huge reason why I didn't want to engage in another relationship with anyone. Putting in time and effort to find that right fit was too much work and too tasking on my already fragile mental and emotional health. Also, what if I just ended up getting hurt again in the end? Having a relationship with power dynamics wasn't everyone's cup of tea, and I didn't want to dance around the whole self-discovery thing with a man who'd never looked at this lifestyle and community before. If my situation were different, I wouldn't have minded, but I wasn't up to putting the small pieces of my heart up on the chopping board again.

A sharp inhale from Adam pulled me out of my head, making me zone back in on him with cautious eyes and bated breaths.

Maybe this was the part where he'd snap.

I didn't mean to reply like the way I had; it kind of slipped naturally from my tongue when I heard the slight command in his deepened voice. I felt a little ashamed about how easily I turned over and showed my belly to him, but at least the regret hadn't hit yet.

If I hadn't been so caught up in my own anxiety, then maybe I would've enjoyed the praise and want in his eyes. I'd been quiet and awkward for too long and ruined the mood and whatnot.

My body instinctively flinched in response to his hands coming at my face, and I couldn't help but offer him an apologetic look. His hardened gaze softened slightly in appeal as his hands slowed. Even though his eyes sparkled with adoration, there was an underlying flare of lust, which became more evident the closer his face grew. It was undeniable when he was a mere inch from me.

His forehead rested against mine, and my head remained still in his hands. The air around us grew hot and heavy as our drawn breaths mingled with each other. Our lips were a mere inch apart from what I could see through my half-closed eyes. I was afraid we might touch in a chaste kiss if my body twitched from how hard my heart drummed in my chest.

But we never did. Not once did our lips touch, not even when Adam's hand caused my head to tilt a little with a downward movement.

Against my gut, I let my heart take over. Just for a moment wouldn't hurt, right?

Naturally, my head leaned back into his touch when one of his hands slipped to the back of my head. Shivers of delight trickled down my body at the feeling of his fingers threading themselves through my dyed locks, and my breath came out airy with the faintest sigh of pleasure. Then, it hitched sharply at the feeling of his rough hand sliding down along the column of my neck. With heavy, trembling breaths, I looked at him with eyes full of wariness and excitement as the warmth of his hand coiled around my neck.

Anticipating a squeeze, I closed my eyes and waited for the pressure, cutting my oxygen off. Yet, it never came, much to my disappointment. Adam merely settled his hand around my neck firmly, making his presence known.

He was testing me, testing the waters. His gray eyes were nearly black from his dilated pupils, and it felt like he could see through every layer of me, right down to my vulnerable soul as he studied me so deeply.

Goosebumps followed my shudders at the feeling of his thumb brushing against the thrumming pulse in my neck. I wanted to tell him to continue, to choke me until my eyes rolled to the back of my head, but no words came out of my stunned mouth.

Another gasp of pleasure slipped from my trembling lips in response to the blazing trail of fire his thumb left as it moved up the underside of my jaw, over my chin, and to my lips. "I'm afraid to kiss you." His hot words fanned across my pouted lips and the lower half of my face.

Before I could ask why, he continued, "I don't want this dream to end. The moment I kiss you, I feel like everything will shatter because you're not ready yet." Taking a deep breath, he slowly closed his eyes and pulled away reluctantly with a soft frown. "Your pace, that's what I agreed to take this at," he reminded me with controlled smile.

The hot tension in the air faded in an instant with his soft chuckle. "Eat up, *mia rosa*, before your food gets cold." His head nodded at my plate before he left for the fridge to grab a small bowl of baby food. "I got the little munchkin handled, so relax and enjoy your dinner for once," he urged, lightly stroking my cheek with the back of his finger.

As if that was possible after he'd just mind fucked me. Okay, he hadn't, but it damn well felt like it. It was almost impossible to simmer down while I ate my dinner. Sitting there with my aching cunt pressed against my pants and the chair, getting the softest waves of pleasure every time I leaned forward to take a bite of my food, made it impossible to collect myself fully.

Of course, the world really wanted to rub it in my face because seeing Adam interact so well with Asher melted more of my icy-cold heart towards the charming man. Seeing how well Asher took to Adam was the cherry on top. It wouldn't matter if I was fine with

Adam, and a relationship between us worked out more than perfectly. If Asher and Adam didn't get along, or God forbid Adam hated kids, then none of it would work. Also, vice versa, if Asher despised Adam for some reason, then I'd throw Adam back out into the open ocean.

Fortunately, neither of those scenarios seem to be likely, and I hoped they never would. Everything felt perfect. If anyone had peeked in on us at that moment and had no idea about us, they'd probably think we were the perfect couple with a lovely family. Well, maybe that would become the case in the future, but I wouldn't jump the gun with Adam.

After all, he still had twenty-seven ish days left. Yes, I knew he could very well pretend for the whole duration, but surely, he had to crack sometime in the month if anything festered underneath, it would crack through in that time. Besides, there was no faking his connection with Asher. One look in both their eyes was all I needed to know; everything between them was wholly genuine from deep within their very beings.

A short while later, all of us were fed and full. Surprisingly, Adam managed to feed Asher in record time. Not gonna lie, I was a little jealous at how fast he managed to feed my little man. But it was the playful kind of jealous, not the scathing kind.

Once we were all done, I tried to clean up and do the dishes, but Adam wouldn't let me. He was insistent on cleaning up his own mess and giving me some time to myself and Asher. So, I was effectively barred from the kitchen and dining area until he had the place spotless again.

While he was a busybody in that part of my home, I played with Asher for a good while before giving him his nightly bath. When he was all clean and smelling good, I got him dressed up in his pajamas and was ready to settle him in his car seat to do my nightly delivery runs, but Adam stopped me.

He plucked Asher out of my arms, making me look up at him with a scrunched-up face. "Nope, no late-night runs for you while I'm around, or at least, no taking Asher out with you," he said rather definitively with a stubborn look. "If you have to go out, then go. I'll be here with Asher and make sure he gets to bed and everything."

Huffing and scoffing, I crossed my arms and glared up at Adam. "I can't afford to not do my other job and putting Asher into a new routine won't be healthy for him if you won't be around after you're done with me," I snapped, turning my head away in shame when I realized the last bit that came out.

Yes, I still had my doubts, but I couldn't be blamed for it.

Seeing the broken look shatter Adam's eyes did little to ease the shame and guilt which threatened to drag me down to the depths of darkness. The knife only dug in deeper at his dejected sigh, and when he reached out and grabbed me by my waist, I thought that this would be it... Until he spoke, "Eliza, I will never be done with you, not even when we draw our final breaths in this world."

Jerking my body up against his, his shadow crowded me as he leaned down and nudged my head with his. "I'm going to be honest. Even after the thirty days are done, I'm still going to be hanging around you every single day. Even if you try to lock me out of your home and life, I will still be there every morning with breakfast ready for you, be there to take care of Asher for you because I love the little dude."

I didn't know what to say. All I could do was stand there like a stupefied idiot and stare at him as he continued, "Every night, you will come home to a home-cooked meal that will leave you more than satisfied." His hard head continued to lightly nudge mine until our eyes were locked. "And if you refuse my help and keep your second job as a delivery driver, then I will stay the night with Asher until you come back."

"W-what happened to taking things at my pace?" I squeaked with a hitched breath. "You already seem pretty sure about everything and how you want to take over my life." Which, not gonna lie, kind of appealed to me.

It was a broken bridge, but maybe it might be okay to cross again one last time. I mean, Adam wasn't a bad person, right? He just wanted to take care of me, so where was the harm in that? Besides the fact that it all sounded too good to be true.

Sighing softly, Adam looked at me with conflicted eyes as his arm tightened around my waist. "You are in control of everything but me in your life. I already swore to you that I won't harm you, and I won't. Me being present in your life, making sure you eat, take care of yourself, and have quality time with Asher doesn't harm you in any way." His convincing smile had me lowering my walls involuntarily. "And just because I am present doesn't mean I'm going to cross any boundaries. I won't touch you without your permission or do anything that will make you overly uncomfortable."

Damn him for hitting all the right things and being such a charming asshole. God, there was no way out of this for me.

As if I wanted a way out.

Taking all he said into account, and really thinking about it, it wasn't all that bad, honestly.

Relenting with a sigh, I leaned into him, resting my head against his chest. "I'll just be a bit." I didn't want to go out without Asher, but I really couldn't afford not to pick up a few deliveries.

Sure, I could take Adam up on his offer of providing a little for me, but I couldn't do that to him. It didn't feel right, nor did I want to be indebted to him.

Looking up at him with a wary smile and chuckle, I asked, "You really aren't going to leave me alone, are you?"

Giving me an amused chuckle in return, he shook his head. "No, I'm not." The way his voice gained a possessive edge, with a slight darkening in his eyes sent shivers down my spine.

Did I make a grave mistake?

If I hadn't feel like trapped prey before, then I definitely did then.

The wild look on his face was fleeting, enough that I questioned whether it was real. If it weren't for the dreadful feeling in the pit of my stomach, the one that told me to shove him away and run—an instinct I knew came from my time with James—then I would've thrown my doubts away.

My string of thoughts snapped at the feeling of his warm lips pressing against my temple. "Be safe out there, alright?" The genuine concern that warmed his eyes into molten steel made my paranoia feel stupid as I forced it away. "And, if you're hungry and want a late-night snack when you get back, then let me know so I can whip something up, alright?"

God damn you, Adam. I'll find something distasteful about you sooner or later.

Humming, I nodded my head in response before kissing Asher goodbye and hugging Adam briefly. "He likes the book—"

What came out of his mouth next should have been a blaring red sign. "I know, the one with the farm animals and the sounds."

How on earth did he know that?

Chapter 12
Adam

~2.5 weeks later~

"Adam, it's eight in the morning on my day off," Eliza whined with a pout when I went to wake her with Asher.

"I think someone's becoming a little spoiled," I joked with a chuckle, slowly pulling her sheets off and sitting on the edge of the bed with Asher in my lap.

"Mama up! Up! Go!" Asher's excited energy lit up the room with smiles as the two of us looked at the toddler. "Out! Go!"

With a tired and sad smile, Eliza sat up in bed and held Asher's hands. "Honey, bad weather, no park today," she told him in a baby voice, making Asher frown and shake his head.

"No! Out!" he demanded, slapping his hand against my thigh and gesturing at me.

Chuckling, I reached out and tucked her messy strands behind her ear. "I told him we were gonna go out today, and we are, just not to the park," I clarified, not wanting her to get into an argument with the toddler and set him into a tantrum. "I'm taking both of you out to Portland today. Get a little shopping in to spruce up your closet and whatnot, eat out, just have some fun in the city."

No matter how hard she tried to hide her excitement, it warmed its way onto her face with big, bright eyes and a lovely, grateful smile. "Adam, you really don't have to." And here came the little tiff again,

133

the one I always won. I knew her argument by heart, but I always won in the end.

"I'm spoiling you, and that is it. Besides, going to the local thrift store is not a shopping trip," I deadpanned playfully, leaning over and kissing her forehead. "And remember, you agreed to this trip," I reminded her with a smug smirk, causing her to roll her eyes and smack my leg.

Scoffing, she rubbed the sleep out of her eyes and yawned for a second before remarking, "I only said fine to shut you up."

"Still an agreement," I retorted with a victorious snicker.

Standing up, I helped her up and hugged her tightly with one arm. "Go eat breakfast, then wash up. I'm going to finish getting things ready for our outing." I gave her a tentative pat on her bubbly ass in encouragement, chuckling a little from the pouting glare she threw back at me.

After flashing a bright smile at me, she leaned up on her tippy toes, and gave my cheek a soft, shy peck before going over to the dining table.

For a moment, I stood there and admired her lovely body, the that was filling out nicely with how I'd been making her eat properly. It wasn't a huge change since it'd only been about two weeks since she'd been eating properly, but I could definitely see a subtle change. Not only did she have a healthier glow to her, but the way she carried herself was more confident.

As she ate, I kept Asher on my hip while I packed his bag for the day. "Do you have an idea of what you want for lunch and dinner? I know we're going to be at the mall, and the food court will be right there, but there are so many options in Portland, so I don't want to limit us to the shopping center," I asked, breaking the peaceful silence between us.

Now, I expected some generic answers like 'I don't know' or 'Oh, you pick', something along those lines, but she surprised me with actual answers. "Can we get dim sum and Korean? Doesn't have to be that order, but I've been kind of having an itch for those two."

I wasn't gonna complain about my life being made easier. "Whatever my little rose desires," I replied warmly. "Besides, if I wasn't fine, then I would've just picked for us or not asked at all."

Rolling her eyes, she giggled and looked at me longingly for a moment before returning to her food. "That's a fair point." Sipping at her juice, she grinned at me from behind her cup. "And thank you for breakfast."

"You don't have to thank me for everything, *mia rosa*. But you are more than welcome." Her gratitude for everything I did for her really threw me for a loop, more often than not. I had expected it to stop after the first few days, but nope. Although, I couldn't help but wonder if she was expressing her appreciation or if it was a habit.

"W-well, too bad. You're stubborn with staying in my life and making a whole new routine for us, so I'm going to keep thanking you to show you how grateful I am for you butting into our lives," she stammered, her voice trailing out toward the end as she stuffed her face.

Biting my tongue, I kept my words at bay as I smiled at her tenderly. I didn't know if it was intentional or not, but she'd said 'for us' just then. Perhaps she was coming to terms with things faster than I'd anticipated, which was a good thing. It would make the next step of my plan a whole lot easier, too.

Once I was done packing, I sat on the couch and watched Asher play with his toys. Thankfully, Eliza wasn't one to take forever to get ready. So, it wasn't long until we were in my Lamborghini Urus and on the road.

Peaceful silence filled the car as I drove, with the occasional baby noise from Asher—who was entertained by a show on a tablet I'd jerry-rigged to the back seat. Obviously, I was busy driving, and Eliza kept to herself, staring out the window contently.

Honestly, it felt like a nice family trip. Hopefully, I'd be able to call her and Asher my family sooner rather than later. Thinking about the three of us being together always brought the happiest smile to my face from the sparking bliss that lit up every nerve ending in my body.

"Would you still want me if I were a criminal?"

That was one way to pump the brakes on my happy train. Her question came out of nowhere and blindsided me. Seriously, I almost hit the actual brakes to jar myself back to reality.

Was that what was up with her? Was she a criminal?

Snapping my head to the side, I took a quick glance at her before training my full attention back on the road. "I'm sorry. I think I might have misheard you," I mused with a wary chuckle. Maybe I did because I was so deep in my mind that her words didn't make sense.

The sound of her clearing her throat cracked at the tense air for a moment before the leather set creaked with her shuffling. "Would you still want me if I was a criminal?" she repeated herself loud and clear, making me feel like I'd been slapped in the face.

Unable to help it, I threw a question back at her rather than an actual answer, "Are you on the run?" She seemed calm and put together for someone on the run, and honestly, I couldn't see it, no matter how hard I tried to imagine it.

Granted, I shouldn't be one to judge people based on appearances and shit, but there was no way Eliza could be a criminal. My little rose could barely throw a decent punch, let alone hold a knife to stab someone enough to kill them. That, and she got so torn up over the littlest things. Forgot to pay for an item? She'd let her anxiety eat her up until she went back to either pay for the item or put it back. Someone bumped into her? She'd be the one apologizing.

My Eliza didn't have one bad or mean bone in her delicate body.

So, there was no way she could be a criminal.

"Uhh, that's not exactly an answer..." she drawled out awkwardly.

"Answer mine first, then I'll answer yours," I quickly bargained with an amused chuckle.

Huffing, Eliza grumbled something incoherent under her breath before replying, "No, I'm not, but why the heck did you even ask that question? Why is that the first question you ask?"

Playfully pretending to be taken aback, I leaned back slightly in mock disbelief. "Well, you're the one who asked the most random question out of nowhere. I mean, I get the whole 'would you love me if I was a worm' shit, but a criminal?" I kept my tone lighthearted and playful to prevent her from misunderstanding me and thinking I was accusing her of something. "But how else should I respond? I mean, I gotta know if you're in danger to plan and act accordingly."

Then, I remembered that I didn't answer her initial question, the one that threw a wrench into my running gears. "But to answer your previous question, yes. Yes, I would still want you if you were a criminal. Unless your crimes are heinous, then that might be an issue."

As if I was a saint myself. It'd be very hypocritical for me to judge her for being a criminal—if she was one—given the fact that I was a damn mafia boss. Yeah, I would be the last person to scold her for living a life of crime when I lived it 24/7, practically.

"Is there anything that would put you off from me?" She sounded curious but also a little defeated, as if her fate with me was starting to sink in.

Humming in thought, I pretended to think for a few seconds to tease her a little. "Besides very deplorable things like you being a serial child abuser or something that bad, nope." Honestly, she could be a full-blown serial killer, and I wouldn't be bothered one bit.

Reaching over, I blindly felt around her thighs until I found her hands. A little haphazardly, I wiggled our fingers around until our hands were intertwined with each other. Holding her tightly, I smiled to myself. "*Mia rosa*, there is nothing that will deter me from you, and sorry if this is going to sound..." Insane? Absurd? Downright deranged? So many words to choose from. "A little out there..." Yeah, sure, let's go with that rather than the other words. "But I am determined to make this work between us. Even if you decide to keep me in the friend zone after next week, I won't let you have any other man in your life."

I already had a whole list of murder plans for anyone who dared to come around Eliza with me in her life. If it ended up being the whole damn town, then so be it. There was no harm in having more bloody bodies under my feet. My hands were already bloodied, so I might as well drench them for a good cause for once.

Bringing her hand up to my lips, I inhaled her scent there and kissed it longingly. "I know you feel it too, little rose, this fire between us." Glancing at her with burning eyes full of desire and adoration, I smiled against her soft skin. "The undeniable chemistry. And if you try to deny any of it, then I'm going to have to call bullshit on it because I see the sneaky little looks from you when you think I'm not looking." That got her to freeze up and blush madly. "And I see the way your eyes light up at the sight of me, the calm that washes over you, the bliss, everything."

Yes, she was a little jumpy at times, but she'd improved quite a bit. Of course, I was more than mindful of any sudden movements around her, along with knives, particularly big ones. She actually scared me with her a panic attack the first—and only—time I turned around to face her while holding a kitchen knife.

It was a few nights back. Eliza came home a little early while I was in the middle of making dinner, and surprised me. My hands were covered in juice from the meat I was cutting up, so I merely pivoted towards her and offered a short, but sweet hello. Had I planned on greeting her properly, I would've put the knife down and washed my hands, but I didn't want to stop what I was doing and have dinner be late.

Eliza had smiled back at me, but it only lasted a second before her face paled as if she'd seen a ghost. Even at a slight distance, I could see every inch of her body lock up as she turned into a statue. I could've sworn the sound of my heart cracking and shattering at her fearful whimpers when I stepped toward her could be heard for miles at that moment.

Of course, stupid me took too long to figure out what triggered her because it was a little hard to follow her trembling eyes to a specific object. I instantly discarded the knife onto the counter when the dots connected, though. I never did get an explanation that night when Eliza had calmed down, after I held and soothed her for a long while. She kind of went aloof to the whole thing, so I dropped it to discuss later.

Which, I guess, meant now because, hey, what else were we gonna talk about on an hour-and-a-half-long car ride? Well, maybe later will be a little later into the car ride because I didn't want to ruin our good little moment right now.

I had her in my hands, so I had to charm her some more.

Tucking the knife topic back into the recesses of my mind, I glanced at her tenderly and sympathetically. "And I also see the hesitation in your eyes, which I'm not mad or upset about." She had every right to be wary of me, considering my actions thus far.

Turning my head, I gave her a reassuring look. "And I just want to let you know that you have nothing to worry about." Holding our hands against my chest, I basked in the blissful warmth filling me as I spoke, "All that I have done, the new normal for us, the way I dote on you and Asher, everything good that seems too good to be true, is not some ploy to get you. It's not some stupid honeymoon phase for us."

Bringing her hand up for another kiss, I looked at her fully to show her the intense conviction that stemmed from my soul. "It is our life."

Fuck I wanted to grab her cute face and turn it stupid with a kiss. I wanted to plant my lips against hers until her eyes would go dopey with a matching smile. But no, I couldn't because I was fucking driving!

"As I said before, I will never treat you any differently or less just because we are officially together. I'm not the type of man to trick someone into a lie of a life." Cruel mafia boss or not, I was always upfront with people.

I never hid anything from anyone, as shocking as it may sound.

Now, if someone got into shit with me because they didn't read the fine print or asked the right questions, then it was on them.

"And I know you may find it hard to believe, and I don't blame you one bit for that. But just know you can trust me and the life I am promising you," I said in such a tender and teeth-rotting sweet way as if I was giving her any choice in the matter. Of course, she had no idea who she was agreeing to.

She already lost the game the moment I decided to have her.

A long and soft sigh dragged out of Eliza before her deflated words followed. "I know, and that's what scares me." I could feel her resolve weakening. "I want to believe you, let you in, give you that chance, but I'm just so scared because of what's happened in the past.

I've been promised so many things and tricked down so many paths that I just don't want to trust anyone now."

"Understandable, and I don't hold anything against you for your feelings toward this whole situation because of past experiences," I told her with full belief. "But, I'm just reassuring you that I'm not a two-timing bastard, promise."

An understanding silence floated between us for a while until I ripped the band-aid off. "Speaking about past experiences..." A quick glance and guilt swallowed me into an endless pit when I saw Eliza's slight panic as she withdrew from me. "I didn't bring it up that night because it didn't feel right, but I can't let it go, and I completely understand if it's too much for you. Just tell me so, and I'll drop it. But the thing with the knife, you really worried me, and I just want to know what happened for you to react like you did."

And I needed to know who to kill for mentally scarring her like that.

I didn't feel too confident about getting an actual answer from her because I had a strong feeling about the subject being an iffy one. So, I couldn't help but smile proudly at Eliza when she gave me something.

"It..." I didn't push her when she struggled to get her words out. She needed to do this on her own, and all I could do was stand right beside her as support with a listening ear. "An ex of mine... He... Uhh... He... It was..." Her fingers picked and pinched at my hands nervously as she trembled in her seat. "I got into an argument with him, and he didn't like it. So, he grabbed the kitchen knife I'd been using to prep dinner and lashed out at me..."

My tongue ached with the desire to press her for more details—get the whole truth. There was truth to her words, but I could sense a lot went unsaid. Her voice was too empty and shaky as if she was avoiding things.

Prodding would have to wait for another time, though. I didn't want to make her more uncomfortable or, God forbid, set her off. As much as it bothered me, I couldn't for her sake and ours. Though, also, this brought up another problem...

"Did you drop-kick the asshole across the ocean? Did you have to go to the hospital or anything?" I tried to jest with my words, but they came out a little harsher than intended with my scoffing.

Chuckling dryly, I caught the slight movement of her head shaking. "I wish I had the guts... And it was bad enough I ended up in the hospital, but nothing serious enough where I had to be admitted."

Where the hell was that visit in her records then? The only medical records I had in her file were her annual visits, pre and post-natals, well-child checks with Asher, and of course, her hospital visit for Asher's birth. There was nothing about any emergency or urgent care visits. Trust me, I had her whole life on paper memorized from the moment she came into this world to now.

There was no way Max, or I, missed something, especially something so significant. So, what the hell was going on? How did we fuck up that badly? What else had we missed?

"Does it bother you? How I am?" Her small voice cracked at the thick tension in the air. "I mean, it's been what? Three weeks or so, and I haven't even let you kiss me yet." I hated how bothered she sounded, as if she was blaming herself for some nonexistent fault.

I never indicated being irritated or upset about the lack of intimate contact between us. Hell, I was more than elated with the hugs and short cuddles she allowed, and I nearly popped like an overinflated balloon from being so overjoyed when she started kissing my cheek in the recent week or so. Honestly, I took what I could get and never complained or whined for more.

Letting go of her hand with a sigh, I traced along the length of her arm to her nape, gripping it softly until I felt her body give under my hold. "My little rose, if I was bothered, then I would have left long ago. I already told you before and all the other times you've asked, but I will keep telling you until you get it through your pretty little head; I will never be bothered by you setting boundaries and sticking by them."

She still had some issues with digging her feet in sometimes, but she got better at voicing her own thoughts and opinions and sticking by them. Although, if I pushed hard enough, sometimes she caved—this was still a work in progress.

"I know the road to recovery and shit isn't easy or fast, and I accepted that fact before I decided to chase you. If I couldn't handle it, then it would've been a shitty move on my part to butt into your life," I remarked with a chuckle while rubbing the back of her neck with my thumb. "So, what if you haven't kissed me yet? Not like I'm going to die if you don't. Besides, there's no law to dating that you have to kiss within a certain time frame."

Soothing her with subtle squeezes and strokes of my fingers, I kept my hand around her nape as I drove. "Also, it's very bad practice for a man to not respect his girlfriend's boundaries." An amused smirk spread across my lips at the feeling of her shuddering and the sight of her cheeks blushing. "Especially if the relationship is more of a Dom and sub dynamic." Probably not the best time to bring up her not-so-sneaky Googling the other day.

"D-do we have to bring that back up? It's so embarrassing, and I honestly can't believe you peeked over like that." She flustered with a huff.

My stifled laughter slipped into a light chuckle when I couldn't hold it back. "I'm sorry, your face was too cute to not see what was causing it." She sat there for a good while with a scrunched-up face and pouted lips.

Taking a deep breath, I steadied my voice to speak in a calm and comfortable manner. "There is nothing wrong with being into BDSM after you've been through trauma. It doesn't make you a fucked-up person or messed up in the brain or anything like that, and if anyone says otherwise, then you flip them off and tell them to get fucked." It was one of those things that was easier said than done. "Just because you like pain does not mean you like to be abused, nor does it mean anyone has permission to lay their hands on you. There is a huge fucking difference between flat-out abuse and a controlled session or consensual play involving pain. Yes, the lines can be easily blurred and misconstrued, which is what a lot of abusers and fake Doms use as an excuse and manipulation tactic, but that is all bullshit. So, don't you dare let anyone try to tell you otherwise."

Guess this car ride would turn into a BDSM 101 talk. Totally not awkward. "Even if people are more accepting in this day and age, BDSM is one of those touchy subjects that a lot of people still grossly misunderstand. It's also misrepresented and gets a bad rep more often than not, so don't listen to the chatter in the air because it's stupid shit from mindless monkeys." Why the hell was I doing that to myself?

I should've stopped the conversation and saved it for a more serious or intimate time, or at least a time where the option to physically walk away from the other was present. If things took an awkward turn now, then, well, we were stuck in the car for at least another hour.

On the other hand, since we were already on the topic, we might as well dive deeper.

"Here, tell me this." I waited until I felt her eyes bore into me before continuing. "Why did you get into BDSM? Or what got you interested? Any aspect or idea or dynamic? Just what sparked things for you?" Maybe leading with such questions would've been a better start.

Besides the various kid songs coming from the back, the sound of her thoughtful humming and soft clicks of her habitual nail-picking occupied the car's cabin. "*Mia rosa*, what did I tell you about picking your nails?" I wasn't bothered or disgusted by her habit; I didn't want her engaging in it because it was destructive. If I let her go on, she'd chip away at her nails until she hit the bed and bled.

The soft clicks instantly stopped. "Sorry." Her quick apology came out sheepishly. "But your question... I... It... Hmm..." Irritation strangled at her words as she fidgeted in her seat. "Sorry, it's just a little weird to talk about... My ex always ridiculed me for it so..."

Remind me to cut his tongue out and feed it to him before I break his face.

Eliza's body stiffened under me. "Huh? What?"

Shit.

"Hm? Sorry, just a thought that slipped, don't worry." Hopefully, she didn't hear it. Otherwise, that'd be a not-so-fun conversation to be had.

Shaking my nerves away, I recollected myself, and cleared my throat. "Eliza, if I was going to ridicule you, which I won't ever do, then why would I have engaged in this conversation?" I brought us back to the talk at hand. "Also, you are going to have to start forgetting about your shitty ex and all he's told you because he sounds like an absolute bastard, and you should never listen to one," I joked with a dry chuckle.

A soft sigh fell from her lips before I felt a slight shrug from her. "I don't know. Maybe you're asking so you know what to use to ridicule me for," she answered in a dejected voice. "That's what James always did."

James.

The leather of the steering wheel cried under my tightening grip. I finally got something out of her about her damn ex. At least I had a name to start my hunt.

Breaking the tension with a warm chuckle, I relaxed my outstretched arm, letting it slide down her body to her thighs. Of course, I couldn't help myself from squeezing a handful of her soft thighs once my hand was there, making her giggle and squirm a little. "Stop it." She lightly smacked my hand. "I know they're getting fat. You don't gotta rub it in my face." The strain in her playful voice made me frown internally at the tugging feeling in my chest.

Sighing, I shook my head.

God, this woman.

Every time it felt like I had put a piece of her back together, I'd find a whole other pile after the rubble cleared. Discovering more broken pieces of her wouldn't deter me, though. On the contrary, it made me want to hold her closer and cherish her more because she needed and deserved it all.

It was hard to fathom how anyone out there could've been so cruel to my sweet Eliza. Yes, I knew shitty people filled the world, and they would do anything to get a leg up. I just hated how Eliza was unfortunate enough to be on the receiving end of abhorrent treatment for Lord knows how long.

"Eliza, you are but a pile of sticks. You need to get some meat on your bones before you become an actual skeleton." I chided playfully, chuckling rather forcefully to hold back my disdain about her lack of self-esteem. "Besides, I love plush thighs. They make the best pillows, and it feels quite nice to have my head squished between them when I go down on a woman." Okay, maybe I should've left out that last part because it felt a little sudden.

I was about to apologize and tell her to forget about it, but she caused my eyebrow to raise with her next words. "You like to go down on a person?" she squeaked, sounding a little embarrassed.

Unable to help it, I chuckled rather heartily in response. "Yes, I do. I love making my partner squirm and scream under me with pleasure from just my mouth and tongue, and something about the taste of a woman drives me crazy." Giving her a wary glance, I debated my next mouthful carefully for a few seconds before going fuck it and spilling it. "It might sound a little dirty and shit, but I'm going to be honest with you. I've thought about going down on you so many times. Jerked myself off to fantasies of how wonderful you're going to taste. How your delicious lips will moan out a special song just for my ears, and how amazing it's going to feel making you shatter with every orgasm I make your body have."

The thought of slamming my head against the steering wheel was very tempting right now.

My fucking God! That did not sound hot! That sounds creepy as fuck! Oh, my fucking God, Adam. If you didn't blow your chances by now, you definitely just did!

Heat burned my cheeks as I sat there with a fake smug smile plastered on my face, not wanting to make a whole fucking idiot out of myself in front of her. I was sure her hand would come across my face any second now, or a stern scolding, or she'd probably tell me to stop the car or turn the fuck around. Any second now, the rejection was just over the horizon.

"You really think about me that much?"

"Yes, that was cree—huh?"

...

I sat there with my mouth hanging open like an absolute idiot as the wires in my brain struggled to connect. The apology I'd formulated burned to ashes when I didn't get a mouthful of seething words from Eliza. Or maybe I'd hallucinated it, twisted her actual words in my mind to something more favorable.

Shaking my head in disbelief, I tore my eyes away from the road to look at her. I'd already braced myself to see a disgusted scowl or horrified look, so I was in no way prepared to meet her awed eyes. "I'm sorry... What? I... You're not going to slap me for being a lewd prick?" I barely managed to get my stunned words out as I looked at her cynically.

Going red as a cherry, Eliza stammered, "W-well, it was sudden and intense... and a little revealing... But, I don't know, I'm not upset or anything. I'm more shocked at the fact you even think about me in such a way because, well, I'm not much to fantasize about."

Reaching down, she gripped my hand in her lap, fidgeting with my fingers. "No one's ever thought of me like that for so long... The last time anyone had any kind of fantasy about me was back when my ex and I were dating in high school, but I'm pretty sure it was more or less to get into my pants now that I think about it." The bright little spark of excitement of hers started to fade as realization dawned on her face.

Not wanting her mood to dampen, I quickly joked with a chuckle, "If you peeked into my mind and saw how much you plague it, you'd run for the hills." Not sure if it was a good joke, but it got her to smile and giggle.

Then, she went silent with a brooding expression that slightly worried me. Yeah, that rejection was probably coming right about...

"This might be a big ask, but could you show me later?"

Now...?

Huh?!

That was not the reply I had anticipated, not one bit!

Holy shit, was I really that off my game? I mean, I thought I had Eliza mostly figured out, but she was throwing me curveball after curveball!

Suddenly, our bodies were thrown to the side and jerked forward. I had to pull over and slam the brakes because there was no way any of this was happening.

My body spun around in my seat after I threw the car into park, and my hands shot out to hold her confused face. "A-are you serious? Please tell me you just said what I just heard, that I'm not dreaming," I demanded in a deep and breathy voice, desperately searching her eyes for any indications of deception.

The muscles in her neck popped with her hard swallow as her head nodded firmly in response. "Y-yes... If you're so crazy about me, then I want you to show me tonight. Prove to me you can do what you just confessed just now. Show me how serious you are." Her eyes were resolute, making me smile rather arrogantly.

Letting out a breathy chuckle, I leaned in and kissed her forehead. "God, I could kiss you right now if you—"

My, my, Eliza was chalked full of surprises today.

I loved it.

The boldness of her strength in which she grabbed my face and pressed our lips together sparked a newfound passion for my little rose. My grip on her face faltered for a split second because she caught me off guard, but the second I recovered, I gripped her face tightly, kissing her back with vigor. "Fuck, Eliza," I groaned against her lips heavily after we parted. "You have no idea how long—mhmph!"

Someone needed to stab me in the gut right now to prove this to be a reality because in no way did my sweet Eliza just shut me up with another demanding kiss. God, I could feel my very soul leave my body because of how starved she was. But, fuck me, she could take it. I didn't care—I was in Heaven.

Fucking paradise.

Her lips started to ease from mine, but I didn't want it to end yet. So, I tightened my hold on her face to keep her locked against me. Protesting, Eliza pawed at my chest with some light hits, making me chuckle against her as I forced my tongue into her gasping mouth.

Fuck, I couldn't get enough of her! Every swipe of my tongue against hers gave me more and more of her intoxicating taste.

Groaning, I let go of her face and slipped a hand down her body to her waist, anchoring it there while my other slid around her neck. Having her locked in place, I finally released her from our dizzying kiss.

Slowly, our lust-dazed eyes caught each other's, causing our swollen lips to curve into blissful smiles. No words needed to be exchanged between us as we got lost in one another. Our little moment couldn't be disturbed; not even the little kid tunes in the background could touch the invisible barrier of solace and adoration we'd inadvertently put up.

Fear gripped my body when I saw Eliza's tongue swipe across her lips while her eyes averted slightly. "You wanted to know what got me interested in BDSM?" I could feel her pulse pick up with my fingers against her carotid. "I was curious. Curious about why people liked and wanted to get hurt, to submit, and have no control over their lives. I wanted to know why I found the idea so thrilling and cathartic." Looking away in shame, she hung her head slightly. "I wanted to know what was wrong with me because I shouldn't get excited at the thought of someone having such control over me, belting me until I orgasmed, calling me every deplorable name in the world while using my body, and being treated like nothing but a body to fuck."

Sucking in a trembling breath, she breathed deeply for a moment while chewing her bottom lip. "I wanted all of that, but I also wanted to be cherished," she admitted with a long exhale. "I mean, after a lot of research, I found everything to be quite normal and shit, but it still didn't really ease the feeling of shame in me." Smiling sadly, she reached a hand up and loosely wrapped it around my wrist. "But I couldn't go back once I started. James seemed fine with it all, and we both learned and experimented with each other. He got off on the power, being in control and everything, and I was more than content with someone being in control while still loving me." Her wary eyes peered back up at me almost distantly as if she'd prepared herself for a blow from me.

"Oh, little rose." My voice barely came out above a whisper as I leaned in and pressed my forehead against hers. "Is that what you want? Deep down, you crave for me to take control, so you no longer have to worry?"

She practically melted at my words with how she leaned into me. Her eyes fluttered shut, and her whole body relaxed fully. "But I'm scared..."

"I understand." I truly did.

I assumed her ex completely fucked up her view and understanding of Doms, and honestly, he deserved a few blows to the gut with a metal club for that shit. I wouldn't be surprised if she never wanted to engage in the lifestyle with anyone ever again after such a horrible experience.

My only problem was how the fuck would I convince her that I was different?

Life was not going to make this easy for me, was it?

Sighing softly, I leaned in and pressed my lips against hers in a slow and sensual kiss. "Eliza, I know it may be hard for you, and I completely understand if you don't want to give me a chance, but I will never wrong you as your Dom. I've lived the lifestyle for nearly half my life now, and one of the very first things I ever learned and had drilled into me by everyone decent in the community is that the Dominant is never in charge." A bit of an oxymoron if you asked me, but it wasn't anything complicated. "Nothing happens without a submissive's permission. The Dom can hold and pull the leash all they want, but the moment their submissive says stop, that leash is dropped faster than a burning pan."

The whole D/s dynamic and relationship could be rather precarious, but if done right, and with the right match, everything would turn out perfect.

Stroking the side of Eliza's neck with my thumb, I let her take her time digesting the information. All I could do was offer an understanding silence and comfort.

"Do you have anyone who can vouch for you?" Her small voice almost got lost in the background music. "Like a past sub or someone like that who I can talk to?" Once again, she looked away in shame until I jerked her attention back to me.

Chuckling, I nodded and kissed her softly before replying, "Yes, and if you want to talk to them, then I can get into contact with them." Her eyes grew hard and sharp with rage at my words. "I don't keep them as booty calls or anything if that's what you're thinking." It was hard not to discern the boiling jealousy in her eyes. "A lot of them work at my various business establishments, too, so I have their contact because I'm their boss."

Pursing her lips out in a pout, Eliza huffed and rolled her eyes before jerking her body away from me. Fully turning her body straight in her seat, she crossed her arms and grumbled under her breath.

Snickering, I placed my finger under her jaw and turned her to face me. "Don't worry, little rose, they have nothing on you. So, don't let that little green-eyed monster hang around you for too long." My teasing words earned me a smack to my laughing chest.

"Oh, shut up and drive." She sneered, slumping down in her seat.

"You are it for me, Eliza, just know that."

Chapter 13
Eliza

"YOU ARE IT FOR me..."

Even after several hours, his sure words wouldn't leave my mind, along with his certain eyes. The moment he uttered those words, the soft gray of his eyes hardened to stone. He was an unmoving statue on the matter. Nothing shy of a wrecking ball would shake his decision up.

As much as it scared me, there was a part of me that relished in the bubbly feeling. No one had ever been so firm and decisive about me before. He didn't declare his undying love for me, but I could see it in his eyes. The way they sparkled as his passion burned brightly was all I needed to feel secure with him.

"How about this one?" His question jarred me from my foggy mind, making me whip my head around to see what article of clothing he held up this time. "It's only a few months until summer, so the weather's gonna start warming up a bit."

Of course, Adam had to be even more perfect. Damn man actually had a good fashion sense. Thank you, God—not. If I planned to reject him, then the big man in the sky would not have made it easy for me. I might not reject him, but that didn't mean I wanted our soon-to-be official relationship to speed down the tracks like a train with no brakes.

I admired the cute dress he held up for a second before faking a smile to hide my disappointment. Unconsciously, I gripped my arms and rubbed at them. "I don't like the color," I lied, slowly letting out a strained breath, my heart clenching in my chest.

I loved the color. Call me cliché and girly, but pink, especially a pastel or any kind of softer pink, was my kryptonite. I wanted to say yes to the dress, but I couldn't. I didn't do short sleeves or sleeveless.

Sighing softly, I turned around to continue browsing the store. There was so much I wanted, and I know Adam told me to buy whatever I liked, but I didn't want to spend his money like that. Also, where the hell would I even put half the shit? If I bought everything I wanted, then I would need a whole-ass closet the size of my apartment. So, I was mindful to keep my shopping spree to the bare minimum.

Buying nothing wasn't a choice, especially because of Adam's pressure, but I also needed new clothes due to my recent weight gain. I hadn't blown up like a beached whale, but my current wardrobe felt a little too tight. Hell, the worn seams on some of them gave recently, with a few snaps and rips, when I forced them onto my body.

My head craned back when Adam spoke up. "Alright, well, once we finish up with this store, we'll hit the dim sum spot before more shopping," Adam informed me with a warm smile as he pushed Asher along in his stroller behind me.

"Mhmm, okay," I replied with a small hum before going back to the seemingly endless racks of clothes. "I won't take long. I'm just about done." To satisfy Adam's desire to spend his funds on me, I picked out two additional items of clothing before checking out.

A short car trip later, we arrived at our destination, a bustling dumpling house. Shockingly, when we arrived, we were seated right away, despite the place being packed to the brim. Seriously, I don't think I saw an empty inch of the floor, let alone an empty seat. Yet, we were ushered back to a nice little booth the moment Adam gave the hostess his name.

Once we settled and had our tablet handed to us, I couldn't help myself from commenting, "That was... fast."

Smiling at me, Adam waved a small hand. "I called ahead to reserve a spot for us." If it weren't for the flatness of his eyes and expression, I would have been inclined to believe him.

He didn't give me a chance to voice my doubts with how fast he shoved the tablet into my hands, urging me to figure out what I wanted. "Whelp, go ahead and order whatever and however much you want. As long as you are full and happy, then that's all that matters." Turning his attention from me, he focused on Asher, who was occupied with some straws. "Just order me whatever you're getting or anything," he told me with a quick glance and smile.

Not wanting to waste my breath prying at a metal wall, I dropped it and busied myself with looking through the menu and ordering our food. "What do you want to drink?" I asked, peering up from the tablet.

"If you can get me one of the spiked tea lemonades, then I'll love you more than I already do," he teased with a cheesy grin, making me roll my eyes at him. "And you get yourself something other than water," he quickly added, with a raised brow and pointed look. "If I see only water, then you're going to be in trouble later."

His words made me suck in a sharp breath and shiver from a burst of excitement. He'd probably meant nothing by it but given our conversation on the car ride earlier, I couldn't help the direction my thoughts went—dirty. "What are you going to do? Spank me?" I snarked with a bratty little smirk.

Something in his eyes ticked as he ran a hand across his jaw. "After we have a very long conversation, yes," Adam bit back with gusto, sinking his darkened eyes deep into mine. "Better start thinking of a safe word."

Gulping involuntarily, I shivered again in my seat. God, this man would be the end of me, I swear. We hadn't done anything, yet I was already clenching in anticipation, something I hadn't done in so long.

Fuck, when was the last time I got turned on by a man without a drop of alcohol in my system? Usually, it took a lot of booze and fantasizing about anyone other than James to get me in the mood. Of course, I couldn't even be bothered to try most of the time because there was no point. I wouldn't enjoy it either way, so why try? It's not like it'd change the outcome or his treatment of me afterward.

So, it was refreshing to feel aroused around Adam—naturally aroused. I hadn't admitted anything to him, but there had been nights when I thought about my desire for him guiltily—especially since we'd spent quite a bit of time around each other throughout the weeks.

Having him around on a near-daily basis chipped through my resolve, and I couldn't really imagine a day without him. It was more than lovely to wake up to breakfast by him, come home to his and Asher's smiling faces with dinner ready, and go to bed with his comforting presence embracing me protectively. Honestly, I haven't been this happy in so long, and I didn't want it to end.

If being with Adam is a mistake, then at least it'll be a good mistake for a while.

I still hadn't found anything wrong with Adam, besides the fact he had too much time on his hands and was a bit of a homebody. Granted, I didn't exactly take a deep dive into his background, only a surface-level media search on Google and the web. The only things that had come up about him were various articles about his businesses, some news articles about his little escapades, and kind of typical rumor mill shit. There wasn't anything *bad* about him, besides a few misdemeanors for disrupting the peace with his parties and whatnot. No murder or hard crime scandals that I could find, so he had to be mostly safe.

Needing to get out of my head, I set the tablet down, reached over the table, and grabbed Adam's hand to get his full attention. "Are you going to get mad at me if I do use my safe word?" Better to know before it happened, so I could mentally prepare myself for a worst-case scenario.

Adam physically reeled back at my question, staring at me quizzically as if he was waiting for me to go, 'Ha, just kidding' or something like that. When I offered nothing but a confused look in return, he sighed heavily with a shake of his head. "*Mia rosa*, no, never, and no proper partner should ever get upset at you for using your safe word. It is there for either of us to use if anything becomes too much or crosses into some unknown territory in which we feel the slightest discomfort." His heaving breaths increased the more he spoke until he was raking his fingers through his dark tresses.

Warily, I watched his jaw clench after a click of his tongue with a bated breath. I nearly jumped out of my seat when he lurched forward and grabbed my face. "The only thing I will ever get upset at you for is if you *don't* use your safe word when I cross a line, or you feel uncomfortable." His eyes narrowed sternly. "That word is there for your safety and well-being, so don't you ever hesitate to use it. If you abuse it, then that's a different story, but I'd rather you use it more than needed as opposed to letting me think everything is fine and inadvertently damage our relationship."

A deep breath in, and his whole body relaxed. Pulling me forward a little, he leaned his forehead against mine. He kept us like that for a moment as he took in some more drawn-out breaths. "Promise me that you will never hesitate, not even for a nanosecond, to use your safe word if such a moment comes," he demanded in a firm but soft voice. "Promise me that you will use it and that we will talk it over after I'm done fretting over you. I need to be able to trust that you'll to use it, if this is going to work between us."

My cheeks ached with how wide my lips spread in a reassuring smile. A soft caress of warmth bathed my whole body from head to toe when I settled my hands over his as I nodded in response. "I promise." Surprisingly, my words came out confident despite my churning stomach, which made my heart tumble around in my chest.

The paranoid side of me wanted to doubt him, pick at him until he'd inevitably snap, but I wasn't having any of it. I didn't want to listen to a single whisper from my overly cautious self, the one that constantly screamed at me to have no life and be a damn hermit with Asher. It was nothing but a buzz kill, honestly. I mean, it had its uses, but regarding Adam, it felt stunting rather than beneficial.

Intense heat pricked at my cheek as his thumb brushed against it tenderly. "And promise me that you will always communicate with me, not that you've had many issues as of yet, but there will be uncomfortable subjects and topics that you might become hesitant about." A playful chuckle left his shaking head. "And as I said before, I'm no mind reader, and I always overthink when it comes to you. So, I really need you to tell me one way or another. I don't care if it's a few short sentences or words strung together haphazardly, or hell, you could write it down on a piece of paper or through a text. I don't give a shit, as long as it gets through to me clearly."

Chuckling, I nodded my head with a sure smile. "You really are a saint sometimes, you know that?" Kinda fitting since it was his last name.

Adam's shoulders shook with his amused laugh. "Well, I mean, when I want to, I can be a saint," he joked between his laughter.

For some odd reason, I couldn't fully join his amusement. All I could offer in return was a half-hearted laugh as my wariness picked apart the flash of irony I saw in his stony eyes.

Then, I found myself saying something a little out of character. "Well, as long as you're my saint, then I don't care whether or not you are to others." Okay, maybe it wasn't *too* out of character.

Before I was beaten and battered into a shell of myself, I had quite a bit of spunk in me. I might not have been the snappiest person or the best at comebacks, but I was petty enough to give a nice, backhanded compliment every now and then. Also, I'd had *some* confidence, or at least enough to have friends and boys chasing me.

That part of me had been hidden for so long that I was surprised to find it peeking its head. To be honest, I thought it was dead the day James carved me up. Or maybe it had died, but Adam's patience, understanding, and unrelenting attention had worked a miracle and brought it back to life

Don't get me wrong, I wasn't back to my full self or anything, but I'd noticed bits and pieces here and there. Adam had as well, and he'd been more than a gentleman in coaxing more and more of me out.

Not to feed into his little rose analogy of me, but he was the gardener nurturing the dying flower back to life. No, I hadn't told him about that, because I knew he'd tease me endlessly about it.

Besides, it'd only give him more reason to call me little rose. I wasn't bothered by his pet name for me, it just felt a little weird. The only things I'd been called were useless, piece of shit, whore, fuck sack, and whatever horrible thing James's idiotic mind could come up with that would gouge at my dying heart.

"Well then, you're my little rose, and I'm your saint." The light-hearted smile on his face sharpened dangerously with his eyes as he leaned in, brushing his lips against my ear. "But I'll be your god after tonight with how much I'm going to make you scream."

Oh, God! Oh... God...

How the hell was I supposed to respond to that!?

Holy shit, he was really going to be the death of me.

"A-Adam...!" I stuttered through my shock, lightly smacking his shoulder. "We're in public...!" As if I hadn't just brought up a whole conversation about safe words and the BDSM lifestyle.

Chuckling, he huffed a hot breath against my ear before pulling away. Situating himself properly in his seat, he smiled innocently at me. "I really advise you don't skimp out on the food." Then, for a split second, his eyes gleamed with lustful cheekiness. "You're going to need the energy."

"Don't act like you're going to go for more than an hour," I snarked, rolling my eyes.

Pump, dump, and done. That's how it always went.

Or so I thought.

The way Adam laughed arrogantly made me question things.

"Oh, *mia rosa, ti scoperò finché non sorge il sole.*"

Chapter 14
Eliza

"Adam, I'm not having sex with you for the first time in a sex club," I deadpanned, clinging to the back of his shirt tighter, as my heart raced faster and faster.

I also didn't want to lose him and get lost in this damn place!

Seriously, what the fuck was he thinking?!

A sex club was the very last place I thought he'd take me after our wonderful day today! The rest of our mall excursion was perfect, and dinner went by so smoothly that it was the damn cherry on top of this perfect sundae. Then, when I thought we were about to make the drive home, he turned a few corners, drove down a few streets, and stopped at a rather fancy dark building with a neon sign saying 'Barred Out.'

Come to find out, it was one of Adam's many business establishments. Particularly, one of his more mature establishments. I refused to go in, even though he promised the trip would be very quick, but he wasn't having any of it. He literally hauled me out of the car, threw me over his shoulder, smacked my fucking ass while laughing at my struggle, and walked in like he owned the damn place! Okay, he did own the damn place, but I was referring to the way he'd walked in so damn proudly.

What about Asher, you ask?

Well, apparently, there was a kiddie care place attached building. When I asked Adam about it, he said it was something he came up with, because so many of his employees had children and struggled to find childcare. I mean, getting past my frustration about him dragging me into the place, I found that rather sweet of him. Of course, I didn't say jack shit because I was supposed to be mad at him.

Eventually, he put me down once I stopped hitting his back and begged him to. It was so embarrassing to be carted around like a sack of potatoes—people were staring!

So, there we were, me clinging to the back of his shirt like a terrified child while he led us up to the third floor.

His body trembled under my hold, and I had to focus very hard to catch his amused chuckle over the deafening music in the place. "Little rose, I wouldn't take you in one until our twentieth date or unless you begged me to." That made it sound like he had plans on taking me in the club at some point. "But also, what I've got at my place is more than enough for both of us."

The fuck did he mean by that!?

Oh God, and why the hell did I just get so heated at those words?

Did he have a sex dungeon at his place? Okay, stupid question because he basically just hinted at that.

Something strong snaked around my waist, forcing me to take a few large strides. Following the arm, I visibly relaxed when I saw who it was attached to. Someone random could've grabbed me for all I knew.

"Breathe, no one will touch you here unless you give them explicit permission," he assured me with a warm and confident smile. "This is an exclusive club, and everyone gets vetted and signs an agreement before being accepted and granted access. It's more relaxed on the dance floor, but everyone here is pretty mindful. So, it's typically harmless touches unless the recipient allows further touching."

If my faith in humanity was better, then I'd have no problem believing him, but people kept staring at me so intensely. I wanted to crawl out of my skin and hide in a dark corner somewhere because of it. On the other hand, they might've been hungering for me, but none of them made any indications of advancing. There was this edge of control in their eyes, a mutual understanding and respect.

I wasn't some piece of meat, a conquest to be taken. Under their gazes, I felt like an actual person.

Taking a deep breath, I squared my shoulders and lifted my chin a little as I walked side by side with Adam. It felt a little weird, not gonna lie, to be acting as if I was confident—like I belonged.

"There's my little rose." Adam's praise cooed against my ear, making me shiver from the waves of delight. "God, seeing your thorns come out makes me so proud and crazy for you."

It was a struggle to keep my steps from faltering as I kept up with Adam. The constant ache between my legs became more annoying by the second, and with each step my jeans kept rubbed right up against my throbbing clit.

Slowly, the music faded out the higher we went up the stairs. By the time we reached his office on the third floor, it was nothing but a very soft buzz in the background.

Leading me over to the black leather couches, he settled me down before draping his jacket over me. Kneeling before me, he cupped my knees and rubbed them softly for a moment. Then, his head looked up at me with a lopsided smile. "I just have to attend to something really quickly with the managers here and grab some things," he told me with an apologetic smile. "I thought it could wait until tomorrow because I didn't want to cut business into our day like this, but it's something important."

Securing his jacket with one hand, I reached the other out to stroke his cheek. "It's okay," I assured him with an understanding smile. "Just try not to keep me waiting too long?"

Placing his hand over mine, he stroked the back of it with his thumb. "Thirty minutes." He sounded and seemed certain enough to ease my doubts. "Feel free to help yourself to anything and everything in my office," he told me while standing up.

Then, leaning down, he kissed my forehead before leaving me to my lonesome self.

Unsure of what to do, I tucked myself into the couch, hugging my knees to my chest. I wasn't exactly thirsty for more alcohol so soon after having a few spiked lemonades with dinner. So, I just sat there in a ball on the couch, and that was my plan until the heavy wooden door crept open.

At first, I thought it was Adam, but then a series of giggles shot that down. The fuck was I supposed to do?! He didn't say anything about me getting barged in on! Nor did he say anything about girls coming in!

Oh my God, what if he came back with a woman? Or what if his employees decided to sneak away for a little quickie in here!?

Gulping, I buckled my nerves down, and reluctantly turned my head to face the cracked door, where three girls had their heads peeping through. "H-hi, uhh Adam's not here right now."

So much for sounding confident.

"Oh, we know, we just wanted to see the cutie Adam's so whipped about." One of the girls giggled with a friendly smile. "And let me just say, you are just a perfect little thing!"

Unsure of how to respond, I offered a friendly smile back with an awkward chuckle. "T-thanks?"

Was that a compliment?

Another girl scoffed at the first, smacking her arm. "Girl, you're scaring her," she scolded playfully before looking at me with a warm smile. "Sorry, we're just all a little too curious for our own good. I'm Sara, by the way, and these two are Amy and Ann." Sara gestured at the other two girls with her introduction.

"Yeah, sorry, but we really wanted to meet Adam's mystery woman who he keeps gushing about." The short blond-haired woman, Ann, commented with a cheeky grin. "And I can see why he can't get you off his mind. You really are such a cute and beautiful thing."

All the sudden attention caused a rush of heat to fan over my cheeks. "H-he talks about me?" I couldn't imagine it; it wasn't as if I had a lot about me to mention.

Amy, the darker blonde, instantly prattled on, "Gurl, all the time! He's always prattling on and on about how cute and dedicated you are to everything! Everything you do, he talks about. He even gushes about how you walk because your hips sway just right and your tight ass is so cute to watch. And gurl, don't even get me started on how lovey-dovey he looks when he talks about how he imagines you three as an actual family."

She kept going, but I couldn't focus on a single word that came out of her mouth after hearing the last bit.

One of the main reasons why I never had an inkling to date, besides being on the run and in hiding, was because I didn't want to worry about my partner and Asher. I mean, not everyone was keen on taking on a kid that wasn't theirs. I've heard and read so many horror stories of single parents dating only to have their partner and kid not work out, for mistreatment to happen, or that the blending didn't go well.

Hell, I didn't know how I was going to tell Asher the truth about James when the time came for him to ask questions about his dad.

Also, what if Asher bonded with Adam well enough to the point where he saw him as his dad? What would I do then? Lie to my kid? I mean, no one knew about Asher's dad, so it's not like anyone could tell him about James. On the other hand, we could drive a wedge into everything by telling him that Adam wasn't his real father. Then, what would I tell Asher?

Yes, I knew I couldn't keep everything from him forever, but that was an issue for later. I wasn't fond of the fact it would all happen eventually, but who knows, maybe Asher just wouldn't even want to know—I was banking on that idea badly.

But, Asher aside, I also worried about Adam. Yeah, he and Asher got along more than grand, and watching the two really brought me a whole different sense of peace... But what if Adam got tired of Asher in the future and didn't want to deal with him anymore?

Shaking my worries away, I zoned back into reality. "Have you guys worked for Adam long?" Maybe I could pry some secret information from them about my soon-to-be boyfriend.

"Think all of us have been working for him for about like seven or so years? Just about. Discounting the year or so we each subbed for him," Sara answered, after pondering for a moment.

Well, that certainly piqued my attention. "You guys were his subs?" All three at once? I didn't want to ask that because the thought of Adam being a master Dom, roping around three women at once didn't settle too well with me.

Chuckling, Sara nodded as she and the other two came into the office fully. "Yeah, at some point in our years knowing him, we were his submissives. Think it was me, first, and the other two knew him through me. When I ended our relationship, the others kind of slowly filed in."

So, not all three at once... I think... I hope.

Embarrassment and discomfort inched around my body, right under my skin. "If you guys don't mind me asking, umm how is Adam? As a Dom?" I felt awkward asking such a question—it felt too personal to me.

The three of them stared at me in confusion for a moment as if I were some lost duckling. "Uhh are you two not Dom and sub?" Amy asked, tilting her head and looking at me with furrowed brows.

Slowly, I shook my head. "N-no, he's been kind of... courting me? We aren't fully official yet or anything, and we haven't really had sex or done anything of the sorts... We've had a bit of a talk about how our relationship might look and work once we make things official, but I haven't given him the full go yet because I'm just wary about the lifestyle after my past experiences left a rotten taste in my mouth," I admitted almost shamefully as I rubbed the back of my neck.

"Oh, sweetie, you're going to love Adam then. He is like one of the best." Ann gushed with a nostalgic smile. "He's so patient and caring, and he used to be a mentor too, so he really is perfect for a beginner or anyone curious about the lifestyle, or in your case, just anyone who needs a reset," she assured me with a bright and calming smile. "I thought the lifestyle wasn't for me after a string of bad and abusive Doms, so I understand where you might be coming from. And if it wasn't for Adam, I probably would be a lost and frustrated potato out there on the streets."

With a warm smile and giggle, Sara said, "You are in perfect hands with Adam, so don't worry about a single thing. He's not too soft, nor is he hardcore. He's just the right middle ground." The added assurance from the middle-aged woman comforted me some more.

Before another peep could come from the three women, a deep and smooth chuckle took our attention. "Girls, you're not trying to cause trouble or steal my little rose, are you?" Adam stood there at the open doorway, leaning against it with his arms crossed.

"Don't go giving us ideas now," Sara joked with a small laugh. "You better not fuck this up 'cause she's a keeper, and you know I'm never off about these things." I was a little surprised at the authoritative tone she used with Adam while her finger jabbed his way.

Looking past the women, he settled his adoring gaze on me. "If I do, put me six feet under," he joked back, keeping his attention on me.

Pushing off the door, he politely made his way over to me. Getting comfortable on the couch, he coiled his arm around my waist and held me close to him before looking at the three women. "Your partners still treating you well? How about the guests?" His voice was full of genuine concern and curiosity, which made my heart melt a little because he cared.

All three of them flashed him reassuring smiles and waved at him dismissively. "Perfect as peaches." Amy giggled with a giddy grin. "Don't worry. You'll be one of the first to hear if anything happens."

Grabbing the other two women by their arms, Ann tugged them out the door. "Well, we'll leave you to your girl." Ann snickered, closing the door behind her.

Adam chuckled amusingly. "Those three are always up to something. Should've known they'd peek their heads in here." Then, his full attention went back to me. "They didn't say anything bad about me, did they?" he asked in a teasing manner.

Shaking my head, I chuckled. "No, only good things. It seems like they were more or less curious about me." At least they were friendly, and even though our conversation was very brief, it shed a lot of light on my questions.

Smiling up at Adam, I let a burst of boldness take control. For once, I went 'fuck it' to the consequences as I slid onto his lap, straddling him. Leaning in, I ghosted my lips against his. "Swear you'll treat me right?" I whispered breathily against him while, my hands slowly inched down the front of his body, coming to a stop at the waistband of his pants.

His jaw ticked with his sharp inhale, and his eyes closed for a quick second. A rough hand traveled up my body and wound around my neck. Growling softly against my lips, I felt him pull back slightly and his eyes opened back up. The sharpness of his lustful eyes sliced through to my core, making me gasp and shudder at the sudden rush of excitement heightening my arousal. "Yes and no." His deep voice rasped as his lips curled into a feral grin.

Tightening his hand firmly around my neck, he kept me still for a moment while his other hand grabbed my hip. A sudden jerk of my hips, and I found myself pressed right up against the growing tent in his pants. "I will treat you right, treat you like a fucking queen, but..." He chuckled deeply against my lips as he swept his tongue against my bottom lip. "There will be moments where it'll seem like I don't love you."

Why did his words not strike the fear of God into me? Why did they arouse me so much? My body felt like an inferno of lust was consuming it as I thought about the dark edge of his words.

His lips kissed my jawline to my ear, where he continued to spin such sinful scenes. "The nights when I tie you down in such lewd positions to fuck you like my good little slut, when you'll be strapped to a spanking bench until I've turned your sweet ass beet red, or when I just treat you like you are nothing more than a fuck doll for me."

I didn't even realize how desperate I'd become until I felt his grip tighten on my rocking hips. "Look at you, already humping me like a bitch in heat at just a few words." He chuckled deeply in my ear, biting the shell of it rather harshly, causing a sharp, gasping moan to slip from me. "I fucking love it," he growled proudly, thrusting his hips up into me.

"Oh fuck," I gasped with a whimper at the sudden shock of pleasure from his hardness rubbing forcibly against my covered sex.

His fingers around my neck inched a bit so he gripped my face. Dangerously, his smug and devoted gaze hovered over me as he continued to teasingly roll his hips into me. "I swear, I will cherish and love you like no other, and you will feel nothing less than perfect. But there will be moments where I will wreck your sweet body until you are a moaning and babbling mess, until your holes are stuffed so full of my cum that you are constantly leaking me for days after I'm done with you. But even then, I do all of that because I love you, and that's just another way for me to show you how much I fucking need you like I need air."

"Those better not be your wedding vows," I joked with a snort and roll of my eyes, earning a harsh jerk from him.

"We haven't even made it official between us, yet you're already thinking of tying the knot?" he teased back with a cocky grin, making me want to quickly backtrack. "Don't worry, you'll be crying at the altar, but they'll be tears of joy because of how much of a sap I'll be," he promised with a chuckle.

Well, shit.

He actually seemed serious about the whole thing.

For fuck's sake, we weren't even boyfriend and girlfriend yet. We shouldn't even be joking about something so serious as marriage until at least a year or two into the serious relationship.

"Still want to keep going with me, knowing how I'll treat you all sweet and spicy?" he asked with a chuckle against my lips, keeping them just a hair away from fully kissing me.

Licking my lips nervously, I nodded. "As long as it's more sweet than spicy at first." I might run for the fucking hills if he pulled out the hot sauce right now.

His lips softened against mine in a warm smile. "Everything will be at your pace. I will push a little just to get you to act and become more confident, but I will never do anything that you deem out of bounds once we have a thorough conversation later tonight or tomorrow," he assured me, sealing it all with a deep kiss that pulled a soft moan from me.

Breaking the kiss, he smiled at me deviously, making me lean away from him warily. "What do you say to having a toy on you for the drive back?" His bold question made me slam my brakes, and I looked at him dumbfoundedly.

Was I going to regret it? Probably.

"W-what toy?" I wanted to slap myself for even entertaining him and not outright shutting it down.

My slight regret deepened with fear when his smile grew wider with excited victory. "I'll let you pick since you agreed," he told me, chuckling softly as he stood with me in his arms.

"W-wait a minute—hey!" I lightly smacked his chest in protest. "I asked you what toy. I did not give you an agree... ment..."

Fuck my life.

I couldn't help but stare in horror-filled wonder when Adam pulled open the drawer of a standup dresser I hadn't noticed in the place. The whole drawer was lined neatly with so many sex toys! Like, holy shit, I didn't know vibrators came in so many different shapes and sizes, from wired to wireless, all the colors of the damn rainbow, and from the size of a quarter to the size of a fist.

There were so many!

It was impossible to not be curious and reach out for one to inspect it closely. I wasn't too fascinated by the bullet vibrators because I'd seen a ton of those on the web and in sex stores when James and I used to go to them early in our relationship. The others, though, especially the ones with a little protrusion thing on them, were new to me.

Holding up the object tentatively to Adam, I asked with a flushed face, "What exactly does this do?" The object was about the size of my hand, pretty thin, shaped almost like an oblong seashell, and had a small well thingy at one end.

Chuckling softly, Adam took the toy from me and grabbed my hand. "Here, I'll show you," he told me before covering the little hole of the protrusion with the pad of my index finger. "Typically, this goes on your clit, but you could also use it on a nipple," he said, before a soft click filled the air.

Instinctively, I jumped at the strange feeling of the toy. Intrigued, I studied the toy closely as the little hole suckled on my finger. "It's supposed to stimulate oral sex, or at least a part of it. A lot of people like it because the clitoral stimulation gives them their big orgasms fast and strong," he informed me after I took the toy back from him to play around with the buttons.

"Shit!" I gasped in surprise when I hit a few of the buttons, and the thing sucked harder *and* vibrated.

Chuckling, Adam clicked a few buttons and turned it off. "It's also pretty fun to use for training on the more extreme-ish end, in my opinion."

Curious, I set the toy back into the drawer while looking back at him. "Training? What kind of training?"

Rubbing his hand across his jaw, he did his best to hide his smile, but I could see his cheeks rise. "Orgasm denial, orgasm control, orgasming on demand, punishment, so many things." He sounded a little too excited listing things off, and there was also a glint of hope in his eyes as he looked at me warily.

Turning my head away to hide my red cheeks, I swallowed nervously. "W-will you do those things with me?" Okay, maybe I should have worded it a little differently, because it sounded like I was asking him to do those things to me right then, when really it was me asking if he had plans for it in the future.

His powerful presence crowded my space, making my breath hitch. Warmth closed around my hips, and his breath wafted against my ear. "Only if you want to. Like I said, we will talk about things thoroughly either tonight or tomorrow before we jump into anything serious. If I am going to be touching you tonight, it will all be soft play." Leaning his head around, he kept his face inches from mine. "And at any point, if you tell me to stop, I will."

Offering a certain smile in response, I nodded my head before leaning in and kissing him quickly. "I'm definitely going to have to Google a lot of shit for a list," I joked with a chuckle, before going back to browsing.

I really shouldn't be entertaining his idea of having a toy on my body for the drive back; it was so dirty, but that's what I craved about it. From what I could see, there was no harm in the activity.

Having made up my mind, I quickly picked up the light pink toy I kept eyeing over and over. It was a soft silicone vibrator, one of the clit sucking ones, and it was kind of like the other he demonstrated earlier, only a little different in shape and size. This one was shorter but wider with some grooves to it.

"Wait, are you...?" Adam's lip twitched in a struggle to hide his growing smile of excitement as he eyed me like a dog watching their owner hold a leash.

Biting my bottom lip, I turned around fully and nodded at him with an eager but shy smile. It was impossible not to chuckle at his amused reaction, though, with how he bounced a bit on the balls of his feet. "Okay, okay, calm down. It's not like you won the lottery or something," I mused with a chuckle as I reached out and took his hands.

"Anything with you is a win and always the best feeling." He beamed with a happy grin.

Rolling my eyes, I leaned up and gave him a quick kiss. "Do you think you can help me with it? I don't exactly know how to position it..."

If I thought he was elated before, it was nothing compared to the way his eyes lit up like a damn Christmas tree at my request. They were so bright that they made me want to step away to avoid being blinded. "Adam, it's just a vib—mhmph!"

Well, I couldn't exactly finish because I was too busy choking on his tongue that he so generously shoved into my stunned mouth. If he wasn't such a damn good kisser, then I would've shoved him off. His lips were so addictive. I couldn't get enough of him.

"I'm not excited about the damn toy. I'm fucking happy you agreed and even more so that you asked me to help." He groaned against my lips breathlessly, before picking me up by my ass and setting me on top of the table next to the dresser. "So happy that you're giving me permission to touch your precious body more." His smile was brief before it became lost in a lustful kiss.

As he distracted me with a mind-numbing kiss, his hands frantically worked at getting my jeans undone and yanking them off like the nuisance they were—panties, too. His lips and tongue attacked every inch of my jaw and neck as his hands caressed my thighs, making me sigh pleasurably. "You are a damn dream come true, and I'm barely touching the surface." His chuckling words tickled my neck with his heavy breaths. "You smell so good, so damn intoxicating." He growled possessively against me before scraping his teeth along my slender column, pulling a gasping moan from me.

Leaning back up, he hovered over me again, looming into my personal bubble as his fingers danced along the inner crease of my thigh, dangerously close to my aching cunt. "Please tell me I can touch you, that I can finally get a small taste, just a little, please," he begged in a desperate voice full of lustful need.

It confused me for a second because why the hell was he asking me for permission? Why wasn't he just going for it?

His watchful eyes softened with a sad smile. A rough hand came up and stroked the side of my face before holding it tenderly. "Just because I have your pants off and just because you asked me to help doesn't mean I have explicit permission to do anything besides help get the toy on you. Unless you are clearly begging me to touch and fuck you, I won't do anything besides what was agreed on."

Fuck me, and fuck him for being so goddamn perfect!

Melting into his touch and gaze, I smiled affectionately at him. "Just a little. I don't want to keep Asher waiting for long, nor do I want us to waste our night here." It would also ruin my little surprise for him, so I really didn't want to get distracted too much here.

Slowly, he leaned down and kissed me languidly. "Thank you," he whispered against my lips, then dropped to his knees before me.

With a firm shove, he spread my legs wide, exposing my lower half to him completely. "Fuck, you're so fucking perfect." I faintly heard his hungry words before he leaned in and kissed my inner thigh.

Letting my head fall back, I breathed heavily as my eyes closed halfway with bliss. Peering down at him with hooded eyes, I watched him eye my cunt hungrily as his fingers parted my throbbing sex with a satisfied groan. "You're so fucking wet already." He chuckled darkly as he stroked the length of my cunt with the tips of his fingers, pulling a breathy gasp from my lips.

He spent what felt like forever stroking every inch of me, working me up until my patience grew ice thin. Thankfully, he acted before I broke and begged him. Well, I did break, but it was in a much better way.

A body-aching crash of pleasure rippled throughout my whole body at the sudden sensation of him licking my clit as his finger entered me deeply. "Adam!" I moaned sharply, my body arching and thrusting at him instinctively as I felt myself teeter on the edge already.

The vibrations of his chuckle made me shudder and tremble under him as my head fell back fully. Searing hot pleasure closed around my swollen clit, and I was in pure fucking ecstasy with how he sucked and licked at my clit so carefully. He wasn't sloppy with his finger, either. Every little swipe and thrust felt purposeful, as he brushed right against sweet spots I never knew I had.

Honestly, I half expected him to stiffly rub my clit raw with his tongue while jamming his finger in and out of me haphazardly. I wouldn't admit it out loud, but I was one hundred percent ready to fake the whole thing. I had the fake and exaggerated moans ready, the sweet nothings to spur him on. Guess those could go in the trash because everything was fucking real.

Gasping loudly, my hand shot down and grabbed the back of his head to push him closer to my rocking hips. "Oh! Just like that, move your tongue like that again!" The sudden surge of pleasure was maddening when he circled his tongue around me, and I wanted more.

Repeating the motion, he curved his finger oh so sweetly against my sensitive walls, making me moan happily at the building orgasm. God, it'd been way too long since I'd felt such pleasure I'd forgotten how addicting chasing that high could be. "Baby, more, please, please, I'm so close," I struggled out between my panting moans.

I felt a familiar pressure begin to build when he targeted a different spot inside me, causing my body to go a little rigid. "W-w-wait, Adam, not there," I whimpered while trying to force my body to pull back, to no avail. "If you do that—fuck!"

Too fucking late now.

My legs ached as they tensed to the point I felt like they'd cramp from the shock of my orgasm. Mind-shattering pleasure crashed into my body, throwing it against the rocky shores of lustful bliss as my orgasm took full hold. Unconsciously, I threw my head back and moaned loudly, nearly screaming, as my squirting cunt got no reprieve from his skillful tongue and thrusting finger.

I tried to warn him to prevent this from happening.

God, he's going to be disgusted with me.

Or so I thought.

His deep groan vibrated through my body. "Mhmm fuck, that's it, darling, give me everything." Then, he feasted on me like a depraved beast, licking and sucking every inch of me until another gush came out of me from the constant stimulation.

After my second orgasm, he slowed down, pulling his finger out of me with a satisfied grin. Popping his finger into his mouth, he groaned deeply as his eyes rolled slightly. "Just when I thought you couldn't get more perfect." He grinned happily up at me as he leaned back in to give me a few more languid licks.

Getting up, he grabbed my face and planted a sloppy—but hot—kiss on my lips, making me groan at my own taste mixed with his. "I am so having you for breakfast every morning and a late-night snack before bed." He chuckled deviously against my lips. "Thank you so much for letting me have a taste."

Grabbing his face in return, I grinned at him through my orgasmic haze. "If you give me orgasms like that, you can have a taste whenever the hell you want. God, you can just have me. I don't care what you do. As long as you give me more of that in the end, I'll be your damn slutty bitch on a leash."

Holy shit, where did that come from?

I was a little mortified at my filthy boldness, because I definitely did not mean for any of it to slip out of my mouth. What terrified me more, was how comfortable I was with that idea and how much I wanted it.

His chuckling lips pressed a kiss against my forehead. "That's your orgasmic bliss talking, my rose," he commented before picking the toy up from the table and settling it against my throbbing cunt. "You are going to be so overstimulated," he remarked as he parted my folds to settle them into the grooves. "This one stimulates nearly everything externally."

Maybe if I was in a better state of mind, I might've told him to stop and pick a different toy. Too bad I felt a little too needy for more orgasms. "It's fine."

No, it was not.

The moment he turned it on, my whole body jerked and stiffened with shocking pleasure. I don't think it was even thirty seconds before an orgasm trembled from my body at the combined feeling of the vibrations and suckling of my clit. "Oh fuck, I'm going to soak everything." Maybe I should've put a stop to it, because there was no way I'd survive a long car ride, but I didn't.

Laughing smugly, Adam pulled my pants back up and fixed them. "I'll give you breaks," he told me in an attempt to ease my nerves. "But if it becomes too much, just let me know, and I'll cut it out," he said, waving the little remote control in the air. "And for your sake, I'll keep it on low the whole time."

With all the sass I could muster, I rolled my eyes at him. "Well, gee, thanks for having some mercy on me," I remarked sarcastically.

Something in his eyes ticked, and I caught his finger twitching at the buttons on the controller. Conflict stormed in his eyes as he looked at me with playful malice. "You are so lucky we haven't discussed your limits and shit yet..." he grumbled, taking his thumb off the button.

"Well, guess we got something to talk about on the car ride then."

Chapter 15
Adam

As I ROLLED INTO a parking spot at her apartment complex, I killed the toy along with the car's engine. She probably wouldn't appreciate the fooling around with what she was about to see next.

"Thank you so much for today." She smiled at me gratefully before leaning over and kissing me. "I didn't think I needed a day out like this."

I loved how energized and content she looked after the day, and no, it wasn't because her face was flushed from her arousal and orgasms. She honestly looked so much better with how her eyes smiled naturally.

Fuck, seeing her like this made me feel bad about what was next. I mean, it was a little too late to put a stop to my plans since they were well underway. Granted, it's not like she'd ever know the truth about them. So, what did I have to worry about?

Silently apologizing to her, I kissed her forehead before urging her out. Pulling an empty smile on my face, I looked at her for a moment before looking back at the sleeping toddler. "You go ahead first. I'll bring Asher in for you with his whole car seat," I told her with a nod toward her place.

I had no intention of bringing Asher in.

Patiently, with a fake smile, I sat there and watched her leave the car and open the door to her place. It was a little hard to see in the dim lighting, but her body went straight as a pin as she stood at her front door. The seconds counted by in my head torturously as I waited for her to spin around and run back to the car in a panic.

Cracks formed in my heart at the sight of her tear-strewn face when she threw the car door open. "Adam, call the police!" she cried through a soft sob. "Someone broke in and completely trashed my place, and so much of my stuff is missing!"

Pulling out my nonexistent acting skills, I forced my lips to frown as I got out of my car. Cycling through my emotions, I kept working myself up until I felt worried enough to act right. Rounding the car, I quickly pulled her into a tight hug. "Oh, baby, I'm so sorry." Hopefully, my pity was believable enough to fool her.

While I rubbed her back soothingly, I peppered her forehead with empty kisses. "Go sit in the car with Asher. I'll call the police and get them down here." I also couldn't bear to see her broken face right now, knowing it was my doing.

Every sob that ripped out of her felt like a stab to my heart, and I had to keep reminding myself that this was for her own good. This whole plan needed to be followed through for our sake. I was doing it all for her—for us.

Taking in a shaky breath, Eliza pushed away from me and slipped into the car without a fight. Guilt gripped at me like the chilly air bit my face as I stood there for a moment to collect myself.

It's nearly done. Just one phone call, and everything will go accordingly. Eliza will finally be where she belongs, and we can finally start being a family.

My thoughts played on an endless loop for what felt like an eternity, before I worked up the nerve to pull my phone out and call the police. I wasn't worried about the call or conversation with law enforcement; they already knew about this whole ordeal as I'd let them in beforehand and paid them off.

Faster than usual, a cruiser came by, and an officer came out. The next moments blurred as the officer spoke to Eliza, gathered details, swept the place, and told her she needed to find temporary shelter. Soon, she was back in my arms, sobbing away and ripping my heart out layer by layer.

"What am I going to do? I have nowhere else to stay or go to," she sobbed into my chest, her body shaking in my arms.

With a deep breath, I pressed away the nagging feeling in my chest to smile strongly for her. "Hey." I curled a finger under her chin, forcing her to look up at me. "Come live with me. My home is plenty big enough for all three of us, and it's a lot safer, too."

Her head shook vigorously in denial as she pushed away from me a bit. "No, Adam, I can't do that to you." She looked so guilty as if she was a burden to me.

Dismissing her with a chuckle and shake of my head, I tightened my arms back around her to press her against my body again. "*Mia rosa*, the only thing it would do to me is make me happy. I mean, think about it; we will be in a committed relationship, for one. Second of all, I'm already at your place from sun up to sun down practically, and I've spent most of my nights with you over the past weeks. So, you moving into my place isn't going to be much of a change, if any." Pausing, I turned my head to look at the sleeping Asher, "and thirdly, it'll be a lot safer and better for not only you but

Asher as well." Bringing her kid into it was a bit of a low blow, but it had to be done.

Eliza's body tensed with her bated breath, and I was prepared for some pushback from her, given how stubborn she was. So, it was refreshing to see her have some sense for once when her shoulders slumped with defeat. "But, what about the bills and—"

Immediately, I pressed a finger against her lips to shut her up. "Nope, none of that. The house is already paid off, and the bills don't even make a scratch to my bank account. You can pay me back by being happy by my side and letting me spoil you, alright?" In all fairness, that wasn't much of an equal deal, but I didn't want or need her money.

"All the money you make is your fun fund or for Asher's college and whatnot, alright?" The way she glared at me flatly was telling enough of her displeasure. "Again, I have more than enough to last me lifetimes, and that's after taking care of my whole family. So, please, just let me take care of you and Asher because I really want to, and it would really make me happy."

Please relent already.

I didn't want to have to lay it on thicker, or pull-out guilt-tripping her. The last thing I wanted to do was manipulate her that badly, because then I'd be no better than her rotten ex.

And no, I wasn't counting this little stunt of mine.

Silently, Eliza stood there for a worrisome minute or two before fully leaning into me. "Can we at least grab some stuff right now? I have some important documents and photos that I really want to take if they've been spared." My chest muffled her meek voice, but I caught the words—barely.

Smiling victoriously above her, I leaned down and kissed the top of her head. "Of course, go grab what you need, and we'll go." It was so hard to hold back my excitement, but I gritted my teeth through it to keep my poker face. "I'll stay by the car to watch Asher and you from here."

Her head nodded in response with a heavy sigh, and she tore herself away from me. Watching her drag herself into her home with a hung head felt like a punch to the gut and got my stomach churning a little from the welling guilt.

It had to be done, so quit it.

My teeth threatened to shatter from how hard I clenched my jaw in response to the pain I inflicted on myself by digging my fingers into my arm. I just had to endure the night, and it'd all be over. Once she got settled and I saw her smiling face every day, then it'd all be smooth sailing. This whole thing would be water under the broken bridge in no time.

Thankfully, Eliza didn't take long to gather what she needed, so I didn't have to stew in my head and feel guilty for long. "Did you get what you needed? They didn't take or trash anything important, right?" I might've hired the damn idiots and gave them explicit instructions, but I wouldn't put it past them to fuck up somehow.

Breathing deeply, Eliza smiled at me half-heartedly and nodded. "Yeah, everything important is safe, and I have it all with me." She gestured at the ratty moving box in her arms. "I got all my documents, photos, keepsakes, and Asher's things he can't function without in here. So, I'm all set."

It was kind of sad to see everything important to her, and probably her whole life and Asher's, packed into a box that fit in her arms. It seemed like nothing to me, which made it even more depressing. How could someone have so little in their life? It didn't feel right.

Closing the distance between us, I took the box from her with a small smile. "It'll be fine. Just think of it as a step into a new journey. One, where you won't be walking alone because I'll be right by you." A new path I forced her down, but tomato tomahto.

Once everything was loaded and Eliza was settled back in the car, I drove us home with a silent smile.

Home. Our home.

The notion of home felt right, now that Eliza and Asher would fill up the house. Everything had fallen into place, and I savored the fact that things had worked in my favor. Granted, I always got what I wanted, so I'd had little doubt that my plan would go awry. I was more surprised at how satisfying this all felt.

I knew getting Eliza would be the ultimate high, but this feeling of pure euphoria went beyond my imagination. If I got technical, I still didn't have her fully, but getting her to take up permanent residence in my house was done. The plan going forward was to claim her body and solidify our relationship by putting a ring on her finger.

All in due time, though. Small steps, I had to take small steps with my sweet rose. Otherwise, I'd knock all her petals off and kill her. I needed to be extra cautious from now on until Eliza accepted everything wholeheartedly.

The drive to my—our—place didn't take long, nor did it take much time for us to move everything into the house. Settling Asher in was probably the easiest part of it all, considering how the toddler was out cold the whole time. He did stir briefly when I took him out of his car seat, but he quickly fell back asleep when he realized where he was.

Unlike Eliza, I had gotten Asher used to my place from the start. It started off with short visits to my place to get him used to the house, and having little Adelaide around helped quite a bit. Then, I eventually brought him around for nap time to familiarize him with sleeping in his new room and bed, once I had it set up. Eliza knew about Asher spending time at my place—a brief fib about needing to do some work from home got her to agree easily enough.

Deciding to give Eliza a few moments to herself, I sat with Asher to watch over him for a moment with a contented smile. I know it'd only been a short amount of time, but I truly did love the kid. I didn't know how or why, but he'd taken root in my heart the moment he grabbed me at the grocery store.

I never minded kids, and I had wanted my own for the longest time, before I got deep into mafia life. Dating, women, and the notion of starting my own family had taken the back burner when I was given the reigns and had to drive the trainwreck that things were at the time. Afterwards, I had trouble finding someone when things finally settled to how they were now.

There was nothing wrong with being an independent woman, but there were so many out there who didn't want children to cramp up their lives. Which I completely understood, but obviously, I wanted children, so that took out a lot of the options available for me. Another good chunk had children of their own, and a lot of them were just looking for a cushy bank account to support them. As rich as I was, I wasn't out to play sugar daddy to someone and their four kids.

Not to sound harsh, but most of those women weren't too good either. The few I did meet and go on dates with, didn't bother showing any interest in me, only my bank account. They made it pretty blatantly obvious they just wanted someone to fund a lavish lifestyle of their dreams while they sat around and had their whole cake and eat it. They wanted to party, have fun, and have someone else care for their kids. Now, the occasional break here and there, a night out with friends, a self-care day, I understood, but at the end of it all, you had to come back to your children and pick up your responsibilities again. Going out to party nearly every night or ignoring your children for a 'life' and shit was not okay.

That was something about Eliza I loved. No matter what, Asher was at the forefront of her mind, and she always returned to him at the end of the day to spoil him with all her motherly love. She didn't shrug off her responsibilities as a mother, not even for a second. Of course, Eliza fell into the category of women who needed to take a break for their sake and sanity.

As strange as it sounded, in my opinion, there was a fine balance to be had when it came to parenting. Parents needed to love and care for their children, but they also needed to love and care for themselves. It was good for their mental and physical well-being to find that balance. That way, they could show their kids how to put themselves first and how to take care of themselves in a healthy way.

I adored my niece and Asher, but after nearly a whole day with the little suckers, I was more than happy to let their mothers take them so I could do a quick workout or a chore or two in peace. But after a breather, I didn't mind taking them again so their mothers could have some time to themselves.

Of course, Eliza's problem was she never wanted to take time for herself, even though she needed to. It was a work in progress, but she was slowly getting better—very slowly.

Speaking of Eliza, I probably should check on her. She'd been concerningly quiet for a while. For once, I wasn't too thrilled about seeing Eliza. I was afraid to see the effects of my actions, but I had to face the music sooner or later, and later wasn't much of an option. So, with a sigh, I kissed Asher's forehead and headed to my bedroom, where I had left Eliza to unpack.

I couldn't help but frown at the sight of her sad little body on the floor at the foot of my bed. Breathing deeply, I went over and sat down next to her. Picking up a shirt, I ripped the tag off and tossed it in the little trashcan on the other side of her body. "Little rose, what's wrong?" As if I wasn't the damn cause.

Her heavy head lifted to me, letting me see the small smile she forced on her face. "If I'm being honest... I don't know." Sighing heavily, she set the clothes in her hands aside to crawl over into my lap. "I feel like I should be more torn up about everything, and I am, but not as much as I thought. I'm just kind of shocked something like that happened after such a good day, and of course, I just feel bad about barging into your home like this."

"Our home," I corrected her with an overly warm and excited smile. "This is our home now."

God, that felt so right to say.

Our home.

Cupping her face, I leaned my head down and rested it against hers while stroking her cheeks. "Our house," I whispered against her lips. "Our home." My voice dipped lower as my eyes closed. "Our bedroom." I briefly smirked against her lips before taking them fully in a passionate kiss. "Where I am going to make you *my* woman," I growled possessively with a sharp inhale.

Lowering her down to the floor, I caged her body between my arms and legs before attacking her lips in a frenzied kiss. Taking her hand, I kissed her palm and pressed her hand against my body. "Everything that belongs to me is yours too, and that includes this." Sliding her hand down, I forced her to cup the hard tent in my pants.

Rolling my hips into her hold, I bit out a low groan and looked at her darkly. Exciting fear gripped her widening eyes as her body shuddered under me, causing a wickedly feral grin to pull across my lips. After releasing her hand, mine found its way to her neck, choking her until she audibly gasped. "No more late nights with your fingers or stupid toys. If you need relief, you either come to me on your knees and beg like a good girl, or you just take my cock out and sit on it and fuck it until you are satisfied. You got that?" My face hovered over hers with a dominating gaze. "And if I ever catch you pleasuring yourself without permission from here on out, then I will punish you accordingly. Got it?"

Fuck, I wanted to rip her clothes off and take her right now with how her body squirmed sweetly under me, before she melted into me. I don't know how aware she was, but she had this blissful smile on her face as her eyes softened with submission. "Yes, sir."

"Good girl," I whispered against her lips with a deep chuckle. "What's the safe word?" I asked, keeping my lips a hair away from her trembling ones. "And what will you do if you can't use your word?"

Letting out a shaky breath, she locked her hooded eyes with mine. "Alarm, and if I can't speak, then flash the light," she replied, glancing over at the little keychain flashlight I attached to her wrist.

At least the long drive back was productive in the sense that we came to an agreement on limits and boundaries for our dynamic, along with a safe word and gesture. Surprisingly, Eliza had a good idea of her soft and hard limits, so there wasn't much dancing around there. When we were done discussing everything, I gave her a little keychain flashlight I had in my car to use for the time being until I could get her a better one.

Pulling myself back to the present, I smiled at her proudly and kissed her tenderly. I expected both of us to give in to the kiss, but the way her lips stiffened ever so slightly threw me for a loop. Whatever mood I was in came to a full stop when I sensed her discomfort and noticed her averting eyes. "*Mia rosa*, what's the matter? Do you not want to tonight? It's fine if you don't. Just let me know." I was more than understanding and was careful not to sound empty or pressuring.

She did have a bomb blow up in her face with the apartment, so I really wouldn't blame her if her mood for sex was nonexistent right now.

Her chest heaved with a heavy sigh, tongue darting out and across her lips nervously as she mindlessly picked at the floor with her fingers. "It's not that I don't. I do. It's just... I don't think I'm ready for you to see my ugly body," she admitted in a cracked voice.

Every crack of her voice broke pieces off my aching heart. Gingerly, I took her sad face into my hands and kissed every inch of her face. "You will never be unsightly to me, but if it bothers you that much, then you can keep your clothes on," I whispered against her lips. "Or we can forgo sex, as I said before." I easily smiled at her reassuringly as I stroked her cheeks. "You are in charge—don't forget that," I reminded her with a proud smile.

Grabbing my wrist, she carefully pried my hand off and pushed me up so she could sit. Slowly, she settled her hands on my chest, resting them there for a long while as she hung her head in thought. Then, her head snapped up, and her eyes had a determined look to them. "You know what? Give me a minute to change, and we'll continue well into the morning," she told me with a flash of a grin, slipping out from under me and darting away into the adjoined bathroom before I could reply or try to stop her.

Passing up an easy lay was out of character for me, but I had really contemplated axing sex with Eliza, because it didn't feel like she was in it wholeheartedly. The last thing I wanted was for either of us to have regrets the day after, and I didn't want to risk damaging Eliza more than she already was. Damning our relationship before it even started was not in my plans.

Sighing, I ran a hand down my face as I got off the floor and sat at the end of our bed. Well, I guessed I'd let her know after she came out of the bathroom. Oh, and I guessed I should probably take the toy off since it was pointless... Or maybe I should just put a stop to her before she finished—

"*Porca puttana.*"

My mouth refused to pick itself off the damn floor as I stared at my lovely Eliza in a complete stupor. Her creamy legs were on full display from the lacy black body suit she wore, and if I was being honest, they looked so much better in contrast to the dark fabric. Also, I think the black heels she had on helped in the sexual appeal department, too. *"Oh, cazzo. Sarai la mia morte, piccola rosa,"* I whispered in a daze, watching her hips sway as she strutted over to me seductively.

Stopping between my open legs, she leaned down and set the toy down next to me, before settling her hands on my knees. Slowly, she ran them up my thighs to my chest. Her coquettish smile slithered up my body to my lips, where she dangled it like a carrot on a stick in front of me. "Like what you see, sir?" It should be illegal for her to sound so sexy and innocent.

Looking over her shoulder at the dresser mirror behind her, I sucked in a sharp breath when I saw her bare pussy proudly framed and on display with her supple ass. She fucking wore a crotchless piece! God, I couldn't stop staring at her tantalizing body. Even though her whole upper half was covered in a dense lace, her lower half was more than open enough for me to ogle. The lace also thinned out enough on her torso that I could see her dark nipples clearly through the fabric.

Straining out a growl, I reached back and grabbed two handfuls of her ass, squeezing roughly to make her squeal and squirm. Freeing one hand, I snaked it around her body and grabbed her face, training her aroused gaze on me. "All of this for me? How sweet of my little slut." I chuckled against her lips before kissing her with a deep groan.

"I'm not your slut yet, not until you make me so," she remarked with a cheeky smile.

Then, her hands cupped my face sweetly, and her smile softened with tenderness and adoration. "Make me yours, Adam. Make me your woman." Her warm smile grew sharp with lust as she leaned into my ear to whisper, "Then make me your fucking slut."

Fuck regrets.

Grabbing her roughly by her neck, I pulled her onto the bed and threw her down.

If we had any issues afterwards, then we'd fucking talk them out like a normal couple.

Pushing my need to be rough with her back, I closed my eyes to take a few controlled breaths to recenter myself. She needed to be adored and loved right now, not fucked. I had to remind myself of that a few times to fully simmer into a sweet mood before I could continue.

Sitting back on my knees, I looked down at my sweet rose with wonder. Taking my sweet time, I let my eyes sketch every inch of her body into my mind. God, I couldn't wait to see her fully naked to have that image for my fantasies. A nagging thought tugged at my brain when I noticed how the lacy sleeves of the bodysuit covered her arms.

It had bothered me earlier when we were shopping, and it was earlier on that I noticed her choice of clothing never revealed her arms. But I never questioned her about it because it seemed like a personal preference, not a necessity.

No matter, that was a topic for tomorrow.

"You are so beautiful, Eliza, so fucking perfect," I mumbled with a happy smile, leaning down and capturing her lips in a sensual kiss. "Are you sure about tonight?" Damn my caring nature for her.

With a sure smile, she nodded at me with trusting eyes. "Yes, I am. I want you to take me, Adam."

Alright, no more questioning it. Otherwise, I'd ruin our night before it started.

Pushing my reservations aside, I graced her body with my hands, stroking every bit of her to make a perfect map in my mind. Once I was certain I'd touched every part of her, I focused my hands on her breasts. I took my time cupping, fondling, and tweaking her nipples.

Fucking hell, I wanted to feel more of them! But the stupid lace proved more of a barrier than I'd like. Instead of ignoring her obvious preference to stay somewhat clothed, I did the next best thing and grabbed the front of her outfit, ripping two holes for her small breasts to spill out of. Eliza protested, but I heeded none of it as I was too busy licking and sucking her hard nipples.

I know I was supposed to be sweet, but I couldn't help the ideas zipping through my mind. Looking up at her with a sheepish grin, I lazily flicked at her hardened nipple with the tip of my tongue. "How would you feel about nipple clamps?" She had he cutest, perkiest, and most perfect-sized nipples for a pair of clamps to pinch beautifully.

Her cheeks flushed red with her stammering words. "I guess they wouldn't hurt to try."

Holding back my laugh, I forced myself to grin innocently at her words. The irony of them poked at my sadistic side. "Oh, the plans I have in store for you." I chuckled darkly, kissing down her body to her sopping wet cunt.

Carefully, I rubbed her sex with my fingers, spreading her juices everywhere. "For now, you have permission to come all you want, but when our sweet moment is over, I expect you to be a good girl and beg for your orgasms." We needed to work on controlling her orgasms, but that would have to come later.

"Alright, thank you, sir," she replied so sweetly, so perfectly.

Fuck, training her to be my perfect little submissive was going to be one hell of a ride for us both. I was used to training subs, but never to keep them permanently. So, Eliza was going to be a first for me in a sense.

Closing my mouth around her clit, I slid two of my fingers into her. Carefully, I spread my fingers inside of her as I thrust them in and out slowly. She was so fucking tight; I needed to stretch her to make taking me less painful. My hope was to draw out an orgasm or two to slicken her up and relax her walls.

Fortunately, it didn't take me long to pull two orgasms from her quivering body, and I even got her to gush a little.

Leaning back onto my knees, I kept my scissoring fingers inside of her as I undid the buttons on my shirt and pants. Before I pulled my fingers out, I reached back, grabbed the toy she had set down earlier, and swapped it for my hand. I didn't want her arousal to die down, so I needed to keep her stimulated. After I turned the toy on, I kept it in place with my knee while I quickly shed my clothes.

"Holy fuck!" Eliza gasped loudly, close to shouting.

Although, I didn't know whether it was in reaction to me or her orgasm. Deciding to take some mercy on her, I turned the toy off and tossed it aside. Not like I needed it now that my aching cock was free.

Leaning back over her, I lowered myself down to her entrance. Settling my cock against her wet cunt, I rocked my hips to coat myself in her juices. As much as I wanted to bury myself in her, I needed her to lube up my cock some more. Otherwise, this would suck for both of us. I could've spit on my dick, but the thought of getting her to gush or squirt again sounded more fun.

"Oh God," she whimpered, trying to buck her hips away from me. "You're fucking huge, like porno huge." She managed to squirm about an inch away from me before I grabbed her shoulder and pinned her down.

Teasing her with a laugh, I shook my head in disbelief. "Oh, now you're just trying to stroke my ego." I was being an asshole. "It's only nine inches." I probably sounded a little too casual which made it come out rather arrogant.

"Average is fucking five or six!" she remarked with a glare. "There's no way you're going to fit in me." She squirmed in protest under me as I continued to rub my girthy shaft along the length of her cunt. "You're going to hit my fucking womb or some shit." Her fisted hands lightly hit my chest as she pouted up at me.

My body wouldn't stop shaking with laughter at her words and reaction because she was being a little ridiculous. It was adorable. "Well, guess we'll see if you like getting your cervix smashed or not," I teased with a smug grin, earning a firm slap to the pecs from her.

With a roll of my eyes, I grabbed her flailing hands and pinned them down, intertwining our fingers. "Darling, I'll be gentle. Don't worry," I assured her with a comforting smile. "I know what I'm do-ing, so don't worry." I wasn't an idiot when it came to sex, thankfully.

Lowering my head, I kissed her deeply with a smile. "Breathe and relax," I murmured against her lips as I positioned my tip at her entrance. "Breathe," I hissed through gritted teeth when I felt her tightness squeeze the life out of my throbbing cock. "Fuuuuck you feel like fucking Heaven, Eliza."

Shuddering, I gripped her hands tightly as I inched myself inside of her with soft and short thrusts. I was too greedy to stop because I craved her heat around my dick, even when tears spilled from her rolling eyes. "That's it, baby, fucking take it. Break for me. Let me ruin your cunt with my cock," I snarled softly with a few hard thrusts, jerking her body.

Forcing her hand down, I pressed it against her stomach when I bottomed out inside her. Kissing her tears away, I trailed up to her ear, whispering deeply, "I'm all in, little rose. You feel me deep in you?

Your body knows who it belongs to and took all of me so perfectly." Harshly, I pulled at her ear with my teeth. "Keep your hand there. I want you to feel me take you for the first time. Feel my cock move in and out of your lovely body."

I half expected her to pull her hand back and slap me or something, but she impressed me by complying. I had to give her some credit where it was due. Her chest heaved with her trembling breaths as she looked at me with worried but trusting eyes. My hand that still held hers was crushed by her grip, but that was a small price to pay on my end.

Smiling proudly at her, I adorned her face with sweet kisses as I praised her, "That's my good girl. You're taking me so well, and you're doing amazing." I growled softly into the kiss against her lips. "I am so proud of you." I couldn't hold the wicked grin from my lips as I jerked my hips against her whimpering body. "You're going to make such a good little slut for me and only me."

Pulling my hips back, I paced myself and gave her long and slow thrusts. I needed to give her a little mercy after getting ahead of myself and bullying my cock into her like that.

Fucking hell, this woman was going to get me pussy whipped for her.

The control I had over my own body slowly ebbed with each thrust the more I got drunk off her bliss. "I can't fucking wait to start your training, and you're going to do so well for me, aren't you? Because you're my good girl who wants to do nothing but please me and make me proud, huh?" I chuckled teasingly against her lips as I rammed myself into her harder.

Through her moans, Eliza nodded her head vigorously in response. I waited for her words to come, but when they didn't, I grabbed her face to steady her attention on me. "Words, little rose. I always want to hear your responses, so I know you understood." I didn't mean to sound as harsh as I did, but I was trying to hold back a groan when I spoke.

Whimpering out a long moan, her head bobbed again in response. Unlike before, her struggling words followed, "Y-y-yes, sir."

"Shit!" Gritting my teeth, I forced myself to stop moving when I felt her tighten around me. "Fucking shit." I felt like a complete joke with how fast my resolve crumbled away with Eliza.

I was no one-minute wonder, and not gonna lie, I prided myself on that aspect. Yet, seems like Eliza might make a fool out of me tonight.

As much as I tried, I couldn't keep my release at bay for long. Not with how Eliza bucked her hips and rolled her body against me so needily when I paused to collect myself. "No, don't stop, please." Her pouting face leaned up to mine, and the faintest brush of her lips spurred me into action.

Relenting to her demands, I released her hand to firmly grasp her hips with both of mine. "Wrap your legs around me, darling," I commanded her with a deep breath, waiting for the constricting feeling of her legs around my waist before going at her.

Eliza's hands immediately shot up and gripped my shoulders the moment I started thrusting into her again. It wasn't long until I felt the sweet sting of pain shiver throughout my body from her nails digging into my flesh as I continued to jerk her body with my forceful thrusts.

"Oh God, you're too much," she whimpered through her moans and soft orgasms.

Feeling a bit mean, I slammed into her a little more forcefully during every other thrust. "Who's too much?" I asked with a cocky smirk. "Last I checked, it's not God who's cock you're cumming on." Oh, I was so going to get smote for that, probably, but fuck it.

"So." Thrust. "Try." Thrust. "That." Thrust. "Again!" Thrust.

She practically screamed with pleasure as her nails raked down my arms, leaving blotchy, beady trails of blood in their wake. "Adam! Oh fuck, Adam, too much! It's too much!" Her whole body shook under me and her walls squeezed me so tightly during her orgasm, that I couldn't hold my own back.

"Fuck!" My own pleasureful groan caught in my throat as I blew my first load into her. "Take it all, Eliza, fucking take it." I strained out a groan as I jerked my hips sloppily into her.

Letting go of her hips, I wrapped my arms around her, holding her sobbing body tightly against me. "Hey, shh, hey, breathe," I soothed her while stroking her hair. "I'm here. I've got you," I assured her with butterfly kisses to her face. "Breathe and come back to me, little rose."

Her jagged breaths slowly paced out evenly the longer I held and comforted her. Seeing her overwhelmed like this made it impossible not to give her some grace. The nagging need I had to turn her around, get her on all fours, and pound away at her like there was no tomorrow disappeared at the sight of her struggling through her sobs. She needed a moment, and if I didn't give it to her, then she might break.

"Maybe we should stop for tonight." Nothing wrong with throwing in the towel, and it wasn't as if I'd make fun of her for it. Hell, as much as I wanted to subject her body to wicked acts, I knew both our limits.

Shockingly, Eliza refused with a firm shake of her head. "No, I'm fine." She didn't sound too convincing with how airy her words came out. Clinging to me tightly, she buried her face into the side of my neck. "I don't want to stop yet, but I just need a minute."

I wasn't entirely sure about it, but if she wanted to, then who was I to deny her? I'd still keep a close eye out, and if things went beyond my comfort, then I'd call it off.

Giving in with a soft sigh, I kissed her forehead before pulling her up with me to site fully on my bed. A sharp wince left her gritted teeth at the sudden movement, and I quickly apologized before covering her face with kisses to distract her. With us settled comfortably, I grabbed the water bottle off my nightstand and pressed it to her protesting lips that clamped shut.

Looking at her sternly, I forced her lips apart. "Little rose, if you don't drink, then I will find other ways to make you," I threatened in a voice full of promise. "You are going to drink to rhydrate, then you are going to eat what I feed you because I will not have you pass out on me. If you don't, then no more sex tonight, only cuddles and kisses." Those were the only options I'd give her, neither of which I minded.

Yes, it'd be nice to keep fucking her until both our bodies gave out, but I'd be just as content lazing around with her safely in my arms and against my body. Call me a damn sap or loser, but cuddling with my Eliza was the next best release for my body.

Glaring up at me, Eliza grumbled under her breath before reluctantly parting her lips and sipping at the water. "That's my good girl," I praised her with a teasing smile, earning a very deep eye roll from her. "If you don't stop that, then I'll give you a damn good reason to roll them after this little break," I threatened her with a playful but serious voice.

Biting her lip seductively, she tightened her arms around my neck. "Oh? Is that a promise of a grand time I'm hearing?" She giggled alluringly, looking up at me with a coy smile.

Whatever little concern I had for her well-being flew out the window at her renewed spunk. So, grabbing her hips, I threw her off me onto the bed on her front side. Pressing a hand against her upper back, I kept her pinned while I jerked her backside up until she was on her knees. Unable to hold back the urge, I let my hand lash across her creamy ass cheek, turning it pink.

Just as I positioned myself behind her, I gazed down with a proud smirk. Seeing her quivering cunt leaking my cum down her thighs snapped at my primal heartstrings. "Hope you got enough of that sass to last you all night," I bit out smugly before thrusting myself fully into her eager body.

Eliza whimpered and squirmed violently under me as I kept myself fully buried in her, pressing my tip against the entrance of her womb. Rolling my hips, I lightly pressed and rubbed myself against her cervix, making her gasp and cry out. When she showed no signs of stopping me or signs of pain, I grabbed ahold of her ass and started to ram myself in and out of her.

"The only thing these pretty legs of yours are gonna do after tonight is remain spread for me to fuck you whenever I want," I barked out a rather snide laugh as I continued to pound into her moaning body with abandon.

"Better start learning how to take my fucking cock, my sweet slut."

Because I'm not anywhere near done with you, my sweet rose.

Chapter 16
Adam

~1 month later~

"Can you walk?"

Alright, laughing at her struggling to move around on her jelly legs probably was a little mean of me, but she rejected my offer of help.

Throwing her head up, she tossed a glare at me. "S-shut up," she whimpered, still clinging to the wall for support as she inched down the hallway.

Of course, Asher being the sweet boy his mom was raising him into, wiggled himself from my arms to waddle over to Eliza. "Mama owie?" His big eyes widened with concern as he looked up at his mother with a soft frown.

The fake smile Eliza plastered on her face easily stretched to a real one as she leaned down and hugged her son. "No, mama, okay. Mama a little tired," she assured him sweetly before turning his chubby little body around and urging him forward with a few pats to his backside.

Once Asher was out of earshot, she trained a playful glare on me with her deadened expression. "I hate your stupid dick," she snarked.

Laughing in response, I turned around fully to go to her pouting side. Leaning down, I leveled my face with hers. "That's not what you were saying last night," I teased with a knowing smirk, earning a smack to the chest from her. "Don't forget the cock you're a slut for now, little rose," I reminded her with a cruel but playful smirk. "Unless you need a lesson and reminder already."

That seemed to have gotten her. Eliza's face instantly paled for a split second before it went red as she sputtered while crossing her legs in an attempt to shield herself. "You're a bully," she remarked after she gathered herself back together.

Leaning down some more, I slipped my arms under her knees and around her shoulders, picking her up despite her protests. "Well, maybe next time you'll think twice about being a little brat to me. I mean, I did warn you that if you didn't behave, then your punishment wouldn't be fun." I did tell her what would happen if she continued to defy me about not finishing the snack I had prepared for her.

"You're going to get me fat—ouch!" Her body jerked with a yelp at the impact of my hand on her ass. "What was that for!? It's true!" she retorted with a glaring pout.

"Call yourself fat again, and I will strap you to the spanking bench after breakfast," I threatened her, rolling my eyes a bit. "You gotta get a better outlook on your beautiful body that is filling out very well."

Okay, so maybe she was getting a little fluffy, but I loved that! I loved how she had more to grab at, to hold, and to love. Also, I definitely wasn't complaining about her ass getting bigger. I fucking loved making it jiggle by fucking her nice and hard, and smacking it was heaven.

"I am nearly one-thirty, you jerk... I don't want you to get mad at me when I lose my body and look like a blob." Her dejected words made me frown deeply internally.

Sighing heavily, I set her down at the dining room table, settling her in a chair. Then, I kneeled before her, taking her hands in mine and rubbing the back of them with my thumb. "Darling, I am not a shallow asshole like that. So, what if you're getting a little more plush? I love you and your body how it is. I love having more of you to hold and adore," I spoke with my whole heart, smiling lovingly at her with nothing but genuine honesty and passion in my eyes.

Her sparkling eyes, full of wonder, widened at me in awe as a big smile spread across her face. Her lips trembled with her voice, "Y-you love me?" And there was some fear in her eyes as I felt her body clam up a little.

The sweet warmth that shrouded us slowly chilled with her paced breathing. Seconds felt like hours as I watched her eyes grow a little wary, her body timid. "W-why?" A broken look of rejection made her eyes grow somber as her head turned downward.

Letting her hands go, I carefully reached up to cup her face, tilting her gaze to me. "Eliza, you are the best thing that's ever happened to my life, and you never cease to amaze me every day with your spark. I loved you the moment Asher grabbed me and put me on your path, and I am never going to stop." I couldn't help the dopey, lovey-dovey smile on my face as I looked at her like she was my whole world.

Actually, scratch that, she *is* my whole world.

"I know it's a little fast, and I didn't want to say anything about my love for you until you were more comfortable with us." Sighing softly, I smiled at her apologetically. "But it kind of came out, sorry." I did feel bad for dumping it on her like this and not in one of the overly romantic ways I've thought of. "And you do not have to say anything back to me, and please don't feel pressured to if you don't feel anything yet. I want you to arrive at your own terms and pace. Just because I've said something doesn't mean I want to hear it back from you, nor do I want you to pressure yourself to love me back when you are not ready."

Slipping a hand to the back of her head, I brought her down into a soft and deep kiss. "I won't get upset or angry or anything like that either for what you feel and what you don't. If anything, I'll get upset if you force yourself into something because of me." I kept my voice soft and assuring as I spoke, "Nothing you do or say will ever get me to change how much I love you and Asher. I know you've been hurt in the past by your ex, and I swear, the day I find him, he's going to wish he was never born."

I wanted to wring the fucker's neck out for the pain he inflicted on her. Unfortunately, I had no name to go off of, and no one in her damn profile or social network knew anything about the damn douchebag.

Slowly, I let out a deep breath to calm myself and shove the subject away. I couldn't think about that right now because there was no point. Besides, the day's barely started, so there was no point in dirtying it.

Focusing my attention back on Eliza, I smiled at her tenderly as I stroked the back of her head. "You and Asher are my life now, and I know it sounds crazy and scary, but you two really have made a home in my heart." Maybe I should start to find a way to make her forget all of this because it kinda made me sound creepy or deranged the more I thought about it.

Stunned, she sat there staring at me with an unreadable expression for—what felt like—an eternity before some stale words filtered out of her mouth. "I... I don't know what to say." Reaching a stiff hand out, she brushed my hair aside with trembling fingers while looking at me with an unsure smile. "You feel too good to be true, and I'm so afraid that the moment I let you in, accept everything, I'm going to wake up from this dream."

"Oh, *mia rosa*." Pecking her lips, I smiled happily. "I am your dream come true."

As long as she didn't find out the truth, then I might become her nightmare embodied.

Looking at her as confident as possible, I admired her for a few seconds before giving her a long kiss. "Like I said, take all the time you need. I will always be here for you and Asher, patiently waiting for the moment."

Relaxing with a smile, Eliza stroked my cheek gingerly with the tips of her fingers. "You really don't mind, Asher?" Her smile wavered a little with worry as her smooth strokes jerked to a stop. "I mean, I know you said you don't mind him and all a bunch of times, but if this thing between us is going to get serious..." She didn't have to finish her sentence; the way her body shied away from me a little and how her eyes shut me out was telling enough.

If I was honest, which I would be a little later down the road when she wasn't a flight risk, I already saw her as my wife and Asher as my own son. Yeah, no way would I tell her that right now, not unless I was prepared to chain her in the basement to prevent her from fleeing me.

So, I settled for smiling at her reassuringly. "My sweet rose, I already see Asher as my own son. He is such a bright kid, even if he's still very young, but I can see what an amazing person he will grow up to be." Licking my lips nervously, I looked past Eliza for a split second to look at the toddler a little way from us with his pile of toys. "And I am so happy and blessed that you allow me in his life. I know you two are a package deal and shit, and I didn't care about that. You are mine, so therefore, Asher is also mine to love and care for."

What came out of her mouth next caught me off guard. "What if I want you to be his father?" I couldn't read her nearly blank expression.

Was she serious? Was she pulling my leg? Was this some fucked up game to her? No, she wasn't a malicious little thing who got her rocks off on such things. Honestly, she was one of those people who wouldn't harm a fly, let alone fuck with someone's mind and feelings.

Forcing the bad thoughts away, I smiled at her gratefully. "Then I would be so fucking honored, I might just propose to you right now." The ring was ready to go.

All I needed to do was pop the question, and I was more than ready to do that whenever Eliza was ready.

"Of course, if that's gonna be so, then we're going to need to be more than girlfriend and boyfriend," I teased with a cheeky grin.

Eliza's hand lashed out against my chest playfully. "Oh, stop it, you."

Chuckling softly, I grabbed her hand and kissed it. "What? I can't help it. I mean, you, Asher, and me being a little family." It was picture-perfect, and it was what I wanted—what I'll have in the end.

Another tick faltered her growing smile, saddening it. "What if we end up having our own child?" Worry weighed every inch of her precious face down.

I knew what she meant with her question, and I didn't fault her for having such troubles in her mind. "Darling, if or when I knock you up, then that changes nothing besides the number of children we'll have in our family." Smiling at her confidently, I stroked her cheek with my thumb. "I'm not going sideline Asher, treat him any less, or not see him as 'my kid' just because we'll have a biological child. Blood-related or not, I will always see Asher as my own son, and I will not treat him any different than one who comes from my family jewels."

I couldn't imagine treating Asher any differently just because he wasn't biologically mine. Unfortunately, the same couldn't be said for other men, so I completely understood her reservations.

"The moment I accepted Asher into my life, accepted my responsibility to him, meant that I accepted my part to treat him right as I do you." Neither mother nor son deserved any less than perfect from me, and I would stop at nothing to give them the whole universe.

Suddenly, a thought crossed my mind when I thought about her question again. "Wait, you're not pregnant, are you?" Was that why she was worried about how I would treat Asher if or when we had more children? We hadn't exactly been careful in terms of using protection with our sexual activities, and by not being careful, I meant no measures were used.

Eliza wasn't on any birth control, though we did have a brief talk about it. Or rather, she made it known to me that she was getting on birth control because she wanted to have everything sorted out before opening the possibility of having children with me. All of which I had no qualms with. No matter how much I wanted to breed her sweet body, that wasn't my decision to make alone—not my body, not my choice.

Also, there was a lot to unpack with Eliza. Nearly a month into being official, and despite us laying down a rule of not keeping anything from each other, she dragged her feet a bit. Now, I've been more than understanding and given her the space and time she needed. She needed a firm hand with some things, but her past and personal secrets weren't it. No matter how irksome it was to have her keep me out, I'd rather her arrive at things at her own pace than force her hand only to have her shut me out completely.

Reeling back a little, Eliza quickly denied me with some vigorous shakes of her head. "Oh, God no, no," she replied with a forced chuckle. "I was just curious since we were somewhat on the subject, so I just wanted to know for future plans."

With a relieved sigh, I smiled softly at her. Yes, I wanted her pregnant with our child, but not right now. Our relationship was still trying to smooth itself out, so this would be the worst time to bring a child into the world.

Kissing her forehead with a smile, I stood up to grab Asher. "Did you see the doctor about birth control yet?" I asked after picking him up and bringing him to his highchair.

"Yeah, I got my patches already and started them basically the same day," she replied with a quick smile. Turning to Asher, she played with him while I busied myself in the kitchen for a bit.

Blissful chatter and laughter filled the dining and kitchen area for a long while as I made breakfast. Not much about our daily routine has changed besides the shift in scenery and such. I still made us our meals, her lunches if she had work, took care of Asher while she was out of the house, and when she'd get back then I'd handle my work for the day before spending time with them both before bed.

Honestly, life was fucking perfect. Okay, it was almost perfect, but the little details didn't dent the situation too much. Plus, it was only a matter of time before everything would be checked off the list.

With the plates of food in hand, I made my way back over to my lovely woman and child. "What does your schedule look like for today?" I asked, feigning some curiosity in my voice.

I kept my eyes set on her, letting her know I was listening even as I set the table. "I only have two houses today. My third one had to reschedule, so I should be back a few hours before dinner," she answered after a moment of thought.

Her pursed lips relaxed into an appreciative smile when I set the plate of crepes in front of her. "Oooh, are they the fruit-filled ones?" Her bright eyes trembled with excitement as she bounced a little in her seat.

The sheer energy from her pulled a chuckle from me as I sat on the other side of Asher with my own plate. "I know those are your favorite, so there's one with strawberries, blackberries, and raspberries, while the other is a mix of mango, kiwi, and peaches." At least she was more than good with eating her fruits; vegetables were a whole different story.

Giggling enthusiastically, she lightly clapped her hands before leaning over the table and kissing my cheek. "Thank you." And her genuineness would never grow old or tiring to me. "What are the plans for today, then?" Her face softened with curiosity as she settled back in her seat and started on her breakfast.

A coy little smile curled at my lips as I fed Asher a bite of his food. "Well, before you get home, text me. When you do get home, you're going to go take a nice bath that I'll have ready for you before putting on the outfit I set out and coming to my office." Seeing her smile widen unconsciously while her cheeks flushed up brightly made my desire for her grow until I had an aching tent in my sweatpants. " I'll give you more instructions when you come to the office."

I couldn't give them to her now because I still hadn't decided what I wanted to have her do. There were so many things, and eventually, we'd get to them. To pick one for now was hard, though. Also, I might decide later based on how tired she seemed and depending on how much sass she'd give me.

Our more intimate activities have been going rather well, more so than I'd expected. Things were slow and steady, but I didn't want to put too much on Eliza's plate or scare her off. So, I've been taking her training slowly and at her pace, as we agreed. I've also been keeping it simple and mild in nature, mostly having her wear outfits of my choosing, keeping to our set schedules, making her take time for herself, having her do more self-care, and having her do certain things around me.

"Alright, sir." Her breathy reply, paired with her eager smile, brought a sense of pride to my swelling chest.

"Brava ragazza."

Chapter 17
Eliza

Nᴇᴀʀʟʏ ᴀ ᴅᴀᴍɴ ᴍᴏɴᴛʜ later, and I still couldn't bring myself to tell him.

But how the hell do I even begin?

I needed to let him in, but how? How could I without unraveling everything? Anything and everything personal about me was tied to my old life, which shouldn't exist anymore. If I cracked that can of worms, I'd have to come clean to Adam about everything, which I didn't exactly want to do.

For once in my life, everything felt like it was finally fitting together. Adam was beyond amazing, and I didn't want anything to ruin our budding relationship. Yes, it was still young, and we were still working things out, but everything was sailing smoothly. Of course, the fact we haven't exactly argued probably should be a red flag... But I was considering that it's only been what? Two and a half months, give or take? So, was it too soon in a relationship to really argue?

We've had some intense conversations—the one in the car about limits, another the day after I settled into his—our—new home, covering rules, schedules, splitting chores. Meager things, really. Granted, we didn't really have much or anything to argue about. Finances, he handled things, and I still had my job and own funds. If anything, I argued with him to let me help, but he always shot me down. Chores? He wasn't a slob or anything, cleaned up after himself, and given how he was home most of the time, he took care of a lot of it while I was away. So, I didn't even have a chance to do any of it, and when I asked him to leave some for me, he always played the 'well, I'm bored at home when Asher's asleep' card on me.

Actually, my job has been a bit of a tension point for us. Adam didn't want me working so much or at a job that was so physically demanding with less than average pay. Of course, that conversation usually led into the whole subject of my lack of college education, career aspirations, and why I should go back to do what I wanted. I wouldn't call the whole thing an argument per se, just a very irritating and emotional talk.

Adam hasn't brought it up in a while, or ever since I snapped at him to quit it the last time about a week or so ago.

It's not that I didn't want to return and get my pharmaceutical degree—I couldn't. As real as my fake records were, I didn't want to put them to the test through the system. The last thing I wanted was to end up in jail for identity fraud or some shit like such. Well, if James didn't find me first somehow.

Even if he didn't press about my past, how long could I keep it hidden? I mean, such things were important to divulge to your partner. Granted, I could lie and make up a fake ex to tell him about. What was Adam going to do with the information? Go out and kill the man for being a raging asshole to me?

It'd have to come out eventually, either on my terms or when we'd get married. That would be disastrous because, well, telling your husband-to-be that you're not who you've claimed to be and that the wedding can't happen because, surprise, surprise, you're still fucking legally married in Idaho to some douchebag wife-beater of a cop!

Still, it didn't feel fair to hide my real self from him, not when he was so forthcoming with me. I practically knew my boyfriend from the moment he was born until now, and he knew nothing real about me. Well, maybe saying that was a little extreme because all my likes and dislikes, limits, personality, and attitude was all me. Nothing about any of that had been a lie or remotely fake about me.

I mean, he didn't have to know about my past, right? The past was in the past; that's what all people say, right? So, no point in digging it up.

Yeah, and what's gonna happen when James finds you? Then what?

My brain really needed to shut up and not work sometimes, I swear. My ex finding me was always a risk as long as I was on the run, but it wasn't a guaranteed thing to happen. I mean, people have disappeared before in history, and criminals have broken out of jail and assumed a whole new identity successfully.

It wasn't as if I was reckless, either. I kept myself from social media, never ventured out much or any, and lived in a quaint town that wasn't too bustling. Honestly, what even were the odds of James finding me? Especially with the alterations to my appearance. Shockingly, going from dark blonde to dark brunette changed my look quite a bit, and the same went for Asher. Well, I wasn't so worried about Asher because his appearance wouldn't stop changing until he was a teen, basically.

Groaning, I ran my hands down my exhausted face before slamming it against the steering wheel a few times.

What do I do?

Sitting in the car brooding to myself didn't help. All it did was make me more frustrated.

You know what? I'll just mull over it in the bath!

It almost slipped my mind; the bath Adam had waiting for me. A lovely bath, and Adam's baths were always lovely, sounded perfect for helping ease my mind. Seriously, he always added extras to the water to make it all the better. Oh! Especially bath bombs! I seriously hoped he left one out for me today. I loved plopping them in and watching them fizz out and turn the water fun.

A small surge of excitement gave my aching legs the energy they needed to step out of my car, into our home, and into the bathroom.

God, that was still a little strange to think about.

Our home.

I never thought I'd call a place home with another man in my life. I thought 'our home' would be with Asher and me, not us two and Adam. Not that I was complaining, just thinking about how strange my life has turned out so far.

A giggle chirped from my bouncing body when I saw a line of bath bombs lining the grand tub, and I eagerly snatched one up and tossed it into the bubbling water. While I watched it dissolve, I quickly stripped myself and put the other bath bombs away into the basket on the floor before slipping into the jetting tub. "Fuck, this is perfect." I moaned happily as I sank into the water, stopping when it reached my chin.

Oh, this is Heaven.

The soothing floral scents of the bath bomb paired with the hot water eased my aching body to bliss. I could stay like this for hours or forever. Too bad I couldn't without turning into a prune.

Shame.

Sighing, I let my head fall back over the tub's edge, resting it against the cushion. I probably shouldn't have stayed as long as I did, considering how tired I was. Seriously, I nearly fell asleep and drowned myself a few times. The most recent, when I was fully submerged, drove it home for me to get my ass out.

Begrudgingly, I dragged myself out of the warm water with an internal groan. God, guess I was more exhausted than I thought. Even though I only had two places today, there was a lot to be done. I thought the nice bath would reset me, but my body felt heavier for some reason. It felt like someone chained anchors to every joint of every limb right now.

Maybe I'll be good and see if Adam will let me nap in his lap or something like that because, lordy, I did not feel up for any funny business. The energy to pull on this little lingerie dress felt nonexistent as I struggled to work out the lace of the corset top.

"Ugh!" Frustrated, I threw my hands down and my head back, letting out a long, raspy groan.

The thought of marching my ass down to the office half-dressed to ask Adam for help crossed my mind quite a bit, and I nearly did it. Actually, I would've if it weren't for the sudden heart attack.

"El—!"

My heart leaped out of my chest with a sudden startle to my body. It felt like my thumping heart ping-ponged around in my chest from the violent grab from a familiar pair of rough hands.

Panic chilled me to my bone, making my body freeze up as my breath choked itself in my throat. All I could do was stare at Adam's worried and rageful face with wide eyes and a gaping mouth that refused to let any words out.

Concern softened his gray eyes, but then the wave of pure wrath sharpened them into a jagged stone the next second.

All I could do was brace myself to be the punching bag for his words and hands. I mean, why else would he look at me so angrily? I didn't even have it in me to think about what I possibly did to deserve this because it was probably everything. Maybe he finally snapped. People did that, and why would Adam be any different?

The way his peeled-back lip relaxed while his eyes boiled more and more with such seething vexation unnerved me because how could someone be so calm but so furious? Then, his voice was so controlled that it felt like some calm before the storm—worse, the eye of the storm itself.

Finally, his words... They felt like a stab to my face with how shocking they were to me.

"Who fucking did this to you?"

Chapter 18
Adam

SECONDS STRETCHED TO MINUTES, then to hours. No, I wasn't being dramatic; it really was hours that Eliza spent in the bath.

I'd heard the front door open and saw her through the camera when she came home. Her little gleeful giggle and squeal from the bathroom didn't elude me either. I also might've snuck a peek here and there because I couldn't help myself. Then, I lost myself in my work for a while, and time kind of flew by. By the time three hours came and went with no signs of Eliza at my side, I grew a little worried.

Fearing she might've dozed off; I scrambled out of my seat to go check on her. She was fine when I last peeped at her. Granted, that was a long while ago...

Much to my relief, she wasn't floating in the bathtub. Unless she had, and this flustered person before me, with lingerie haphazardly donning her body, was the ghost of Eliza. I was about to leave her be, but something on her arm caught my observant eyes.

For a split second, I played it off as a trick of the light, but when I focused my attention on her arms, all of that went sky-high. Heat exploded in my chest, cascading in harsh waves over my body. The bomb of rage veiled my vision with red as instinct took over my actions. Some unknown force pulled my feet in her direction, causing the distance between us to close in the blink of an eye.

Before I could control myself, I watched my hands shoot out, wrapping around Eliza's forearms. Feeling her body go stiff as a statue under my unintentionally harsh grab was enough of a shock to my system for me to grasp my strings again. As much as I wanted to apologize and remove myself, I couldn't.

It was too late.

The way her eyes looked like they'd shatter into pieces when she looked up at me in utter fear nearly broke me, and it would've if I weren't so enraged and concerned.

Seeing the discolored lines scattered across her arms and feeling the roughness under my fingers set off some kind of dynamite of pure fury in me as my trembling eyes raked every inch of her scarred arms over and over. Most of the concentration of scars were on her forearms with only a few scattered higher up.

I was so torn. Half of me wanted to take her to bed, hold her tenderly in my arms while I kissed every one of her scars, and tell her how much I loved and adored her. The other half, the one that won, wanted vengeance for her. She could be spoiled later. I wanted—no, needed—answers, now!

Taking a deep breath, I pulled myself together. I needed to be strong and calm for both of us. I'd already spooked her barging in the way I had, and I didn't want to trigger her into a panic attack.

After a few seconds, I felt the tension in my face ease with my controlled breaths. Even though my shoulders had relaxed, I could still feel a slight ache threatening to tighten them back up. With every heaving breath, I fought the suffocating grip around my chest—the one that demanded I take vengeance for my woman.

Once I thought I had a good cap on it, I spoke up. however, the brewing anger slipped from my tongue and spewed out of me like venom, and my voice turned deep and raspy with it.

"Who fucking did this to you?" My grip on her loosened slightly, and I slid my hands up to her shoulders, holding her comfortingly and longingly.

And I refused to let her slip away this time. Having seen the horrors done to her body, I wanted the name that belonged to the body I was going to carve up to match what had been done to my little rose. For every scar they inflicted on her body, I would double on theirs. Then, once I'd scored their body like some lump of meat to be marinated, I'd take them out to sea and make the sharks happy.

This wasn't a matter of if, either. It was only a matter of time.

I will get a fucking name from you, Eliza, one way or another.

But by God, I wanted to melt at her feet and apologize for being so demanding when her eyes teared up.

No! Stop it! No more!

I couldn't cave. Not this time.

Softening my gaze a little, I looked at her demandingly but also with concern. "Eliza, *mia rosa*, no more. You need to tell me. I have been more than patient with you, and I want to keep giving you the time you need, but if you're hiding something like this from me... I don't know if I can keep hanging back until you are ready. I mean, how long were you planning to wait before telling me? How long until you stop wearing long-sleeved shirts?"

Granted, I should've pushed the issue a little more. I mean, did I find it strange how she always wore long-sleeved tops? Maybe. But we were on the Oregon Coast, not like it was bustling hot or warm to the point where a lack of sleeves was needed.

Easing my grip, I slid my hands around her body, pulling her tightly against me. "Please, let me in, even if it's just a little, or at the very least, tell me who did this." Because I needed to kill the bastard; otherwise, I could forget about getting a good night's sleep any time soon. "Who hurt you?" I pleaded against her head with a kiss.

Eliza's body eased in my arms, and a soft weight pressed against me when she slumped and sobbed. "It was my ex, but I don't want to talk about him... Please... I just want to forget. I don't want to go back to that night." Her muffled words sobbed against my chest as her body shook like a scared bunny.

Her head snapped back in an instant, and her sadness and worry cut through her tears like a knife into my heart. "Please don't be mad at me. I wanted to tell you. I did, and I'd planned to do it the morning after I moved in... But I couldn't bring myself to. I didn't want you to be disgusted with my already flawed body." Her small hands fisted the front of my shirt as if she was afraid I'd pull away from her revelation. "I didn't, and don't, want to lose you. I couldn't risk it, so I continued to hide it."

"*Oh, mia piccola rosa, no, mai.*" A flurry of kisses to her face followed a soft shake of my head.

Picking her up in my arms with a smile, I went over to the end of the bed and sat down with her in my lap. "The only thing I'd do is praise you for being such a strong woman and for getting yourself through such an ordeal, and that is what I am doing now." While my lips remained in a proud smile, my concerned and angry eyes had a mind of their own as they fixated on her arms. "I can't even begin to imagine..."

There were so many. I tried to count them all, but I lost track after fifteen because there were so many small ones that they kept blurring together. Of course, trying to count them didn't quell my anger. If anything, it only made it worse because the more I looked at them, the more I could see the differences in the discoloration.

She was attacked on more than one occasion, and that pissed me off to an entire universe.

Who was this bastard ex of hers who'd dared to inflict such suffering onto her, and more than once!?

When I get my hands on him, he'll wish he never existed.

Kissing her forehead, I kept my lips pressed against her while I breathed in her soothing scent. "I can never be upset at you or see you any less. Besides, you've seen my body and its scars. So, who am I to judge when my body isn't perfect itself?" Chuckling, I cupped her face and wiped away her tears with my thumbs. "You will never be less than perfect to me."

A look of defeat crossed her eyes momentarily before she closed them and leaned into my touch. "I don't know how or why I let it happen so many times." Her voice cracked a little as she spoke. "He was so sorry the first time, and I was stupid enough to believe him... Once, twice, three times. He was always tired from work, a few drinks in his body, and it was my fault for not being more diligent with having dinner ready or the house proper."

Her tired body trembled against me with her pathetic laugh. "And I was so stupid to let it go on for as long as it did." Her laughter picked up in volume, and it had the same pathetic and disbelieving pitch to it. "Ten fucking years, and to think it could've been forever if it weren't for Asher."

Keeping a comforting smile plastered on my face, I let my thoughts brew in my turbulent mind. "You got out, that's all that matters. You found your strength and will, and you got out. Not everyone can say they did, nor can everyone in your situation find it in themselves to think about escape."

I knew what I wanted to tell her, but everything mixed in my mind. Thoughts about who this ex was, how I fucking missed uncovering such a fact, how much she must have endured. For fuck's sake, ten years! That's how long she was with the damn bastard, yet nothing came up in my search.

No way would something like that have gone under my radar. I was more than diligent with digging into Eliza, so a ten-year relationship would've come up. There had to be something else at work here because I refused to believe that Max and I were that careless.

Using Eliza to distract myself from my own mind, I mindlessly kissed her temples. "You took that important first step, and you are still walking to a better future. Even if it's inch by inch, it's better than nothing and much better than being stuck in an abusive relationship." I was too numb to put much thought into my words, but Eliza needed such comfort right now, even if it was a little empty.

At least something genuine filtered through my haze of rageful paranoia. "I am so proud of you for how far you've come. It truly makes me appreciate you that much more because I couldn't be prouder to call such a strong woman mine." It might not seem like much to a lot of people, but to do what she did took a lot of courage.

Leaving a bad situation was never easy, despite what people might think. Yes, the door might be right there; hell, the door could be wide open with a bag of cash sitting next to it. The notion of walking out was simple enough, and the act of it was fairly easy. Yet, a lot of people failed to consider the storm underneath the surface.

Physically, nothing could stop them. Abusers didn't have to beat their victims twenty-four-seven to keep their compliance. Just the one time to really knock them down and force them into submission was enough. There were no chains or ropes needed to tie a victim down to their abusers either.

No, everything was always mental and emotional. The diabolic manipulation of a victim's emotions and mind would eventually mold them into believing they are nothing without their abuser. Threats of harm to loved ones hanging at the forefront of a victim's mind could be enough to keep them in line as well. Then, after a while, they accept it. Whatever the abuser has done, their routine, it all becomes normal to the victim. They can't see the bad situation before them because, to them, it wasn't bad. It was why most victims often returned to their abusers or a similar person or lifestyle if they ever got free.

Stepping out of the cycle and preventing relapses took a whole different strength and willpower entirely.

I mean, fuck, ten years with the damn bastard in such a relationship. No wonder my Eliza was so guarded and afraid. I really couldn't blame her for being so hesitant with me. Whatever life she made with the scumbag became her livelihood.

Taking her face into my hands, I brought her into a deep kiss full of promise. "I'll take care of you, my sweet rose." Inhaling a breath full of her calming scent, I let my nerves settle a bit. "I'll cherish you as you should have been all those years. I'll love you so much that you'll have a whole new set of standards that no other person on this earth will ever meet." As if I'd let her try to find another person in this damn universe.

With a smug smile, I took her hand and moved it down to the front of my pants. Pressing her hand firmly against my bulge, I rolled my hips slowly into her palm. "You feel that, *mia rosa*?" I whispered against her lips. "You think I'd be turned on and all hard for you if I didn't find you attractive? Even after seeing your arms, I'm not in the least bit turned away." Grabbing her face, I squished it a little between my fingers as I forced her to look into my intense eyes.

"So, don't you ever say you aren't pretty or that you look disgusting because of those scars, understood?"

I fucking loved how her eyes and body melted under me with submission, so much that I felt my cock twitch and strain in its confines. "Yes, sir." Her trembling voice fanned across my lips and lower jaw.

Crowding over her, I laid her down on the bed, trapping her under me. "That's my good girl. Just let me take care of you, alright? Let me show you how much I adore you and this body of yours. How crazy you drive me," I whispered sweetly with a hot breath as I kissed her face and neck. "Let me get you bare and show you exactly what this body of yours does to me." Grabbing her lingerie, I pulled at it harshly, loosening the bindings of her half-done corset. "Show you what I want to do to you."

A sharp gasp slipped from her smiling face when I yanked the piece off her in one swift movement. "God, you have no idea how many nights I've thought about getting my hands on your bare body," I spoke against her body as I adorned it with kisses. "Fuck, you feel heavenly." I groaned deeply, taking a moment to collect myself before I continued to take in every inch of her body greedily with my hands.

I adored every inch of her body with my hands and lips, not leaving any part untouched. Then, I returned to her arms, giving them special attention. Every scar got a long kiss pressed against—every single one. "I love you for everything. Perfectly flawed, so perfect for me," I whispered against her arms as I continued loving them.

"W-what are you going to do to me?" Her voice trembled with nervousness and excitement as her wary eyes looked down at me.

Crawling up her body, I looked down at her softly, with eyes full of ardent sweetness. Stroking her cheek with the back of my finger, I smiled at her for a moment. "I'm going to show you what sinful things this lovely body of yours makes me want to do." Running my finger along her jaw, I sharpened my smile lustfully. "I'm going to show you the burning desire the sight of you brings me."

Grinning like a wild animal, I jerked her body around after shooting off the bed. "Spread your legs," I commanded in a guttural voice, looking down at her shivering body with starving eyes, "and touch yourself."

Her eyes bugged out of her head as she looked up at me with a stunned mouth. "W-what?" She looked at me with such disbelief, and I wanted to chuckle a little at how adorable and clueless she looked.

Dragging out an exhale, I grabbed her by the neck, pulling her off the bed a little. "I didn't stutter, and I know you heard me well enough. So, don't make me repeat myself, or I'll tie you down and make you come until you cry." Or do; I won't mind either way.

Her throat bobbed with her hard swallow before her head nodded in response. "I'm sorry, sir."

Letting go, I settled her back down with her head hanging over the edge of the bed. "No coming." The way her pouting face palcd with a complaint nod made me stifle a laugh as I helped her spread her legs.

Standing over her, I watched her with mesmerized eyes, only losing site of her as I removed my clothes. Her shy hand slowly slid down her body, cupping her breasts and fondling them with a soft moan. "That's it, darling. I love watching you play with yourself," I told her in a proud voice, running my rough hands along her inner thighs to help arouse her some more. "I love how confident you've gotten." She wasn't overly bold or anything, but she was more than willing to expose herself at my command after some coaxing and training.

Biting my bottom lip with a low groan, I breathed out heavily as I watched her deft fingers slide down her inner thigh to her twitching cunt. "Part those sweet lips for me, baby. Let me see how wet and needy you are for me," I encouraged her by reaching down and palming her tits roughly.

"I love how good you are for me. How obedient you are. Such a good girl." Smirking cruelly, I pinched her hard nipples between the gaps of my fingers. "Such a good fucking slut."

Unable to help it, I removed a hand from her soft breast to take her hand away from her pussy briefly. With her cunt fully exposed, I pulled my hand back and brought it down on her hard, filling the room with her yelp and the wet slap of my hand slapping against her juicy pussy.

"You drive me insane, Eliza. Every time I see you, all I want to do is hold you and worship you." Which I did. Not a day went by where I didn't spoil her with as much affection as possible. "But seeing your sweet body tease me makes me want to ruin you all over again."

Love her, then fuck her like I didn't. That's how it worked with us.

My chest rumbled with another growl as I spanked her pussy again, and again, and again. Every jerk of her body from my impact was like a tug at my heartstrings. Her sweet yelps a lovely melody for my ears—only my ears. I couldn't stop spanking her cunt. Every swing of my hand felt automatic, and I felt myself growing too excited at the sight of her sex twitching and reddening with each spank.

With one final spank, I let out a deep breath through my smiling lips as I looked at her heaving and twitching body. Praising her, I brushed my thumb against her parted lips, "Good girl, you didn't come once." Controlling her orgasms was still a work in progress, but she'd made good progress thus far; of course, there was the occasional slip-up here and there with certain activities.

"Now, touch yourself again while I put your mouth to good use."

Eliza's eyes went wide along with her mouth, and I might have been a bit of a jerk to use that to my advantage. "Wha—augh!" Her words choked off around a gag when I rammed myself into her mouth and down her throat.

Holding her head with one hand, I wrapped the other around her throat, keeping her in place so I could fuck her face. "This is what I want to do to this pretty little face of yours every time I see it, especially when you get a little sassy with me. Fuck, I just want to shove you down to your knees and fuck your face just like this, so you know exactly what your mouth is good for." My words strained out in a groan as I violently bucked my hips at her.

Feeling her nails scrape against my body while her body squirmed and choked on my cock was the best sensation ever. The bite from her nails sent sparks of pleasure throughout my body, and the tightness of her throat clenching around my aching cock with her struggles felt almost as good as being in her cunt.

"Just breathe, darling," I instructed her, laughing a little when she purposely smacked my thigh in response. "Just focus on touching and fingering yourself to be distracted," I remarked with a chuckle.

Squeezing the sides of her neck, I choked her softly as I continued to face fuck her roughly. Besides the sounds of my balls slapping her face, the room was filled with her sucking, gagging, and choking on my thick cock; it all bled together and drowned out the sweet sounds of her juicy cunt being fucked by her own fingers.

After slamming into her rougher a few times, I pulled back abruptly. With my throbbing cock hanging over her face, I watched her suck in sharp breaths between her coughs. Once I was sure she got enough oxygen, I let go of her neck to grab her messy face, gripping it roughly to jerk her attention to me. "Tell me, what's this mouth of yours good for, little rose," I demanded with a wicked grin.

Her dazed eyes struggled to focus on me as she breathed heavily. Nothing came from her gaping mouth as she opened and closed it, and I didn't know if she could formulate her words or if she refused to answer. Either way, it didn't change the outcome.

Slap!

Redness darkened her already flushed face from my hand lashing across it, and her head hung to the side after it was whipped in that direction. It wasn't a hard slap; I was more than coherent enough to hold back when I brought my hand across her face. I only wanted to jolt a little sense into her, not hurt her.

I half expected her to shout her safe word at me or flash the light in my eyes when she didn't respond after a few seconds. Hell, I was about ready to call it and check on her, when her teary eyes looked up at me in bliss. Closing her parted lips, she swallowed roughly while pacing her breathing out. Then, she smiled at me seductively while licking her lips.

"My mouth is only good for you to fuck, and to suck your cock, sir."

Chapter 19
Eliza

I needed more of the euphoria Adam's proud and lustful eyes brought me. I wanted him to keep looking at me with such desire. Such wanton eyes from a man, something I never thought I'd experience, something I never thought I'd want after all those men before left a bad taste in my mouth.

Grabbing his hand around my jaw, I slipped his fingers across my lips and into my mouth. Closing my eyes, I sucked and licked his fingers with a soft moan before looking up at Adam with a happy smile. "All I'm good for is being your slut, holes for you to fuck and dump your cum in."

Oh my God, where the fuck did that come from!? How did I become so lewd?!

Adam's face lit up with my words, absolutely beaming as if I'd just said yes to marrying him. Both his hands grabbed my face, bringing me up into an eager kiss. "God, you make it impossible not to love you when you say such filthy things like that." He chuckled breathlessly against my lips. "Fucking love how much of a good girl and a slut you are for me."

Leaning back up, Adam's hand flew across my face again, this time a little harder. A sharp gasp slipped from my smiling lips, my hips digging into the bed from the surge of hot arousal that cascaded from the site of impact straight to my aching cunt.

Then, another slap sent my head snapping the other way. "You fucking like that, my little whore?" Adam asked with a mocking laugh, slapping my blissful face again, and again, and again until the stinging pain started to numb out into pure pleasure.

"Yes!" I gasped in pleasure, moaning softly while writhing in delight. "I love it so much."

Wow, I never thought I'd ever like being hit. Granted, this was a completely different situation and circumstance. Adam didn't mean it in a harmful way, and he definitely wasn't hitting me very hard. He wasn't slapping me for the sake of it or to intentionally hurt me or to make me obey. It was hard to grasp, but it was different, and I loved it—that's it.

Fisting my hair and grabbing my face, Adam forced my mouth open and thrust himself deep until his balls slapped my face. I tried to keep myself calm, breathe whenever I could and in whichever way I could, but having a thick ass dick, like some damn sausage bar fucking my throat deeply, made breathing quite difficult. At least Adam reveled in my struggle with how fucking feral he got. Seriously, I wouldn't be surprised if he started foaming at the mouth with how crazed his whole face was becoming with his eyes.

"Keep edging yourself, darling, keep yourself ready to come on my command." His deep voice sent shivers down my body and pulled a moan from me as I struggled to keep my fingers moving.

The whole training me to orgasm on-demand shit was hard! Or at least, it wasn't fun for me, because of how much on edge I had to be kept. Actually, holding back my orgasm was the most annoying part. At this point, I didn't give a damn because things were how they were.

Even if I didn't want to, my damn body had a mind of its own whenever it came to Adam. His word was law to it. If he said no coming, no matter how much I teetered on the edge, I couldn't get myself over. Granted, it wasn't like that initially, but after the first few times, my body got the gist of it, kind of.

"You better swallow every drop of cum I give you. You got that?" His growly words trembled throughout his body and into mine.

Not a second later he told me that, he picked up his pace, slamming into my aching mouth and sore throat relentlessly. It felt like my body would go into sensory overload with the assault on both ends of my body, and just when I was about to cave, he gave me the reprieve I desperately needed.

He strained out through gritted teeth, "Come. Now!" Groaning deeply as his hips jerked out of rhythm for a few seconds before his spurting cock stilled in my eager mouth.

Everything that happened over the course of the next minute (possibly more, I didn't count) was all instinctual. Control over my body ceased to exist the moment the painful tension in my abdomen snapped and I pushed my orgasm over the edge, letting it freefall into oblivion.

Shockwaves of pure ecstasy crashed into my jerking body while my mind went blank. The feeling was scary. Everything felt so perfectly blissful. If floating on a cloud was possible, then I was pretty sure that would be how it felt. No worries, no nothing. Seriously, my mind was as blank as a sheet of paper, just ready for Adam to write out whatever he wanted on me.

"Ro... Ome... E..."

Huh? Was someone saying something?

"Ar... Ing... Come... To... Me..."

That voice... It sounds familiar... It's so soothing.

Safe. That's how that voice made me feel.

Fuck, I haven't felt safe in so long.

The dots were there, but they did not want to connect. Well, more like I couldn't tie the thread between the two thoughts because I was so out of it.

"Little rose, my darling, come back to me."

Adam.

It was Adam's voice that beckoned me back to reality.

But fuck reality.

I didn't want to go back! I wanted to stay on cloud nine forever. This bliss was amazing, and I didn't want it to end. It's never been this intense before. Pure euphoria was all I felt at that moment. I'd come close to that state a few times with Adam before, and there was a very small handful of times when I'd experienced something very similar to it, but not as intense.

"Eliza, darling, you need to come back to me." His voice was calm, but there was an edge of worry to it.

As much as I wanted to cling to this high, I couldn't let Adam worry over me. So, reluctantly, I let go.

It didn't matter how much I braced myself for the impact of the crash. Everything shocked my whole body as if I'd been in a hot tub and then dropped into the freezing waters of the Artic or some shit like that.

My whole fucking body ached like I'd been hit by a speeding train and then tossed into the spin cycle of a washer. Every nerve ending in my tense body felt like it was on fire! I was a mess and a half, and I could do nothing about it.

No matter how much I tried, the tears wouldn't stop streaming down my face. My chest clenched tightly with every breath, sending sharp waves of nail-biting pain throughout my body. Desperate hands slithered around my man's body for purchase, gripping, pinching, and scratching him in my frenzy.

Why am I such a mess?

It felt like such a bad breakdown, and I didn't know how to process it. I wanted to feel embarrassed for losing my shit like that in front of Adam, but it was buried under some kind of cathartic release.

I shouldn't be sobbing my eyes out like a child, but God did it feel good.

"P-pl-pl—" Fucking hell, I couldn't even speak.

Every time I tried to utter a single word, it'd come out as some sputtering mess.

Of course, being the perfect fucking lover he was, Adam kept me safe in his loving arms. Every brush of his fingers across my hair and body caused calm ripples to settle throughout. While his soothing touch warmed my body, he whispered sweet words into my ear in both English and Italian.

A long stretch of time passed before I found myself eating and drinking whatever Adam pressed against my lips. I don't know if I stopped sobbing because my crash evened out or if my body had grown too exhausted to continue. Either way, I didn't have the energy to do anything but give in to him completely. Besides, some water and food wouldn't harm me. I mean, it was nice and caring of him.

Granted, Adam was always the best when it came to aftercare. He was always there for me after a scene, holding me, feeding me, bathing me if my state called for it, cuddling me until I felt better or fell asleep.

"*Mia rosa.*" His soft but demanding voice commanded my attention fully to his worried eyes. "You did amazing, and I'm so proud of you for taking that fucking like my good girl. You were wonderful with edging yourself and holding back. So fucking proud of you..." But? There was a but coming; I just knew it. "But please, talk to me."

Well, at least it wasn't a bad but.

Heh, his butt isn't a bad thing either.

Okay, I needed to get ahold of myself, because it was not the time for such thoughts.

Taking a deep breath, I snuggled myself more into his comforting body. Inhaling a lungful of his intoxicating scent, I let my nerves settle more before opening my mouth to try and speak. "Fine... Tired..." Those were the only two words I managed to get out in a small voice.

Adam pressed his lips against my forehead in a brief kiss before loosening his hold on me. His face came into my field of vision, letting me see his relieved expression. "Let me get you cleaned up and dressed, then I'll let you nap on the couch while I make dinner, alright?"

All I could manage was a nod and hum in response to him before buddling the sheets around me to replace his warmth when he left for the bathroom. I don't know how much of a nap it'll be because I felt like knocking out completely for the rest of the day from the heavy drag of exhaustion. But, who knows, I might surprise myself with some kind of power nap.

Minutes after leaving my side, Adam returned with some washcloths and a bottle of my lotion. Slowly, he unraveled me from my blanket burrito and wiped my face clean, before moving down my body. He took his time freshening up every inch of my body, before giving me an impromptu massage as he applied the lotion to my body.

Once he was done, he slipped a pair of panties and one of his t-shirts on me before picking me up in his arms and taking me to the living room. Gently, he settled me on the couch, propping a throw pillow under my head, covering me with the heated weighted blanket he'd gotten me, and leaving me with the TV remote after kissing my head.

No surprise to me, I fell asleep before the opening credits for Criminal Minds finished playing.

What did surprise me, was the lack of exhaustion and burst of energy that surged through my body when I was startled awake by Asher. His tiny but hefty, little body slammed right into me, winding me. "Mama! Mum mum! Mum mum!"

Forcing a laugh through my strained groan of pain, I cuddled my struggling toddler against me while I recovered. "You're going to squish me one day, baby," I commented with an adoring look.

"He'll make the best wrestler," Hailee, Adam's sister, remarked through an amused giggle. "Don't know what you guys feed the little guy, but he's built like a damn tank."

Sitting up with a winded breath, I held Asher in my lap for a few moments longer before letting him down to play with Adelaide. "Honestly, I have no idea where he gets that chunk from." I wasn't a big person, and neither was James.

Sighing softly in thought, I shook my head to clear it. "Was he good today?" I asked Hailee after looking up at her.

"Perfect as always," Hailee replied with a big smile. "Seriously, he's more well-behaved than Adelaide."

"That's because Adelaide is a carbon copy of you," Adam snarked teasingly with a laugh from the kitchen. "And you're a little demon, especially when you were little."

Hailee stomped her foot while fuming slightly. "Oh, like you were any better! You used to catch bugs and put them in people's food and drinks until mom whooped your ass the one time she drank a mouthful of them," Adelaide retorted with a soft scowl. "You're lucky Asher's a good boy, otherwise I'd teach him to stick a squirrel down your pants so it can eat your damn nuts."

Fire scorched my throat and nose. I'd mistakenly taken a sip of my water before she spoke, and fire scorched my throat and nose when I choked and spat out my water at what Hailee said. Adam's footsteps were drowned out by my coughing fit, and I barely felt his back pats and rubs until everything subsided a little. "Hailee!" Adam half-shouted with a slightly red face.

"What? Not like you'll need them. Besides, Eliza only needs the part hanging off your body," Hailee remarked evilly with a grin and laugh of her own.

A scurry of pitter patters rushed over to us in an instant, and each of our kids hugged our legs. "Mama puppy, plwease?" Adelaide grinned up at her mother, who paled a little with a nervous smile and chuckle. "Big pwuppy fo cuddles!"

From the corner of my eye, I saw Adam's lips curl deviously before he leaned down and beckoned his niece over with a wave of his hand. "Addy, come to uncle Adam and you can tell me all about this puppy." Adam actively ignored the scolding glare from his sister as he continued to sweeten his niece up. "Uncle Adam will get you all the puppies you want, a whole room full of them, yeah?"

"Oh, you are so evil," I commented under my breath with a breathy chuckle and shake of my head.

Poor Hailee, there was no winning this time, not with how her daughter took off towards Adam. Her blabbering mouth ran a mile a minute, prattling off about all the dogs she wanted, the size, the color, how many, and how she would ride them around the house. Not gonna lie, I felt a little bad for Hailee because either she'd either break this little girl's heart later when they got home, or learn how to live with a few dogs. I wasn't gonna bank on Adelaide forgetting this conversation any time soon or ever, and knowing how much Adam adored and spoiled her and Asher, the dogs were going to happen sooner rather than later.

"Mama." Asher swung around my legs with a sheepish smile on his face. "Woof woof? Want woof woof."

Oh boy.

Hailee's eyes snapped to me with a knowing look full of sympathy because both of us would have our hands full soon. Yeah, this was not gonna be fun.

Sighing, I bent down to Asher's level and took him into my arms. With a somewhat regretful smile, I swayed him back and forth a little. "No doggy, baby, mommy has her hands full with you and Adam."

"Oh, Eliza darling, don't worry." Adam piped up, grinning innocently and excitedly at me. "I'll take care of the dog. Besides, I've been thinking about getting one recently. I just never got the time to talk to you about it."

Rolling my eyes, I deadpanned at him. "Uh-huh, that's how it always starts before I end up with a child on four legs who licks their butt," I remarked sarcastically.

Of course, Adam being Adam, flashed me a knowing smirk. "Darling, when have I not been a man of my word?" he retorted like a little smart-ass.

Well, I couldn't argue with him there. Of all the people in the world to doubt, Adam was not one of them. If he said he'd do something, then I could bet my ass he'd do it to the best of his abilities and then some.

"Bub, you have work still on top of basically being a stay-at-home parent to Asher," I replied with a lopsided smile. "I don't want you biting off more than you can chew."

"She has a point, you know. A dog is just like another child." At least Hailee was on my side, but she was probably in it to prove a point to Adelaide in hopes of making the 'we're not getting a dog' talk easier later.

"It's not like I'm getting a puppy," Adam threw back at us, rolling his eyes softly. "Besides, I get things done with time to spare more often than not currently."

Again, no arguing with him there because he was right. Even though I gave him breaks when I came home, he mainly used them to get ahead with work. Rarely did he ever have to play catchup with his career, which I had to give him props for. Also, I envied the little shit a bit because I wished I had my life that organized.

"Eliza, darling," Adam begged me with pleading eyes.

A tug at my shirt deterred my attention from my boyfriend to Asher. "Mama." God damn it, Asher, not you, too. "Pwease? Dada dawggy?"

I felt my jaw drop and hang there in the air at his words. The glimpses of everyone's shocked reactions were caught in of my periphery, but I paid them no attention as I was too busy looking at my son like some stunned idiot.

Maybe I'd misheard. "What? Honey? What did you just say?" Although judging from how everyone else reacted, I doubted that.

I mean, how was I supposed to react to that? Neither Adam nor I had taught him the word or indicated that Adam was his dad. Also, I was in no way prepared to deal with that broken-down bridge yet because I thought I'd have a few more years to formulate an answer and straighten it out. So, to have Asher blurt it out of nowhere like this was like a bucket of iced water to my face.

Just as my stupor died down, anger was quick to replace it. Had Adam been teaching Asher or referring to himself as such around him? I mean, how fucking convenient was it that this happened right after Adam made it very clear about how he wanted to be a father to Asher this morning? Had the conversation this morning been an attempt to soften the blow for me? I mean, it's better to ask for forgiveness than permission, right?

We'd never had an in-depth chat about Asher and Adam's relationship before. The furthest we'd gotten in that department was a few late-night talks where I made it clear to him that I didn't want to touch that can of worms yet. One thing was clear, though: we'd both agreed to let things unfold naturally to see how much damage control we had to do. But I made it vehemently clear that I didn't want Adam butting in, which he very clearly agreed to.

"Ah Dawm dada," Asher repeated himself with a proud grin.

Asher's repeated words had Adam smiling so brightly with teary eyes, but it only lasted a flash of a second before realization straightened his face in horror when his eyes landed on me. "Eliza, darling, listen, it's not what you think," he quickly said with a frantic wave of his hand. "This is as much of a shock to me as it is to you. I swear, whatever you're thinking to make you upset, it's not true. I didn't cross a line or anything, I swear."

Well, at least the fear in his eyes was genuine enough to make me believe him, even if it was possibly a lie.

But his words did nothing to change the boiling rage bubbling in my chest.

The anger I'd wrongly displaced onto Adam shifted back to where it belonged.

Me.

Chapter 20
Adam

~2 weeks later~

Whatever turmoil churned inside of Eliza never subsided as the days went on.

Things haven't been sailing too smoothly since the night Asher called me "Dada". Now, don't get me wrong, I wasn't upset about that by any means. If anything, I was more than elated, and I still felt the same pure joy whenever Asher called me that. I was worried about Eliza and how she took all of it.

Every time I brought things up to her, she'd brush me off, which I hated. I never pushed her about the issue, even though I wanted to. I could practically see her visibly wince every time Asher called me his dad, but she refused to talk about it. Shy of manipulating her somehow or turning it into an ultimatum with punishment (which would be the completely wrong thing to do), I didn't know what else to do besides give her time and space to arrive at things at her own pace.

"What's got your panties in a bunch?" my friend Rowan asked with a mocking sneer.

"Pretty sure that's my question to you, considering how you're here." Lincoln City was quite a bit of a drive from Seaside, and I might call the police captain a friend, but we were merely acquainted because of his cousin, Max.

With the way his face dropped with a heavy sigh, I was sure I got him back good. Soon, an awkward silence filled the area until Max cleared the tension with his throat. "Come on, guys, we're all on the same level here." He chuckled awkwardly, bouncing his eyes between his cousin and me.

Unable to help it, I coughed out a curt laugh before sipping at my drink. "Oh, please, the almighty police captain of Lincoln City could never be on the same level as us no-good mafia thugs," I snarked, flashing a dirty scowl at Rowan.

Max's cousin made it damn clear in the past that he didn't appreciate us doing what we did, but he left us be because we didn't create any problems for him, nor did he have any cause to arrest us. Well, that and Max was his good cousin who had done more good than not for Rowan.

Straightening my face out seriously, I peered at him past the rim of my glass. "So, what brings the good captain around?" He only ever showed his face if there was some big celebration that Max dragged him to.

Well, there was the occasional visit from Rowan if very shady business was involved, or if he needed something shady done for the better good. "Who do you need implicated this time? What confession needs some pulling? Or do you need someone gone finally?" I mocked him with a smug smirk, leaning back in my seat at the armchair across from him.

Rowan's jaw ticked with a click of his tongue, and his jaw clenched for a second before he threw down a manilla envelope on the coffee table. "That's payment for later..." he grumbled, averting his eyes from me.

Max's hands clapped against his thighs, snagging my attention. "Rowan needs some lessons on how to charm a woman, and I suggested you because you're the most charming guy in the whole state," my friend deadpanned with a sheepish smile. "And I thought, 'Hey, why not kill two birds with one stone' and whatnot because we were kind of getting stuck with our Eliza case."

My eyes narrowed sharply at Max as the nasty feeling surfaced and chewed at my sternum. "Get to the fucking point, Max," I demanded in a low voice.

Holding his hand up, Max leaned back in surrender. "I was having some trouble with pulling some files, so I asked for Rowan's help, given his knowledge and expertise." His smile fell with his long sigh.

"You better start from the beginning before I chuck this drink at you," I threatened somewhat playfully, clinking the ice in my glass for extra effect.

"Long story short, I was coming up with some roadblocks with the facial aging and recognition program, needed to work some of the kinks out, so I turned to Rowan for some help pulling some things..." Max's face lit up with interest, his little flat frown turning upside down a little too much for my liking. "Now, I'm pretty confident with the information, but again, take shit with a grain of salt and whatnot."

Reaching out, Max picked up the envelope Rowan plopped down, waving it in my face rather tauntingly. "Gotta say, your girl is interesting." There was an edge of sympathy to his intrigued voice that hooked my interest fully.

Setting my drink down, I reached out and snatched the file from Max. Keeping my eagerness hidden under a collected exterior, I pulled the contents out and slowly flipped through them.

Never thought I'd be excited about some ink on pressed wood, but I felt like I'd finally hit the jackpot. To be fair, I did because my Eliza has been nothing but a mystery to me thus far. Well, correction: everything about her life and history has been a mystery. I've no doubts about her personality and attitude being faked, not with how vulnerable and genuine her eyes were whenever I gazed into them.

"And before you ask, yes, it's all true," Rowan said, his voice low and weighted with frustration. He let out a huff, leaning back as if the confirmation had drained him. "I called a buddy of mine on the force in Idaho Falls to fact-check, and he verified everything Max and I uncovered about your girl." The way he said it—*your girl*—carried a bitter edge, but I could tell it wasn't directed at her. It was the frustration of chasing shadows for so long. "And before you say anything, my friend's solid. Actually..." He let out a sharp, humorless snort. "He can't stand the piece of shit she's married to. From what he says, nobody does."

Elisabella. Elisabella Stone.

The name felt foreign and familiar all at once, as though it both confirmed and unraveled everything I thought I knew about her. My gaze dropped to the file in my hands, a storm of papers filled with details I hadn't dared imagine. Reports, histories, fragments of a life she'd hidden so carefully. It wasn't everything—I knew that much—but it was enough to paint a picture I couldn't ignore. Enough to finally give a name to the woman I loved beyond reason.

"And before you ask," Max interjected, his voice cutting through the tension, "I've got every shred of Elisabella Stone's life boxed up on your desk, ready for you."

"Thanks," I muttered, not looking up, my focus locked on the file as if it held the answers to all the questions she hadn't been ready to give me. Frustration and relief churned together in my chest, a storm of emotion I couldn't quite settle. She'd been a mystery to me from the start, a puzzle I couldn't solve but couldn't let go of either.

And now that I finally had the truth in my hands, one thing was clear—I'd still choose her. Every time. No matter the name, no matter the past, she was *mine.*

After a moment of somewhat tense silence, I peered over at Rowan. It was sudden, but the change of topic was needed. "Quit being an ass to her. If this is still the same girl, the one you bullied throughout all of your guys' childhood and school years, then lay off." The man didn't have a lick of luck when it came to dating and courting partners with how rough and tough he was.

Well, maybe that might be a bit harsh to say. He had a game, just not when it mattered.

"Take her on a fucking date, whatever she likes. Dinner and a movie, movie and a dinner, shopping and meals, a picnic, hike, hike and a picnic, take her shooting if that's her thing. Honestly, the options are endless. You just gotta put your little brain cells into it." Sometimes, I felt a little bad for the poor, fumbling man when it came to his relationship endeavors.

Groaning exasperatedly, Rowan slumped in his seat on the couch, throwing his hands up in defeat and letting them drape across the back of the leather furniture. "I can't just take her out on a fucking date," he bit out with a frustrated scoff.

Lowering the papers, I quirked an eyebrow at him. "Why not?" Seriously, what was so hard about shoving a girl into your car and dragging her out to a restaurant?

Shooting up from the couch, he glared at me softly before flipping me off. "Because I can't. Cele won't just go on a date with me just because I ask nicely," he grumbled with a deflated exhale.

"Then don't ask, just do," I told him nonchalantly with a carefree shrug of my shoulders. "I mean, you've shoved her around enough. What's the harm in shoving her into your car to take her to a nice dinner gonna do?" I seriously don't see why he was having such an issue with such a mundane thing.

Although, I guess I could give him better ideas that were less... Barbaric... As some would say.

Sighing, I set the papers down on the table, leaned over, and propped my elbow on my crossed knees. "'Kay, here's what you do if you want to be a charming sap." Well, the idea in my mind seemed charming enough for him to pull off. "Get someone to babysit her kid, or plan a kid-friendly date, sweeten her with her favorite flowers, tell her to get dolled up because you're taking her out, and you're not taking no for an answer."

"See, what'd I tell you, Row? You just gotta be assertive with her like you always have," Max chimed in with a playful scoff and hit to his cousin's shoulder.

Rolling his eyes, Rowan let out another long groan. "The point of me charming her is so I'm not bullying her anymore." Running his hands down his face, he gripped it for a second before letting them fall into his lap. "I don't want to shove her around like that, especially after she got out of a shitty relationship with a guy who did just the same, only worse."

"Then you do it more gently and lovingly," I threw at him in a 'no-duh' kind of way. "It's the intention behind the actions." Of course, that was easier said than done, but if he was serious about this woman, then he'd pull it off. "Or just stick to what works with you two. I mean, if you've pushed her away before with your bullying, then pull her towards you with the same methods. Bully her into loving you. Problem solved."

Grumbling to himself, Rowan sulked for a good while before directing his attention to me. "What are you going to do with Eliza and the information?" He sounded a little too interested in my diabolical plans for a man of the law.

Keeping quiet, I stared at the stacks of paper for a quick minute before letting out a defeated sigh and running a hand through my hair. "I don't know." It was the honest answer.

"Are you going to confront her about it? I mean, she's been lying to you this whole time," Max commented with a lopsided frown, clearly not envying me.

"But for good reason." Surprisingly, Rowan took a side rather than stay quiet. "I'm not saying it's right, but she kind of has a right in this situation. If she's hiding from that piece of work and trying to start anew, then I kind of don't see too much harm."

"Oooh, someone's becoming a bad cop," I teased with a snickering chuckle. It was a bad attempt to displace myself, but I felt like a floating boat in the middle of nowhere.

I was torn and confused.

A part of me wanted to be upset at her, but the reasonable side of me, the half that loved her dearly, made it impossible to hold any ill feelings towards my darling Eliza. Rowan also had a good point, not that I'd admit it out loud.

What harm did Eliza's omission cause?

It wasn't as if she hid it because she had some malicious intent. She hid things for her sake and Asher's. I mean, if I had a past like that, I'd want to forget it ever happened.

The only reason why I was even remotely upset was the fact she didn't trust me enough to let me in.

Also, I was upset because I had no idea what to do in this situation. Should I confront her about it? If I did, then how would I even go about it? Things like this didn't pop up with a simple Google search, so I'd have to figure out some lie or elaborate story of sorts as to how I even found out despite her efforts to hide it from me.

On the other hand, leaving this alone didn't feel completely right, either. Something had to be said, no? Even if it was her past, it was still a huge part of her life that I deserved to know about.

"Don't even think about dusting the bastard. He's a lieutenant in criminal investigations over there, so if you try anything, someone is going to notice," Rowan commented with his flat eyes trained on me. "Not that you should be doing that shit in the first place."

"As if you're one to talk," I remarked, glaring at him smugly. "Don't forget who you're associated with and what we've done for you." Not trying to blackmail him or anything, but I wanted to knock him back down to my level.

He may be a damn man of the law, but his actions have bloodied his hands as much as mine. Directly, he's never murdered anyone, but he's called on many favors from me over the recent years by having people implicated for his cases or straight up asking me to get rid of some scumbag. So, the good ol' police captain wasn't oh so lawful.

"Well, knowing you, you're not going to let the poor sap live." Rowan rolled his eyes and scoffed at me.

"Oh, as if you're going to let your girl's husband get away with beating her black and blue," Max commented, shooting a knowing look at his cousin.

Scowling, Rowan turned his head at Max, burning his beady green orbs into Max. "Don't sound like you're innocent in any of this either. You have any idea how paranoid I was after covering up for you?"

Clearing my throat loudly and purposefully, I garnered both of their attention. "Listen, we're all in the same boat." Rowan's tense shoulders earned him a pointed look from me to keep him quiet. "Whether we like it or not, what's done has been done, so there's no changing any of that fact. All we can do now is think of what to do moving forward."

"You mean plan another murder?" Rowan snarked in a very sarcastic voice.

"IF!" I hardened my glare at Rowan. "If it comes to that, then yes."

Alright, it wasn't a matter of if but when, because like hell would I let this bastard get away with harming Eliza. I just didn't know how I'd do it yet. The fact that James was quite high in ranking with the police department and probably had a very well-known presence would make his murder trickier to pull off.

Sighing heavily, I ran a hand through my hair before standing up. "Well, you two go make yourselves at home. I'm going to get some business done while Eliza and Asher are still napping," I told the two before walking away with Eliza's papers in hand. "I'll be in the office if you need me."

I needed some time to myself to mull over this new information and formulate a plan to get rid of her soon-to-be ex-husband. Also, I needed to figure out what to do about Eliza and her past. I debated mentally whether or not to pry at her or just let it slide. Either way, things could or would get messy; it came down to which mess I wanted to clean up.

God damn it, Eliza darling...

I wasn't frustrated or upset with her because there really wasn't anything reasonable to hold against her. There had been no harm in her keeping all of this from me. Unlike my secret, which I intended to never let her in on. The moment a word about Eliza got around, my enemies would make her a target to get at me. Reasonably, I should let her know so she could decide if she wanted to stay in this relationship or get out... But I was never reasonable when it came to Eliza, so too fucking bad, for her that was.

I mean, if worse came to worst, locking her away in the house was always a viable option. She didn't need to work, and she could get plenty of fresh air and sunlight through an open window.

No way would I ever let Eliza go. If it came down to it, I'd deal with her hatred for me controlling her life. She could be mad at me all she wanted if it got to that point, I'd gladly take it to keep her alive and happy.

Just as I managed to pull myself out of my thoughts long enough to focus on Eliza's actual files, my office door opened following some soft knocks. Irritation furrowed my brows for a split second before the sight of Eliza dissipated it. Her small and tired voice barely carried through the air. "Bub? Can I be with you right now? I'm lonely." Slipping in, she rubbed her eyes lightly as she waited for my response.

Relaxing with a smile, I nodded and waved her over. "As if I can ever say no to you." Call me a fucking simp for her, I didn't care, but as long as she was satisfied, that was all that mattered to me. "Is something bothering you, little rose?" I could feel concern weighing my face down as I watched her shuffle over to me.

Eliza chewed at her bottom lip for a minute before sighing heavily. "I feel stupid for being bothered by it, though, so I don't want to trouble you when you're working," she admitted with a small frown before plopping herself down in my lap.

Slipping her legs around me, she straddled my body and fitted herself right into me, relaxing after burying her face into my neck. "You smell so good, like wood and hot chocolate," she murmured against my neck. "And like fresh laundry."

Chuckling, I stroked the back of her head a bit before wrapping an arm around her, leaving a free one to work. Was it kind of risky to be going through her file with her literally right on my lap? Probably, but it wasn't as if she'd paid any attention.

Turning my head, I kissed the top of hers. "Take my cock out and sit on it, darling," I spoke against her, making her squirm a little in my lap. Nudging my nose around, I found my way to her ear, nipping at it playfully before whispering, "I want to feel you around me while I work, and I want to be ready to throw you on my desk to fuck and fill you after I'm done."

Her tired hands were quick to scurry down my body to my pants, pulling the waistband down to pull my soft cock out. While she hovered over me, I carefully pulled her panties off from under her outfit—one of my shirts on her fun-sized body.

My arm around her waist tightened at the feeling of her hot tightness surrounding my cock. It was a bit of an awkward struggle for a moment, to get my soft cock inside her, but she managed. *"Brava ragazza,"* I praised her sweetly, kissing her neck some. "I won't be long, promise."

Humming softly and nodding, Eliza kissed my cheek before leaning against me again. Soon, her soft and even breaths tickled my neck, and I had to look down to check if she was awake or not. A small frown of concern pulled at my lips when I saw her sleeping face. How tired was she to fall asleep so easily against me like this? Usually, she stayed awake for her fucking whenever I had her warm my cock.

Oh well, more fun for me.

I studied her profile for a long while until I felt the words blur in my mind. As much as I wanted to keep chugging the information in, nothing stuck. So, that was a clear indicator to stop for the day. Besides, it was not like it was anything dire. Knowing about Eliza's past was more of a personal thing that satisfied my curiosity.

Pushing all of that aside, I looked down at my sleeping beauty for a loving minute before opening one of my drawers to pull out a bottle of lube and a small vibrator. Carefully, I shifted down a little in my chair to get her ass in the air and exposed. God, the temptation to spank her juicy ass ached at my hands and fingers as I took my sweet time looking down at her round globes.

I felt kind of silly for staring so long to the point where I almost forgot what I'd planned to do, but I couldn't help it. Her creamy ass was too much to resist, especially when it bounced from my thrusts when I'd take her from behind.

Throwing my head back with an internal groan, I let my need for her booty win. With a mind of their own, my hands slid down her body to her plush bottom, gripping handfuls of it and squeezing until her cheeks paled. I had to resist spanking her, though. I didn't want to wake her quite yet.

So, reluctantly, I released her ass cheeks. I kept one arm anchored around her while I grabbed the bottle of lube with my other hand. The soft crack of the bottle opening filled the air for a split second, making my heart race when Eliza squirmed a little against me. A second passed, and I let out a breath of relief when my beauty stayed sleeping.

Carefully, I squeezed some lube onto her ass before closing the bottle and setting it back on my desk. Slowly and gently, I spread the lube with my fingers, paying special attention to her little puckered hole. Steadily, I slipped a finger into her tight asshole, gritting my teeth to hold back my groan of victory as I enjoyed the feeling of her forbidden walls around my digit.

Dragging out a sharp breath, I slowly fingered her ass while biting my lip to keep myself quiet. The thought of what I'd do next brought a dark grin to my face as I continued to work her tight hole. I might get some bite from her later about it, but it was all fair game to me because I wouldn't be breaking any limits of hers.

After a few more careful thrusts of my finger, I pulled out and grabbed the small anal toy. Rubbing it against her, I used the smeared lube and her natural juices to coat the small dildo-like toy before mindfully inserting it into her. I doubted she'd stay asleep through this, but I wasn't sure.

That hope flew out the window the moment her body squirmed under me with a sharp breath and small groan. A part of me wanted her to slump back against me and slumber away so I could indulge my somnophilia some more, but the other half wanted her to wake up and fully react to her ass being taken by something other than my finger for a change.

The latter desire won out as her eyes fluttered open and she whimpered in my arms. Her looped arms tightened around my neck, and the feeling of her nails biting me through my shirt followed shortly after. "No, it's too much." Her hips jerked away from the toy, but she didn't get very far since the movement only dug her deeper into my body, and further onto my aching cock. "I can't take your cock and that at the same time." No matter how much she whined, she made no move to try and stop me, nor did she utter her safe word.

Keeping my other arm slung across her back, I trapped her against my body while I pulled one of her ass cheeks apart. "Just a small toy, you can take it, little rose," I whispered deeply and sweetly against her temple with kisses for extra effect. "You're doing so good already. It's more than halfway in, and your greedy ass is trying to take more." Alright, maybe the part about the toy being small was a bit of a lie, but it was when compared to my cock.

"Just breathe, darling, breathe. Just a little more. You can take it. I know you can." Leaning my head back a bit, I nudged her face to look at my proud smile. "You know why?" I asked in a smooth and warm voice.

Biting her bottom lip through a trembling gasp, she looked at me with melting eyes. "B-because I'm your good girl...?" Her eyes brightened with eagerness for praise as she leaned her face closer to mine.

Nodding with a smile, I leaned down and kissed her softly. "Exactly," I groaned lightly against her lips before biting her bottom one. As I spoke again, my voice gained a rasp to it. "And why else?"

Her breath shuddered against me, her body pressing into me ever so slightly. I half expected her to avoid answering, so when her tiny voice came out, I couldn't help but smile wide and proud. "And because I'm your good little slut." Her body gave a little shiver as the corner of her lips twitched into a flash of a smile.

My smile broke out into a full grin as I kissed her deeply and proudly. "That's my girl." I chuckled against her lips as I pushed the last bit of the toy into her ass, making her gasp and whimper.

"Fuck," I hissed out between gritted teeth when I felt how eagerly her body pulled it in and her tight ring snuggly hugged the base. "So fucking full and tight, darling." I could feel the toy pressing against my aching cock through the thin wall between her pussy and ass.

Turning the toy on low, I held her squirming body tightly with both arms as I looked down at her darkly. "You're going to keep that in until I'm completely done with you tonight, got that?" A groan bubbled in my chest as I felt the muffled vibrations through my cock. "I'm going to fuck and fill this cunt." Snaking a hand down her backside, I walked my fingers along her inner thighs until I found her clit. "Then I'm going to stuff and plug it up with a toy so all my cum stays inside of you while we go eat dinner." Teasingly, I rubbed slow circles against her clit, making her moan softly.

Eliza hid her blushing face into my chest with a gasping nod of her head. "Yes, sir." I loved how compliant and submissive she was when tired.

Don't get me wrong, I loved her little bratty bite at times, but I much preferred her melting at my feet. A part of me felt that she liked that, too, even if she denied it.

Outside of Asher, the only time I'd ever seen her truly at peace was by my side without a worry in the world. She was at her best when she knelt by my side or sat in my lap, listening and obeying my every command without any pushback. Sometimes, I wished she'd let me take care of her more so that she could enjoy her life more. Especially since fully submitting to me brought her so much solace.

The way her body naturally relaxed, not a note of tension to be strung across her body, nor any spec of worry in her dilated eyes. I wanted her in that state always, not flustered and worrying about whatever trivial thing ran through her mind.

Pulling my mind out of my mental hole, I let my senses take in my lovely Eliza as she moved against me in her little struggle to settle. "It feels so weird to have something in both holes like this and something big, too." Her small voice brushed against my sensitive neck right before the feeling of something wet and sharp pricked along its length.

Gripping her bubbly cheeks with a low groan, I rolled my hips into her, giving some lazy thrusts to encourage her. "Ride me a bit, darling. Slowly." I needed to get my mind in a better space before I could fuck her properly.

I knew it'd be a tight fit and feel fucking amazing with her ass stuffed, but fuck did I underestimate how delightful it'd feel. If I bent her over my desk now and went at her, I'd blow in a few thrusts.

Shakily, Eliza lifted her hips with a breathy moan. "I might come if I ride you," she whimpered with a soft cry, staying up and refusing to bring herself back down on my impatient cock.

Sliding a hand up her body, I stroked her cheek lovingly. "No," I said in a firm voice, smiling at her warmly in a smug way. "You won't because I said so, and your body knows better than to disobey me." At least her training had been good so far.

Once she managed to get ahold of herself, there wasn't an orgasm out of line. Speaking of training, though...

Her body shuddered at my wicked grin as I leaned up to her. The small struggle from her to move away caused me to quickly grab her face to hold it firm. Teasingly, I brushed my lips across her trembling ones, kissing the edges of her lips but never fully taking them. My lustful eyes locked with hers in an intense gaze, and my tongue danced in my mouth with a need to utter a single word as she slowly rode my cock.

Not yet though.

Seeing her bated breaths as her nervous eyes looked at me with such anticipation was too sweet. Also, the more tension, the better the orgasm, in my opinion.

Salacious ardor filled my mouth as the word hung on my tongue, ready to dart out like a snake's tongue. Tightness clenched at my chest as my breathing paced out to match my lover's the more I tortured myself for my own enjoyment. My throat threatened to strangle itself as the ache of my dominant voice fought to be let out.

"Crash."

Chapter 21
Eliza

"*CRASH.*"

And that I did.

The crushing pain of rapture assaulted my body the instant he said the command in that deep, dominating voice of his. Every fiber of my being bent to the single word, snapping. And all I could do was moan helplessly while I rode out the waves of my orgasm.

I don't know how or when it became possible, but somehow, we'd managed to condition my body to orgasm on command. I felt a little stupid for laughing and mocking him about the whole thing when he first brought it up. The idea had sounded like he was going to Pavlov me or some shit, which seemed ridiculous.

Yeah, not so ridiculous, obviously.

Thinking about the process behind it all made it sound like a fantasy you would see in porn or read in fiction. I mean, to go from nothing to an orgasm because of a simple word or command? Come on, saying it still sounded weird and unbelievable. Yet somehow it happened.

I could be sitting there on the couch doing nothing but watching TV, completely not aroused in the slightest, but the moment he said *that* word in a very specific tone, my entire body ignited. It might not be as intense as an orgasm gotten through hard work, but it was an orgasm nonetheless.

Biting my bottom lip, I sucked in a sharp breath and let my hips drop back down on him the moment my orgasm simmered down. "Sir, please, don't," I begged him with desperate eyes when I saw the way his clouded up with so much dark and playful lust.

It was so hard to keep ahold of myself right now with him in my cunt and the vibrator in my ass. Then, the way my hard nipples brushed and scraped against the shirt I wore didn't help to keep my body anchored. I burned with an all-consuming passion from the endless assault of pleasure coming at me from every angle.

I couldn't escape. There was no escape.

All my holes were occupied—the toy in my ass, his cock in my cunt, and my mouth was busy keeping up with his lips and tongue. The whole front side of my body was in a constant state of stimulation as I rubbed against him with every little movement, and my poor nipples burned with so much pleasure I wanted to rip my shirt off to pinch at them. His deft hands started to love on every inch of my imperfect body as if I were a masterpiece to be cherished, and I was addicted to the way he adored me despite my flaws.

"That's it, darling, nice and slow," he smugly encouraged me with a chuckle and some butterfly kisses. "Just keep moving, and no coming." I was jarred a bit from his 'little' encouraging thrust, causing my body to slap against his with a small yelp.

Getting a grip on myself, I steadied my hands against his chest and shoulder, holding on to easier slide myself up and down his thick member. It was hard to keep my movements smooth, because I was too focused on the strange but pleasurable sensations in my ass. Of course, just when I thought I'd gotten to a point where it felt somewhat normal to have both my holes stuffed, he pulled out a new trick.

Tension tightened my body as I instinctively clenched around the toy when I felt it move. "Adam!" I squeaked, gripping the front of his shirt with a moan as I jerked my hips, attempting to escape the toy's thrusts.

"Oops, forgot to mention it does more than vibrate," Adam mocked me with a laugh before hauling us up.

In a swift motion, he swiped everything to the floor and laid me out in the cleared spce. "Legs on the desk. I want them spread nice and wide for me," he said in a husky voice, slapping my ass to move me along.

Oh God, it was so weird. I was so afraid the toy would slip out as I propped my feet up on the edge of the desk. That or that it would come out somehow when Adam started to fuck me senseless.

A trembling exhale left my parted lips, my body flinching at the feeling of his lips against my nervous body. "Eliza darling, relax. You are safe with me. Whatever happens, happens." His reassuring voice and kisses soothed my racing heart with each passing second until my breathing evened out.

Slipping a finger down between my parted legs, he sought out my swollen clit and softly stroked it with the pad of his thumb. "Breathe. That's it. That's my good girl." His raspy praise shivered my whole body with ease and pleasure. "Settle."

Oh God, fuck you.

My body immediately complied. All the tension in my body melted away like ice thrown into a fire at the command.

Besides 'Crash,' the other command he'd conditioned me to follow was 'Settle.' It was kind of straightforward. Settle was a command that got my body to relax fully and fall into a state of constant arousal, and it was typically given whenever I was to kneel by his side or be on his lap while he worked. Well, there were some other occasions, like when I'd get a little too feisty, and he wanted me more compliant to really fuck me to another headspace—subspace.

Hooking my fingers around the edge of the desk, I braced myself the moment I caught the dark glint in his eyes. Settling his hands on my inner thighs, he squeezed them with a bite of his lip before pressing my legs wider. With a firm yank, he jerked my body toward him until my ass hung off the edge.

A few soft clicks of a button echoed, and I felt my face twist with shock. Everything happened so fast that I couldn't process it. One second, there was nothing but the slight thrust and buzz from the toy and no movement from Adam. The next thing I knew, tidal waves of pleasure rushed me. I could feel my mouth open, but no sound came out.

Or so I thought.

The sound of my moans, Adam's grunts pleasure, our bodies slapping against each other, his dirty and degrading words, and the desk scraping against the floor didn't hit me until seconds later, when I got my bearings. Apparently, during my daze, he ripped open the front of my shirt too, exposing my breasts and grabbing them. "Hey, eyes on me, slut." His harsh words made me snap my eyes to his grinning face. "That's it, such a good girl for listening to me." He chuckled almost mockingly as he continued to pound away at me. "You're taking me so well, darling, and the toy too. So, fucking good for me."

Fucking hell, I hated how he could easily switch from being mean with his tongue to licking my wounds. I should probably look more closely at myself for liking the degradation and praising. Like, I really couldn't pick one or the other. It had to be both.

"It's so much," I whimpered, feeling the wood under my palms creak a little with my death grip.

Chuckling, he stilled himself in me for a moment to breathe. "If it makes you feel any better, feeling the toy moving and vibrating against my cock doesn't make it easy for me to hold back." Yet, he still reached over the remote control and turned the thing on higher—jerk!

Throwing my head back, I let out a long moan. "Please, sir, can I come?" The knot in my body ached so painfully, and every thrust of the toy and shock from the vibration did nothing to help the rising tension. "Please." I knew the pleading and sweet look only worked half the time, but I had to try to get some relief.

Unfortunately, it didn't work this time.

"No, not until I do or say so," he told me in a firm voice before his hips started moving again. "I wanna work you up until you really can't take it. I want to see your whole body shake, your eyes roll, your mouth screaming open, and her cunt milking me when you finally snap."

Oh fuck.

A shiver of excitement trickled down my spine at the thought of the intense orgasm to come, and honestly, I couldn't complain because those were the best. "Okay, sir." One big orgasm... I could hold out.

Of course, that was easier said than done. Just when I thought he'd give me a little mercy, he grabbed my hips with one hand and angled them to easier ram his fat cock right into my cervix. Surprise, surprise, it turns out I love having my cunt bullied to no end, cervix smashing included. Seriously, what was wrong with me? I shouldn't be enjoying the jolts of toe-curling pain that made my body purr with delight.

"Just a little more, darling. I'm almost there." Adam's heavy breaths strained out between his forceful thrusts. "Fuck!" His hips started to jerk out of rhythm with his erratic breathing. "Now! Come, right now!" he groaned through gritted teeth. "Crash! Now!" The dip in his tone, the subtle switch, was the final push I needed, along with his permission.

Every inch of my body ached painfully from my orgasm tensing my muscles. Any control I had over my body disappeared as my hormones and instincts took the strings. All I could do was accept the endless waves of soul-shattering ecstasy. At least it wasn't a full trip to subspace this time. Otherwise, I'd be fucked. The euphoria was enough to take me on a small spin as I floated on cloud nine, giving me a good bit of a high before the drop came.

On the upside, I easily ignored the drop this time. The downside to that upside: I ignored the fall because of Adam, who shoved a whole fucking dildo into me! Also, the toy in my ass never stopped either; it still vibrated my sensitive walls and rubbed at areas I never knew were pleasurable.

Only a second passed before I felt myself being strung up again. "S-sir, oh fuck, I can't sit through dinner like this." It'd be torture!

The dildo in my freshly fucked cunt twisted around and thrust inside of me while the outer part latched onto my poor clit. All I wanted to do was sit there with my legs spread and orgasm to my delight. Fuck dinner. There was no way I could focus on anything else besides my next orgasm.

Like the little asshole he was, Adam smiled innocently at me as he picked up my discarded panties and pulled them back on me. "Don't worry, you don't have to sit through the whole thing. Just eat, finish at whatever pace you want, and then I'll take you to our room." Even though he had a kind smile on his face, his tone inferred something much different.

This night has barely started. This fucking just now was only the damn appetizer. I've yet to have the main course and dessert. Correction: Adam's yet to have me for the main course and dessert. Yeah, I was the fucking feast, and he was the starved beast to devour me.

Fuck me.

And make that fuck me a double because if I had known he had guests over, then I would have tried my damn best to keep my mouth shut or keep my voice down. God, it was so fucking awkward to walk out—correction, to be carried out—to two snickering men in the living room. No doubt in my mind they heard me and pieced things together. It was even more awkward to sit around a dinner table with everyone having idle chit-chat with toys shoved up my pussy and ass. At least Adam was merciful enough to turn the toys down to the lowest setting.

Tsk, as if it's any help...

Also, at least I didn't have to worry about feeding Asher because Adam and his buddies took turns with making sure my son had his fill of food.

"Eliza, are you okay? Or was Adam a little too mean to you in there?" Max teased me with a cheeky grin and snicker, his hand still mindlessly waving Asher's toy before him.

Sinking into my chair in embarrassment, I glanced over at Adam for some help as I sat there red as a cherry. Thankfully, he didn't let me suffer much. "Alright, knock it off. I don't go teasing you and your girl, so leave her alone to finish dinner in peace." He chided his friend while hiding his smug smirk.

Rowan leaned over to Max, nudging his arm with an elbow. "Cause it's the only peace she's gonna get tonight." I faintly heard him snicker to his cousin, who sputtered out a laugh that he quickly covered up with a cough.

Someone kill me right now.

I silently begged the high heavens to save me from the tragedy as I scarfed down the last bites of my food. Although, speaking of my food... I gnawed on the prongs of my fork a little as I stared at the empty plate. I was full but not stuffed like usual. If I really thought hard about it, I could've sworn there was less on my plate today. Unless I've gotten used to him upping my portions again, which I doubted.

"Finish your drink, *mia rosa,*" Adam commanded me, drifting his eyes over to the half-finished glass of juice sitting before me.

Down turning my eyes, I picked up the glass and downed the rest of it before looking back up at Adam for some help. Like hell would I march my ass to bed with vibrators up my holes. I probably won't be able to make it two full steps without needing to lean on something for support or full-on crumpling to the floor in a trembling mess.

Adam's eyes softened in a silent praise, making my lips curl in a happy smile. Keeping quiet, I watched him get up and go over to me. "I'll be right back. I just need to get her settled into bed because she's had a long day." I assumed his words were meant for the others, even if he didn't look directly at them when he spoke.

"I thought her long day err night barely started," Max joked with a quick laugh, earning a pointed look from Adam.

Without a reply to his friends, Adam swiftly picked me up in his arms. Chuckling, he looked at Asher and called out to him. "Asher, say good night to mommy," he told the toddler in a soft and baby like voice.

Asher's head peeped up at us, his little toothy smile spreading wide as he waved at us. "Nigh nigh!" Yeah, that was as good as we would get from him for now, but it was more than adorable.

"Mama!" he called out after us, making Adam stop mid-step so we could both look at Asher.

As loudly as possible, Asher blew us a kiss with a huge grin. Then, he went back to his toys on the tray of his high chair as if we didn't exist—typical Asher.

Rolling my eyes, I lightly patted Adam's chest to urge him back to the task at hand. "Are you going to get him to bed in a bit?" I questioned with a tilt of my head.

His body trembled with his soft chuckle as he kissed my head. "Yeah, I'll get him down after I get you situated," Adam assured me with a warm smile. "The others will take care of him in the meanwhile."

Melting into him with a content hum, I admired him through my lashes with obsessed eyes. "Thank you," I muttered through my big and grateful smile.

"For?" It was adorable how genuinely confused he was.

Keeping my appreciative smile, I stared at him adoring for a few seconds before replying, "For everything, especially when it comes to Asher." I still didn't know what to do about that whole subject. "I know you said you're fine with him calling you 'dada' and all, but..."

Was I comfortable with it? I don't know. I truly didn't know. I couldn't work out that mess in my mind without throwing myself down into a spiral.

It was cute and sweet that Asher saw Adam as his father, and it was even more damning and heart-melting how Adam was fully excepting of Asher and wanted to take on that role in Asher's life.

Honestly, if my left wasn't such a fucking mess, then I'd have no issues with it. If James didn't exist or if we had actually divorced and he left me the fuck alone, then it wouldn't be a problem either. Too bad my life wasn't that simple.

"Eliza darling, if you aren't fine with it, then please let me know so we can start correcting Asher sooner rather than later." Adam was so understanding, and that made my frustration fester more. "As much as I love Asher and want to be in his life in a bigger capacity than his mother's lover, you are his mother, so you have the final say."

God damn you, you fucking perfect asshole! Ugh! I gotta punch you in your handsome face to make some part of you unlovable!

Clenching my jaw, I held my anger in as I let out a deep breath. "I don't have a problem with you wanting to be more to Asher, and if I'm being honest, I want that..." My voice trailed out with my train of thought.

"But?" Adam urged with a curious and concerned voice as he carried me across the threshold of our room.

But I'm still a married woman with a killer ex out there looking for me, and I don't know how to tell you the truth without losing you.

Well, I don't know if James wanted to murder me, but I was more than willing to bet my life on it, given his temper and personality.

Giving Adam a pressed smile, I pushed the subject aside with a shake of my head. "Another time, please." I looked at him pleadingly in hopes it'd get him to agree.

Reluctantly, he nodded his head with a flat hum. Even though he agreed, I could see through his flat smile and his jaded eyes. He wasn't happy with it, but he held his tongue. The disappointed glaze over his eyes felt like a damn punch to the gut, though, and I wanted to go curl in a corner and wallow in my shame.

Without a word, he took me over to the sex chair in our room, setting me down on the padded furniture. Then, he stood before me, looking down at me with an unreadable expression for a long minute that got my heart clenching in fear as it raced in my chest. Before I could ask him anything, he spoke, "You've been doing so well, little rose. It's time for a reward."

Uh oh. I did not like the cheekiness in his voice.

Leaning down, he trapped me between his arms, making me face my predator. "I am going to strap you down, spread your lovely legs, put a toy on your clit and tits, and have the machine fuck both your holes while I handle some business with the boys." The way his eyes grew more feral with his crazed grin got me shrinking away from him into the chair with a nervous whimper. "I don't want you holding anything back. All your orgasms, all your moans, your screams, everything, I want it all. If I don't hear you clear across the house, then we're going to have some problems tonight. Got that, darling?"

Whimpering, I leaned my head away from his wild grin. "H-how is this a reward? It sounds like torture." It was torture!

Fuck, I could already imagine all the mind-searing pain from the overstimulation. Just the mere thought of orgasming so many times back-to-back made my whole body ache with exhaustion. I should put a stop to this insanity before it starts, yet I couldn't bring myself to. Just one word, one word, and this would all end.

But no.

The crazy part of me wanted all of that to happen. I wanted to be in a world of endless euphoria. Not a thought in the world besides when I'd come next. Pure fucking bliss.

His eyes calmed along with his lip-splitting grin. "If at any point you need a break or want it to stop, just shout the safe word and I'll be in here faster than you can blink," he told me with a calming smile. "And there will also be a quick release and emergency shut-off for you too." His eyes drifted over to the arm of the chair, where a flip latch was located. "I'll be keeping an eye out for you as well, through the camera." His body leaned to the side, and his head turned back to look at a small camera propped up on a little tripod.

Swallowing the lump in my throat, I looked at him with trembling eyes as I fully propped my legs up on the padded straddles. "You won't be long, right?" If he planned on going out to the club or bar for hours on end, then fuck this shit.

Amused, he chuckled and shook his head. Reaching up, he stroked the side of my head and cheek. "No, maybe two hours or so," he replied before proceeding to strip me and strap me down to the chair with the built-in restraints.

Once he had me situated, he flipped the safety a few times to make sure it worked before looking at me. "Can you reach and operate the safety?"

Turning my head, I peered down at my wrists and the latches on either side that sat next to my fingers. With a small wiggle of my hand and digits, I easily hooked my fingers under the latch and easily flipped it open. Focusing back on Adam, I flashed him a reassuring smile. "I'm good." Well, as good as a girl was gonna get with an impending orgasm fest on the horizon.

Leaning down, he kissed my forehead before leaving my side. Seconds later, the sliding of drawers and shuffling of objects filled the air, making my nerves ramp up in anticipation at the thought of what he was grabbing.

Adam looked like a damn kid on Christmas coming back with an armful of sex toys and a machine in one hand. Beaming at me with jittering excitement, he eagerly attached the vibrating nipple clamps to my already hard buds, making me wince a little when he tightened them a little too much. "Ouch, a little looser, please." It bit me just a tad too much for my liking.

"Sorry," he apologized, quickly adjusting them. "How about now?" His worried eyes peered up at me as he kept his fingers around the clamp.

Breathing slowly, I relaxed as much as possible, letting the slight sting of pulsating pleasure spread throughout my body. "Yeah, it's good," I replied after a few seconds of debating. "You can continue."

His studious eyes lingered on my face for a long moment before he slowly moved down my body. He wasted no time pulling the toys out of my cunt and ass, making me groan and hiss a little at the sudden emptiness and lack of stimulation. Bracing myself, I shut my eyes in anticipation. I caught a glimpse of the dildos he picked out, and it would be a tight fit.

Much to my surprise, the feeling of my cunt being stuffed wasn't what came. "Oh, Adam, fuck..." I gasped happily, relaxing at the feeling of his warm tongue against my aching pussy. "Oh, bub, you don't have to," I moaned breathlessly as he lapped at every inch of me.

Leaving me hanging on the edge, he got up to his feet and stood over me, looking at me with eyes full of animalistic lust. My trembling lips parted further when he reached a hand up and grabbed my face, and he didn't let me budge one bit when he leaned down and smashed his lips against mine in a sloppy kiss.

Oh fuck.

The taste of his cum mixed with my juices invaded my mouth the moment he forced his way into my mouth and fed me nearly a mouthful of it.

God, it was so fucking filthy but hot. I was a fucking slut for his cum, so I couldn't help myself from tangling my tongue with his and shoving my way into his mouth to get every last drop. I got so caught up in our addictive taste that I found myself leaning toward him when he pulled away.

Then, with a chuckle, he stroked my cheek with his thumb. "I'll fill that pretty mouth of yours later if you're too sore to take me in your cunt or ass," he assured me with a wicked grin.

Stepping away from me, he picked up a strappy leather belt and put it on me. An internal groan dragged its way through my body when I realized what it was. A damn orgasm belt. Yeah, this would be the longest two hours of my life or the fastest, who knows.

A reflexive flinch jolted my body when I felt the head of the wand vibrator press firmly against my sensitive clit before it got strapped in place with the belt.

Breathing deeply, I balled my shaky hands up when I felt something thick rub against my tightened asshole. I might be overreacting a bit, but the thought of a dildo going up my ass for the first time was a little nerve-wracking. It was longer than the toy earlier and a little bigger, but it paled in comparison to what Adam had in his pants.

"*Mia rosa*, breathe. You have to relax. Otherwise, it won't go in easy." His soothing voice did nothing but make me tense up more. "You'll be fine, darling. You're going to take it so well. I know you will." Don't know if his little encouragement helped either. "Come on, be my good girl, and relax." His words whispered across my lips before he took my breath away with a passionate kiss.

For a moment, we kissed and made out with each other heavily, which, I'll admit, got me to relax. At least, it was enough for him to slip the tip of the toy in. "Oh fuck, wish you could see yourself right now. Your tight little ass looks so wonderful stretched around this toy." His marveling eyes refused to leave my ass as he pushed more of the toy into me until I begged him to stop because I felt so fucking full.

Of course, what a fool of me to think that'd be it. Damn asshole proceeded to pull the toy back and fuck me slowly with it for a bit before leaving it be to grab the last toy he had brought out.

This time, I couldn't hold the exasperated groan back when it clicked in my brain. "Babe, you're going to break me. There's no way that'll fit with my ass this full." Whimpering, I tried to buck my hips away when he teasingly rubbed the tip of the dildo against my entrance.

Out of all the toys he could've picked, he just had to go with the replica of his fucking cock. He could've been nice and picked a smaller one, considering how I'd be double stuffed.

Fucking asshole.

Looking at him nervously, I felt my breath hitch in my throat when he smiled at me innocently in a wicked way. "Don't worry, we'll make it fit." Then, I felt the burn of pleasure as he pushed the tip in, stretching my crowded cunt.

"Ahh! Fuck! Adam!" Stunned, I gripped the armrests and writhed in my spot as I stared up at the ceiling with wide eyes. "Adam!" Oh fuck, it hurt so much, but there was a twisted joy to it.

The undeniable rush of pleasure slammed my body, making me tremble through the aftershocks. "See, you're loving it," Adam mocked me with a snarky sneer. "My little slut can't deny a good cock to her cunt." With a forceful thrust, he shoved the rest of the dildo into my orgasming body, ripping a silent scream from my tensing body as another orgasm shattered me.

I couldn't muster up enough energy or brain power to respond to him. I was too lost to this newfound pleasure that ravaged every inch of my body. This was shit that only happened in porn, so the fact it I was in this situation boggled my mind. Hell, we could probably record this whole thing and throw it up on a porn website and blow up.

So lost in my thoughts and sensations, I didn't realize Adam connected the toys to the fuck machine until he turned the damn thing on. The fucking gall on my man! While I struggled to adjust to having both my holes fucked at once, he stood there grinning like a madman. "Fuck, your slutty little holes are stretching so much to take them both so greedily. I'm almost tempted to stick myself into one to really push you over the edge."

Reaching down, he grabbed the front of his pants, where a very noticeable bulge was, and palmed himself a bit. "If I didn't have plans..." His body shuddered with a shaky exhale. "I'd take your mouth right now. Give my little cum slut a nice load."

Fucking hell that sounded so insane... I fucking loved it. Which was an even more crazy thing. I wasn't this lustful or lewd of a person, so what the hell happened to me? It was crazy how far into things we got sometimes.

Some nights were filled with never-ending passion that was so tender, while other nights were filled with nothing but raw and dirty fucking. As much as I enjoyed our nights of making love to each other, I always found myself craving for the more twisted things deep down. The nights when I was nothing but his little cum dumpster, his whore, his good little slut; those were the nights that really satisfied me to no end.

I craved and loved being nothing but his little fuck doll, only to have him treat me like a fucking queen after he was done slapping my cheeks red and pounding my pussy until I'd be too sore to twitch a muscle. He spoiled me so much after every scene; it was fucking addicting.

Shuffling footsteps pulled me out of my head, and I looked over at Adam in a daze. He pulled his phone out of his pocket and swiped and tapped away at it for a second before looking at me with a mischievous smile. I didn't have enough time to question him because I was too busy moaning at the feeling of all the vibrators turning on and stimulating my nipples and clit. Paired with the increased speed of the machine, I snapped and spiraled into another orgasm.

Thankfully, everything simmered down to a low buzz and slow speed.

Adam's dark and cheery laugh rang through the air and melted in my ear, causing shivers of warmth and excitement to zip through my body.

"Remember, no holding back. If I don't hear you, I turn things up, and if I peek on you and don't see you dripping wet, then I turn it up."

Chapter 22
Adam

IT WAS IMPOSSIBLE NOT to display my smug smirk as I listened to Eliza's cries of pleasure as I went about with Asher's nightly routine. Getting him down for bed was easy, like always. Knock on wood, he's never fought any of us when it came to bedtime.

Once Asher was tucked away, I joined the others in the living area.

"You are one sadistic asshole, you know that?" Max chuckled, shaking his head in mock disbelief at me after Eliza's sobbing died down. "No wonder no girl has lasted with you," he joked with a playful scoff, earning a jab to the shoulder from me.

No, my little sadistic streak was not the reason for my past relationships failing. All of my past engagements have all ended amicably. Also, I really didn't feel deeply for any of the past women I've been with. The only person who has ever lit any kind of spark or pure desire within me was Eliza.

Scoffing, Rowan picked up his beer from the coffee table. "And you both call me cruel," he grumbled with a roll of his eyes.

Both Max and I couldn't help but turn our heads at Rowan with a look of utter astonishment. Once, twice, the two of us stared at him in a brief silence before Max broke it with a dry chuckle. "Now, I mean this in the best way possible, but you treat your girl like a sack of shit in the sheets." With a smug expression, Max leaned back on the couch, beer in hand.

Unbothered, Rowan gave us a shrug of his shoulders before taking a few swings of his drink. "Can't help that we both get our rocks off to it." Sighing, he relaxed and slumped a bit in the armchair. "Not like we're that bad. We keep things mostly in private or at the club, and it's not like she enjoys any of it from anyone else. Also, not like it goes as far as me pissing on her or anything."

"You can do all of that, but can't ask her out on a fucking date?" I asked in disbelief, eyeing the grumpy police captain suspiciously.

Sighing, he ran a hand down his face and stared up at the ceiling. "I don't want to be fucking bully to her all the time, and yes, our relationship is hot as fuck, but it's just missing that softer touch..." His words trailed out into a string of grumbles. "I want to be nice to her, but I don't know how."

Leaning back in my seat, I threw my arms across the back of the couch. "Does she want you to be nice to her?" I questioned with a quirked brow.

Rowan's face twisted in irritation and confusion for a split second before he sputtered a bit in his spot. "O-of course she does! What girl doesn't want their man to be charming and nice to them? What kind of stupid question is that?"

"A stupid question you need an answer to before you go and make a fool of yourself," I deadpanned playfully with a roll of my eyes. "Some girls find nice and charming annoying, some appreciate it to certain extents, and some just want things how they are."

Yes, girls always wanted the nice guy, but as I've learned over the years, there were always stipulations to it. "Just talk to your girl to see what she wants." Communication was the key to every relationship. "My suggestion: take her out on a date, don't give her an option, just give her a date and time to be ready by, take her out, and either have a chit chat with her to lay down the foundation or to lay down the law."

I didn't know much about his girl, so I couldn't give him a firm direction. Maybe she was a headstrong and independent woman who took no shit; if that was the case, then him wrangling her by the neck might not blow over well. On the other hand, if she was like that, then communicating effectively with her to come up with a middle ground would work perfectly.

"Honestly, just tone down the jerky assholeness with her for a night, work something out, then proceed from there." That was probably the best advice I could give him as of now.

"Is that what you did with Eliza?" Rowan asked with a deflated sigh.

Unable to help it, I coughed out a laugh and shook my head. "Oh, fuck no, I didn't." Taking a few seconds to snicker and get the ridiculousness of our situation out of my system, I had to take a few deep breaths to reset myself before speaking up again. "My Eliza is lovely and all, but she's kind of indecisive and stubborn. So, I just kind of took the reins with her."

Running a hand through my hair, I turned my head to look down the hallway for a moment as her moan echoed throughout. "She wouldn't have let me into her life, so I forced my way in." Looking back at Rowan with a lopsided smile full of pity, I continued, "But, like I said, I don't know your girl and your full history with her. So, being forceful like I have been with Eliza might not be the best way for you and her."

Rolling his eyes, Rowan dragged out a low groan before nodding his head in defeat. With a curt chuckle, he looked at me quizzically. "How long do you plan on torturing the poor thing for?"

Flipping my wrist, I checked my watch. "Oh, a while more. I mean, the game's barely started, so might as well enjoy some of it." I chuckled deviously before turning up the volume of the TV—just a little.

I paid no attention to the UFC fight flashing across the screen; my eyes were trained on my phone screen. Lustful hunger for my little rose burned through my veins from seeing Eliza's body writhe as the various toys and machines assaulted it. Fuck, I couldn't wait to have more fun with her using the damn sex-machine. The endless ideas clouded my mind in an instant as I thought about all the ways I could have more than one of her holes stuffed while I'd occupy one or even just sat there to watch her fucked out face.

Keeping to myself for the next torturous hour or so, I counted the long seconds by as I sat there and stewed in my raging arousal. I did think about going to Eliza sooner, but I wanted to see how far she could be pushed. With each orgasm her body shook through, I half expected her to flip the safety or shout her safe word. Yet, she never did, surprisingly. She'd moan loudly or scream, jerk against the restraints, throw her head back and shake it about, but after her orgasm would pass, she'd sink back into the chair.

Now, I did take it easy on her a bit at times, slowing the machine down and turning the intensity of the toys down from the controller on my phone. Of course, there were times when I was a total asshole; watching her scream and freak out with everything turned up to maximum was too much fun for me to stop at one time.

Sighing softly, I got up from the couch. "Alright, well, you guys enjoy the rest of your night." Flashing the two a knowing smile, I made my way to the hallway. "You know where the guest rooms are if you guys want to stay the night."

"Do us a favor and gag Eliza," Max joked with a quick laugh. "Some of us actually want sleep and don't wanna hear your girl be bullied by your monstrosity."

Sneering, I flipped Max off before turning my back to them to go to my bedroom. Standing right outside the door, I stayed like that for a moment to listen to Eliza's sweet moans, letting each cry of pleasure wash down my body to my aching cock. Honestly, if I could—well if I really wanted to—then I'd record her to keep things for my late nights. I threw the idea out, though, because why would I need some virtual thing when I had the real thing right in front of me? Pulling her sounds of pleasure from her with my own hands brought a sense of satisfaction that made my pride swell.

Taking in a deep breath, I centered myself for a second before letting the soft creak of the turning knob falter my anxious heart. Eliza's dazed expression, full of exhaustion and bliss, turned toward me when I stepped in and shut the door behind me. Purposedly taking my time, I stalked up to her with a growing smirk.

The sound of the leather creaking and the metal clinking banged against my heightened ears when I came to a stop inches from her. "Enjoying yourself, darling?" I teased with an evil smirk.

Instead of words coming out of her mouth, a strangled sob of agony and rapture left her sweet lips when they parted. If only I could capture her beautiful face right now. God, I wanted this image of her to last forever. It was so arousing to see her whole body arch as much as possible with her head thrown back in a silent scream. Her sweet brown eyes were nowhere in sight with how far they rolled to the back of her head. Then, her face, fuck, her face was something else.

The way her lips smiled through the shocks of her orgasm and how her tongue stuck out just enough to give her that perfect fucked out expression.

Fuck!

A low growl rumbled from my chest as I quickly stripped myself down to nothing, eager to get my painful cock buried inside of her for some relief.

Guess I wasn't the only one, either.

Eliza instantly kicked into a struggle against her restraints, her hands needily grabbing at the air as she reached in the direction of my twitching dick. "Cock. Your cock, sir. Please... Stuff me, please. Need you so badly." Her words came out jagged with her breaths. "Please," she continued to beg incessantly through her sobbing moans and tears while her body trembled through the shockwaves of pleasure.

Silently, I moved between her legs, careful not to hit the machine. Looking down at her pleading eyes, I waited until another orgasm ravaged her body before stopping the piston going at her cunt. Removing the dildo, I moved the arm of the machine out of the way before fucking her hard and fast with the silicone replica of my dick, making her squeal and whimper as I rammed the thing right into her g-spot.

Abruptly, I pulled the toy out when her body tensed painfully, discarding it onto the ground next to us as she squirted all over the both of us. Not giving her any mercy this time, I quickly pressed my fingers against her clit, rubbing her poor love button vigorously to keep her squirting and gushing. When she started to slow down, I plunged my fingers deep into her, finger fucking her sweet spot hard and fast before withdrawing and rubbing her clit to bring her to another squirting orgasm.

"Sir, please, too much, sir, please." She fumbled out those words between her choking moans and breaths.

Too bad all she could do was take and suffer the pleasure I inflicted upon her.

I pulled a few orgasms from her until both of us were quite soaked with her juices and until she begged me for some mercy. With a few slaps to her quivering pussy, I slammed myself into her with a feral groan as I dug my fingers into her plush thighs. "Oh, this is it, darling. Your body was fucking made for me." So tight and amazing, no matter how many times I fucked and stretched her.

Growling with content, I wasted no time bucking my hips wildly at her. "You're made to be my fucking cock sleeve, aren't you, darling?" Mocking her with a laugh, I reached out and slapped her jiggling breast. "To be my free use whore."

"Yours, all yours," she sputtered helplessly with a long moan. "I'm your personal whore."

Pressing her head back against the chair, she bit out a strangled scream of pleasure as her tight walls gripped me in an orgasm. "Fucking shit!" I hissed through gritted teeth as my pace faltered a bit from the sudden tightness. "I'm not going to last long if you keep squeezing me like that." I seethed in a low growl at her.

I doubt she'd last much longer, though, so maybe it'd be a good thing my fuse would blow sooner rather than later. Gritting my teeth, I slowed my thrusting down and leaned over her body, undoing the leather bindings. Hooking her legs around my waist, I tightened them until she locked them around me. Then, I carefully picked her up, making her groan when I pulled her off the fucking machine.

Whimpering weakly, she threw her arms around my neck and shoulders, clinging onto me for dear life. "Sir, I'm so sore," she mumbled against my neck.

Chuckling softly, I kissed the side of her head as I carefully laid her down on the bed, hanging her ass off the edge. "If you aren't sore after that, then I'd have to give you a lot of props," I teased with a playful shake of my head. "Just a little more, darling." I kissed her tear-stained cheek. "I still need to fill you full of my cum before bed."

The temptation to rip her birth control patch off to give me a chance of knocking her up itched and ached at my fingertips before I shoved it into the recesses of my mind. No children on the plate... yet. As lovely as it would be to get her pregnant and make our family more perfect with our child and sibling for Asher, it was clear that Eliza and I had a lot to work out before we could approach that road.

Leaning down, I pressed my body flush against hers by wrapping my arms tightly around her plush body. Brushing my lips across hers, I looked into her adoring eyes with my tender ones for a long minute. "You are so fucking perfect," I whispered with a doting smile. "I love you so much."

I closed the distance between us with a deep and passionate kiss that stopped time. Nothing mattered at this moment but us, but my Eliza.

Lies and all, she was perfect.

"I." Kiss. "Love." Kiss. "You." Kiss.

Slowly, while I kept my lips locked with hers, I moved my hips. I wanted to indulge both of us for a moment tonight, a little break from our usual wild and crazy fucking. "I love you," I groaned breathlessly against her lips as I continued to make love to her.

It didn't take long for the room to fill up with the sounds of her breathy and blissful moans as I took her with long and deep strokes, being mindful to rub and press my cock against her sweet spots to really draw out every ounce of pleasure from her.

Time became nonexistent as the two of us got lost in each other's loving eyes. Eliza's never said them, those three little words, but she didn't have to. I could see the endless depths of her love for me every time she looked at me, and I caught her. There was no faking the way her eyes lit up with happiness and amazement every time she glanced at me, nor was there any faking the way her whole being would glow whenever we got lost in each other's eyes.

Her love for me was real, and never in a million years could it ever be faked.

And that's all that mattered to me.

She loves me.

I had to remind myself that her adoration and devotion was clear as day in her eyes whenever she looked at me. There was no faking the sparkle and wonder in her eyes with every gaze.

"Bub... Adam, I'm close," she whimpered against my lips. "I don't think I can go anymore after this."

From how exhausted she sounded and the way her eyelids took longer and longer to open back up after every blink, it would surprise me if she didn't pass out after this next orgasm.

Luckily for her, I only had one in me tonight.

Releasing an arm from her body, I slid it up her body to cup her face gingerly. "Then you better give me all you got." I chuckled, smiling against her lips before kissing it.

Picking up my pace and force for the last few thrusts, I brought us both to and over the edge. As we both free-fell into an eternal inferno of pleasure, I felt her squeeze the life out of me. "Fuck!" I strained out a groan into the kiss. "That's it, darling, squeeze out every last drop I got for you."

The searing ecstasy filled the air, warming it up as the two of us remained tangled in each other's arms in our post-orgasmic daze.

I was tempted to roll off her, pull her into my arms, and slumber away. I probably would've if it weren't for her soft hand stroking my cheek, which pulled me back to reality. "Adam." Her fading voice breathed life back into me.

Reluctantly, I peeled myself away from my little rose, pushing up onto my arms to look down at her. "Yes, Eliza darling?"

"Adam... I love you."

Chapter 23
Eliza

~1.5 months later~

"Asher, it's too early for this," I complained playfully with a groan as Asher continued to crawl all over Adam and me while the three of us lounged in bed.

"Not too early for our little chunkers," Adam mused with a tired chuckling groan of his own.

God, it was still a little weird to hear Adam refer to Asher as our kid or his kid. I didn't have any problems with it, and it didn't bother me, honestly. It was a little bit of an adjustment still, and it was more of a personal thing for me.

Adam accepting Asher and treating him like his own child kept the problem about James and my personal life at the forefront of my mind. Yes, I could continue to lie to both Asher and Adam for the rest of my life. I could very well lie to Asher about his biological father when or if the time came when he'd question me about him;

it wouldn't be hard to tell him his father died or left him. The only thing that would eat at me is my own conscience.

Now, as grand as that plan was, it'd blow up in an instant if James showed up out of the blue. Banking on him forgetting me or letting me go was a long shot, considering how much of a control freak he was. Also, updates from Eve thus far made that belief scant. James was very actively searching for me; he still posted missing posts on social media, playing the heartbroken husband. It sickened me so much to see the shit he put out to the world knowing the truth about him.

All the tears he shed were nothing more than crocodile tears. Those heart-wrenching sob stories were as fake as his expressions. Nothing was real, yet everyone fell for his pathetic acting. Seeing it all was enough to make me want to drive my ass back to Idaho just to strangle the life out of James after making him make a public confession to all the horrors he'd put me through the past ten fucking years.

Unfortunately—for me, not him—I was the better person. No, I haven't forgiven or forgotten; I probably never will if I were honest. All those years of being beaten down to nothing, to where I saw myself as less than dirt beneath everyone's feet. James tore every part of me to shreds. Emotionally, mentally, physically, everything.

A wave of sentiment consumed me, choking my breath in my throat and causing my eyes to sting with the welling tears. Throwing my arms out, I coiled them around my son with a sad but grateful smile. "I love you so much, Asher," I spoke into his belly, making him laugh from the ticklish sensation.

Thank you.

My gratitude for Asher was something I'd never be able to put fully into words. If it weren't for my baby boy, then I'd probably never work up the nerve to leave James unless it was in a body bag.

I knew it wasn't healthy to bank on my boy, to do everything and live for Asher, but that's all I could do right now. As long as Asher turns out to be a good man years from now, then I'll be more than content with my life.

But how can my son be proud of me when I'm a fat liar?

The thought threatened to flip my smile upside down, but I forced it to remain on my aching face.

How would Asher react when all the lies came to light? Sure, maybe I'd get lucky, and things stay buried forever, but again, I didn't know if I could take all the mental guilt.

But a mother's gotta do what a mother's gotta do to protect her children... right?

Sighing softly, I released Asher when he started to struggle and push against me. Flopping his body over to Adam, he body slammed a winded grunt out of the grown man. "Dada mum mum." He was very cute when demanding things of Adam.

Adam strained out a groan and chuckle as Asher bounced against him. "Alrighty buddy, food." He breathed heavily, recovering from being a human trampoline.

Grabbing Asher, he held the toddler still as he sat up. Then, turning his grinning face to me. "Good morning, little rose." Leaning down, he pressed a quick kiss against my lips. "Any requests for breakfast today?" he asked as he leaned back up, settling Asher in his lap.

Sitting up with a groan, I slumped a bit in my spot while rubbing my eyes. "Can I just have something light today? Maybe scrambled eggs and bacon and toast or something?" I didn't have too much of an appetite the more I thought about food for the day, but I knew going without breakfast wouldn't fly with Adam one bit.

With a soft smile, Adam nodded in response before kissing my forehead. "I'm going to get Asher ready first," he told me before slipping off the bed with Asher in his arms. "Don't keep us waiting too long, alright?"

His face wrinkled with worry as he looked at me with a softening smile. I could hear the question churning behind his eyes. When he opened his mouth, I half expected him to ask if everything was okay or what was on my mind, but my heart eased when he shook his head and covered everything up with a quick smile. "Scrambled eggs, okay? Or any specific way you want them?" he asked somewhat awkwardly.

Smiling at him gratefully, I nodded in response. "Yeah, scrambled eggs sound perfect." Getting up myself, I stepped up to him and kissed his cheek. "Good morning, and thank you." I changed the subject to something a little more lighthearted.

Chuckling, Adam shook his head with a smile. "I already told you many times, Eliza darling, no need to thank me. I'm just doing the bare minimum." Yet, he still smiled and blushed every time I did show him gratitude.

Leaning up to my tippy toes, I gave his cheek another peck, giggling with a grin as I walked away to the bathroom.

Honestly, besides all the mental games I played with myself, everything was perfect. If there was a fairy godmother out there or some miracle worker willing to give me that one performance, then I'd very much appreciate their appearance in my life right about now. I wanted to wish away my past life and have it stay buried for the rest of my life and beyond.

I didn't want to worry about James anymore. Hell, I shouldn't be worrying about him popping his head around the corner any day now; I shouldn't be looking over my own damn shoulder every minute of each day. I didn't want to worry about Asher's safety when he'd start school. The fear of James finding us and whisking

Asher away from school one day constantly gnawed at the back of my mind.

Sighing heavily, I leaned over the bathroom sink, staring at the marbled pattern to help settle my growing nerves.

I need to tell him...

Glaring at my reflection, I mentally scolded myself for being a damn coward over the whole situation. I needed to rip the bandage off before it got too saturated and messy. Adam needed to know the truth sooner rather than later. He deserved to know who he was with. Besides, the sooner I tell him, the easier it'll be. If I continued to drag things out, then we'd fall deeper in love with each other, so it'll hurt so much more to uncover everything later down the road.

But what if he leaves me? What about Asher?

Could I do that to Asher? He finally had a male figure in his life, and even though he was young, having an unstable life when it came to personal relationships wasn't a healthy thing.

On the other hand, it'd be better to separate them sooner rather than later, too.

Fucking hell!

Letting out a frustrated groan, I ruffled my already messy bedhead as I paced around the grand bathroom. "God damn it, Eliza, get a grip of yourself," I mumbled out loud, slumping over the counter with my head in my hands. "Just tell him, tell him, and take the consequences of your shit storm."

Better to hurt yourself now than later.

After breakfast, it'd happen after breakfast. It had to.

Unfortunately, it did not happen after breakfast... nor did it happen after lunch... or dinner.

I kept chickening out every time he'd look at me with that stupid smiling face. No matter how much I worked myself up, it'd all go up in flames the moment a peaceful moment settled between us. I couldn't bring myself to ruin the only good thing in my life right now besides Asher.

Too bad my cowardice wouldn't let me live things down. Every time I tried to push things off, a surge of guilt would grip my chest until it felt like I was suffocating. By the time late evening rolled around, I felt dead.

My whole body, especially my chest, ached with a tightness. I felt like a strung-out string, ready to snap at the slightest touch. Every breath I took to try and ease my anxiety and guilt resulted in more suffocation. I felt like I'd pass out any given second from the lack of oxygen. Well, it felt like a lack of oxygen to my dazed mind. Physiologically, I was fine. My whole body perfused oxygen just fine, but mentally, it felt like I was getting nothing.

Honestly, I might faint before this damn movie was over. It's not like I paid any attention to the moving figures on the flat screen—I couldn't!

Mentally, I was in a whole other stratosphere.

"Eliza darling?" Adam's concerned voice sounded so distant even though he sat right next to me.

The muscles in my head and eyes strained to move my head and gaze at him, and I felt like a damn stupefied zombie staring at him blankly. Mustering up any kind of energy to push my nonexistent emotions to the surface was impossible with how turbulent my mind was. Well, if I was honest, my whole mental health had been in the shit hole for a long while now.

Pressure and warmth wrapped around my body, and I could feel myself being jerked one way until I was seated elsewhere but on the couch. "*Mia rosa*," he spoke up again, this time with more worry. "I don't want to push you or anything when it comes to you opening up to me, but you have to give me something."

Something rough and firm cupped my face, turning my head about until my eyes focused on a familiar pair of stony ones. "I know you need the time and space to process things and arrive at them at your own pace and shit, but you need to give me something right here, right now." His soft empathy hardened demandingly. "You are worrying me with how distracted you've been, so please, talk to me. Give me something." He sounded a little torn with his pleading, as if he wanted to rip my confessions from my very soul.

His grip on my face tightened slightly as his jaw clenched, and a heavy breath pressed out of his body. "I am so torn between letting you go about your merry way with some light nudging and strapping you down and belting you until you talk through your tears and sobs." I don't think I've ever seen his eyes become so dark with intent and so broken with care until now.

The whole world came crashing down on me. It felt like a bomb went off and blew my dam apart. It started as a shiver; then it moved into a tremble before my whole body broke out in a full sob. "I'm just so exhausted," I managed to strain through my uncontrollable crying. "I don't know what to do or what I want, and I just feel lost and so tired and so ugh!"

Finding the right words to describe the turmoil within me was difficult, and what I threw out just now didn't come close to scratching the surface. "And I'm just so scared."

Things between Adam and I were getting serious, and that terrified me. Everything was so perfect, and I didn't like that. Things shouldn't be perfect! Not when it was all built on a lie. Yes, I wanted and needed a new life, but it was killing me every day to keep my past from Adam.

In hindsight, it might not matter since it was the past. Most of it shouldn't affect us, but I felt such guilt over keeping it all from him the more he opened up to me about his life. I wanted to tell him about my boring life growing up when he'd talk about all the fun times he had playing sports growing up, but I couldn't. Instead, I had to feed him spoonful after spoonful of lies about a quaint life in a place I've never been to in my life.

Holding me tight and close, he kissed the side of my head. Soothing me with soft shushes, he stroked the back of my head while occasionally wiping away my burning tears. "What are you scared about?"

Through my pathetic sobs, I managed to get my strangled words out. "Of losing you... Of losing all of—" I waved an arm around, gesturing at everything around us and the two of us. "This."

Adam's eyebrows furrowed together slightly in irritation and concern as he stared at me for a long while. Before I could question him about it, he pulled me into a tight hug, shoving my face into his chest. "You won't." He sounded so certain, and that worried me.

Why did he sound so sure? Why wasn't his answer calming me? Having such assurance should've settled my nerves. Yet, I couldn't find any solace in his firm words.

"You will *never* lose me." His usual soothing strokes to my hair and back did nothing but raise my hackles this time around.

Taking in a shaky breath, I pushed myself away to look up at him warily. "Don't say that." For once, I didn't feel safe around Adam, not with how his hawklike eyes bore right through me. "You don't know what I'm hiding from you to say something like that with such certainty."

Cupping my face with both his hands, he focused my gaze on his unwavering one. "Tell me and see if I run." It was almost a command as it was a challenge with his smug and strong tone. "Because I can promise you—no, I swear to you, that I won't end our relationship no matter what comes out of your mouth the next minute."

There was an edge of excitement to his voice that made fear grip at every single one of my nerve endings until I could feel the chill of it down to my bones. None of this felt right. I felt... trapped almost. It felt like Adam was some predator cornering me, toying with me until he was ready to pounce.

Further pushing him away, I slowly backed away from him by scooting backward on the couch. "I-I... I-I'm not who you think I am..." Everything pounded within me as I continued to nervously back away from Adam, who slowly advanced on me. My heart rammed against my chest like a raging bull wanting out, and every pump of blood rushed against my eardrums as my every breath became white noise. "I haven't—"

A sharp gasp cut my sentence short when Adam suddenly lunged forward, causing me to squeak and lay flat on the couch with him looming over me. "I know."

In a flash, his hand shot and wrapped around my neck, holding me down as he pressed his body weight against me. Adrenaline surged through my body, burning through my veins like lava as I struggled against him, attempting to throw him off. My hands clamped themselves around his wrist and forearm, clawing and prying at it. "Adam, you're scaring me," I whimpered through my quickened breaths.

His face leans down close to mine, looming a mere inch from me to where every inhale was a lungful of him. A chilling shudder choked my body out when I caught the way his sharp eyes softened in a split second. "Eliza darling, I'm not going to hurt you, nor am I angry or upset at you." His thumb slowly stroked at my pulsating neck, making me calm a little instinctively.

Letting out a controlled breath, he uttered a single command, "Settle." Instinctively, every fiber in my being snapped until not an ounce of tension remained. "Talk to me, *mia rosa*." His hand released my neck, and he stroked my tear-stained cheek with the back of his finger. "Let me in," he pleaded with a needy and broken voice. "It's okay. It will all be okay. Nothing you say will change my love for you," he assured me with a genuine smile full of ardor.

An ache twisted my lips into a frown. "You can't say that." My voice croaked and cracked as my throat felt like it was closing in on itself. "You love the person I wanted you to love, not—"

His hard grip on my jaw made it impossible to move it. "Elisabella Stone." The sound of my legal name made my body freeze up with shock. "I love you, Elisabella Stone, and I love you, Eliza Huyen." The depth of the fondness in his voice was as endless as the warmth in his stony orbs. "I love the woman you have bloomed into. All those smiles, the laughs and giggles, the wonderful and doting mother, the amazing girlfriend who only ever looks at me with pure happiness and gratitude."

All the turbulent fear and emotional turmoil simmered out the more I fell into his comfort. "Who you were before doesn't matter to me because you are here with me now." Soft waves of warmth rippled throughout my body from his touch against my cheek. "I love my Eliza, the one who has been around me all this time." Leaning down, he kissed my cheek. "My Eliza darling." Then, a kiss on the edge of my lips. "My little rose." A deep one right against my lips, one that steals my whole soul away. "And don't you try to deny any of it either. I know it's easy to act and fake things, but there is no way to imitate genuine emotions in the eyes or hide micro expressions or any of those natural and instinctual things."

There was no denying or arguing with him because he was right. I lied to him about my real identity, but my true self was something I couldn't hide from him. Thinking back on it all, as much as I tried to deny it to myself, it was impossible. Everything from his lips hit the truth right on the head.

"How can you love me? If you know the truth somehow or anything about my past, then you should very well know that I am nothing but broken goods." The next wave of words caught in my throat for a moment until I forced my nerves back down. "I am nothing but a used body full of baggage."

The next few seconds blurred by, and nothing hit me until I felt Adam's hand on my bare bottom. It felt like everything happened in a blink of an eye. One second, I was on the couch. Then the next, I was hauled up by my neck and bent over Adam's knee with my dress thrown up around my waist and panties bunched up between my ass crack.

It wasn't until the third crack that I snapped out of my stupor entirely. Craning my head back, I looked at Adam with wide eyes filled with disbelief. "Adam! We are having a—ah!"

Another spank from his rough hand promptly shut me up. "We're not done with our conversation, not by far, but we're going to finish it with you over my knee." I barely caught his breath hitching with the next smack that jerked my body. "Just because we are talking doesn't mean you get to berate yourself like that, so punishment is in order for you breaking that rule."

Kicking my legs and grunting in frustration, I lightly hit his thigh with my fists. "You jerk!" I huffed, growling softly with a displeased scowl.

Glowering at the ground didn't last long, not with how he fisted the back of my hair and yanked my head back to look up at him. His stern eyes bore into me, but not in a disappointed or upset way, but in a tough love kind of manner. "You are none of those, and you never will be. Just because you had a rough few years doesn't make you any less of a person, even if it may seem like it. The only people who are trash are deplorable criminals."

Another set of sharp stings bit my ass cheeks, and another yelp jolted out of my body in response. I snapped at Adam through my tears. "There's nothing about me to love, though! I am nothing but a fucking liar! A coward! A bag of useless nothing!" Gripping at his thigh, I chewed at my bottom lip, muffling my pained moans when he spanked me again a few times. "I'm useless. I can't do anything with my life because I'm on the fucking run from my stupid ex. I live in constant paranoia, afraid that the next time I blink, then he'll be right there in front of me."

Once I started, I couldn't stop. All the words spilled from my mouth like the tears from my eyes. "I'm just a useless college dropout with dead dreams and aspirations. I'm not even myself after ten fucking years with James. Ten years of constant pain and suffering, all because I was too fucking stupid to see and admit the truth." Talking became impossible with how my voice kept cracking and hitching with my sobs.

The pressure against the back of my head eased in an instant when he released my hair. A quick spin of the room, I found myself seated in Adam's lap, nestled tightly against him in his arms. "Oh, *mia rosa*, no, no, no," he shushed me soothingly, running his fingers through my long locks. "You are so much more than you think," he said while rocking me softly. "You may see yourself as some failure, but I don't. Nor would anyone else if they were to find out." He paused for a second to take in a deep breath and press a kiss against my temple. "You are everything to me. I don't see some broken person whenever I look at you. All I ever see is my wonderful woman, who is going to be my wife one day. My wonderful wife-to-be, who is the best and most amazing mother ever. My Eliza darling, who is too stubborn and independent for her own good, but those are qualities I fucking love about you."

His body trembled with his chuckle before a warmth of peace blanketed us for a moment. "I only see my little rose blooming every day." A finger curled under my chin, lifting my face to a pair of loving lips. "Little by little, you blossom better and better. You might have been lost before, but now you have direction." He dazes me with another kiss before continuing, "You have me now, and I want nothing but the best for you and our family."

A minute of solace embraced us as we became lost in each other's never-ending wonder and adoration. "You went through Hell, but you pulled yourself out. Not everyone can do that, so you have to praise yourself there," he told me with a proud smile while brushing my hair out of my face. "You work your ass off for Asher, and that's another thing to be proud of right there." His smile grew with his words as his fingers stroked my cheek and jawline. "You are a wonderful woman, Eliza, and I am going to make you see it by making you love yourself as much as you love me."

I couldn't help but giggle and roll my eyes in response to his cockiness. On most men, it was annoying, but Adam had a charming way about his arrogance that made it work in his favor.

Adam's face lit up with a victorious grin at my little sound. "There's my Eliza darling." He quickly stole my breath away with a quick kiss before speaking again in a very warm and affectionate voice, "I will be the sunlight to warm you back up, the water to nourish you, the fresh and healthy soil you need for a new life, and

I'll be the keeper that protects you and preserves your unique beauty for all of eternity."

Unable to help myself again, I rolled my eyes at him. "You and your roses," I teased with a chuckle. "But thank you." I didn't know what else to say in the situation.

Smiling gratefully in return, Adam shook his head. "No, don't thank me when it's supposed to be me kissing your feet for allowing me into your life." The awe and joy in his eyes made me melt with a wide smile. "Never thank me for giving you the bare minimum and what you deserve."

Chuckling softly, I let myself relax against him. "Well, it's not like you gave me much of a choice with how you barged into my life and basically set up camp," I remarked, looking up at me with a playful smirk. "But as flustered as it made me... I needed it." Otherwise, we wouldn't be here right now.

"Hey, I couldn't let you slip away from me, so I needed to encroach on you a bit." He grinned smugly with a cheeky chuckle. "But, I know, that's why I'm a little firmer with you compared to others in my past. You need the guidance, the firm hand, and you thrive off of it." The pad of his thumb arched across my cheekbone slowly. "But, back to the point of everything. You are worth everything, and you will see the greatness that is you and accept it."

Resting his forehead against mine, he smiled against my lips. "I will be there to drag you through it all until you do. When you are down, I will pick you up and carry you through until you can walk on your two feet again. Even then, I will be right next to you or behind you to guide you and protect you." A sweet kiss graces my lips, melting my whole heart and being into Adam.

I fucking loved how true his smile was as he beamed at me. "You are an amazing woman, Eliza, and I am so proud to call you as mine." Kissing me deeply for a long moment, he softly attacked my lips until they ached and swelled up. "I will always love you, no matter what. Even when you can't find it within yourself to appreciate yourself, I will do it for you because I am wholly devoted to you."

Swallowing the reluctance, I fisted the front of his shirt before kissing him with trembling lips. "I can't handle being broken again, so please, don't smash whatever is left of me," I whispered in a broken voice, letting my stray tears run down my cheeks.

Taking my face into his hands, he wipes the tears away with his thumbs before planting a promising kiss firmly against my lips. "Never. I will never hurt you. I'd rather take a thousand bullets to my body before putting a scratch on you."

God, I love this man. I truly, with my whole heart and soul, love Adam.

Never has such a thought and feeling felt so right. Such raw devotion and adoration that felt so natural, like breathing, had always been so foreign to me—a mere dream.

What I felt for James, what I thought was love, paled in comparison to the fire and passion I felt for Adam. James was stupid puppy love if it could even be categorized as love. Hell, it was nothing but a mere crush compared to Adam.

Everything I felt with Adam was the real thing: the blissful happiness that filled endless pages of romance novels, the soul-snatching feeling that so many people swore by, and that 'the one' feeling that devoted people always spoke about.

Adam was it for me.

He is my one.

Chapter 24
Adam

"Darling, you're not well, so rest, please." At this point, I was about to throw my pleading out the window and tie her down to the couch, so she'd stay put.

Stubborn as always, Eliza groaned and smacked my hands away from her groggy body. "I'm fine. I just need to wake up some more," she insisted while struggling to push herself off the couch.

Rolling my eyes, I forced her back down onto the couch with a sigh. "Little rose, you're like a zombie right now," I remarked with a soft frown. "Just nap for a little bit, darling. We were up late last night, and you had a good cry, so your whole system is still trying to recover."

Even though she slept well into the morning, she was still rather pale and sickly with her swollen eyes and cracked lips. After a light breakfast meal, she was still a little out of it. She wasn't too happy when I made her call into work, but there was no way I'd let her go out with half a functioning brain cell and a nearly empty tank of energy. Her boss made no fuss about it, though, especially after I spoke to her about it.

Shoving my worries to the back of my mind with a sigh, I leaned down and kissed her forehead before helping Asher up onto the couch. For a second, I watched the toddler crawl into his mother's arms and snuggle into her. "Just cuddle with Asher until he's tired, relax. I'll make a smoothie for you to help pep you up, get you some snacks and all too."

Eliza glared at me softly but relented, especially when Asher rubbed his face into hers with a sloppy kiss on the cheek and a few cute babbles. "Only because I don't want to leave Asher right now," she argued with a pout at me before turning her full attention to Asher.

Appreciating the warm scene for a moment, I gave both a kiss on the head before busying myself in the kitchen.

Things have been calm since last night, which I expected. I had already accepted Eliza and her past, and I knew all there was to her before she cracked and spilled everything to me before we both went to bed. From the bottom of my twisted heart and soul, I really didn't give a shit about her past.

I didn't see her any different after reading through her whole file. I didn't care about her past marriage to some abusive bastard; she may argue that fact made her less of a woman for me, but that wasn't the case for me. There was no such thing as 'used goods' because of the past. Hell, she could've been a sex worker for all I cared, and I wouldn't see her as anything but perfect.

Women aren't objects, so to say they were 'used' or 'not good' anymore after being married or using their bodies was beyond stupid. Women are meant to be cherished and worshiped by us men. Us men were the lowly humans, while women were the fucking gods of this world. Call me extreme, but I was raised right by my parents to treat a woman more than properly and to view them as above.

My father always liked to joke the world would crash and burn if it weren't for women, and I couldn't agree with him more.

If it weren't for Eliza, then I wouldn't really be alive. A breath of fresh life, as many would say. Day in and day out, I went about my routine like some robot, just living for the sake of living. I never truly felt content or alive until I happened upon Asher and Eliza.

"Hey, bub?" Her curious voice rang out, making me look over at her.

Eliza had sat up and rested her head on top of the couch. "How did you find out about my past? How long have you known?" She grew wary again with how distant and shielded she sounded, making me frown internally.

"I have a lot of friends who work in the system and such, and I've got means and such with the money I have." It wasn't a complete lie. I got her information through my means and connections, though it might have been my more illicit ways, but those tiny details didn't matter.

With the smoothie cups in hand, I went over and sat beside her on the couch. "I've known for a few months, and none of it bothered me, really." Giving her a reassuring smile, I kissed her cheek before giving her the smoothie. "It only made me admire you so much more." I couldn't help the goofy smile from spreading across my lips as I looked at her adoringly.

Sadly, the bliss didn't last long when I caught her lips sagging. "*Mia rosa*, what's wrong?" I questioned with furrowed brows.

Had I done something?

No, that was silly because I literally haven't done or said anything to make her upset.

"I'm happy you know and all, but..." Her tongue darted out across her trembling lips. "But it doesn't change the fact that James is still after me and Asher... Knowing him, he's not going to give up until he has both of us back, or at the very least, Asher." I hated how defeated she looked, like some beat-up puppy on the streets.

Keeping a strong front for her, I set the cups down to pull her into a comforting hug. "Hey, don't worry about your pathetic ex. If he ever shows his ugly face around here, then I'll take care of him." They weren't empty words, but she didn't have to know my true intent. "He will never lay a hand on you again, not while I'm around," I assured her, kissing her forehead.

Letting her go, I held her face firmly to let her see my promising smile. "I will always protect my family, which is you and Asher. I don't want you to think or worry about James anymore from now on, alright?" Of course, she opened her mouth to argue back, but I shut her with a finger pressed against her lips. "I will handle James if he comes around. I want you to put him in the past, where he belongs. He held you back for so many years, so don't let him keep on pulling your life through the mud when he's not even here."

Soon, he'd cease to exist, but again, she didn't need to know about my nefarious plans regarding her damn ex. Well, that and I hadn't exactly figured out a completely foolproof plan yet, so there wasn't anything to tell.

As much as I hated to agree with Rowan, he was right. Given his standing in society, James wouldn't be simple to deal with. A known police lieutenant disappearing would raise some heads without the proper setup.

Fortunately for James, I wasn't God. Otherwise, I would've smote him down the moment I came across his name in Eliza's file. Deplorable bastard. I have so many plans to make him suffer before ending him. His days were numbered, and it was only a matter of time before he'd come for my trap.

"Bub, no." Eliza frowned deeply with a few shakes of her head. "I can't let you handle my problems like that. I mean, it's one thing to take care of me by feeding me and such, but James is a whole different animal altogether. He's not going to go away just because you throw money at him or charm him. He won't stop until he gets his twisted ways, and he's not above murder either."

With each quivering word, her face paled and dropped with terror. By the time she was done talking, her eyes had this glazed-over look as if she wasn't present. "I can't let him take you away from me. I won't. He's already taken away so much, and I've watched him ruin so many lives by taking them... I don't—"

Her next words became muffled from the kiss I forced on her. I didn't let up until she kicked into a full struggle to pull away from me, but at that point, I needed to breathe, so I let us go.

Reaching out, I snatched Asher up and brought him into a tight hug with Eliza. "I can swear with certainty that you will never lose me. Of all the things in the world I can guarantee you, James taking me out is never going to happen." That I could say with a full chest.

Letting my expression relax to a more serious one, I tilted my head slightly. "You don't have to answer me if you don't want to, but from your reaction and answer, has James killed before?" My curiosity itched at my brain, and I started to wonder if there was any dirt I could use to rub into James's wounds. "And I mean outside of duty."

She seemed fearful enough to hint at something wrong, and if her ex was as loose of a screw as Eliza made him sound, then it wouldn't surprise me if he had bad blood on his hands.

Eliza's head hung with a heavy sigh, her shoulders slumping as her body dug itself into mine. "Yes... And he has the means to get away with it... That's why I'm so worried about you." Her small voice whimpered into my chest.

Clenching my jaw, I withheld the excited smirk from showing itself on my face. Forcing out a soft hum, I rubbed the back of Eliza's and Asher's heads before letting them go. "Just trust me on this, alright?" I pleaded to Eliza with a warm smile and trusting eyes. "Let me worry about James, and you live your life to the fullest with me, alright?"

Pursing her lips, Eliza looked at me with unsteady eyes for a long while before giving in with a sigh. "Alright, sir," she mumbled, giving me a quick hug before sliding off the couch to the floor to join Asher. "Promise we'll be okay? All of us?" Her hopeful eyes sparkled with anticipation as she looked up at me with an eager smile.

With all the confidence in the world, I smiled and nodded. "I swear to it." James might be a formidable foe when the time comes, but he was no match for me.

After all, a mere man stood no chance against an angel.

And I say it's time this bastard meets the Angel of Death.

Chapter 25
Eliza

~5 months later~

"Oh, this is going to be so perfect! They are going to be so adorable! Ugh! I can't believe they're turning two already!" Hailee gave out a long, nostalgic sigh as the two of us continued our shopping spree.

Well, I wouldn't consider the thing a shopping spree since we weren't really having a grand time buying things for ourselves. It was more or less a chore run because we needed to get things together for our children's birthday party this upcoming weekend. The only thing that made it feel like a shopping spree was the fact Adam gave us his card and the whole day to do and get whatever our hearts desired.

I only zoned back into Hailee's next question because she grabbed my arm and shook it excitedly. "Ooooh, what cake should we get them? How big?" I had to grab her shoulders and maneuver her around the open door of the diner to keep her from getting hit and to move her into the place.

Chuckling softly, I patted her shoulders and smiled at her briefly before looking up at the hostess with a warm smile. "Two, please, and a booth if possible?" It felt a little weird to ask for a booth, but I wanted a cushioned seat to sit and chat with Hailee.

Thankfully, we didn't have to wait more than a few seconds because there were a few spots open. "God, this is so nice and needed. I mean, don't get me wrong, I love my little Adelaide, but I just need a break sometimes, ya know?" Hailee's body deflated in her seat the moment she plopped down.

Agreeing with a lopsided smile, I nodded my head reluctantly. "Yeah, I do. I don't like being away from Asher, but..." I didn't need to finish my sentence before I got a sympathetic look from Hailee.

"Mom guilt?" Hailee chuckled dryly with her own crooked smile.

Silently, I nodded my head while I rubbed at my chest to try and ease the choking knot in it. "I've never been away from Asher until I met Adam, and he kind of forced me to spread my wings a bit." I wasn't thrilled about it back then, but I was more than thankful for it now.

"He has that way with people. He just knows what buttons to push and how far to push someone for their own good." Chuckling, Hailee leaned onto the table, crossing her arms in front of her. "Thank you for giving my brother a chance. I know he's not the easiest man to get along with in the world, with how stubborn he is."

Memories of Adam basically bullying his way into my life got me chuckling and smiling unconsciously. "He didn't really give me much of a choice, but he's lucky that's something about him I've come to love." Honestly, I appreciated his bossiness and control.

Much to my chagrin, he hit every nail on the head when it came to me. I thrived off the control Adam exerted over me and my life. I was tired of having to plan my days out down to the second, exhausted from having to be completely responsible for everything. Adam dictating my schedule, meals, and activities eased my anxiety so much. And I guess the best part of it all was the autonomy I maintained throughout it all.

Yes, Adam was in charge, but I had the final say. It was a little strange to think about our whole Dom/sub dynamic, but it made sense to us. That's all that really mattered, though, right? Our relationship didn't need to be understood by anyone but us, and it didn't matter as long as it worked for us and we were content.

Hailee's hand brushing across mine pulled me from my thoughts. "I'm really happy that you're getting a second chance at life and that you're just so in love with Adam as he is with you." At least Hailee was an angel, so no more monster in-laws for me down the road. "And trust me, your slimy ex won't want to show his face around you after he sees Adam as your man."

Sighing, I shook my head with a sad smile. "I know you both assure me and such, but you guys don't know James like I do." I wasn't as paranoid and anxious about James, but the hairs on my neck stood at times at the thought of him.

"I know Adam can handle himself, and I know that he has the money and power and such, but James just..." Groaning in frustration, I shoved my face into my hands, rubbing it a few times before running my hands through my hair.

Unless Adam was some politician or the damn president, he stood no chance of getting away from James unscathed. One way or another, James would find a way to meet his goals. He always wins. Even if I wanted to think otherwise because Adam assured me so, it was hard to after seeing all the shit James has gotten away with over the years.

Yet, Adam and Hailee weren't bothered by it one bit. I don't know if something didn't connect in their brains or if they knew something I didn't. Of course, I doubted the latter because what could they even have up their sleeve that could put James in a bind if he ever found me and came after me?

"Don't think about that loser," Hailee said, patting my arm. "We have a nice little girl's day to enjoy after a nice lunch."

Not wanting to dampen the mood, I shoved everything away with a smile. "I don't think it's much of a girl's day if we're going around buying stuff for our kids' party," I mused with a chuckle. "And you can pick the cake flavor. Asher's not picky about anything, so if Adelaide has something she prefers, then we should go with what she likes."

Seriously, a plate of trash could be put in front of my kid, and he'd enjoy it like some grand feast.

"Also, I don't think we're going to need that big of a cake. I mean, it's just us, really, right? And some of your guys' friends?" Not like I had anyone to invite over. Eve was back in Idaho, and the few people I did make some connections with here were already on the list because of Adam.

"Well, our parents are coming in—"

The water I'd been sipping at burned my nose and throat from how hard I spat it out. I didn't mean to, but the shock of hearing their parents were coming had me doing a spit-take. "What!?" I strained through my coughing fit.

Hailee frantically patted my back as I coughed nonstop from the water I'd inhaled into my lungs. "Uhh I'm guessing Adam didn't tell you?" She chuckled sheepishly with an apologetic smile.

"No!" I barked out after a cough. "Oh my God, when do they get here?!"

I was in no way prepared, mentally or physically, to meet their parents! I needed at least seven business days to properly get my mind in the right headspace, and I needed that much time to make sure I looked physically okay. Not to say I looked like a slob or horrible, but maybe a nice haircut to spruce me up a bit, a facial, or something like that.

How Hailee's eyes widened before they averted from me with her wary smile made the stone in my gut sink further. "Weeeelll..." Uh oh, I didn't like the sound of that word being dragged out. "Umm... Hypothetically..." Nope, definitely didn't like the sound of this one bit, especially with how her lips kept twisting with worry. "How much would you freak out if I told you they were coming like... Today... In a few hours..."

Oh my God!

Slumping down in my seat, I cowered and covered my head with my arms. "Why the fuck didn't any of you tell me anything?!" I hissed with a somewhat playful glare up at Hailee.

Holding her hands up in defense, Haliee leaned back a little in her spot. "I thought Adam told you already." She offered me an awkward, apologetic pat on the head before sighing. "If it makes you feel any better, they already love you from what Adam's told them, and they're really lovely people."

Dragging out a groan, I lightly banged my head against the table. "What if they don't like me after they see me? I mean, what kind of parent wants their child to be with someone who has a kid and a shit ton of baggage?"

From what Adam and Hailee have told me about their parents in passing, they sounded like lovely people, truly. But what kid wouldn't praise their parent? Granted, I didn't talk much or any about my parents, but it wasn't as if there was anything to say about them really.

Needless to say, I had little to no fond memories of my parents. They weren't the worst, but they also weren't the best. At most, they were decent. Growing up, they provided for me and made sure I was healthy and whatnot, but they weren't the warmest when it came to giving me mental and emotional support. Sometimes, I wondered if they only had kids for the sake of having kids because it was the 'family' thing to do.

Sighing softly, I lifted my head and flashed a quick smile at Hailee before taking a huge gulp of water. "What if they don't like me and don't want Adam with me?" I worried out loud with a deep frown.

Dismissing me with a cheery laugh, Hailee took my hands in hers, squeezing them reassuringly. "Eliza, they love you already. You really have nothing to worry about. They know about your past and everything, and they aren't turned away by it one bit." She widened her smile after another squeeze of my hands. "They aren't the type of people to care about things like that, and they're the kind who believes in second chances and shit. They feel for you and are more than happy that you found your way with Adam and are headed towards a better future." Grinning excitedly, she bounced a little in her seat. "Seriously, they absolutely fucking adore you and Asher. Lord, I didn't think they'd be excited about another child like Adelaide, but Asher's right up there with her."

Letting my feelings surface, I didn't bother stopping the smile from spreading across my face. Maybe I was overthinking it quite a bit. I didn't want to disappoint his parents because I knew how important they were to Adam. Also, not like I've had a good run with parents when it came to my partners.

Taking a deep breath, I picked up my soda and took a few sips of that, scrunching my face and wincing a bit at the bubbles fizzing in my face. "Well, here's to hoping for the best," I mumbled to myself, exhaling sharply.

"Are you sure? Your parents liking me? And Asher? What has Adam told them? Have you told them anything?" Might as well pry to see what has been spilled to them. Besides, it was better to know and prepare myself just in case they tried to blindside me.

Staring off into the distance, Hailee smiled like a goof for a moment before getting distracted by the waitress when she came by to drop off our appetizers and refill our drinks. Picking at a few fries, she hummed to herself for a moment before speaking to me. "Nothing bad, but it's not like there's anything bad to say about you because you're just an angel." Relaxing in her spot, she lazily pushed the basket of fries at me. "Adam absolutely gushes about you, about how beautiful you look doing everything, how wonderful you are for just existing. He talks about how amazing of a mother you are and how he loves waking up every day to you and Asher. Honestly, just take all the lovey-dovey shit from all the romance movies and books out there, shove it all into one person, and you got Adam. Honestly, girl, my brother is head over heels for you, like bad."

The thing was, I could see all of that perfectly. Adam doted on me and loved to brag about me to other people whenever he got the chance. To have someone love me like Adam was unbelievable and amazing. I didn't know how Adam did it, find qualities to me to adore, little things that I didn't even know existed until he pointed them out.

Picking at some of the appetizers, I thought back on our time together so far. I know it hasn't been too awfully long, but everything about Adam felt right. Actually, maybe not everything, like maybe about ninety-eight percent of Adam felt right. There was that sliver, the tiniest part, that nagged at the back of my mind. Something about Adam didn't fit properly, kind of like a piece of a puzzle that you kind of jam in there and force it to fit because it looked similar enough to the actual piece.

But what is it?

What about Adam was off? He was perfect... A little too perfect... But I couldn't for the life of me figure out what that flaw to him was.

On the other hand, did I want to find out what was wrong? Did I really want to shatter this glass house of mine? It wasn't healthy to live in a lie, but what harm was this lie doing to me?

I've never been happier in my life, and if being a little delusional was what it took to keep this reality up, then so be it.

Chapter 26
Adam

"You so owe me big time for this," Max grumbled as he struggled to balance the two toddlers in his arms.

"I'll make sure to make it extra messy and painful when I do get to the good part," I joked with a chuckle as I zipped my jacket up. "I won't be long, though, just a quick jog to startle the bastard."

If my calculations were correct, then by the time I made it across the river to where the girls were, then I'd catch James just in time. My sources just informed me of Eliza's ex entering the city, and there was no doubt in my mind he'd have no problems tracking her down. Well, he shouldn't have any problems with the trail of breadcrumbs I left him.

Fortunately for me, James was stupid as he was determined. So, luring him here to Seaside was a breeze, especially after the shit I stirred up for him in Idaho.

The good ol' cop wasn't so good, not with all the bodies he had buried in his backyard—courtesy of me. Let me tell you, though, it was a fucking bitch in the ass to track down his victims and un-cover their bodies to relocate them to his backyard over the past few months. The number of bodies he's dropped over the past ten years didn't make that task any easier.

After shifting things into place, all that I needed to do was turn in a nice little—big—tip to the police, and Lieutenant James Stone was placed on immediate administrative leave. Then, since his home was a crime scene, he had to go hunker down elsewhere until everything was done.

Of course, that was merely the beginning of his planned down-fall. His job and reputation as a good lawman were good as gone, but it wasn't enough. No, he had to be completely ruined before things could progress. So, I did what I do best—fuck shit up.

Some drugs here and there, a snap of a picture or two—okay, maybe more like a few pictures—and James's reputation continued to tank once the images were released all over the web. Of course, the explicit and inappropriate pictures that followed aided in dragging him down to the same level as a druggie pimp.

After a few months of the whole city turning their backs on him and despising him, I finally threw out the line. An anonymous tip about his wife's whereabouts hooked him good. According to my source, the one I paid to be the tipper and stalker, James practically made a straight shoot to Seaside. The eager man only stopped for gas over the thirteen or so-hour drive.

I'd expected him to take a bit of a break or something once he got to Seaside, but guess I was wrong. I wouldn't have sent the girls out for the day if I thought James would go after Eliza right off the bat like this. I might've used my girlfriend as bait for her piece-of-shit ex, but not directly.

No way in hell did I want James to find Eliza. Well, maybe I should reword that a little. I didn't want James to show his ugly face to Eliza's eyes. Me luring him here to get rid of him did not include Eliza finding out about his presence in Seaside at all. Things would get kind of messy if Eliza found out about my plans or James's appearance. Poor thing might have a damn heart attack if she knew James was in the town.

I darted off after giving Asher and Adelaide a kiss on their tiny foreheads. No idle dawdling for me; I needed to make this visit with James fast. A little scare for him to keep his distance from Eliza was all I needed to do. I'd have my men pick him up tonight, hold him in the yacht, then take an impromptu trip after the birthday party this weekend.

I had so many plans for Eliza's pathetic ex, and I couldn't wait.

For every scar he placed on my darling Eliza's body, I'd double on him. The only thing that won't be feasible is torturing him for ten years straight. If I was determined enough, then maybe I could drag shit out for that long, but it was way too risky. So, a week on the yacht would have to do.

Thankfully, tracking him down wasn't hard. Granted, I got lucky because he happened to be very close by. The diner Hailee and Eliza decided to sit down at for lunch was literally right across the river, so James quite literally appeared in front of me in a sense.

Slowly, I stalked up to him, keeping a distance as I hung back to watch him. I half expected him to march right into the place and drag Eliza out, but I guess I overthought things a little. It would seem like James here had more control than I wanted to credit him for.

No matter. As long as he stayed put and made things easier for all of us, then I didn't care. The only issue now was snatching him up. I had to lure him into a less crowded area, preferably down an alleyway, but I needed to wait for the girls to leave first. I wasn't supposed to be out, so running the risk of being caught by Eliza was something I wanted to avoid.

So, without much choice, I waited around rather begrudgingly. My sister and Eliza probably didn't take long to eat their lunch, but it damn well felt like forever until they finally paid their bill and got up.

Unfortunately, James decided to move his ass the moment the girls made their way to the exit.

Calm and collected, I got up and closed the distance between him and me with a few long strides. As I approached his backside, I carefully pulled out my handgun, being mindful to keep it hidden under my jacket.

Before he could get a chance to call out for Eliza or make much of a move toward her, I stopped him by digging the muzzle of the gun into his back. "Go ahead, buddy, fucking try it," I said smugly in a low voice, pressing my weapon harder against him until he visibly winced. "I dare you."

"You have three seconds to remove that gun from me, or I will have you arrested." His head twitched with the intention to look back at me, but a firm poke from my gun made him change his mind. "Do you know who I am?" It was laughable at how empty and shaky his supposedly threatening words were.

Chuckling darkly, I grabbed the back of his shirt with my free hand to direct him elsewhere. "Funny, it should be me asking you that," I replied in a low voice, jerking him a bit toward the other street. "Walk," I demanded, jabbing him a bit with the gun for encouragement.

Clicking his tongue, James relented, letting me steer him down the smaller street and into an alleyway. "You know J-Boy, I gotta say, luring you here was so much easier than I expected. I mean, I knew it'd be a piece of cake, but damn, You took the bait like a moth to a flame." I rubbed it in his face with a haughty chuckle before shoving him face-first into a dirty brick wall.

Whirling around, James cocked his arm back, ready to swing. Only, it never came. In an instant, his face dropped and paled as if I was some demon standing before him. "Y-you..." His stunned eyes blinked slowly a few times as he stared at me in disbelief.

"Not so tough, are ya?" I taunted with a dark laugh, holding my arms out. "Too bad for you, I'm not some girl half your size." A familiar ache pulled my face taut, causing my lips to curl into a crazed grin. "Come on, I'm giving you a free swing."

Lowering his clenched fist to his side, he took a step back. "I'll have your ass thrown in jail!" He stammered out his threat in a trembling voice.

My voice became a little unhinged with my head tilt. "Jail? For what? Tell me, what laws have I broken?" Okay, that was a rather sardonic question, given my mafia profession.

Dodging the question, he narrowed his eyes at me accusingly. "Was it you? The bodies in my backyard, was that your doing?!" He jabbed a weak finger at me with a daring step forward.

Laughing him off, I feigned innocence. "Well, it's not nice to litter, so I was merely gathering it all up for you and giving it back." There might have been an extra body or two in the pile, but not like it mattered.

His shoulders shook with his deepening scowl. "What do you even want with my bitch Eliza? How do you know her? What does she have to do with you?" he spat with a sharp tongue.

Softly clicking my tongue, I lunged at him in a blink of an eye. My arm shot out, laying across his neck. With some forceful steps, I shoved him back up against the wall, choking him with my forearm until he went red in the face with rolling eyes. If I didn't have torturous plans for him, then I would've pressed on until his body was lifeless at my feet.

Fortunately for him, I needed him alive.

"Tsk." Releasing him with a scowl, I watched as he slumped to the ground with a coughing fit. "Say one more thing that's remotely bad about my Eliza, and I will cut your tongue out and feed it to you." Now, that was a promise, not a threat.

Jerking my leg, I land a quick kick into his stomach before taking a deep breath to keep myself collected. "You are going to regret every lash of your tongue against her, and you are definitely going to regret every time you laid a finger on her sweet body." Unable to help myself, I lashed out at him with another hard kick to the stomach.

Flipping my wrist, I checked the time with an irritated scowl. I had to head back to the house before the kids tore it down with Max, but my men weren't here yet to pick up this sack of shit.

"Eliza's not going to stay with you once she knows the truth," James strained through his dying coughs. "You better enjoy your last seconds with her before I take her back with me."

I tried to stifle my amused laugh, but it slipped out completely. "Oh, she's never going to find out, and she's never going back with you." Giving him a sorry look, I shook my head with a few tuts of my tongue. "She won't even be going to your execution." I don't think she'd appreciate me murdering her ex, no matter how much she hated him and wanted him gone.

In the blink of an eye, James lunged for my legs, hooking his arms around the back of my knees and buckling them. Caught off guard, all I could do was brace myself properly for the tumble to the ground. Landing flat on my ass, I threw my arms back to try and recover fast, but him scrambling atop of me sent me to the ground completely. He wasn't a small man by any means; height-wise, he was a few inches shorter than me, but he beat me in the muscle department by being built like a solid chunk of meat.

Anticipating a few blows to the face, I instinctively threw my arms up to guard my face. It was a good call on my end because the blows did come for a moment before I struggled back. I waited until there was an opening between his punches to strike back with my own punch to his face, causing him to reel back with a groan.

Grabbing the front of his shirt, I threw him off with a grunt of effort before scrambling at him to try and get on top to pin him down. Unfortunately, he was a tad bit faster, narrowly escaping me as he got onto his feet.

A quick scuff and James kicked a puff of dirt and gravel right into my face. "Fuck!" I seethed through gritted teeth, rubbing my eyes in an attempt to clear them. "Damn it!" I cursed under my breath when the sounds of retreating footsteps echoed through the air, along with the sight of a fading figure from my line of vision.

Scurrying to my feet, I took off after James with two left feet. Stupid fucking grit in my eyes burned like hell! What made things more frustrating was that I lost James after a few turns. Damn asshole blended into a crowd of people crossing the street, and I lost him after that.

The defeated trip home was filled with nothing but me grumbling to myself while trying to clear my stinging and aching eyes. Hopefully, one of my men could snag him before he went around and caused too much trouble.

Letting out an angry cry, I kicked at a boulder along the river, knocking it into the water with a huge splash.

I have to find him before he goes to Eliza.

Eliza can't know. She can <u>never</u> know the truth about me.

If James cracked open my vault of skeletons, then I'd be done for with Eliza. She was much too sweet to understand my lifestyle. I really didn't want to resort to forcing my hand with Eliza, but if James spilled my secrets, then I'd have no other choice.

Chapter 27
Eliza

"Eliza darling, they're just my parents, nothing to fret over." Adam's soothing voice did little to calm my buzzing nerves.

Sighing, I lightly shrugged his hands off my body to pace around our room again. "I still would've appreciated a heads up! I want to make a good impression on them! I could've walked out with bad bedhead and in gross pajamas or just your shirt and undies if Hailee didn't say anything!" Okay, maybe that was a bit of an exaggeration, but it wasn't out of the realm of possibility.

"*Mia rosa*." Adam chuckled, grabbing me by my shoulders and pulling me into a tight hug. "My parents already adore you, and they haven't met you fully yet. You have nothing to worry about, honestly." Grasping my chin, he brought my face up into a feathery kiss. "Just be yourself. You are more than perfect to me and them."

Frowning and pouting slightly, I fisted the front of his shirt tightly. "But what if they change their minds when they actually meet me for the first time? What if they tell you I'm not enough?" The negative words hung on the tip of my tongue, ready to swing out of my mouth the next time I opened it.

The bucket of bad comments would've spilled all over if it weren't for the pointed look from Adam. "I am not opposed to taking you over my knee, little rose, so be careful with what comes out of your mouth next." It would be the only warning I'd get from him on the matter. "My parents don't get here for at least another hour or so, which leaves me plenty of time to punish you and get a little slice of cake for myself." His mischievous face leaned down closer to mine, and his lips ghosted over the edges of my trembling mouth. "On the other hand, that also means an hour of possible fun for both of us."

"B-bub, this is not the time to be thinking about—ah!" A surprised squeal squeezed out of me when Adam suddenly hiked me up and threw me backward onto the bed. "Adam! You can't—"

"Spread your legs." The depth of his soul-shattering command made sparks of excitement zip down my whole body to my sensitive areas.

I shouldn't entertain him, but fuck, I couldn't help but obey. My body had a mind of its own when it came to Adam, not that I minded. Honestly, my legs propped up and spread wide before my mind could fully process everything. Adam was so dangerous for me, but I lived for that thrill and solace.

"Good girl," he praised me with a heart-melting smile as he positioned himself between my thighs. "Pull your dress up a little more. I don't want to get it dirty." His dominating eyes never left me as he undid his pants to pull out his heavy cock.

Mindlessly, I fumbled around with scurrying hands, bunching up the skirt of my dress around my waist, exposing myself to Adam. The only thing between me and Adam were my panties, which didn't stay on my body long. Adam yanked them off me hastily and threw them aside without a care.

Smirking down at me, he lazily swiped the tip of his dick along the length of my sex. When I tried to buck my hips away and squirm away, he shot his hand out and coiled it around my neck firmly, holding me in place. "You're going to relax and let me get you in a better mindset. The only thing I want to hear coming out of your mouth while my cock is claiming your cunt is 'thank you, sir' for every orgasm I grant you, got that?" His thumb stroked the side of my thrumming neck calmingly as he looked down at me with a dark smile.

Taking in a deep breath, I nodded softly. "Yes, sir." There was no fighting him. Well, I could, if I wanted to spice things up a bit, or if I really wasn't in the mood, then putting a complete stop to all of this was on the table also.

Fisting the sheets, I sucked in a sharp breath and whimpered as Adam eased himself into me with a few rough thrusts. "Shit! You gotta relax, darling," he strained through gritted teeth.

I wanted to quip back at him, but I was too busy keeping my jaw clenched. God, it hurt so much because I wasn't completely prepared to take him. My eyes burned a little as my tears welled up and stung at my glassy orbs. Pressing my head back into the bed, I shut my eyes tight to bite through the discomfort.

The soft feeling of lips kissing my stray tears away made my eyes flutter open. "It's okay, *mia rosa*, it's okay." He shushed and soothed me with sweet words as he continued to decorate my precious face with kisses.

My body fought against his as he slowly thrust in and out of me with slow strokes, and my body naturally clamped down on him because it needed more time to adjust. No matter how many deep breaths I took, how much I let my eyes wander around the room and his stony orbs, I couldn't relax enough.

Whimpering and gasping, I reached out and grabbed his forearms. "S-sir, I don't think..."

His lips brushed against my ear, making me shudder when his chest rumbled against me. "Settle." His deep voice instantly calmed my turbulent waters. Leaning back, he smiled proudly down at me. "*Brava ragazza.*"

Our sweet moment lasted just that, a moment. "Crash." Nothing could've prepared me for the way my body gave in to his command.

Every fiber of my being, from head to toe, tightened and tingled with a surge of pleasure. The shock of my orgasm blindsided me, and all I could do was take it and ride it out. A soft haze clouded my mind as I breathed my way through the ebbs of my orgasms, and I barely caught Adam's next words. "Remember what I told you before we started." There was a faint edge of amusement to his voice, I think; it was a little hard to tell with how muddled everything was.

Without putting much thought into it, I let my gratitude slip from my lips. "Thank you, sir." I shuddered through a whimper as I came down.

Well, at least it made things a little easier. All the pain bled out into pleasure the more he slammed himself into me. Every orgasm he pulled from my body heightened me to new levels until my damn head was high in the clouds.

The constant knot in my stomach didn't bother me one bit as it lingered after every orgasm. My body was conditioned to be ready for the next snap, and Adam did well to keep me strung and up in the air.

I don't know how long we kept at it. It wasn't as if I kept count of how many times he commanded me to orgasm or how many times I thanked him afterward.

"Crash." His voice growled, making me tremble as I felt him speak to my soul.

"Thank you, sir," I whimpered between my moans. "Sir, please, too much." Everything ached so bad, and if he kept going, then he'd drive me insane with all this pleasure and lust.

"One more, darling, just one more for me." I could tell he was close with how heavy and paced his breathing had become.

Holding me tightly against his body, he jerked his hips into me forcefully, ramming his hard tip right into my cervix. I gasped sharply as my legs twitched instinctively. "Fuck!" My toes curled out of my control; they tightened up so much that I could feel the strain in my muscles and tendons as Adam caused jolts of painful pleasure to ravage my body.

Clawing at his back, I whimpered at him pleadingly. "Please, Adam, please, no more, please, please." It was incessant, and I couldn't control my words. "It's too much."

My whole body jumped at the sudden slam of his hand next to my head. "Crash." He shuddered, groaning deeply and arching his body into my when I dug my nails deeper into him with my anguished cry of pleasure. "Fuck! That's it, darling, get every last drop."

It felt as if my whole body would snap in on itself with how much my muscles tensed up. "Adam!" I cried out through a choked sob. "Adam..." I didn't even bother trying to fight my body, letting it writhe against him through the crashing tidal waves of my orgasm. "Oh Go—"

I choked out a gasp at the sudden hand necklace from Adam. "Finish that, and I'll fuck you so hard that you will see him before I pull you back to Hell to be with me forever," he threatened darkly with a chuckle, making me moan and squeeze him harder. "Or maybe I might take some mercy on you and make you get down on your knees and worship me, make you remember who your god really is."

Oh God.

Suddenly, he pulled out of me, causing a small gush of my juices to spray out before he shoved his fingers into me.

Keeping his fingers in me, he got off the bed, hauling me to the edge of it. I couldn't help but panic a little because I thought he'd pull me to the ground and face fuck me until another load filled my mouth or painted my face because I'd said my thought out loud.

So, much to my relief, I found myself being forced to take his half-hard cock into my mouth instead of what my mind cooked up. "Clean me off." His gruff command came from above before his hips gave some soft thrusts.

Moaning deeply, I reached up and grabbed his hips to help keep myself steady as I sucked and licked his throbbing cock clean of our mixed cum. Just as I was done cleaning every inch of him, he pulled back, making me whimper a little. I didn't whine and pout for long, not with how he shoved his cum coated fingers into my mouth.

Shoving his digits deep into my throat, he made me gag and choke on them while holding my face still with his free hand. "That's it, get every drop of us." I faintly caught the sight of his mad smile through my tears. "I love how much of a cum slut you are for me." His dark chuckle sent shivers down my body as I eagerly cleaned his fingers.

His fingers pulled out with a soft smack of my lips with how much I sucked at them. "You're so fucking beautiful." His words were filled with awe and love as he admired me from above.

A tender moment fell upon us as he stroked my cheek ardently. "I really can't get enough of you." He started with an overly warm smile, getting down on his knee to hover his face above mine. "Your lovely eyes." His words faded out as he kissed my eyes. "This cute nose." I could feel his lips graze down my nose bridge before they kissed the tip. "And these lips." He took his sweet time claiming my lips in a passionate kiss.

Loosely wrapping my arms around his neck, I tangled my fingers into his dark strands as we let our tongues dance with each other hotly. Through heated breaths, he smiled lovingly at me as his hands mapped out every inch of my body. "Your body is a fucking masterpiece, my masterpiece." He growled softly against my lips before taking them again in a heated kiss.

When he pulled away, I expected some more sweet and doting words or his cheeky smile. So, seeing the nervous scrunch on his half-smiling face made my mood and expression fall into a dark pit as my anxiety hiked up to the damn skies. "Bub? What's wrong? Why are you looking at me like that? Did I do something?" I certainly didn't say anything because I haven't peeped up one bit.

Flipping onto my front side, I pushed myself up onto my haunches. Gingerly, I reached out and held his wary face, brushing his hair out of his face with trembling fingers. "Adam? Bub? Please, what did I do wrong?" It had to have been me because what could he possibly do wrong between us?

His face relaxed with a reassuring smile before his head shook. "Eliza darling, no, nothing like that, no." The vibrations of his chuckles tickled my palms a bit as I held onto his face for dear life. "It's nothing bad or anything of your doing," he assured me with a strong smile.

I watched his shoulders rise and fall deeply a few times before his flickering eyes settled on his pants on the ground next to him. Without prying himself from me, he reached out and snatched the piece of clothing up. After a quick second of fishing around in the pocket of the pants, he pulled out...

No...

Please, no...

"Adam..." I could feel all the color drain from my face and trickle down and out of my body as I stared at him with bugged-out eyes and an agape mouth.

Adam's face twisted in confusion for a split second before he broke out laughing, which had me looking at him with a twisted expression. "Oh, darling, please, no, it's not what you think." He stammered out between his laughter.

Skillfully, he popped open the small, black box with one hand while taking my hand with the other. "I'm not proposing to you," he assured me with a firm smile that quickly turned cheeky. "Yet." He snickered softly before kissing my stunned lips. "It's just a promise ring, something for you to have around your finger to look at whenever you are not next to me."

Again, with one hand, he pulled the delicate platinum ring out of the box and slipped it onto my left ring finger. "Whenever you are feeling down or having doubts about anything with yourself or us, I want you to look at this ring," he told me with a soft and tender smile. "This ring is so much more than a promise from me to you about making you my wife one day. This is a reminder of *all* the promises I am making to you and of those you will make to yourself."

Slowly, I pushed myself up into a sitting position when Adam stood a little and sat beside me. His arms shot out, wrapping around my waist and pulling me into his lap. "I swear to you, what we have, our relationship, is not temporary. I have every intention of making you my wife when I see that you are ready. You are my forever, Eliza, my paradise. I swear, I will always treat you right and do right by you as I have been, but I will always be trying to do better and better every day for the rest of our lives." His lips sealed mine with a breath-taking kiss before he continued with a big smile, "I swear, our family will be nothing but perfect by our standards. I swear, I will always provide for you in every aspect: physically, financially, mentally, emotionally, and anything else you can think of. My heart belongs to you, and I am your home." My whole heart melted with his ardent gaze full of promise. "Our life will be a flawless love story. I will love you until my dying breath and beyond."

God damn it!

Tears burned at my eyes as they squeezed out of my eyes and streamed down my cheeks. "Adam." Grabbing his face, I pulled his face into a kiss. "I love you so much," I whispered against his lips with a big smile.

Taking my hands in his, he looked down at them with a dreamy smile while he rubbed the ring with his thumb. "I also want this ring to be something of a promise to yourself as well," he said, looking deeply into my eyes. "I want you to promise me you will stop putting yourself down, saying that you aren't good enough for me, that you aren't worth anything."

Lifting my hand up, he lightly shook it in front of my face. "This ring right here should be more than enough proof to you that you are worth it because I would never put a ring on someone who wasn't worth my time, someone who I have no intentions of spending forever with." Bringing my hand to his lips, he kissed it. "When you have your dark moments, you look at this ring and remember the future that you are promised, the life that you have in front and ahead of you."

Setting my hands back into my lap, he cupped my face again, stroking my cheeks with his thumbs. "I love you, Eliza, and nothing will ever change that. I am beyond serious about you, and not only do I want what's best for us, but I want what's best for you, too."

Giggling and grinning like a girl in love, I placed my hand over his and leaned into his touch. "My bub is just the sweetest."

God, I really don't deserve this man, but he's so crazy about me that I can't help but take and keep him.

Holding my hand out in front of me, I admired the ring with bright eyes.

The small band was made up of waves like the ocean, closing in on a pink pearl with a ring of white diamonds around it, all of which sat in the center of a rose. Then, on the band next to the pearl were our names, his being on one side and mine on the other.

I spoke in awe as I continued to marvel at the ring, "Can't I just have this as the wedding ring? It's so perfect already." Seriously, the only thing that was missing was the second band to make it a wedding set.

"If that is what my darling Eliza wants, then I guess," Adam relented with a teasing chuckle and roll of his eyes. "But I'm adding some fancy bands to make sure your finger is completely decked out, and I'm proposing to you with another ring that will be a part of the whole set."

Sensing it to be a pointless battle, I rolled my eyes in defeat before kissing his cheek. "Nothing too fancy. You know I'm not one to make a huge statement." Call me simple and cliché or whatever, but I preferred lowkey and delicate jewelry.

I was more than happy with the promise ring because the pearl wasn't huge or anything, maybe about the size of a pencil eraser, and the ring of diamonds around it was dainty.

"Don't worry. I know what you like and what you don't." At least his confident grin was reassuring enough for me.

Getting off the bed with me in his arms, he brought me over to the vanity and set me down, straightening my dress out. "Now, let's get you put back together before my mom sees you like this and goes after me for making you such a mess."

Chapter 28
Adam

THE WAY ELIZA'S FEET shuffled in her spot was rather adorable. I mean, her nervous energy wasn't cute, but I didn't have any tricks to ease her nerves, unfortunately.

Leaning down, I kissed her forehead and squeezed her jittery hand tightly. "Darling, breathe before you pass out." I could see the quickening rise and fall of her chest with each breath; she was a few seconds away from full-on hyperventilating. "My parents are going to adore you, especially my mom."

It probably didn't mean much coming from me because they were my parents, but I spoke the truth. They adored Eliza the moment I told them about her, and even after I told them about her past and Asher, they still loved her. Actually, after they heard about everything, I was pretty sure they loved her more.

They weren't judgmental people by any means. The only thing they cared about was if Eliza was a good person on the inside and if I was serious about her. When those two check boxes were ticked off, they went full in with loving Eliza and Asher way before even meeting the two.

"Eliza, they already love you, so don't sweat it." Hailee tried to calm Eliza by rubbing her shoulders, but that only seemed to make Eliza tense up more.

Asher lurched out of my arms, wrapping his tiny ones around his mother's neck to comfort her with a baby hug. "Mama?" Of course, poor little Asher had no idea what was going on; just here for the ride.

Breathing deeply, Eliza plucked Asher from my arms to fully snuggle him. "What if they—"

She didn't get a chance to finish her worried thought with how the door practically flew open with my mother's excited greeting. A flurry of Italian was thrown our way, along with my mother's arms and kisses.

Hailee and I were instantly suffocated by our mother's scrawny arms that were somehow stronger than a damn python. Our faces weren't spared from how much she smothered every inch of our faces in smooches. "Oh, my babies, I missed you so much!" Stepping back, she looked at us up and down with her observant eyes, her lips twisting a bit in a frown. "You two have gotten so skinny! You need more meat on your bones!" She grumbled something in Italian about how we were walking sticks and that we had no love on our bodies for others to appreciate, as well as other stuff along those lines.

In an instant, her head snapped over to Eliza and Asher, both of whom stood there with a dumbfounded expression. Of course, the moment my mother's attention landed on them fully, their faces widened a little with shock when she somewhat tackled them with a hug. "Oh, you two are just the sweetest-looking things!" My mother gushed.

Eliza's eyes drifted over to me in a cry for help as my mother sweetened them with compliments that were almost teeth rotting. Sighing, I settled my hands on my mother's shoulders. "Mamma, you're scaring them." Chuckling nervously, I pried my mother away from Eliza and Asher.

"*Mia rosa*, this is my mother, Maria." Adam chuckled, smiling proudly.

With a nervous chuckle of her own, my mother simmered herself down to a more doable energy level; hopefully her toning it down a bit would be enough to not overload my poor Eliza. "Oh dear, I'm sorry. I'm just so happy to finally meet my little Adam's woman and my new little grandson," she apologized in a softened voice, reaching back out and hugging Eliza tightly. "You look so much better and prettier than the pictures Adam showed me. Really, you are such a doll."

"Mamma, you're making her blush." Hailee giggled, smiling happily at the scene with me.

Laughing softly, my mother released Eliza to give Asher her full attention. "Oh, and this little man is just the most handsome thing ever," she spoke in a baby voice while wagging a finger at Asher. "Hi there, my little one. You are just the plumpest grape in the field now aren't you."

At least Asher wasn't too freaked out with my mother. Granted, I didn't have any doubts about Asher taking to anyone because he was the friendliest child ever. Sometimes, his lack of stranger danger terrified me, if I was honest. The amount of times he's followed and gone up to basically anyone remotely friendly looking scared the hell out of me because I knew how fucked up some people could be. At the very least, Asher never strayed too far from me, Eliza, or anyone who was his immediate caretaker. Still, the fear of him being kidnapped or going missing was always present whenever we went out.

The fact James was now out there didn't help ease my anxiety over the whole situation any. Thinking about that bastard getting his hands on Asher made my blood boil and the veil of red cloud over my vision. If that ever happened, then that'd be a nightmare come true for all of us, especially Eliza. I didn't want to imagine the devastation Eliza would go through if such news were ever to reach her ears.

She knew nothing about James being in the city, and she never would as long as I could help it. James *will* be a thing of the past, and he *will* no longer be a problem for much longer.

Any minute now, a message from one of my men informing me of James's capture would buzz on my phone.

"Wait, where's papa?" Hailee interrupted the warm moment with her confusion.

A hard knock at the door pushed it open, and in came my stumbling father, who nearly tripped over all the bags and luggage he had in his arms.

Instinctively, my feet scrambled over to my father, and my arms shot out to catch him before his body hit the ground. "Dad, I have men for a reason, and I'm also here to help. I don't want you throwing out your back or something at your age," I fretted, pushing all the things away from my father so he wouldn't grab at them.

"Just because I'm old doesn't mean I can't whoop your ass still. I'm more than capable of handling some bags and your mother's luggage," he shot back at me with a sneer.

"Your stupid pride is going to put you in the grave, I swear," I grumbled with a roll of my eyes. "Why do you guys have so much stuff?"

While using me as support, he patted my chest with a hearty chuckle. "Then you better watch out for this pride as well 'cause you are just like me," he remarked, letting out some winded breaths. "And all that stuff are things for the kiddos." He tried to wave it off, but Hailee didn't let it slip.

Groaning rather playfully, Hailee ran her hands through her hair before looking at our mother with a flat glare. "Mamma, Adelaide has way too many toys and clothes."

Rolling her eyes, my mother swatted a playful hand at Hailee, dismissing her while keeping her eyes on the two kids who occupied her arms. "Oh, there's no such thing as too many toys and clothes for these little ones." She giggled, tickling the toddlers with her nose.

"Oh, just let your mother be a grandma. It keeps her sane and off my ass," my father joked, barking out a laugh that earned him a few kicks to the shin from my mother.

Nudging my father's hand, I nodded at my nervous rose. "My little rose, Eliza." My voice swelled with pride as I smiled at her lovingly.

Then, I flickered my gaze from her to my father. "Darling, this is my father, Antonio."

Lightly tapping my mother out of the way, my father stepped up to Eliza, hugging her comfortingly. "Welcome to the family, Eliza," he greeted her warmly, releasing and stepping back. "Sorry for my wife's eagerness. She gets excited very easily, especially when it comes to our kids' love lives."

My father remained quiet for a moment, studying Eliza carefully while maintaining a friendly smile. "Are you sure you can put up with my son? He's got a hard head that one, and I would know because he got it from me," my father asked with a diffusing chuckle. Then, his expression turned serious. "Is he treating you right? If he's not, then I want you to tell me so I can set him straight," he told Eliza sternly, throwing a glare my way, the one that meant I better be the proper person he raised me up to be.

Turning her loving eyes to me, I watched as Eliza's nervous face lit up with a tender smile. "Adam is perfect, and I mean it. He's done nothing but treat me so right and proper." Tearing her eyes away from me, she looked at both my parents with eyes full of utmost gratitude. "I hope I can raise Asher up as well as you two raised Adam."

Letting out a happy sob, my mother set the kids down to attack Eliza with a tight hug. "Oh, you are too kind. You and Adam will raise your little boy just perfect, don't you worry."

Now, I did feel a little bad for Eliza when my mother pulled her off to the living area, asking my poor darling every question possible on God's green earth. A part of me wanted to help Eliza out, especially when she threw me those panicked eyes like some deer being caught in the headlights, but my father dragged me off to the patio before I could step in. So, all I could do was hope that Hailee would save Eliza if things got a little too deep and far.

Even as my father dragged me away for some privacy between us, I couldn't help but keep my gaze trained on Eliza until a firm slap to my back forced my attention elsewhere. "How are you, son?" my father asked in a tired voice, with an equally tired smile.

Sucking in a deep breath, I rolled my head back to look at the clear skies for a moment. I knew what he was asking. It wasn't a simple question to see how I was doing overall. "Perfect, honestly," I answered truthfully with a big smile. "Business is going smooth as usual, and I'm just basically doing light admin work. I've got so much time to myself and Asher, and honestly, my life couldn't be more perfect right now."

"Then why do you look like your face just ate shit?" My father deadpanned.

Opening my mouth, I quickly shut it because correcting my father was pointless. "It's just a little hiccup, that's all, but it should be handled pretty soon." Hopefully.

"Adam, what did you do?" he pressed me with a heavy sigh. "It's never a little hiccup with you."

Grumbling internally, I rolled my eyes a little before deflating with a huff. "Eliza's ex got away from me earlier, and that was kind of not the plan..." Trying to hide things from my father was pointless because he'd either pry it out of me with his own hands or find out some other way. "And Eliza has no idea about any of that... Or my plans."

Sighing heavily, my father gave me a grave look. "Does she know about... *that* side of you?"

The air around us instantly mugged up with a heavy tension. My father didn't need me to verbally answer him, my grim silence being enough of one. "Adam," he sighed heavily with a disappointed groan and shake of his head. "You cannot keep things that huge from her. I know it's not easy, but it's better for you to tell her sooner rather than later." Crossing his arms, he looked at me pointedly. "You need to tell her before she finds out by other means, and that's when things will really get messy."

Running a flustered hand through my tousled hair, I huff out an exasperated scoff. "I know, but... I don't know how to tell her or even start letting her in, and what if that pushes over the line? I mean, Eliza is just... Perfect. An angel. If I told her that the man she is with is a mafia boss, she's going to run for the hills." Sighing in defeat, I hung my head in my hands and shook it.

"I wish I could tell you the right thing to say, but I'm at a loss myself for that situation." My father flashed me an apologetic smile, patting my shoulder. "Just tell her the truth, and if she really is the one for you, then she will stay. I know it's probably not what you want to hear, but that's the most basic foundation. If a person really loves you, then they will learn to work with all your bad as well as your good."

My father's head turned to look at my mother through the patio door, a nostalgic smile gracing his face. "No one is perfect, even your mother and I, but a huge part of making a relationship work is communication and compromise." Looking back at me with a warm smile, he squeezed my shoulder. "You cannot build a relationship on lies, nor can one survive on an untruthful one. No matter what, she deserves to know *everything* about you."

Unfortunately, I had no response because my father was right. I mean, the only thing I could do was agree with him, but I couldn't tell him that I'd tell Eliza right away or something. Yes, I knew I needed to tell her, but I was still iffy about it. Call me a bad, horrible person, but I seriously debated keeping my mafia life a secret from her even after my elderly father advised me otherwise.

Things probably would blow up in my face like a shit bomb when she finds out, and I should try to mitigate all of that by being upfront with her now rather than later. But I couldn't do it. I felt like a complete prick, but I wanted to keep her in the dark forever.

"Adam." My father's stern voice pulled me from my thoughts. "I know what you're thinking. You have that stupid face on you right now, and whatever you're thinking, don't."

Sighing heavily, I dropped my hands to my sides, shoving them into my pockets. "But what if—"

"No!" My body shook a little from my father's firm shove. "Lies never belong in a relationship, and omissions count as lies, too. Nothing good ever comes from that toxic sin."

Hanging my head, I peered up a little at my father with a pathetic look, watching as his tense shoulders relaxed with a deep breath.

"It is going to hurt, but how much it does, and the damage can be controlled by you."

Yet, I swore to never hurt my darling Eliza.

Chapter 29
Eliza

"Mrs. San—"

"Eliza!" Maria cut me off, snapping at me lightheartedly. "How many times do I have to tell you? It's Maria or Mamma. You are family," she reminded me with a stern smile.

Chuckling nervously, I rubbed the back of my neck. "Sorry, it just feels weird for me to address someone by their name like that." And it certainly felt weird to address her as my mother when Adam and I weren't married yet or anything—not to mention it's only been a few days since I've met his family.

Nervously, I chewed at my bottom lip a bit as I debated whether to ask the lingering question in my mind. "Uhh I know you're his mother and all, and that you probably don't want to say anything bad about him, but is there anything about Adam I should be aware of?" Just as my words left my mouth, I backtracked with a quick wave of my hands. "Not that I'm looking for anything bad about Adam and all, and he's been very forthcoming with me about my questions, but

I figured since you're his mother, you'd have more knowledge about him."

Dismissing me with a wave and warm chuckle, Maria dried her hands off with a towel before leaning against the kitchen counter with a nostalgic smile. "Oh, Adam, he's a special one. If you haven't figured out by now, then he's very stubborn and assertive." Shaking her head with an amused chuckle, she looked out the patio window at Adam and her husband. "Always getting his way, that one." Sighing, almost sadly so, Maria looked at me with almost a sympathetic smile. "Adam's hard to wrangle with, so he needs a lot of patience and persistence. Once he sets his mind to something, he'll stop at nothing to achieve it. Sometimes such headstrong qualities are good, but at times, it can be very frustrating."

Setting the towel down with another sigh, she came up to me and gave me a side hug, keeping her arm snug around my shoulders in a comforting manner. "Not that he'd do anything bad with you, but I'm just a little afraid that if you don't dig your heels in sometimes with him, then he'll bully you a bit. Adam won't raise a hand or his voice against you or anything like that lest he wants to face my wrath, but with how passive you can sometimes be, I'm just a little afraid of him stepping over your toes sometimes."

Her soft face twisted with slight pensive worry as she looked at me studiously. "He hasn't tried to manipulate you or anything, has he? I would like to believe better in my son, believe that I raised him better than that, but once they are out in the world, there's only so much you can do as a parent, you know?" she worried with a deepening frown, making me panic a little because I had no idea how to respond properly to her. "I won't be upset or anything at you, promise. I just want you to be truthful with me when it comes to Adam."

I slowly reached a tentative hand up and patted hers as it rested on my shoulder. "No, Adam's perfect, honest. He hasn't been mean or pushy or anything of the sort. He has been a saint to me, and sometimes I feel bad that he's wasting his time and energy on someone like me."

Now that last part got Maria whirling around to face me fully with a scolding look, not the bad kind though, kind of like the ones mothers would give their kids to teach some kind of positive lesson. "Now, you listen here, Eliza," she said, holding up a finger at me. "You are not a waste of anything, so quit that about yourself." She started with a huff before grumbling, "I swear, you and Hailee are going to make my head blow up with a headache with your bad self-esteem."

Her chest puffed out with a deep breath that was held for a second. "Nothing of what happened to you makes you any less of a person or any less worthy. As I like to tell my children, we are hidden gardens, and you just have to find or wait for the right person to discover you. The right gardener will appreciate your worth and beauty, and they will tend to you and make you bloom like never before. They will turn you into a wonder of the world for others to marvel upon. Despite all the weeds, overgrowth, thorns, trash, they will put in the effort to clear it all up because they want you."

I couldn't help but notice how Maria looked at her husband with lovestruck eyes. Even after all this time, she looked at him as if it were the first time, and I only hoped that was how Adam and I would look at each other ages from now. "When you find the one." Maria turned her smiling face back at me, patting my arm lovingly. "You just know. It really is a work of wonders that no one can explain, true love, that is. It is just something that our heart and soul know innately."

Her words pulled a chuckle from me as I shook my head softly. "It's strange, but I know what you mean." Sighing, I looked over at Adam with an unconscious smile. "I thought I found love and knew what it was when my ex charmed me and such, but I never felt such liveliness until Adam. Not a day goes by that I don't feel happy to wake up to his snoring face. Just the mere thought of him being mine makes my whole body light up with this fire that I didn't know was possible."

I probably sounded like some lovestruck idiot, but I didn't care. What I said just now was only a fraction of what I felt with Adam, what his presence in my life has kickstarted.

Giving out a bell-toting laugh, Maria hugged me again, this time tighter. "Just don't let my boy get too stubborn and step on your toes too much, and if you need some help, then please let me know because I am not the type of mother to coddle her children or stand behind them when they are in the wrong."

Returning her affection with a hug of my own and a tearful smile, I nodded. "Thank you."

Patting my back, we remained in each other's arms for a moment before she pulled away with a light chuckle. "Go grab our men for lunch while I set the table. Then, we can make them set up for the party after the meal while we 'go pick up the cake' and last-minute supplies." AKA, we girls would be grabbing coffee and treats and spoiling ourselves for a few hours before the kids' birthday party would start later that evening.

"I can't believe you actually got them dogs. Hailee's going to kill you." Unless I killed him first.

Rubbing my temples, I leaned against the wall. "I know we talked about a dog or two, but today? Really?" I slightly glared at Adam tiredly out of the corners of my eyes.

Chuckling dismissively, Adam snaked his arm around my waist, pulling me close for a kiss on the temple. "Well, Asher really liked Bodie when we went to the shelter the other day, and you gotta admit, he's a cute dog," Adam started, grinning at our newest addition, rolling around on the floor with the children. "And besides, I already told you I'll take care of Bodie."

Before I could hold my eyes down, I felt them roll around very dramatically. "That's what they all say before a week later I'm the one picking up his poop, walking him three times a day, letting him out in the middle of the night and whatnot, feeding him, bathing him, and basically doing everything." Pretty sure that line was akin to a tale as old as time.

Snuggling his face up to mine, Adam grinned rather confidently. "Then you can either kick my ass for not keeping my word or tattle on me to my Mamma so she can do it for you."

Words failed to leave my open mouth as I was too busy staring down at the blue nose pit bull fawning at my feet. I had to admit, he was cute and charming in his own special way. Bodie's little white mitts on all four of his paws didn't help either because I found them adorable.

I wasn't against us having a dog or any kind of pet; I was against me having to take care of the pet once everyone would get bored of it. I already had to take care of Asher and worry about Adam and myself, so adding—basically—another child on top of everything was a bit of a headache to think about, let alone live.

Reaching down, I petted Bodie's head and scratched his ear, giggling a little when his hind leg started twitching and thumping against the floor in response. I really had no qualms with Bodie. Well, maybe I was still a little surprised by his size because I thought Adam would bring home some puppy or a medium-sized dog, not some eighty-pound pit bull.

"Bohwdie!" Asher's excitement was cut short by his grunt when he tackled himself into Bodie.

I also couldn't complain because Asher really adored Bodie, and Bodie was more than patient so far from what I've seen with Asher. He was pretty good with all the little kids who'd been climbing all over him, tugging at his ears and tail; the tough fellow just sat there and took it all with no problem. A real gentle giant.

The birthday party for Adelaide and Asher was a little bigger than I expected. It was mostly family and close friends, but Adam and Hailee had quite a bit of family around who came down for the little celebration. Some of their friends came too, and most of them had children of their own.

I was the only odd one out, having no one. No contact with my parents, and even if I did, it wasn't like I could call them down—too risky. Eve was in Idaho, but she sent her wishes.

Sighing heavily, I shrugged Adam's arm off and stepped away from him. "I'm going to step outside for a second. Just need some fresh air before cake and craziness." I watched as Adam's lips tightened into a firm line as if he wanted to fight me a little, but he relented with an understanding nod.

"Thank you." Leaning up to my tippy toes, I kissed his cheek before stepping out onto the patio, shivering a bit at the chilly ocean breeze raking against my bare arms. It was more than warm enough inside the house not to wear a long sleeve.

Soft creaks echoed through the eerily still night as my slow steps worked their way to the railing of the wooden patio. Leaning against it with a deep sigh, I stared out at the private beach backyard, watching the waves go in and out in a steady rhythm like the constant beats of my heart.

This was all so nice, so perfect.

So, why did it feel so wrong?

All this was a dream come true, the stupid magazine family or some shit like that. Beach front house, a rich man who wasn't a jerk, the kid, the dog... the life. This life I was living with Adam, all that I've got, and all that Adam would give me with time, it all felt too surreal.

Click.

There was the pin that shattered everything.

The sounds of the crashing water faded out to nothing as the ringing in my ears intensified until it sounded like some machine was inside my ear. Movement of my chest could be felt, but I couldn't feel the fresh, cold air filling my lungs and moving about my airways. Every muscle fiber of my body tightened as my heart stilled in my chest; not even the faintest thump echoed throughout my body.

"Doesn't feel real, does it?"

The voice of the devil himself didn't sound real, and I refused to turn my head to put a face to the voice.

Unfortunately, that option of self-preservation was taken away from me. "Look at me, bitch." The voice of my nightmares demanded as the feeling of something hard and cold dug into my back. "Turn around and look at me. I want to see *my wife's* face after all this time." He sounded so vindictive, and I was afraid that if I gave in, then his face would be the last I saw on this earth. "Turn. Around. Now!" With each word, he dug the weapon deeper into me until I winced from the bite of the muzzle.

The wood beneath my feet gave with some soft creaks as I slowly turned my body around after holding my hands up in surrender. "J-James, wh—"

Having the barrel of a gun pointed right at my face was a sure way to shut me up. "Of all the people you could've exposed my son to and all the scum in the world you could've whored yourself out to, you choose to spread those stupid legs of yours to a low-life mafia bastard." James's angry face seethed inches from my face as he glared me down.

This was probably not the right situation, but I couldn't help it. The moment I heard his words, a laugh of disbelief sputtered out of me. Emboldened, I shot my hand out, slapping the gun away from me. Stepping right up into his face, I caused him to stumble back a step as I invaded his personal bubble. "Maybe if this had been over a year ago when I was under your thumb and didn't think for myself, then maybe, just maybe, I might fall for such bullshit." I had no idea where the confidence came from, and I didn't care.

It was hella gutsy for me to jab a finger in his face with every word, especially since he still had a gun in one hand. But I refused to stand there and let him spew lies about my Adam. "You know, I don't think you ever could stand me being happy, not even for a fucking second, and that's why you were always such a fucking abusive jerk to me. You hated it when I smiled or laughed because it meant I was enjoying life and that you might lose control of me." Scoffing, I shook my head at him with a look of disbelief. "You would say the most stupid things to break me down, but newsflash: I'm not that girl anymore."

With the adrenaline coursing through my body like a river of lava, I worked up enough nerves to put my hands on James's chest and shove at him, making him stumble back a few more steps. "What? Couldn't come up with some other stupid lie about Adam, so you decided that accusing him of being some career criminal was the way to go?"

Then, James did something that surprised me a bit. Instead of aiming the gun back at me, he looked at me with disbelief and grabbed my shoulders, shaking me as if to wake me. "Have I ever lied to you, though? Everything I've ever told you through the years has been true, hurtful, but true. I know you think this stupid asshole may be your saving grace, but he's not all he's cracked up to be. I mean, I'm a cop, and I know a criminal." His eyes pleaded with me to believe him, but I refused to.

"No." I vehemently shook my head, shoving him away. "You've fed me so much shit throughout the past ten years that lies and truths just all fell into the same pile." Scoffing and laughing slightly like some madwoman, I looked at James in a new light, a new but bad light. "Adam is a successful businessman, and you just can't stand that. You can't stand that I've found someone so much better than you, someone who I truly love." Now, this might have been a bit much, but I was on a high. "Un." Jab. "Like." Jab. "You." Instead of a finger jab with the last word, I firmly shoved him.

Yeah, I shouldn't have gotten so uppity because James instantly retaliated. I was so high on my adrenaline, though, that I barely felt the sting when his hand lashed across my face. Honestly, the loud and sharp slap that resonated through the air sounded more hurtful than the dulling ache against my reddening cheek.

This next hit, I felt, only because it was a fucking metal gun instead of his hand. "You bitch!" His body hid the ground with mine, and the wind was knocked out of me when his heavy one landed right on top of me.

"Get off me!" I shouted, thrashing as much as possible against him.

My legs kicked and bucked wildly like a panicked horse while my arms swung, and hands clawed at whatever they met. I didn't know whether it was my nails that tore or his flesh, but I pushed through the searing pain radiating from my hands as I grabbed and yanked handfuls of him.

Like hell would I go down without a fight this time. If he wanted to kill me, then I'd make damn sure I'd make a mess of him before I went.

Also, I hoped that if I made enough of a ruckus, then Adam or someone inside the house would take notice, and help would come my way.

Throwing my arms around his flailing one, I hugged it tightly against myself, anchoring him to me before biting down on his hand that held the gun. "Fucking bitch!" James howled in pain, punching my head with his other hand.

Despite the blows to my throbbing skull, I kept stubborn. Even as the metallic taste of iron filled my mouth, I kept my jaws locked around his hand until I felt his tendons move and heard the clatter of the gun hitting the ground next to me. Immediately, I let go of his arms and grabbed at his face, digging my thumbs into his eye sockets, causing him to cuss and scream in agony.

I expected him to retreat with the new injuries, but he kept on wailing at me blindly with his fists. He didn't remove himself from me until he was forced to by a big flying boulder. Okay, it wasn't an actual boulder, but with how fast and hard Bodie tackled James, the dog might as well be considered one.

While James was occupied with trying to pry the hound off him, I took the opportunity to snatch the gun up in a nanosecond and scramble to my feet.

"*Mia rosa!*" Adam's voice cut through my thrumming adrenaline haze so clearly, forcing my eyes to lock onto him.

Stuck in place with the gun raised in my hands, I stared at Adam and all the other shocked people gathered around the patio door. "Darling," Adam started, taking tentative steps toward me with his hands held out. "It's okay. I'm here, so lower the gun." His large, warm hand covered both of mine, pressing a little to urge me to lower the weapon. "It's okay. You've done amazing already, and I'm sorry for not being there for you like I promised. But I am now. So, please, let me handle the rest."

My heavy chest continued to heave with my drawn breaths as my wide eyes darted between James and Adam. My vision faded in and out of focus while everything around me spun. I felt so lightheaded with how my adrenaline died down in that instant. Every sharp breath of fresh air felt like pins and needles to my lungs and made my head spin out of control.

Adam's chest puffed out before deflating with a sharp whistle. "Bodie, release! Come!" Surprisingly enough, Bodie obeyed instantly.

With sharp eyes, I watched Bodie release his bloody jaw from James's mangled-looking forearm and run back over to Adam's side, where he assumed a protective stance with his teeth bared.

Coughing briefly, James spat out a bloody glob onto the floor while glaring at me and Adam. "Oh please, bitch doesn't have the guts or skills to shoot me," James mocked me with a scoffing laugh.

"You shut up before I let her use you as target practice," Adam snapped back at him with a deep scowl.

James underestimating me ticked something off in me, making me straighten my arms out again to point the gun at him. "I might not have the best aim, but I can damn well shoot you. You, of all people, should know I can handle a gun, considering how you fucking taught me." Sneering, I scoffed to myself with a pathetic laugh. "Or do you not remember teaching me the day you got accepted into the police academy? You were so damn excited about it and handling a gun and shit that you took me out back to shoot at cans. And since you were so adamant on me sharing in the joy, you stood right behind me the whole time, teaching and guiding me until I landed my first can."

I don't know if James finally lost it or if I did somehow get through to him, but he looked at me with such a sad smile and longing eyes. "You were so afraid of the noise. I had to pad the earmuffs to dampen the noise more, yet you still squealed and jumped at that first shot. Nearly broke my nose, too, with the recoil." His distant chuckle made me smile forlornly in return.

What happened to us?

That's what I wanted to ask him, but we were far beyond that.

For once in a long time, James felt normal, like the man I fell for once upon a time. If I didn't know any better or had no dignity or self-respect, then I might actually fall back into the whole pit trap.

"Goodbye, James."

Closing my eyes, I flicked the safety of the gun…

Chapter 30
Adam

"I'M SORRY... I'LL CLEAN it out for you, promise," Eliza continued to apologize despite my wishes against it.

"Darling," I chuckled, grabbing my bloodied shirt from her hands. "It's just a shirt." I reiterated, balling it up and throwing it back into the trash.

"But it's an expensive shirt," she remarked with a slight pout.

Rolling my eyes, I reached out and loosely wrapped my arms around her, swaying her around slightly. "And replacing it and twenty others would be nothing but pocket change for me," I threw back with a smug smirk, earning a flat glare from Eliza.

Shaking her little glare off with a chuckle, I leaned down and kissed her deeply. "Do you want to go back to the party, or do you need to call it a night?" I asked her with a concerned frown.

It'd barely been an hour since her encounter and attack with James, something I still beat myself over. I was supposed to be there to protect her, and she was supposed to be safe in our home. Yet, here she stood, looking like she'd been tossed into some fight ring with her beat-up face, scuffed-up arms, lacerated cheek, and banged-up head.

Also, she'd been rather reserved ever since my men whisked James off, and that concerned me quite a bit more than her physical appearance. The doctor said she was fine, maybe a mild concussion at best, but other than that, the surface wounds would heal with time. Mentally and emotionally, that's where I worried about her because those injuries could take forever to heal. Knowing Eliza and how she could be, I worried that she might not ever heal, or if she did, then I was afraid of the impact it might have on her personally and on our relationship.

A small silence ghosted over us before Eliza's long sigh ripped it away. "I think I might call it a night." Her blunted words felt like a punch to the chest, especially with how she shrugged me off and turned herself away.

"*Mia rosa*, what's wrong?" I prodded with a concerned scrunch of my face. "You haven't told me what exactly happened with James out there..." Obviously, they got into a tiff. Otherwise, she wouldn't look like she went a few rounds with a kangaroo.

Also, did James just attack her, or did she attack him? Did he say something to trigger her? Or did she say something to make him snap? There were so many what if's that I had no answers to.

Silently, Eliza slipped into our bed, bundling herself up with the covers. "I mean, there's not much to say about it. James showed up, shoved a gun at me, ran his mouth about hateful things like he always did, tried to talk me back by telling me some lie about you being a part of mafia." She scoffed and let out a laugh of disbelief. "I didn't believe any of it though because, well, I mean, come on." Shaking her head, she leaned up on her elbows, looking at me with a lopsided smile. "You? Mafia? Organized crime? No way."

Forcing out a stale chuckle, I shook my head in denial. "You don't believe him, do you?" If this wasn't a sign from the universe for me to spill my guts, then I didn't know what was.

Unfortunately, I never listened to signs.

This would bite me in the ass later, and I'd deal with the consequences then. Besides, now would be the worst time to tell her the truth. She just went through a lot of shit in such a short amount of time, so me showing her my walk-in closet full of bodies and skeletons was a huge no-no. So, for her sake and mine, the truth would have to wait.

Rolling her eyes, Eliza shook her head. "No, that's just a ridiculous thing for him to accuse you of. I mean, the only thing mafia about you that I can put a finger on is the fact you own some guns, but even then, that's a stretch because half the people on this planet own a few guns." Her dismissal made me let out a sigh of relief as I walked over to her and sat on the edge of the bed. "Besides, you don't have a mean bone in your body. I can't see you beating some man up for not paying you, nor can I see you ripping families apart and shit. Honestly, you're just too wholesome of a man."

Oh, my darling Eliza, if only you knew...

Keeping a smile on my face, I reached out and stroked her hair. Neither of us said anything for a small while, just basking in the muffled silence. "But, how are you, though? And I understand if you want to put off talking about things until tomorrow, but I need to know how you are doing." How much damage control did I have to do?

Taking a deep breath, she looked at me with hesitant eyes for a few seconds before scooting over to make room for me and patting the area lightly. Usually, I'd make her use her words, but after her stressful night, giving her a pass wouldn't hurt. Giving in to her demands, I laid down and pulled her into me, holding her securely.

Snuggling into me, Eliza took some controlled breaths for a long while, so long that I thought she fell asleep because her breathing became so rhythmic. I almost opened my mouth to ask, but she spoke up before I could. "I don't know... Kind of... I just... I don't know, a part of me is like exhausted because of the whole thing, but another is damn proud and satisfied that he's finally going to get his dues." Peeling her head away from my chest, she looked up at me with a thankful smile. "Oh, can you tell Rowan thanks, and to keep me updated as much as possible with what happens to James?"

Of course, there was that other issue. Rowan might've taken James away under the guise of arresting him for assault, but that was the lie we told everyone who was there. James wasn't rotting away in some holding cell right now. No, he was tied up in my yacht, just waiting for me to take him out to sea the moment I could.

Soon, James would cease to exist, and I'd just feed the story of him getting sentenced to Eliza. If need be, then I'd forge up some fake articles and records for her to shift through if she wanted.

"We'll keep you updated about him, don't worry." A sharp pang to my heart made me wince a little.

Lying to Eliza has slowly become rather painful. Hailee liked to call it growing a conscience and shit, and that probably was the case. Unfortunately, I couldn't do anything about it. Alright, well, I could do something about it; tell the fucking truth. Too bad that wasn't the best option given what the lies covered up. So, a lifetime of heartache it was.

It wasn't as if I lied to her often or much. I only omitted my mafia life and, I guess, this whole James situation. But it'd all blow over eventually, right? At the very least, James would be dropped sooner rather than later. The whole mafia secret was a whole different story that I needed to sort out. For my sake, I needed to figure that shit out much sooner and never later. Hell, I was pretty sure if I held out long enough, then one of my parents would tattle on me.

"Tell me what's on your mind, little rose." Maybe hearing her dump everything on me would ease this guilt and pain. I mean, her voice was always so soothing to me, so it had to do the trick.

Her soft fingertips danced across my cheeks while her smile crossed my eyes, and we both admired each other for a long minute before more words came out of her luscious lips. "It's finally over, or at least very close to being all over." Her whole body relaxed with her words. Those little fingers of hers slowly flattened against my cheek until her whole hand rested against it. "As long as nothing happens, then James ends up behind bars, and that's the end of that. Well, I guess it'll be officially over once I file for divorce since I uhh am technically still married to him legally."

"Oooh, my darling, is so scandalous," I teased playfully with a chuckle, earning a smack to the chest from her. "Scandalous." Kiss. "And dangerous." Kiss. "And so fucking sexy." The third kiss was dragged out until Eliza fought against me for some air.

Holding her firm against me, I looked down at her with a rather wild grin. "Seeing you with a gun is probably one of the hottest things in my life." Discount the shock and all those iffy emotions on her face, of course. "Maybe I should take you down to the shooting range sometimes or just shoot in the back with you."

Also, I was low-key jealous of the fact Eliza had such a fond memory with James. It peeved me a little how she recounted that moment with such nostalgia in her eyes, and my irritation didn't simmer out when James seemed to have a moment with her because of that recounting. In a way, it was almost as if reality was reminding me of the possibility of losing Eliza, and I hated it.

Eliza is mine, and only mine!

We weren't temporary. We were forever for eternity.

A surge of possessive anger clouded my mind, spurring me to grab Eliza's face and kiss her hungrily. "If you didn't need rest right now, then I'd screw you stupid until you're nothing but a moaning mess dripping my cum out of every hole on your body," I growled deeply against her lips, letting my chest rumble against her trembling body.

Her soft eyes fluttered shut for a moment as she let out a breathy moan. Then, her whole body slumped a little with a weight to her shoulders. "Alarm." I immediately backed off at the sound of that word—figuratively backed off, that is. "Not right now. I want to, but I can't. I'm not up for it, nor am I in the right headspace for anything intense or intimate. I just need you to hold me, so I know you are real and here for me."

Cradling the back of her head, I pressed her into my chest. My other hand soothed her back with slow rubs while my lips spilled every sweet compliment and kiss to her head.

It was unusual for Eliza to use her safe word. Aside from when we tested her limits, I could count on one hand the number of times she uttered that single word. Usually, it was during moments when she was frazzled and overwhelmed beyond what she could comprehend.

Naturally and rightfully, like any decent partner and Dom, I immediately dropped everything at the single word. There was a time and place for everything, and when Eliza drew that line, that was that. No funny business, just sappy sweetness, support, and love.

"Do you want me to get you anything? Small snack? Drink?" She didn't really eat much during the party, but I chalked that up to her being so busy running around and mingling with everyone. Of course, before I could force her to sit and properly eat, she'd stepped out, and the rest was history.

Humming softly, Eliza shook her head lightly in response. "I'll be fine with my water. Besides, I'm getting really sleepy and just want to snooze." Her voice trailed in and out with her slow blinks.

With a curt hum, I kissed her forehead. "Alright, my darling. I'll stay until you sleep, then I'll head back to the party until it's wrapped up. I'll get Asher to bed and everything as well." I whispered lowly against her head before pressing another kiss to it.

"Good night, bub. I love you," Eliza mumbled against my chest with a smile, closing her eyes and getting comfortable against me.

"Good night, little rose. I love you too."

Chapter 31
Eliza

"I'M GONNA MISS YOU."

Adam paused midair with folding his shirt to look at me with a crestfallen smile. "I'm going to miss you more," my cheeky asshole replied oh so cooly. "It's only a week, and you'll have Hailee and my parents here."

Sighing heavily, I crossed my arms and pouted while trudging up to him. Stopping inches from him, I jutted my chest out and huffed my chin up. "I still don't like it," I grumbled, making my displeasure about his last-minute business trip known.

It also felt strange to not have him around for that long. Sure, we've been apart before ever since we made things official, but nothing beyond two days at most. So, a whole week without Adam made my chest tighten as if someone had punched a hole through my chest and squeezed my heart in a vice grip.

Additionally, I didn't have a good feeling about this trip of his. Dread filled my endless cup whenever I thought about him being out at sea for seven days, but it wasn't the typical bad feeling as I'd never see him again or anything like that. No, it wasn't paranoia or anxiety about some unseen doom. I didn't know how to properly label my turbulent emotions, let alone figure out how to voice them to Adam without sounding like some accusing bitch.

On that note, why did it come out that way? Why did I feel like I'd be accusing him of something? What was there to accuse?

'Maybe it's because you might not know him as well as you thought...'

That stupid voice, James's voice, to be exact, has been haunting me ever since that night three days ago. It was one of the few things he told me before Rowan whisked him off. In hindsight, it was probably nothing, just his last-ditch effort to shake me up. Yet, I couldn't shake it from my mind, no matter how hard I tried.

I hated how cautious it made me around Adam. Never before have I second-guessed him or harbored any doubts. Of course, that was discounting the constant nagging feeling that something was amiss. Actually, that feeling that I thought was hidden away in some dark corner forever came back with some kind of vengeance it felt like.

Mafia.

Ugh, that stupid word. It was nothing but a thing of the past and something in movies and books, so why the hell did it bug me so much? Maybe in other parts of the world, mafia people still existed and reigned, but there was no way something like that would fly by in the States.

I never could see anything before, but ever since James planted the rotten seed in my mind, I'd see flashes of it here and there. What if Adam's late nights were him dealing with shady business? His business trips to the city? What if those were just another nefarious thing?

If it weren't for the way he looked at me with genuine ardor, then I might be inclined to think that he had some mistress in the city that he saw every now and then. But no, I always dismissed that thought because he only had eyes for me. Adam really was wholly devoted to me.

Unfortunately, that was the only thing I could confidently cross off my list.

Whenever I had a moment to myself, memories of the nights I'd catch him coming home a little disheveled always managed to find their way into my mind to plague it. It even got bad to the point where I'd hallucinate him at times with an evil glint in his eyes or him with blood splatter on that handsome face of his.

I wanted to bring this issue up to him, but how? Besides, he'd just dismiss it and shove me off as being silly because he wasn't mafia.

Averting my gaze from him, I looked over at his suitcase to distract myself. I didn't find anything calming about his choice of clothing the more I studied the pieces I saw. It seemed to be all casual clothing, like the outfits he'd wear at home. Sure, there were some cargo shorts that skated the line of business casual if paired with a nice polo, but I didn't see any business-like tops in his folded pile.

"*Mia rosa*, please don't be sad." I could hear the drag in his voice. "I don't want this either, but it's one of those time-sensitive things."

Was it strange that he was having such a serious business meeting out at sea? Maybe? But I mean, rich people kind of lived in their own world and abided by different rules. At least, that's what it felt like to me.

Plastering a fake smile on my face, I looked up at him briefly before deciding to distract him with a kiss. I couldn't let him look at my eyes. Otherwise, he'd see that something was wrong. On the other hand, maybe it wouldn't be a bad thing for him to call me out on it. I could try and guilt trip him into staying. It didn't make me feel good, being a manipulative asshole like that, but then what?

Ugh! This was all so frustrating! I shouldn't be dwelling on anything that came out of James's mouth, yet this stupid bug had burrowed its way in so deep that nothing could rid it but some sensible answers.

Slowly, I lifted a trembling finger to his chest, jabbing it playfully. "Just come back to me, alright? You promised me a lifetime with you, so I expect you to keep it."

Warmth blanketed my cheek as he cupped my face with his large hand. "You know, I don't have to leave quite yet..." Oh, I knew that suggestive tone of his so well at this point. His breath fanned across my face with his soft chuckle. "What do you say to me leaving you something to remember me by."

Rolling my eyes, I lightly slapped at his chest. "Oh, as if I'm not still dripping you down my thighs from the fucking you gave me right before you started packing," I remarked, shifting my legs a little at the sudden gush from between my legs.

Besides, you already have...

Arching up to my tippy toes, I pecked his lips in a fleeting kiss before helping him pack. "Hey, bub, if we have a honeymoon—"

"When we have a honeymoon," he corrected me smugly, shooting me his infamous cheeky grin. "Only a matter of time with us, darling, no if, and, nor, or buts."

Relenting to him, I rolled my eyes and continued my train of thought from before. "*When* we have our honeymoon, do you think we can go somewhere a little tropical? Take your parents, Hailee and Adelaide, along as well. It can just be a big family trip, and when we need some alone time or something, then we have your parents and sister there to watch Asher."

Of course, everything flew over Adam's head by a long mile. "So, when's the wedding? I mean, you're talking about a honeymoon, so that means there has to be a wedding." Of course, that's what he'd think about, damn cheeky asshole. "I still haven't proposed to you yet, so is this a sign for me to hurry it up?"

Coiling up the shirt in my hand, I lashed it out at him playfully, catching the surface of his arms. "Oh hush, I'm just talking about the future for future's sake. Maybe give it about a year before you propose to me. I really want to figure out my life before walking down the aisle with you."

Snickering, Adam threw his arms around me, trapping me against his body and attacking my neck with playful kisses. "But you already walked down the aisle with me," he remarked, dragging his teeth along the length of my neck.

Laughing softly, I grabbed the back of his hair, tugging at it until he removed his face from my throat. "The grocery store aisle doesn't count," I shot back with a smirk of my own.

Prying my hand off, Adam pressed the back of it against his lips in a brief kiss. "It's the only aisle that matters to me because that's where our story began." The dreamy far-out look of pure bliss brought a huge smile to my face.

Even though it sounded silly, it was kind of a sweet thing between us. Also, it meant a lot to Adam, which I didn't really fault him for or anything. A chance encounter at a grocery store aisle was all it took for both our lives to collide and change in ways neither of us could've imagined.

Adam's face brightened playfully, and with how pitched his voice got, I kind of saw where things were going with his words. "What if we—"

Cutting him off with a pointed look, I poked the tip of his nose. "We are not having our wedding be in the grocery store," I deadpanned, chuckling playfully at his slight pout at the end. "We can have a grocery-themed wedding, but it ain't going to be in an actual grocery store, bub. It's going to be either in our private backyard, beach or in a vineyard."

I felt a little silly talking about this subject matter with Adam right now, given how it wouldn't even happen for years possibly. Also, I had other pressing matters to think about.

Now with James officially dealt with, I could have my whole life back. Unfortunately, that left a lot of open doors for me. I didn't know which paths to block off and which to keep open or possibly go down.

"Eliza darling?" Adam's voice pulled me from my head, making me zone in on his furrowed face. "What's the matter? You have that pensive look on your face."

"Still just dwelling on the whole thing with James finally being over and having my life back and all. It just... I mean, I've thought about it a few times, about what I'd do if I got this chance one day... But those were just silly aspirations." Pursing my lips a little in a pouty frown, I sulked to myself a little as my irritation festered.

I didn't bother resisting Adam when he sat down on the bed with me in his lap. "What did you want to do? Tell me about them," he somewhat demanded in a nice and gentle way. Well, and he was genuinely curious with how his eyes sparkled.

Of all the things I've told him and conversed about, my plans and dreams weren't a part of the pool. Well, my true plans and dreams because I honestly didn't place any importance on them, nor did I have hopes for them because James going away was something impossible at that time.

Leaning into him with a sigh, I pulled one of his hands into my lap to play with his fingers while I spoke, "I really thought about going back to school to get my pharmacy degree, but like I said, just a silly dream." Thinking about it now made me feel a little deflated because no way would something like that be possible.

"Then do it," Adam said matter-of-factly, making me look at him with a quirked brow. "What? I don't see why you shouldn't. If that's what you want to do, then do it. I mean, what's stopping you now?"

My mouth was quick to open, but no words came out. There was a whole list of reasons engrained in my mind, but thinking about it now, nearly all of it was irrelevant.

There should be no issue for me to apply to schools and financial aid because I could use my real identity again, and as shitty as it sounded, if I needed funds, then I had Adam to help. I didn't want to rely on him for financial support like that, but it wasn't as if he'd let me not use his money. Quitting my job now and going to school full-time was feasible, and it wasn't as if I'd be too torn over leaving my job.

A kiss on my head pulled the brakes on my train of thought. "We can talk more about it when I get back, alright?" Adam chuckled softly, rubbing my arms a bit. "We can look at schools together, figure things out and all. We'll get things sorted out for you to finish that dream of yours."

Smiling tenderly at him, I stroked his cheek with my hand and brought him into a deep kiss. "I love you, bub, so much," I whispered against his lips. "Please be careful out there."

"I will," he promised me with a confident smile. "You do the same. Take good care of yourself and our boy, alright?"

Our boy... Our family... Everything is ours, secrets included. Whatever you're hiding, Adam, I will find out.

Chapter 32
Eliza

"YOU GUYS, ARE YOU—"

No one let me finish my doubt with how they physically shoved me toward the yacht. "Go." Maria practically begged me with sad eyes as she continued to nudge me closer and closer to the yacht. "Trust us, we're only doing this because it needs to be done."

Well, I didn't like the sound of that, particularly her heavy tone.

Sighing heavily, Antonio shook his head and hugged me tightly. "My son is a very stubborn man, and sometimes, he needs to have his hand forced." He sounded apologetic, and that made my stomach sink. "I know your relationship is none of our business, but you deserve to know who my son really is. It's clear to his mother and I that he won't tell you on his own, so this is for both of your sakes." Stepping back, Antonio smiled at me sadly. "I just hope you can find it in your heart to forgive us for making you take this trip with him."

Before I could respond, Hailee tackled me in a hug. "Get on that yacht, but remember, don't let him find you or anything until you guys are far out," she reminded me in a muffled voice before letting go of me and shoving me firmly at the yacht just a few feet away from me.

Swallowing the lump in my throat, I gripped the bag in my hands tightly, looking at everyone one last time before I let my feet move. "Asher, Mama loves you." I blew him a quick kiss and waved at him, smiling warmly when he returned the air kiss and wave.

"We'll take good care of him. Just worry about you and Adam," Maria assured me with a secure smile.

The closer I got to the ship, the wobblier things became, and it wasn't because of the soft waves rocking everything. I was so afraid that my legs would give out under me when I stepped up onto the ship and didn't feel my leg.

This whole thing was probably a bad idea, sneaking onto the yacht to see what Adam was up to. I wasn't for the idea, but everyone else was. Something snapped at them when I left the room to leave Adam to finish his packing, and they all got this tired look to their faces. Honestly, the way they looked at me earlier was akin to a parent being done with their child's antics.

So, the next thing I knew, they threw together go bag for me and dragged me down to the docks. No one wanted to tell me what was up Adam's sleeve; they kept telling me it was something I needed to hear from Adam. Apparently, this was the only way, according to his parents and sister. So, on a whim, I agreed to their plan, which is why I was on the stupid ship, hidden away in the closet of the master room like some child.

Vibrations tingled my body from the engine turning over, and my body swayed a little bit when the boat started to move. Then, an unknown amount of time passed. Seriously, I had no idea how much time passed because when I decided to sit down to keep myself from throwing up, I passed out into a nap. By the time I woke up and crawled out of the closet, the moon was out high in the sky from what I could see through the window.

Slowly, on very shaky legs, I approached the window, placing my hands against the sill to steady myself. I couldn't help but marvel at the open ocean. Moonlight hitting the subtle waves gave it this eerie and mesmerizing shimmer, like glitter under the sunlight. It was a clear night out, but the stars were shy tonight, it would seem.

If it weren't for the ruckus outside, I would've stayed at the window until someone came in and tore me away.

"Walk." I didn't recognize that voice.

Unfortunately, the next one I did. "What? Going to make me walk the plank? Thought you were mafia not pirates." That was James.

"Man, can I cut his tongue out?" It was that first voice again.

The next person to speak up made all the feelings drain out of my freezing body. "Can a person scream without a tongue?"

Adam... Why is he asking such a question?

"Yeah," the first man answered him.

"Then there's your answer." I didn't know if it was the walls or if Adam really did sound cruel and blunted. "But not here. Wait until we get above deck. Blood's easier to clean off up there than down here."

The faint footsteps faded over the next few seconds, along with the sounds of something heavy dragging and thumping against the floor.

I waited until nothing but the waves filled my ears before peeping my head out of the room, doing a quick sweep to make sure the coast was clear before stalking my way through the hallways to the upper deck. Hesitation stopped me cold in my tracks when I reached the door leading out. The knob felt so slippery in my clammy hands. I couldn't get a grip on it for my life. Unless the thing was locked, but why would it be locked from the other side?

Then again, why was James here on this ship with Adam? Why did Adam lie to me?

Glaring holes into the door, I gripped the knob tightly with a deep breath. I had to remind myself why I snuck on in the first place. It wasn't so I could hide away for seven days like some wimp. I was here for answers, and I'd damn well get them before I set foot back on land.

Every inhale and exhale sent a surge of invigorating energy through my system until my heart pounded at my eardrums. Running away wasn't an option this time. Adam was it, and I wanted things to work out with him. Well, scratch that; I wanted to see if things could work out with him. I couldn't make an informed decision until I knew what this secret of his was.

No turning back, Eliza. You have to do it. Rip the bandage off. You can do it.

Psyching myself up until I was sure I'd go mad, I threw the door open and trudged up the stairs with my head held high. I had no idea what to expect up on the deck, and I thought I braced myself enough to take whatever shit I'd see... But nope.

My last meal churned in my stomach and up to my throat, clogging it up and threatening to spew out when I saw the gruesome sight before me.

I couldn't feel anything but the chill of the ocean air as it wafted against me. Every inch of my body refused to budge despite my nerves aching with a need to run. But hell, where could I run? Back down below where he could corner me? Off the yacht and swim away until my limbs gave out for the ocean's depths to swallow me?

"Eliza." At least I wasn't the only one who was stunned stupid. "What are you..." Adam's face twisted with frustration, and his hand raked down his face then through his hair. "Why are you here? You're supposed to be back home." He was pissed, upset, and rightfully so.

Yet... his voice...

Why isn't he yelling at me?

The burning anger in his eyes was like looking at a picture of a furnace, but there was something off about his glassy orbs. His eyes were locked right onto me, but the storm in his eyes wasn't directed at me.

Who was he angry at?

A glint under the harsh lights flickered in my field of vision before I caught a glimpse of the knife in his hand slipping and falling to the ground with a loud clatter.

Neither of us twitched a finger in the other's direction, let alone move an inch. It might've stayed that way if I weren't an easy startle.

The yacht suddenly lurched, causing everyone to balance themselves. Now, that wasn't what got me. No, it was the bloody stump of a finger rolling across the deck and hitting my foot that got me jumping and screaming.

My actions caused Adam to spur into action. In the blink of an eye, he ran over to me and held me tight. "It's okay. It's okay. It's just a finger," he shushed and soothed me.

In a slight panic, I shoved at him to put some space between us. "Just a finger!?" I looked up at him in shock and horror. "Just a finger? As opposed to what? A head?" Adam reached out for me, but I backstepped and held my hands out for him to stop. "You have any idea how insane you sound? Actually, how the hell can you sound so calm and casual about it?"

Okay, maybe I really would hurl. The staunch scent of iron didn't fully permeate my senses until now, and now my stomach felt like it was in the spin cycle of a washing machine. And, of course, I made the horrible decision of peering past Adam and saw the carnage of my ex.

Unable to stomach it, quite literally, I ran over to the railing and bent myself over the side of the boat. It'd been so long since I felt the burn of acid and digested food burn my throat and mouth. God, and the horrid stench and taste of it.

But the sight of James on the floor with his hands being bloody stumps because his fingers were cut off bit by bit was too much for me to handle.

A hand on my back caused me to reel back and swat at the limb. "Don't touch me!" The look of hurt across Adam's face felt like a stab to my heart. "Don't touch me with the same hand you..." There was no churning tummy this time; everything came straight up. "Oh God..." Leaning back over the railing, I puked... again.

"I fucking told you... bitch..." James's raspy voice cut clearly through the chaos around me, along with his mocking laughter.

The sound of his laughter triggered a rush of anger, causing me to snap. "Shut up!" Whirling around, I glared at James so hard that my eyes strained in my skull. "You shut the fuck up." Something took over my body, and my feet moved over to James until I stood over him menacingly. "I don't want to hear any more shit from your mouth! I've listened to you and your stupid voice and words for ten fucking years too many."

To be looking down at James after all these years felt surreal, and maybe I let the feeling get to my head a little because the crazed laugh that left me scared the shit out of me. "Doesn't feel fun being on the other end, does it, James? Being the one beneath someone's feet, being the one bleeding and pleading," I spat at him with so much venom in my voice that it burned my throat and tongue coming out.

In a split second, I spun around on my heels to face Adam when I felt his presence come up behind me. "And you!" Jabbing a finger right into his chest, I made him stumble back a step. "Talk. Now!" I demanded. "I want the truth. All of it. And if you leave so much as a single word out." I shut my mouth and wretch the promise ring off my finger. "I will throw this overboard along with our future," I threatened, holding my hand back as if I was ready to chuck the ring.

At least all of that seemed to kick Adam's ass in the right direction because his lips started moving like a dancer in the moment. "It's true. I am involved in the mafia... I uhh... I'm the boss here in Oregon and South Washington. I have been for years. I got involved late in college when I was close to finishing my degree. The old boss saw something in me gave me a taste of life. And at that time, I just wanted to be successful, so I took it."

Looking like a kicked puppy, Adam slowly reached out for my outstretched hand, closing his around mine and lowering it. "I'm not going to lie. It's a violent and bloody business, and illegal, but I run it as cleanly as possible. Things aren't how they were back then, and it's not all guns and turf wars like movies make things out to be, promise. I'm mostly hands-off at this point, just running things from the background while my lieutenants handle a bulk of everything."

His regretful and apologetic eyes looked deep into mine as he kissed my hand. "I've done a lot of things, and I won't deny any of it. I regret some, but not all, because I did what I had to do in order to provide and care for my family and future." Carefully, he pried my hand open until the ring was out in the open in my palm. "But there's nothing I regret more than keeping this from you. I have no excuse for my cowardice in keeping my secret from you. I was afraid of losing you, but that's no valid excuse in my book. I kept telling myself I'd tell you, but I kept chickening out and coming up with lame excuses for myself..."

Shoving the ring into his hand, I pushed them away. "Were you ever going to tell me, then? Or would it have been one of those next time moments that never come?" I couldn't bring myself to keep looking at him in the eyes, afraid that my wall would crumble if I did.

Too bad Adam wasn't having any of it. He grabbed my face and forced me to look up at him. "Yes, I swear, I was going to tell you. It wouldn't have become one of those things that slip into nothing. I just really couldn't find a good spot to tell you all of this." Sucking in a sharp breath, he leaned his forehead down against mine and chuckled pathetically. "I wanted to wait until you were stronger to tell you to minimize the risk of you running away from me."

Licking my drying lips, I let out a trembling breath. "What if I ran away no matter what?" No matter how in love with this man I was, a secret like this could've broken it no matter how far along we were in the relationship.

"No." Adam lightly shook his head with another chuckle. "If you couldn't accept me after I told you, then I had a plan to lock you in the basement until you came around." His grip on me tightened, and his trembling lips brushed against mine. "I love you too much to let you go, and I know you love me too. I would've kept you locked away until you learned to love me again because that's how crazy I am when it comes to you."

"You're insane," I gasped, shivering from the sudden chill of fear that cut through me.

He sounded so far out when he laughed in response. "For you, yes. Nothing makes sense when it comes to you. You give me the craziest thoughts and feelings, ones I only ever read about in books and seen in movies. You light up my world like no other. Give it that breath of fresh air and life. You are my everything, Eliza, and I am never letting you go." His eyes were so full of passion and craze that it gave me whiplash.

Fact is, I should be running for the next country over, put as much distance between me and Adam as possible. Yet the need to run staled out.

"Have you ever wanted to lock any other woman in your basement like that?" I don't know what came over me to ask that asinine question, but I had to know. "Am I special, bub? Am I really your girl? Is there anyone else? Has there been anyone else?"

God, maybe I'm the crazy one between the two of us.

Adam's expression softened lovingly as he shushed me soothingly. "Oh, darling, no, no, no." His words danced across my lips. "There is no other woman, never has been, never will be. I am loyal to you and only you. I have never felt alive with anyone else before, only you. You are the only woman who I would ever go to such lengths to keep because you are just that special to me and only me. Everything that I have done for you and Asher has been to take care of you both and keep you safe. It is never my intention to harm you guys in any way, shape, or form."

"Oh my God, are you hearing him!? He's fucking crazy!" James interrupted our sweet moment with his spiteful words.

Annoyed with him, I kicked my foot back right into his face. Turning my head back, I glared down at him briefly. "And I told you to shut the fuck up."

"*Cazzo, sei così sexy, tutta arrabbiata e sicura di te.*" Adam's chuckling words made me turn my head back at him. "There's my little rose with her thorns." His words muffled out with the kiss he pressed against my lips. "I swear, I'll do whatever you want and whatever it takes to make it all up to you. Just please, don't make me lock you in the basement." He murmured against my lips.

God, am I really doing this? Am I really considering forgiving him just like that?

Sighing heavily, I stepped away from Adam and walked a few steps toward the door to the lower deck.

Stopping after a few, I turned my head back to look at Adam with my lips pressed in a thin line. There was a moment of tense silence that suffocated the air before my defeated voice simmered it. "Don't make me wait too long, and don't give me that ring again unless you can promise me without a doubt that you will keep this away from home, away from me, and away from our children. Because like hell am I going to walk into a bloody mess in our living room or have Asher encounter that shit show, nor do I want you to handle our baby with bloody hands. All your mafia business stays away from the family and home."

Closing my eyes, I took in a long and deep breath, holding it in for a few seconds to calm myself a little. Opening my eyes, I looked at Adam sternly. "That is my condition, or I walk."

If I was sane, then I'd call it all off right now and jump overboard.

But the thought of a life without Adam, no matter how dark and dirty he was on the other side, was heart-achingly painful. Thinking about moving on somewhere else made me feel so cold and dead inside.

I love Adam, and there was no changing that.

Our souls have found each other, and we were locked in for life.

Chapter 33
Eliza

LAST NIGHT FELT LIKE some fever dream. If I had woken up to the warm sunlight in Adam's arms to Asher jumping on both of us rather than a rocking boat with my MAFIA boyfriend—or soon-to-be ex-mafia-boyfriend—then I would've chalked it up to some whackass nightmare.

Sadly, reality was a bitch.

Seeing Adam's face this morning was not a welcome sight. The only thing his goofy morning smile did was bring back the memories of last night. I mean, how could he do it? Commit crimes at night while I was in bed, then smile so innocently at me as if he didn't have any blood on his hands.

God, he touches me with the same hands he snuffs lives out with. The same one that choked me so tenderly was the same one to break someone else's neck!

God, I can't do this!

Without a word, I shoved his arms and body away from me to scramble out of bed. Silently, I rushed my morning routine to get away from Adam. I needed space from him, which was a hard thing to do considering how I was stuck on a fucking yacht with him! Well, at least the floating hunk of metal was more than big enough for us to go about without seeing each other.

Okay, slight correction: it was big enough for us to go about without crossing paths *if* Adam allowed it. He probably did think before, but I only noticed it now because of how on edge I was after last night; I could feel his eyes on my back and see him out of the corner of my eyes. I didn't bother addressing him. Was it annoying to have him stalk me? Yes, very much so, but he wasn't doing any harm, nor was he bothering me.

Breakfast went by very awkwardly, which sucked because the meal was amazing, and the scenery was romantic as fuck. This whole thing was a scene right out of every damn romance movie involving a rich guy charming over a woman. Yeah, rather ironic because I always hated those movies and the stupid women in it because they were so shallow, dense, gave in too easily, yet I ended being one of them in the end.

Shoveling the delicious food down—shame because I really wanted to enjoy it—I left the instant the last spec of food was cleaned off my plate. I thought about shoving the plate of food away, but that'd probably prompt Adam to force feed me because going without breakfast was a sin in our relationship.

How stupid of me to think I'd get rid of him so easily, though.

Persistent jerk was hot on my heels the moment I left the table. I was half tempted to whirl around and snap at him to give me space, but I figured him following me around like a lost puppy for reassurance was better than him killing James in the next room over from me.

Although... Speaking of James...

It was probably a bad idea—oh, who was I kidding, it was certainly a horrible idea, but I found myself standing before a heavily guarded door when I came to it. My feet somehow carried my stunned body back to the root of my problems.

I should turn away. I was done with James. I made my peace with him on the patio.

...right?

Everything around me faded away to nothing the more I stared at the door that grew further and further with each pounding beat of my heart. Maybe that was a sign for me to leave because the door was out of reach, but I stepped forward.

Soon, the freezing metal of the doorknob bit the palm of my hand, and the creak of the gears turning assaulted my ears, along with the hinges giving away.

"And look who came crawling back to me." His heavy but weak chuckle echoed throughout the empty room. "Finally come to your senses?"

Unsure of what I was doing, I remained tight lipped as I approached his bloody, chained up body on the floor.

Groaning in pain, James slowly got up to his knees before spitting his venom at me. "Where's your illegal lover? Off killing the man who looked at you wrong? Finding some other chick who is actually worthy of his time and attention?"

If I had doubts about Adam's devotion to me then James's words might've affected me to some extent. Too bad his attempts won't do anything to shake the foundation that's been laid.

Sighing heavily, I leaned down and started to reach out to James. I never got to touch him, though. He knocked my hand away with a violent jerk of his head and snap of his jaws. "James..." Swallowing the lump in my throat, I looked at him with eyes full of pity. "I am so sorry. I didn't ask or want for any of this to happen, really. I had no idea that Adam had anything bad planned, you have to believe me."

I don't know why I was apologizing. There was no denying the blackhole of guilt that consumed me when I saw James last night. No matter how shitty of a husband he might've been, he was still a human at the end of the day—and no one deserved the treatment he was getting.

...Well, maybe I shouldn't say that because I was pretty sure there were many exceptions in the world...

Either way, James didn't deserve the murder coming his way. I mean, yeah, he may have nearly killed me once... or twice... three times... more...

Still!

A sudden wet slap against my face had me reeling back in disgust when it hit me. The fucking asshole literally spat a glob of bloody spit at me!

"Don't act so fucking innocent. I don't need your fucking pity or apologies for anything. The only thing you should be doing right now is begging me for a second chance, for me to not beat some fucking sense into you after you get me out of here." Taking some deep breaths, he let out a deranged chuckle that border lined a laugh. "And the only damn apology that should be leaving your mouth is how sorry you are for not listening to me in the first place! Because just like always, I was fucking right!"

"I can't believe it." I scoffed in slight disbelief.

Falling back onto my ass, I laughed at myself as I shook my head in my hands. "God." Running my hands down my face, I groaned deeply. "Why did I think for a second that you'd be different? That maybe you actually changed."

I felt so fucking pathetic.

After all of this, after having his hands reduced to nubs, he was still a rat ass bastard. James was still the person I ran away from nearly two years ago.

"It's because you are weak and can't help but love me even after all this shit," James stated coldly.

Surprising even myself, I shot back without missing a beat, "But did you ever love me?"

The eerie silence and his cold stare void of all emotions as his face twisted with utter shock was more than enough of an answer.

"Did. You. Ever. Love. Me." The words came slow, deliberate, each syllable cracking the air like a whip to make sure they went across clearly the first time around. My voice trembled, but not with weakness—with fury.

"Of course I fucking love you!" he shot back, his tone laced with indignation, not tenderness. Not even a flicker of regret. "Would I have married you if I didn't? Had a kid with you? Built a home with you?" His words were sharp, biting, but they didn't wound me like they used to. Not anymore. Then came the final blow. "You're being fucking ridiculous. Do you hear yourself?"

A strange calm washed over me, a quiet clarity that only comes in the eye of a storm. A smile curled on my lips—not from happiness, but from bitter understanding. "No," I whispered, my head shaking slowly as I let out a dry, humorless laugh. "You did all of that for you."

How did I not see any of this before?

"You didn't marry me because you loved me," I said, my voice breaking but steady enough to cut through his silence. "You married me because it fit the story everyone spun about us. The perfect high school sweethearts. You couldn't bear the thought of being the loser who let the 'golden one' get away. That's what it was about, wasn't it? Winning. Keeping me so no one else could." My lips trembled, but my words kept coming, sharp and unrelenting. "You couldn't let me have anything in my life—not a shred of happiness that didn't revolve around you. Not a dream. Not a single goddamn piece of myself."

I stood, wiping the stray tears off my face with one hand, and his spit—the last piece of him I would ever let linger—off with the other. My chest heaved as I fought to steady the storm building in me. "You couldn't let me outshine you. You had to be 'the man,' the one everyone admired. And I let you. I *let* you," I spat, my voice rising with years of pent-up fury. "Ever since we got hitched right out of high school, you've done nothing but belittle me. Tear me down piece by piece until there was nothing left of the girl I used to be."

My laugh was bitter, sharp like broken glass. "I dropped out of college because of you. Because you convinced me—no, you *made* me believe—I wasn't cut out for it. That I was too stupid for pharmacy, for any degree. I gave up my dreams for you! And you—you fed me that bullshit about how life as a housewife was the right choice. The *only* choice. And when I fought back, when I tried to hold on to even a sliver of myself, you got meaner, crueler. Until I gave in. Until I believed the lie and made it my truth."

I paused, my breath coming in short gasps as I stared at him—really stared at him—for the first time. He didn't look like the towering, intimidating figure I had once seen. He looked small. Pathetic. Weak.

"What moments we had—no matter how sweet, no matter how deep—they were never for me," I said, my voice softer now but laced with a newfound strength. "They were for you. To feed your ego, to make your perfect little life shine brighter, to keep you on that pedestal you built for yourself. Maybe some of it was real, maybe there were blips of truth in the mess of it all. But looking back now..." I shook my head, the realization cutting through me like a blade. "You never did anything for me. It was always for you."

The weight I had carried for years lifted as I spoke those words. I wasn't asking for his understanding. I wasn't looking for an apology. I was reclaiming the pieces of myself he had stolen, one broken shard at a time.

"You know," I began, my voice soft but laced with an edge sharp enough to slice through his fragile pride, "if I had asked Adam the same question, he wouldn't have hesitated. Not for a second. Not for a single, goddamn nanosecond." I pushed the stray hair out of my face, a serene smile tugging at my lips as I let the words linger, as if savoring the thought of a love that didn't need to be begged for. "Adam would've dropped to his knees, professed his undying love for me without an ounce of doubt, kissed my feet, and showered me with a passion so raw it'd take my breath away."

I let the moment hang in the air, watching the flicker of something—rage, jealousy, fear—pass through James's eyes. It didn't matter anymore. Not to me.

"Adam would give me the *world* if I asked him to," I continued, my voice steady and filled with a newfound conviction. "He'd move heaven and earth, not because he wants to prove something, but because he loves me. I see it in the way he looks at me—every single time. It's in his actions, in the little things he does, in the way he makes me feel like I'm the only person in the universe."

I inhaled deeply, letting the words settle in my chest like armor. Lifting my chin, I looked James square in the eyes, my gaze unflinching. "You never cared for me. And shame on me for not seeing it sooner. Shame on me for believing in the facade, for making excuses for you, for convincing myself you were enough when you never even tried to be."

The realization hit like a tidal wave, crashing into me with both pain and clarity. "Even after everything—after finding love with Adam, after finally knowing what it feels like to be cherished—I was about to come back to you. To this. To *all* of it." My voice broke on the last word, not from weakness, but from the sheer weight of letting it go.

No more, though. No more hurting over James and what we had.

It stops today.

"I don't wish you death after everything, but everything you have coming to you is all deserved."

This was truly goodbye.

Not only was it goodbye to James, my soon-to-be dead husband, but farewell to my old life forever.

Goodbye to Elisabella Stone, and hello to the future Missus Eliza Santini.

Chapter 34
Adam

To say the next day was awkward would be a severe understatement. We'd both gone to bed the night prior in silence and coldness, and neither of us uttered a single word to each other thus far.

I didn't dare utter a single word to her as I followed her after breakfast. It broke my heart how she shoved me away in bed this morning, as if I was some diseased person—an unworthy bastard.

Ideally, the smart thing to do was actually give her space, but my nerves wouldn't be at ease unless I physically saw her with my own eyes. So, I followed her at a distance throughout nearly the whole morning, not even bothering to keep myself hidden because there was no point.

Much to my surprise—but not—she made her way to James after wandering for a while. I stopped the guards before they could stop her from going through, and I stood right outside the door while she had her moment with James. Was it wise to let her go in there with her abusive ex? No, probably not, but I also knew she needed this.

I tried not to listen into their private conversation, but my curiosity got the best of me. The more I listened to Eliza go off, the prouder I became of my blooming rose.

When she left the room, I let her go off on her own to reflect on my own life with her thus far. I didn't bother with finding her until it was close to lunch.

Finding her wasn't hard, but the spot where I found her was a little tense.

The words pinched at my tongue. "*Mia rosa.*" I didn't feel worthy to say them. "Darling, it's almost lunch."

Not wanting to encroach on her space, I hung back a few feet from her on the upper deck. I kept my beady eyes trained on her backside as she stood there at the spot where James was last night. The whole deck was spotless now, not a drop of blood or a single hair to be found. Honestly, no one would ever know or guess a torture session was held here hours prior.

"Are you really going to kill him?" There was a light tremble in her small voice, and I couldn't help but wrap my arms around her to comfort her.

Carefully, I approached her with slow steps until I was right behind her. "Yes." I wouldn't lie to her, not anymore, not ever again. "He will be disposed of by the end of day seven. Shark food." Again, that last part could've been left off, but it slipped before I could help it.

It was subtle, but she did lean into me. "Is it bad that I don't feel bad? I want to feel wrong about it all so badly, but I can't find it within myself to care enough. I mean, I shouldn't be this fine with the fact of him dying or the fact that you are torturing and killing him." Her head fell back, and her torn, glassy eyes looked up at me. "Am I really that fucked up?"

Gently, I turned her around and cupped her face with one hand, stroking her cheek with my thumb. "No, darling, no. You are not fucked up. You've just gotten to the point of not caring for him because he's given you nothing of him to care about. You are done with him and genuinely don't care about him anymore. That is all," I told her with a firm smile.

Obviously, she wasn't screwed up to me, but I was a little biased. For me, to consider someone fucked up would be rather hypocritical considering things. On the other hand, if I thought they were screwed up, then they might actually be very wrong.

Shaking myself out of my head, I zoned back in on my Eliza to re-center myself. Taking in a deep breath, I leaned down and kissed her chastely. "No more about James from now on, alright?" It wouldn't do her any good to fester on the bad shit that would be at the bottom of the ocean soon.

With a reluctant smile, she agreed with a nod before looking off into the distance. "You're not going to have our children take over your empire, are you?" she asked in a worried voice, glancing at me slightly.

Assuring her with the most confident smile I could muster, I shook my head. "No, never. Asher and any of our other children will never know about my dark life, and I swear that to you." And I was a man of my word, as she should know by now.

Then, with a controlled breath, I got down on my knees with her hands held before her. "I swear, I will never bring any of it home—"

Shockingly, Eliza's hand slapped over my mouth, stopping me. "No. I don't want to hear any of it. I know I told you my conditions last night, and I have to admit, they were said in the moment." Her tongue swept across her lips, and she looked at me apologetically.

"You need to do what you need to do, and I shouldn't get in the way of that. I shouldn't be stomping all over your career with such demands, and I apologize for that."

With a small smile, she ran her fingers through the top of my hair. "All I want you to swear to me is that you will never involve the children, never bring anything home unless you have to, and never talk about anything to me unless I ask. And by bringing things home, I mean bodies. I don't know all you do in your office, and I don't care if it's desk work for your legal business or mafia business, but don't you dare bring anything violent or bloody home."

"I swear, all of it, I swear to it. I agree and swear." I didn't hesitate one bit to agree to all she said. I mean, she wasn't unreasonable with her demands, so I couldn't really argue fairly with her.

Reaching into my pocket, I pulled out the ring she gave back to me last night, holding it out to her. "So, does that mean you'll wear this again?" I asked, holding my hope in with my breath as I stared up at her with a pounding heart.

Giggling, she held her left hand out for me. "Yes, until my finger gets too swollen throughout the next nine months."

Talk about a change of subject?

"Huh?" All I could do was stare up at her with a stupid smile and confused face.

Yeah, call me stupid because it did not click at all for me at that moment.

Grinning at me cheekily, she slipped her finger into the ring before reaching down and pinching my cheek. "And the wedding is definitely not happening until next year because I refuse to walk down the aisle with a belly."

Not knowing what to say or how to respond, I stared at her with a dumbfounded face as I stood up. "W-what are you saying, darling?"

Was it what I thought it was? Or did I overthink because of my want to have a child with her?

Taking my hand, Eliza placed it against her soft belly. "And you have to promise to be on nightly diaper duty and feedings." She added with a blushing smile.

Breaking out in a gleeful grin, I could hear my shout of joy boom through the air as I swung Eliza around in my arms. Attacking her with laughing kissing, I didn't relent this time when she started smacking my chest and shoulders. "Oh my God, really!? You mean it!? You're sure!?" It was so hard to contain my excitement, but could you blame me?

Eliza's mouth moved, but nothing beyond a faint and squeaky 'yes' came out of her nodding head. She kept trying to get it out of her, but her words kept coming out all high-pitched and incomprehensible because of her excitement. I think she eventually gave up when it was clear she couldn't get it through because she just grabbed my face and laid a big kiss on me. "I'm getting you all snotty and teary. I'm so sorry." She chuckled through her sobs and kisses.

Dismissing her with a chuckle and shake of my head, I continued to press kisses against her when she tried to pull away. "They're happy tears, so don't apologize." At least, I hoped they were tears of joy. We were having a completely different conversation before this, and I hoped this wasn't spill-over from it.

Smiling happily at her, I held her still in the air for a moment, admiring how the sun shined down on her and outlined her image perfectly. "When did you find out? Why didn't you tell me sooner? Why didn't you tell me about the doctor's appointment?" My curiosity quickly turned sour because I didn't like the thought of missing out on her appointments regarding our baby.

"Yesterday, I got the confirmation from the doctor." She smiled at me apologetically, stroking my cheek lightly with the pad of her thumb. "And I didn't have a doctor's appointment for this really. I only went in because of that cold last month, and before they could give me any medication, they wanted to double-check. So, they ran a pregnancy test even though I was on the patch, and it came back positive."

Patting my shoulder, she flickered her eyes at the ground a few times before straight-up pointing. Getting the hint, I set her down with a sheepish chuckle.

Loosely, she draped her arms around my waist, leaning against me. "I had to have a few follow-up labs to have my levels checked, and things weren't clear one way or another for a while until the most recent ones where there was a steady increase and clear answer." Her lips pressed into a thin line, frowning a little. "I might be jumping the gun a bit by telling you right now before my first visit with the OB to actually confirm things with an ultrasound, but I have a good feeling, and since we're already on the boat and putting everything out in the open, I figured I should just tell you now rather than when we get back."

Cradling her protectively in my arms, I kissed the top of her head. "If things don't work out how we want, then we can always try again later after more planning."

As elated as I was with the news, we weren't exactly prepared for a child right now with all the craziness happening in our lives. Not saying I didn't want our child, but some more time to fully talk things through with Eliza and mentally prepare myself more. But, no matter, I'd take things as they come.

Sighing heavily, Eliza buried herself further into me. "It's just so much happening at once..." I hated how heavy her voice sounded. "Another baby on top of everything..."

Leaning away a little, I looked down at her with an affirming smile. "Hey, we will figure everything out together, one step at a time," I told her in a calm voice. "One step at a time, that's how we have to take things. No point in sprinting forward for no reason when we can walk and pace ourselves. Let's just focus on enjoying the next few days to ourselves, then the visit with the doctor, and after the results of the visit, we will plan for the next." I had to pace her for both our sakes. "So, breathe for me, alright?"

Eliza nodded in response while breathing deeply. "Sorry..." Her meek apology made me frown a little. "Just kind of over-whelmed." She admitted with a heavy sigh.

Rubbing the back of her head, I dismissed her with a chuckle and shake of my head. "Well, don't think about it too much. Yes, I know it's a lot in a short amount of time, but we'll make it. We'll handle it together, one step at a time." I reminded her with a lopsided smile and kiss to her temple.

Flicking her chin, I poked at her face until she cracked a smile. "Now, lunch, what would my little rose like? Or what does our little rosebud want?"

Eliza's shoulders shook softly with her chuckle before her lips pursed in thought for a moment. "I'm down for anything really right now. I have no cravings or aversions, but maybe something on the lighter end?" Her hopeful eyes peered up at me as she rocked back and forth on the balls of her feet. "And uhh, can we actually do something while we're out here? I mean, it's nice to be on a yacht and all, but uhh I kinda don't want to just be floating out here for seven days with nothing to do."

Unable to help myself, I leaned down and nuzzled my face into her neck. "Well, you got me to do." I teased, grinning at her cheekily.

Her eyes rolled so hard that I was afraid they wouldn't come back around. "You are so lucky I love you still." She joked with a teasing chuckle. "Even if you are some mafia boss." Her face twisted a bit as she looked at me as if she struggled a little with her own thoughts. "God, that's going to take a while to get used to."

Swaying her playfully, I nipped at her neck. "Thought girls dig the bad boy or crime lord image." I prodded a little with a joke, hoping to make light of my newfound secret. "A man who isn't afraid to get dirty and bloody to provide for his family, to keep his woman safe. That powerful man who lives in a gray-and-black zone, willing to do anything and everything at his woman's whims." I whispered darkly with a teasing brush of my lips against the shell of her ear. "The whole world at your fingertips through me."

The way her body shivered in my arms as her breath hitched brought a twisted smirk to my lips. A part of her was enjoying what came out of my mouth, and she may deny it, but the signs were clear to me.

It's time for your thorns to come out, my little rose.

Chapter 35
Adam

~8.5 months later~

"Whoa, whoa, whoa, buddy, careful, hot pot here." My heart flipped in my chest from Asher suddenly charging at me and tackling my legs while I stood in front of the stove frying dinner.

"Mama angwy. Scwarwy." Poor thing looked terrified, which made me wonder just what the heck was up this time with my pregnant woman.

Well, I didn't have to wonder for long because in came a very pissed-off Eliza with a shirt bunched up in her clenched hands—my shirt, to be exact. "This better be ketchup or paint, or so help me God, I will lock you in this house until you learn to beat someone up without getting bloody." Flailing the dirty shirt in the air with a glare, she huffed loudly. "I already told you I don't want this shit in the house. What if our children get into the laundry basket and catch whatever shit is on your clothes? Or what if the dog eats it and gets sick?"

The urge to roll my eyes tensed at the muscles in my head, but I refrained for the sake of my safety. As much as I loved how pregnancy has brought out Eliza's spunk, having it taken out on me wasn't something I appreciated too much. "I wish I could tell you it was ketchup, but..." Pretty sure that was leftover brain matter from the man who got cozy with my fists last night, but Eliza did not need to know that. "I kind of got carried away. I'm sorry."

I had no excuse, and I should've been more mindful and careful. All I could do now was apologize and move on.

Turning off the stove, I moved the pan over before going over to her with open arms and an apologetic smile. "*Mia rosa*, I really am sorry. I was going to take care of it before you can see." I sighed softly with a frown, taking the shirt from her and throwing it into the trash before hugging her.

Huffing and pouting, Eliza hugged me back tightly and smushed her face into my chest. "I just don't want the kids seeing it, and the smell makes me very sick." Uh oh, the way her voice cracked meant tears would follow soon. "And I just hate how fucking queasy it makes me, and I don't like throwing up."

With a very wary grin, I awkwardly patted her back as she broke out sobbing. "Uhh... Shh... Shh... There, there...?" Oh God, this was so awkward!

Soft thumps of waddling footsteps padded over to us, and a pair of tiny arms wrapped themselves around our legs. "Mama, no cry. Why sad?" Asher comforted Eliza with some pats on her leg and looked up at her with a soft frown of confusion.

Reaching up, Asher lightly poked and patted Eliza's round stomach. "Rwosie make Mama cry?"

Eliza chuckled through her tears and wiped them away with the back of her hand. "No, honey, no, Mommy's just being weird." Of course, her answer only earned a confused head tilt from our toddler.

To be fair, that was probably the best and only answer he would get at this moment. I doubt the almost three-year-old kid would understand a whole talk about pregnancy and hormones. Heck, I was a grown-ass man, and I barely grasped the whole concept of pregnancy. No matter how many books I read or how many questions I asked the doctor or my friends and family, nothing prepared me for dealing with it during the moment. Even with my mother warning me about the crazy shit she did while pregnant and what my father had to put up with, I didn't really want to believe it. Well, guess the joke's on me for that.

Bending down, I picked Asher up for a family hug. "Are you excited for your little sister to come?" I asked Asher with an excited smile while rubbing Eliza's stomach with one hand. "Ready to be the best big brother ever?"

"Yeah!" Asher squealed and giggled excitedly, clapping his hands and happily bouncing in my arms. "Dwiapwers, mum mum Dada's food, toys..." And off he went with his incomprehensible toddler babble as he let his excitement get the best of him.

Even though this moment was blissful, I couldn't help but notice Eliza's dull eyes. "Hey." I brushed a finger across her cheek to snag her attention. "What's wrong? Or is it just hormones?" She gave me quite the scare the other day when she started sobbing over her dinner; turns out it was because she was so thankful for me making it and how wonderful it tasted. With how hard she bawled her eyes out, you'd think that she had just witnessed a beloved's death.

Sighing heavily, she directed her worried and sad eyes at Asher. "I'm just worried about his speech, that's all." She voiced her worries out loud with a soft frown.

"Darling, the doctor said that it's fine, that Asher is okay even if he is on the lower end of average. And besides, he is learning two, sometimes three, languages, so it's natural for him to be a little slower because the wires in his brain are trying to cross and connect correctly," I reminded her with a reassuring smile.

I didn't mean to get him into Italian, but he started to pick it up from being around me and hearing me use it with my parents and Hailee at times. It wasn't hardcore or anything; it was just simple terms and conversational in nature. Then, Eliza threw in some Vietnamese phrases and words here and there, so I doubt the toddler was having an easy time with sorting things out in his tiny noggin.

Obviously, I wasn't too worried because the doctor said so. Also, it wasn't as if Asher was completely silent. He loved to talk err babble. It'd start out as actual words, but then it'd trail out to just strings of sounds the more amped up he got. Also, he was only two, well, almost three, so how much could an almost three-year-old even talk?

"But, if you're that worried, then we can take him back to the doctor," I told Eliza with a half-hearted smile. At the end of the day, a mother always knows best, right? Was that how the saying went?

Wobbling her head around with an unsure hum, she shrugged her shoulders and sighed in defeat. "Maybe after I have the baby, and the hormones simmer down. I mean, I get worked up thinking about him growing up," she decided with a lopsided smile. "I'm probably just letting my hormones make my worries worse."

The edges of her lips curved up with her eyes until she looked genuinely happy. "I'm so lucky to have you two in my life." She sighed happily, adoring both her boys with her eyes for a long while before kissing each of us on the cheek.

"I'll go set the table while you finish up in here," she said, stepping away from me and leaving.

If I didn't have Asher in my arm, then I'd grab a piece of that juicy ass of hers. Honestly, pregnancy did wonders for her body, and I loved how plump she'd gotten over the months. Her hips flared out so much; her legs thickened so well that her thighs felt like soft pillows and her lovely breasts swelled so much that they filled my hands fully. Although not gonna lie, I loved her smaller breasts from before; they added a daintiness to her that I really appreciated.

"Food? Pop pop?" Asher leaned a bit out of my arm to reach around and point at the pan filled with oil.

"Frying. Frying food," I told him in a slow and steady voice, making sure to exaggerate my lips for him to see me enunciate the words.

Asher's lips pursed and mimicked mine for a few seconds before he copied me. "Frwying food?"

Eh, close enough.

Ruffling his hair, I kissed his cheek. "That's right, bud! Good job!" I praised him with a wide grin. "Let Dada finish food, then we eat. Go to Mama, alright?"

Asher's chubby little feet took off like a roadrunner the moment I set him down. At least the kid's comprehension seems to be intact, so no worries there. Again, maybe it was because I wasn't his mother that I didn't worry too much. Well, I wasn't one to worry much about anything in general. Things happen as they happen, so no point in stressing out about—

"Dada! Mama owie thummy!" Asher's tank of a body crashed into my legs, making me stumble a little.

Chuckling nervously, I picked Asher up and quickly speed-walked to the dining table, where Eliza was hunched over with a grimace and holding her stomach. "Oh shit." Cussing around Asher was a big no-no, but I say this situation allowed for one slip-up.

Besides, it wasn't like I could control what came out of my mouth when my brain and heart went a thousand miles a minute.

Setting Asher down, I went to Eliza's side, putting my arms around to support her. "Did you hurt yourself? Did you bump the table? A chair? Are you feeling pain anywhere else?" Fretting over her was second nature to me, even before she became pregnant.

"No," Eliza grunted with a worsening frown. "I need to go," she whimpered through gritted teeth.

"Go? Go where?" Did she need help going to the bathroom? The couch? Our bed? A bath?

"Bub, I swear, the one time your little brain cells need to work, they don't." She seethed, glaring at me and digging her nails into my forearm as she let out a pained grunt.

...

Yeah, it took me a very long minute or two to connect the damn wires—sue me.

"Oh!" Forcing myself away from Eliza, I scrambled around the house, running from one room to the next, grabbing keys, bags, and phones.

This moment was not supposed to be like this! I had it all planned out! Things were supposed to be a smooth transition, and everything swooped up in one quick run. But nope. Instead of keeping a leveled head and being in a zen state, I ran around like a maniac chicken with its head cut off.

"W-wait, the baby's not supposed to come for another three weeks!" I stressed as I zipped past Eliza in search of my car keys.

I barely caught a glimpse of her rolling eyes as I passed her again. "Babies come when babies come, and our little girl here wants to come now!" she strained out, wincing and whimpering with her stomach cradled.

The faint sound of metal clinking together nearly drowned out Asher's call for me. "Dada." Stopping in my tracks, I let out a huge sigh of relief when I saw him holding up my keychain with a rather stoned expression as if he were the calm adult and I was the child.

Snatching him up in my arms, I thanked him with a kiss on the cheek before setting him down on the couch. "Aunty Hailee and Adelaide are gonna come to hang out with you for a little bit, okay, bud? Dada and Mama gotta go get your baby sister." Don't know if he fully processed it all with the blank look he gave me, but he didn't budge from the couch when I left him to go open the door for my sister and niece.

"I am so sorry, but dinner's in the kitchen if you want any. I gotta go right now—"

Hailee didn't let me get another word out; she spun me around with a long sigh and shoved me toward Eliza. "If she has that baby in the car because your head is in space, then I'm gonna kick your ass for her when you get back."

Not wasting another second, I helped Eliza into the car and sped to the hospital, breaking probably too many traffic laws on the way.

Thankfully, we made it to the hospital fine and in record time. It wasn't long after our arrival that we were situated in a room. Eliza got all changed into a hospital gown and hooked up to machines in a matter of seconds the moment we got up to the room.

Fuck, it's really happening. Oh fuck, oh fuck, oh fuck.

Being next to Eliza in the damn hospital really drilled it into me that this was reality, that our child would be here soon. Okay, maybe that needed some correction because being next to Eliza wasn't the wake-up call for me. The real kick in the ass was the pain inflicted on me by Eliza squeezing the life out of my hand!

Fucking hell, it hurt like a bitch! I didn't think Eliza had this kind of strength in her to break my hand!

Of course, I had no time to think about my phalanges because I was too focused on my poor darling, who cried out in pain with every contraction. God, every whimper and sob gutted me, and I only wished that I could take away her pain.

"I'm so sorry." I kissed every inch of her tear-stained face as I held her tightly. "I am so sorry for putting you through this."

Surprisingly, she had enough in her to crack a joke, "It takes two to make a baby, so I'm as much at fault as you." But that little bit of sweetness disappeared with her next contraction. "Motherfucker I'm going to stab you in your ball for this!" she hissed through a tightly clenched jaw, slamming our hands against the railing of the bed. "God, I hate you. I swear, if this baby doesn't come out easy, I will fucking kill you."

I took not an ounce of offense at her words because, no doubt, it was the pain and hormones talking. Not another word left me for the next hour after Eliza told me to shut it when I tried to whisper sweet nothings to her. All she wanted from me were cuddles and kisses, which I gave her in full and then some.

After the first hour flew by, a second quickly followed before our little girl decided to make her grand debut into the world. As overjoyed as I was about being able to hold both our baby and Eliza in my arms finally, I couldn't help but feel an underlying guilt for the suffering that Eliza had to go through just now. The pregnancy was a breeze for Eliza, according to her every time I asked, but witnessing her going through labor and giving birth felt like Death ripped my soul out of my body inch by inch.

I hated how useless I was throughout the whole thing. All I could do was give her water, kiss her, hold her, and comfort her however she needed and wanted, but there was nothing I could do about alleviating her pain. What's more shocking was how fine she seemed afterward.

The moment our Rosie came out, Eliza kind of did one-eighty of sorts. Honestly, seeing her exhausted but blissful face right now made the whole labor process seem like some bad acid trip. No way did this woman of mine suffer the worst pain in the universe moments ago with how happy she was. It was like someone hit a reset button in her or something. There wasn't a grimace or cry in place as she cooed and gushed over our daughter.

"Bub? You okay? You're kinda looking a little pale." It took me a second to realize those concerned words were directed at me.

Blinking my fumbling thoughts away, I quickly smeared my smile back on my face. "Y-yeah, just... Overjoyed..." My mouth hung open as my thoughts refused to leave my mind.

"And overwhelmed?" Eliza finished for me with a sympathetic smile.

All I could do was nod in response before kissing her. "It all just happened so fast, and in a way, it almost didn't feel real. I feel like I blinked a few times, and we flashed around to this point in time." That was the best way I could put it. "And I just... I feel so horrible about how you had to go through all that pain, but also, I have this newfound admiration for you."

Holding them both tightly, I leaned my head against Eliza's in a quiet sob. "Just... Thank you. Thank you so much for all you do for me and our family. Thank you for blessing me with another child for me to spoil and love."

And like babies, my tears came when they did, and I didn't care. "Thank you, Eliza darling," I whispered against her lips with a cracked voice. "I love you so much, and I always will until the end of time."

$\mathcal{E}pilogue: \mathcal{E}liza$

~1.5 years later~

Never in my life did I think I'd be doing this again. Hell, I remember swearing to myself that I'd never put on a fancy white gown ever again unless it was for my funeral.

Yet, here I stood, at the end of a fancy, sandy aisle, obscured by some fancy umbrellas so Adam wouldn't see me quite yet. I knew that jitters on your wedding day were normal, and I had them the first time around with James. But, the butterflies in my stomach this time around were something else altogether.

Thinking back now, my first wedding was probably just anxiety and sheer panic because, honestly, I loved James, but it wasn't true love like with Adam. Back then, I got married for the sake of getting married. I basically settled for James because I didn't think anyone out there would find me worthy, and James did. Obviously, I have more self-respect now after Adam showed me my worth to the world.

This time around, it truly felt like how I always imagined it to be. I was excited and nervous as fuck to the point where I wanted to throw up, but it was all the good kind. It wasn't dreadful; it was enthralling and wonderful beyond my imagination. The sparks, fireworks, stars of amazement, the one and only feeling that everyone talks about, I was finally feeling it all for the first time ever.

"Alright, Mr. Santini, if you could turn your body a little and look over your shoulder for me, kind of like you're gazing into the distance." I heard our photographer instruct Adam, which meant my time was now.

The brightness of the white umbrellas curtained away to reveal a lovely arch made of roses and ribbons with Adam at the center. He hadn't seen me yet, which was the point because this was our first look shot for the rest of time.

As if the embellished ballgown didn't feel like a thousand pounds on my body already, standing there behind Adam in anticipation made me feel like the whole thing cemented me to my spot.

Unlike my first wedding, my dress this time around was of my choosing. It wasn't some old, raggedy gown from the 1800s that was forced down my throat and onto my body. This time around, I wore the perfect dress of my dreams.

When I found the dress, I instantly fell in love with the sweetheart neckline and delicate illusion inset. The refined sparkle tulle, glass beading, and sequins gave it just the right amount of shimmer without being too much. Then, the off-the-shoulder long sleeves added the hint of modesty I wanted, and they were made from the softest rose net, with lace accents that felt so romantic. Oh, and I don't even get me started on the floral details—petals, leaves, and vines—and how they gracefully wrapped around my arms, making me feel naturally elegant. And the killer part was the back; the illusion V-back with buttons perfectly accentuated my curves before flowing into the most stunning cathedral train.

It may seem simple to some, but it was more than perfect for me. Hopefully, Adam will think so as well.

Guess I'll find out.

Adam's whole face dropped at the sight of me the moment he turned his head, and his eyes snapped to me. No words left his aghast expression as his mouth hung open. Wide eyes teared up as they scanned my body up and down endlessly, even when he ended up falling to his knees. He just stared up at me as if I was the only thing that mattered in the world, and to him, I wouldn't be surprised if that was how he saw it.

Slowly, in a stupor, he got up to his feet again before reaching out with shaky hands, almost as if he was afraid to touch me. "Oh, darling, my little rose." He whispered with a widening smile.

Slipping an arm around my waist, he held me close and tight. He brought his other hand up to my face, cupping it with tender strokes to my cheek like always. "*Oh, mia piccola rosa, sei così fottutamente perfetta. Sei così eterea, è irreale. Non riesco a credere che questa sia la regina che sarà mia moglie. Non mi sento degna di te, ma ti amerò dannatamente finché non lo sarò.*"

Giggling, I leaned into his touch. "I don't know what you said, but it sounded romantic as hell."

"You look fucking perfect and so much more. I don't know how to put it into words, but you look like Heaven to me," he whispered against my lips with a big smile before kissing me deeply. "Are you ready to officially be Mrs. Santini?"

With a big smile, I nodded before forcing myself away from him so that I could get myself into place before the guests got there.

Standing at the end of the aisle, I watched as the workers finished setting up the last of the chairs and decorations on the beachfront. I knew we had the funds to have the wedding anywhere in the world, but I wanted to have it all in our backyard. I don't know why but having it close to home felt intimate and more heartfelt.

All the seats filled within the blink of an eye, and by the time I blinked again for a second time, I found myself across from Adam at the end of the altar. Hailee and Eve stood a little way behind me as my bridesmaids, while Asher and Rosie sat front and center with Adam's parents.

This perfect family of mine would only grow more perfect with time, and I thrived off that fact.

Our wedding was perfect. Besides Adam's family from all over, all our close-town friends filled the seats, and I even got Eve and her family over for the wedding, too. Well, more like Eve did all she could to make sure she'd be here because, and I quote her, "Like hell am I missing my best friend's wedding!"

"Before we exchange the rings, do the bride and groom have vows they want to exchange?" The priest's question pulled my attention back to the main point of everything.

Both of us looked at the priest and nodded before taking each other's hands tightly. Adam was the first to go, mainly because he spoke up before I got a chance to, "Eliza darling, *mia rosa*, you are the only thing right in my life besides the kids, it feels like. I thought I knew what it was like to live and love, but I realized now that my life never started until I met you and Asher." Taking a moment to appreciate our children with a happy smile, he chuckled a little. "Never thought I'd meet my future in the grocery store aisle, but unique relationships start off as so. From the moment Asher grabbed me and I saw both of you, I knew right then and there that you two were my family. You are the gem that I've been searching for all my life, and I am so glad that I made the last-minute decision that day to go to the store."

Taking a deep breath, he brought my hands up to his lips in a chaste kiss. "I know I am not perfect and hard to love, but I am so grateful that you learned to love me in your own special way. I will never be able to put into words my love for you because they don't exist in the dictionary or in the world. What I will do is show it to you every day for the rest of our lives as I have been every day so far. I will never stop cherishing you each second of each day. Every morning, I wake up to you is a blessing like no other, and every night I get to have you in my arms is a gift from the heavens. I swear to you that I will continue to love you for as long as I breathe, through sickness and in health, through rich and poor, for better and worse, until death can try to do us part."

No matter how hard I tried to hold my tears in, they wouldn't stay put behind my eyelids. Well, at least my makeup was waterproof, so no runny mascara. "Oh, Adam." Dropping his hands, I brought mine up to hold his face. "I'm so thankful you're as stubborn as you are. You knew what I needed long before I did, and you saw my worth when no one else did. Before you, I just wanted to get by the days with Asher safe by my side. I never knew the warmth of life until you graced mine and brought the sun to it. Your selflessness when it comes to me and your family is what I love so much about you. You always looked after me and tended to me until I bloomed into the stunning rose you saw me for. Never once did you ever stop and ask for anything but my happiness in return. As long as I thrived, then you did as well. And I will never be able to thank you enough for all the love you have shown me and continue to show me."

Taking a moment to recenter myself, I brought his head down to rest my forehead against his. "I swear, I will continue to do right by you by thriving like you want me to. I will continue to be a wonderful mother to our children while you continue to be the most amazing father to them. I will never stop loving you for as long as I live and breathe." Cracking a small laugh, I smiled at him in disbelief. "You know, I swore to myself long ago that I would never walk down the aisle again. Yet, I end up finding my forever down an aisle, even if it's a grocery store aisle, and walking down the aisle of life with him. I never would've thought that the hot stranger my son snagged back then would end up being my missing half. I never knew how half-empty I felt until I saw your bright eyes the first time they looked at me, and in a way, my heart and soul knew at that moment in the store that you were the one. And now, I can't wait to continue walking around the path of life with you by my side, through sickness and in health, for rich and poor, for better or worse, until death does us part. I will be with you until the world ceases to exist."

After a quick exchange of the rings, the priest popped the most important questions of every ceremony.

"Before all the witnesses here today and God, do you, Adam, take Eliza to be your wife until death does you two part?"

Without a nanosecond of hesitation, Adam answered, "Yes, I do." So much confidence and pride in his voice and smile.

Then, the priest turned his attention to me. "And do you, Eliza, before all these witnesses and God, take Adam to be your husband until death does you two part?"

And unlike last time, I didn't hesitate one bit with my reply. "Yes, I do."

Closing his book with a soft and satisfied thump, the priest gestured us together. "With the power vested in me by the state and church, I now pronounce you husband and wife. You may now kiss."

Immediately, Adam grabbed my waist and face, bringing me into a soul-searing and breathtaking kiss, dipping me for extra added effect. "Adam!" I squealed against his lips, afraid that he'd let me slip to the floor.

"I haven't let you down yet, darling, and I never will," he replied with a cheeky grin before planting another one on me as he pulled me back up.

The rest of the ceremony went off without a hitch, and a small interlude of pictures and socializing later, the reception was all set up and on its way. Just like the ceremony, it was perfect and went off without a hitch. There weren't any issues with the catering or the food; all the guests were more than happy with the choices and open bar, and the DJ—Max—had all the right jams to keep the mood set. Some table greetings and games later, and it was time to cut the cake by the time I knew it.

If I hadn't been nervous before, then I definitely was now as I let Adam guide our joined hands and the knife toward the tiered cake. The knife cut into the soft cake like a hot knife through butter, but for some reason, it felt like trying to cut a block of cheese with a spoon. Well, maybe it was because I knew.

While Adam's face twisted in pure confusion, mine lit up. "Uhh... Did you change the cake flavors without telling me?" His quizzical eyes bounced between me and the pink and blue slice of cake on the plate in his hands.

Giggling, I shook my head. Not giving him an answer, I picked up the fork, stabbed off a small piece, and shoved it in his parted mouth before picking up the champagne bottle that was all whited out with blue and pink rose designs all over it. "The only thing I'm changing is the size of our family," I told him, placing a hand over my growing stomach that has yet to start showing.

His scrunched-up face stretched out into an excited grin as he set the plate down and took me into his arms, spinning me around with a joyful shout. "Oh my God, I am so elated right now, but Eliza, you gotta stop hiding your pregnancy from me." He chuckled against my neck.

"I didn't know, I swear. I just went in for my yearly physical, and, well, surprise?" Yeah, trust me, I was not expecting that kind of news when I went into the doctor's office about a month ago.

Setting me down, Adam tilted his head at me with a confused twist of his lips. "Wait, how far along are you then?"

Chuckling softly, I leaned up and pecked his lips. Yes, even in some high heels, I still had to lean up quite a bit to kiss my damn husband. "Based on mother nature, about eight weeks, but the OB will confirm next week at our first prenatal appointment," I replied with a big smile.

"Wait..." Looking at the bottle in his hand and the cake with furrowed eyes, he stood there a moment in thought before looking back at me. "Wait, then what's all this gender stuff for? Isn't it too soon to know?"

"No, blood work came back with the gender, so I figured it might as well make our wedding night extra fun with an added celebration of a baby announcement and gender reveal." Also, I didn't want to plan or have an extra celebration for all those things, so I might as well kill all the birds with one stone.

Stepping back, I urged Adam forward more toward the center of the dance floor. "Alright, everyone! What do you think baby number three is gonna be?! Because apparently Mr. Santini here couldn't help but do some pre-wedding celebrations with the new Mrs. Santini here!" Max's laughter caused the whole place to chuckle and snicker before some chaos erupted with how everyone shouted their guesses wildly.

While everyone cheered and shouted, Adam eagerly shook the champagne bottle with a giddy grin like some kid on Christmas day.

And once he shook it more than enough...

POP!

"YES!"

Epilogue: Adam

"Hey, Dad?"

My head lifted from my desk to look at my son, who stood at the doorway of my office. "What's up, bud? What do you need?" Closing my laptop and books, I gave Asher my full attention.

Poor kid, his face was so crestfallen with hurt and confusion. "I made Mom upset..." Asher's voice cracked a little as he spoke, "But I don't exactly know what I did."

My heavy shoulders fell with a deep sigh as I waved him over. As he made his way into the office, I got up from my desk and met him halfway with a hug. "Hey, just tell me everything from start to finish, and hopefully, we can figure it out," I told him before sitting down on the couch with him.

Sighing, Asher curled his legs up onto the couch and hugged a throw pillow. "We were just snacking, and I was doing some homework. I needed some help with this family tree thing for science," he started, his face growing more perturbed with his words.

However, I had a good idea of where this was headed based on what little he had told me so far.

Asher continued after another heavy sigh. "Mom just kind of went quiet, and maybe that should've been a sign for me to drop things, but I guess I was just too curious. So, I asked and pressed.

I asked about my grandparents from her side because I needed to know more about our family's medical history and all. She was quiet and blunt, but she answered things, even if it was a little vague, too." His voice trailed out for a moment as he picked at the throw pillow in a fidgeting manner. "But then, when I asked about you..."

I didn't need to hear anymore, so I held a hand up for him to stop.

Well, I knew this day would come, or a day like it. Eliza knew it as well. It was probably bad on our part, but we both made a conscious decision to keep the truth about Asher's biological father from him.

"Wait here. I'm going to get your mother because this is a conversation that she needs to be involved in," I told Asher before getting up to go fetch Eliza, who was standing out back on the patio.

"Eliza darling..." My heavy words made her shoulders slump. "Asher..." I started but quickly shut my mouth. "We have to tell him. It's time, little rose. We knew a time like this would come, and today is the day."

Obviously, we weren't going to tell him about how I chopped James up and threw him overboard into the mouths of sharks, but the other bits of truth were something Asher deserved to know.

"He's old and wise enough to take it." Asher was a very bright kid, and he was a little more advanced than some boys his age in the mental and emotional department. So, I felt confident about telling him right now.

Sighing heavily, Eliza hung her shaking head in her hand, rubbing her temples. "I just... What if he hates me? What if he wants to meet James?" she worried, still looking out into the distance.

Well, that last part would certainly be a huge problem.

My footsteps thudded against the aging wood deck as I approached her from behind and held her. "We will cross the bridges as they come. For now, we have to let him know about James, minus the seven days at sea." I sighed softly against Eliza's head, kissing it lightly. "Come on, he's in my office waiting right now, and it won't be long until the twins come back with Rosie from their activities with Hailee and Adelaide." I hated rushing Eliza, but this was one of those things that needed to be done now.

Nodding with a sigh, Eliza turned her head back to look at me with a forlorn expression. "I just don't know what to do if he hates me," she whimpered, leaning her head into me.

Assuring her with a smile and kiss on the forehead, I rubbed her arms and shoulders. "Asher's not going to hate you for keeping James a secret from him. Our son is a bright kid and has more functioning brain cells than us combined most days," I lightly joked at the end with a chuckle, hoping to uplift my wife some.

Thankfully, it worked with the giggle she gave in response. "Well, guess we gotta rip the bandage off sooner rather than later, huh?" She sighed in defeat, relenting to whatever fate had in store for us.

Hand in hand, we made our way to my office, sitting down across from Asher, who still sat curled with the throw pillow. I didn't envy my wife, not one bit after I saw the guilt fully set into her dreadful face.

"Asher, there's something we have to tell you about your father," I started, glancing at Eliza to make sure she was fine before looking back at Asher with a serious face, "and it's important that you listen to everything before responding and such, alright?"

Slowly, Asher nodded in response as he grew rather apprehensive of the situation. "I'm not adopted, am I?" he prodded warily and somewhat half-jokingly.

Unable to help it, I cracked a chuckle and smiled while shaking my head. "No, you're not. Well, at least to your mother." Leaning back against the couch, I settled an arm around Eliza, pulling her close while I rested my other arm on the armrest. "I adopted you, yes, but Eliza is your biological mother. Now, that being said, I've always seen and treated you as my own son. You've seen how I am with your siblings, and I don't treat you any differently from them. No matter what, you are my son, and I couldn't be prouder and happier of that."

Asher's lips pressed into an unsure smile, though his eyes softened with genuine gratitude and affection. "You're my dad for all I know, but I'm guessing from all that so far you're not my biological father." He surmised with a somewhat disheartened expression.

Surprisingly, Eliza spoke up before another word could leave my mouth. "Adam isn't biologically your father, you are right, but he's more of a father than your biological one." Peering up at Asher with apologetic eyes, Eliza looked at him for a moment before shedding a few tears. "I'm so sorry for keeping something like this from you, and please don't be mad at Adam for any of it either because I made him promise not to tell you."

With a frown of his own, Asher got up and went over to Eliza, hugging her tightly. "Oh, mom, please don't cry. I don't like it when you cry." His voice cracked as he held his mother. "Listen, if it's too much for you, then you don't have to tell me. I don't care about someone who hasn't been there my whole life. Like I said, the only dad I have and know is Adam, and even if you tell me about whoever I came from, I won't see things any different."

Pushing Asher away, Eliza looked at him with a regretful smile and a shake of her head. "No, you deserve to know about James." Sighing heavily, she moved Asher to sit next to her on the couch. "James Stone, that's your father. He's dead now and for the better. I wish I could say that he was a good man and such, but he wasn't. He was a horrible man who did nothing but manipulate other people to get what he wanted. He was also a violent man, and unfortunately, his wife was no exception." Her eyes drifted down to the faded scars on her arms.

Asher's trembling hands took Eliza's arms, looking at them in a new light. Well, more of a new and dark light. "H-he did this to you? All of them?" He sounded so hurt and horrified. We'd always told him that her scars were from an accident in the past, and Asher had always accepted the answer without question.

"Yes, and on more than one occasion. For ten years, I endured because he beat me down to the point where I really believed that I was less than dirt beneath people's shoes. I was so broken, not only physically, but mentally and emotionally too." Eliza's frown slowly curved into a hopeful and happy smile as she stroked Asher's hair and face with a mother's fondness. "It wasn't until I had you that things really became clear to me. A child wasn't going to fix a horrible man, and he made no attempts to change when you came. Hell, he even made plans to make sure you were as vile as him. And I couldn't let any of that happen to you, so I ran. When you were just a few months old, I drugged him, packed our things, and ran all the way from Idaho to Seaside, Oregon."

"I came into your life when you were a little over one, and I've been there since you grabbed me at the grocery store. I'm not going to lie. The moment you touched me, and we looked at each other, the connection was instant," I told Asher with a warm smile of my own. "James managed to find your mother, and he threatened her, beat her right there on the back porch with a gun held to her. The cops took over afterward, but then we heard that he died somewhere along the way." I quickly wrapped the story up with a bit of a white lie.

The cops—Rowan—did take him away, and he did die along the way somewhere. Asher really didn't need to know the details about any of *that* for his sake.

"Oh, Mom, I'm sorry for asking." Asher apologized, hugging Eliza tightly.

"No, honey, don't apologize," Eliza dismissed him with an understanding smile as she pulled away. "You didn't know, so you have nothing to apologize for."

Then, Asher looked at me for a moment, and he lunged at me, tackling me in a hug. "Thank you, Dad."

Hugging him back, I let a few tears slip as my heart ached with happiness and relief. "You don't need to thank me for doing what's right. You and your mother deserve the whole world, and I wanted to give it to you both."

Chuckling softly, I pulled my wife into the group hug, cherishing the moment for a while before the peace was interrupted by my other three kids. Of course, the three of them didn't bother questioning anything the moment they arrived. Hell, I didn't know the three of them got back until I felt a sudden force and weight slam into me.

"Family hug!" Dario, one of the twin boys, shouted with a laugh.

"Ugh, you're squishing me too much," Rosie complained with a scoff and groan.

"I'm barely touching you," Francis, the older of the twin boys, retorted.

"Guys, dying here," Asher strained out with an exaggerated drag of his breath. "Can't breathe!"

The sounds of nails against the floor drummed through the air, and an excite bark echoed through the room before all our chuckling groans drowned it out. "Bodie!" All of us chuckled at the extra weight of the old hound joining us.

Unable to help it, I laughed loudly to let my joy be known as I captured my family in my big arms. "God, I love you guys so much." They all let out a dying groan when I squeezed everyone tightly.

Then, I looked at my lovely Eliza with starstruck eyes. "But I love you the most, *mia rosa*." Not caring about the kids being present, I leaned in and kissed Eliza deeply.

"Oh, ew, Dad!" All my kids groaned with mock disgust, rolling their eyes and sticking their tongues out.

"Ew, cooties," Dario scoffed playfully, making all of us laugh.

As Eliza's laughter died down, she looked up at me with a grateful smile and eyes full of burning love. "I love you too, bub."

And all of this because I walked down the right aisle.

Glossary

- **Brava ragazza:** Good girl.

- **Brava ragazza, sono così fiero di te:** Good girl, I'm so proud of you.

- **Cazzo, sei così sexy, tutta arrabbiata e sicura di te:** Damn, you're so sexy, all angry and confident.

- **Mia rosa:** My rose.

- **Ti scoperò finché non sorge il sole:** I'll fuck you until the sun comes up.

- **Porca puttana:** Holy shit.

- **Oh cazzo. Sarai la mia morte, piccola rosa:** Oh fuck. You'll be the death of me, little rose.

- **Oh, mia piccola rosa, no, mai:** Oh, my little rose, no, never.

- **Oh mia piccola rosa, sei così fottutamente perfetta. Sei così eterea, è irreale. Non riesco a credere che questa sia la regina che sarà mia moglie. Non mi sento degna di te, ma ti amerò dannatamente finché non lo sarò:** Oh

415

my little rose, you are so fucking perfect. You are so ethereal, it's unreal. I can't believe this is the queen who will be my wife. I don't feel worthy of you, but I will love you like hell until I am.

Thank You

Hope you enjoyed Adam and Eliza's story! If you did, then please take a moment to leave it a rating/review—it'll also do wonders for a small indie author like me!

If you enjoyed the first installment in this cozy dark rom-com standalone series, then I hope you guys keep an eye out for Rowan and Celeste's story! Good cop turned bad for the girl he used to bully throughout all of their school years. Splash of Love will come your way in 2026!

In the meanwhile, I've got many other books published and coming out for the rest of the 2025 year that you guys can occupy your TBR list with!

Also, big shoutout to my editors Annie and Brittany Harris! Big props to Brittany for her last-minute help!

Chapter 36
About the Author

Rose Chase, a dedicated nurse and loving mother to two boys, discovered her passion for storytelling in middle school on online forums and Wattpad. Despite her busy life, she delves into the captivating realm of contemporary romance, with a particular fascination for dark romance and morally gray characters. Through her skillful storytelling, Rose navigates the intricate dance between love, desire, and the shadows of human nature. When not saving lives or caring for her family, she immerses herself in the world of fiction, inviting readers to explore the depths of love and passion while confronting the complexities of the human heart.

www.ingramcontent.com/pod-product-compliance
Lightning Source LLC
Chambersburg PA
CBHW061105310726

48974CB00002B/406